R&B singer C̶h̶a̶n̶t̶e̶l̶ ▮▮▮ D1427908 ss of Love Ballads lost everything. ꜰ ꜰ ꜰ ꜰ ꜰ ꜰ ꜰ ꜰ ꜰ ꜰ ꜰ ꜰ ꜰ ꜰ ꜰ ꜰ ʳᵉⁱ and the death of her mother lead to a career-ending mental breakdown. Then, at the same time, her attorney makes off with *all* her hard-earned fortune. The only chance she has of resurrecting her career is in the recording studio her mother left in her name. . .

When struggling country star Truman Woodley's duet with a sultry young singer falls flat at Chantel's studio, Chantel is faced with a rare second chance—until Truman's vindictive ex-girlfriend turns the pair's sparkling debut into grounds for a custody battle over their son. But Chantel has discovered more than sweet vocal harmony with Truman. She's found something worth fighting for. And when Truman surprises her with a kiss after a live television performance, the whole world will find out just what it takes to be crazy in love. . .

Visit us at www.kensingtonbooks.com

Books by Crystal B. Bright

Mama's Boys Series
The Look of Love
Forget Me Not
Head Over Heels
Published by Kensington Publishing Corporation

Crazy in Love

The Love & Harmony Series

Crystal B. Bright

LYRICAL PRESS
Kensington Publishing Corp.
www.kensingtonbooks.com

Lyrical Press books are published by
Kensington Publishing Corp. 119 West 40th Street New York, NY 10018

First Electronic Edition: October 2017
eISBN-13: 978-1-5161-0468-0
eISBN-10: 1-5161-0468-4

First Print Edition: October 2017
ISBN-13: 978-1-5161-0471-0
ISBN-10: 1-5161-0471-4

Printed in the United States of America

This book is dedicated to anyone afraid of taking a chance on the unknown. Sometimes trying something new and different is a good thing.

Acknowledgements

Thank you to Renee Rocco and Martin Biro for taking a chance on me again. I submitted *Crazy in Love* as a single title. I was shocked when I was asked to make this a series. Thank you for seeing more in me as an author than I see in myself at times.

Thank you to my new editor, Mercedes Fernandez. Hope we have a long-lasting working relationship.

Thank you, always, to Jim Stark. You may be tone deaf and often make up lyrics to songs when you sing them, but you are always music to my ears. I love you.

Author's Foreword

I came up with the idea for this story—of a sexy R&B singer falling for someone who doesn't seem like her type—back when Beyoncé was dating Jay Z. I didn't understand how those two people could be together and, ultimately, fall in love. I wrote *Crazy in Love* to explain the attraction, but instead I changed the hero to a country singer. I liked the idea of mixing the two different types of music and how it doesn't matter when it comes to making great music.

Hope you all find a bit of harmony in this series.

Keep reading,
Crystal***

Chapter 1

"Up. Don't mess up your makeup." Her manager tapped Shauna Stellar's shoulder.

Shauna shivered at his touch. On a day like today, she needed the comfort and resented it. She stared at a picture on her large, rectangular phone. Her mother with her wild mane of chocolate-brown hair and wide, expressive dark eyes smiled in the shot. If Shauna inhaled deep enough, she could smell her mom's flowery scent.

Moments like this, she missed having her mother sit by her side to tell her everything would be okay. Then again, with Shauna's busy schedule, it had been a while since her mother had been able to do that. Now, she would never get that chance again.

Shauna knew Craig would stay around her, hovering, until she complied with his directive. Until she sat up and looked him in his eyes, he wouldn't move on to his next task. Shauna waited a beat before connecting her gaze to his through the mirror.

"Good girl." The large man in an expensive suit winked at her.

She started to open her mouth, wanting to scream at him for so many things right now. Why wouldn't he let her be for a moment? Why did she always have to appear perfect? Why did she have to sing today? Why couldn't she say no?

He held up his finger. "You open that mouth of yours for hot tea or vocal warm-ups. Nothing else until show time. You know the rules."

Yes, Craig George's rules. Shauna pressed her lips together.

"You need tea?" He didn't even look at her when he asked the question. His stare stayed on his diamond-encrusted Rolex.

No. Having tea before a performance reminded Shauna of her mother. Before every dance class and singing lesson, Shauna had shared hot tea and great conversation with Fatima Evans. Tasting the bitter drink now would bring back too many memories and way too many missed opportunities that she didn't want to admit.

Like him, Shauna didn't answer until he acknowledged her again. When he connected his gaze to hers, she shook her head. The diamonds in her drop earrings brushed her cheek.

"You want to do some scales?" He snapped his fingers for her vocal coach who always came with her on the road.

As soon as she spotted him, Shauna felt her eyes get scratchy. She didn't care if tears messed up her makeup. Besides Craig, her vocal coach had been with her from the start of her career at fifteen. Now she saw him as a reminder of Fatima, the woman who had given her life in more ways than one.

Again, Shauna started to say something. She needed to be heard.

"Get out of here." Craig held the coach's shoulders before he could get any closer to Shauna and turned him to the door. He pointed to a makeup artist. "You. Get in there and fix her up. The Princess of Love Ballads has to be impeccable."

A young man scurried to Shauna with a silver-and-black makeup case in hand.

"Make sure that mascara is waterproof. She has to look flawless. This has to be like every other performance." Craig took a seat on a couch next to her, but kept his attention directed to his phone.

His request pushed Shauna to the edge. She waved her hands in the air to prevent anyone from getting too close to her. "Get out." She pointed to the door.

Craig bolted to his feet. Before saying anything, he put his hand on Shauna's shoulder as though to remind her to remain silent, preserve her tool.

"Okay, you all heard her. Everyone, get out." Craig nodded to the door. "Come get her when it's time for her to get on stage."

Shauna shook her head. "No." Now that she found her voice, she didn't want to stop.

Craig silenced her with a raised hand and waited until the room emptied before he spoke to her. "I know you're feeling a little shaken up right now. Raheem—"

The mention of her ex-boyfriend had her head throbbing. Shauna balled her hands into fists before she bolted to her feet. The dangly sequins on her dress clinked together like a wind chime, creating a soothing melody for her. Something had to be on her side.

Craig powered through his speech. "I know the breakup was rough, especially how he did it."

She started to pace in her spindly heels. To say Raheem broke up with her in a grand and humiliating way would be a severe understatement. He crushed her spirit. Everything else that happened to her crushed her soul.

"I made sure he wouldn't be anywhere close to you. According to his recent tweets, he's in California right now." This time Craig held up both hands. "Universe Records has asked that you keep this obligation."

Of course the record label would want her to continue performing no matter what. They needed money to line their pockets. It didn't matter how Shauna felt.

When Shauna worked, which seemed to be all the time now, Craig remained business-minded. It seemed so easy for him to switch from business to personal mode in a matter of milliseconds, a trait Shauna never acquired.

All the laughing and joking stopped with the involvement of money. Shauna ached for a friend right now, someone to commiserate over recent events. Even with Madison Square Garden being packed full of people, she felt so alone.

Craig tried giving Shauna the most sincere look he could muster. "Fatima would want you here doing what you're doing."

Shauna doubted that. The mention of her mother stilled her in her position. She held on to the back of a chair as she regarded her manager. When she brushed her thumb over the wood, she brought her gaze down to it and the rest of the room.

What happened to her large throne-like white velvet chair that felt like a hug when she sat in it? She'd done shows at the Garden before and had had that piece with her when she performed there.

She scanned the room and noticed that the normal all-white furniture she always requested didn't make it to her dressing room. The drab battleship-gray walls brought her mood down even more than the burnt burgundy-colored carpeting with stains in various spots. Where was the expensive Oriental rug that came along with her for every show?

Shauna glanced over to the area where the venue normally had her specialty drinks and snacks. Nothing. No. Not nothing. Bottled water. *Generic* bottled water. She turned to Craig.

As though reading her thoughts, he answered what had been running through her mind. "I've asked them to scale back on some of your perks."

She felt her eyebrows furrow. On a day like today, having overpriced water, bouquets of daisies, and an assortment of Now and Later candies didn't seem like it would be too much to get. Then she noticed how much Craig fidgeted in his spot.

"We need to talk." He took a step closer to her. "About a lot of things. In the morning, we'll see the lawyer about your mother's will." He ran his meaty hand over his shaved head. "Hopefully, she left you something."

The way Craig's voice dipped, it seemed like he didn't want her to hear the last part of his statement.

Shauna's heart raced. Forget preserving her voice. She needed to say something.

When she opened her mouth, a knock sounded at the door before the person came inside.

A young woman wearing a headset glanced at Shauna before dropping her gaze, avoiding eye contact like she had been instructed to do so. "Your stage is set. The second opening act is finishing their last song. You're up."

"Thanks." This time, Craig waved her away. He held Shauna's shoulders as he gazed at her.

The way Craig stared made her feel like a commodity, an art piece he wanted to buy, or a horse he had put his life savings on for a race. She tried taking a step back, not to run but because she needed some space.

Craig must have thought the motion meant she didn't want to be there. He gripped her arms tighter.

"You can do this." He turned to the door. "You have thousands of fans out there cheering for you. They paid a lot of money to see you. Fatima's death was a setback."

Shauna blinked. Did he actually call her mother's death a setback? Losing her mother had been more than an inconvenience. What the hell was she doing there?

"I can see you looking a little unsure." Craig shook his head. "I don't need Chantel Evans right now. I need you to be Shauna Stellar."

The mention of her real name gave Shauna another reminder of how disconnected she had become from her family, her mother. She turned her head and caught her reflection in the mirror, and had to drop her gaze just as fast. She couldn't take staring at a stranger.

Although she understood Craig's hard-nose attitude, she wished he would drop being Craig George, the business manager, and be the nice man who vowed to protect her and her interests when she, at fifteen years of age, and Fatima sought him out to represent her in the music industry. She could be Shauna if Craig would just hug her before she went on stage.

"Don't let the fans down." He pointed to her chest. "You can do it. You're a pro. Always have been. Always will be."

No hug. Not even a pat on her back.

Right now, Shauna didn't feel like a professional. She wanted to rip off her designer gown, take off the skyscraper heels that hurt her toes and probably cost as much as the house she grew up in, throw on a well-worn T-shirt, crawl in bed, and not come out for years.

Craig swiftly moved behind her and pushed her to the door. Like he had to, he guided her through the long hallway, up several flights of stairs, and to the backstage area. Shauna knew the path, although the place now appeared blurry all the sudden.

She couldn't get her eyes to focus, and her head remained cloudy. She had been that way ever since she placed her hand on her mother's coffin before they lowered it into the ground only a few hours ago.

A young man in a dark suit approached her. He looked familiar. Maybe he worked at the funeral home. Even with his blond hair and blue eyes, he looked sinister, like he had an agenda. The dark lighting in the backstage area might have had something to do with it.

"Good evening, Ms. Stellar." He stood in front of her. "I don't know if you remember me. I'm Laz Kyson. I work at your label. We, at Universe, want to thank you for your bravery. You're going to put on a great show." It looked like he had to choke out the last part of his statement before he plastered a fake smile on his face and nodded.

Shauna didn't acknowledge him. She swiftly moved around him to get into her position. Someone placed an earpiece in her ear and covered it with her long, flowing chestnut colored hair that had pieces of fake hair mixed in it. Craig placed a white microphone in her hands and had to wrap her fingers around it for her to hold it. Her dancers ran by her to go to their marks on the stage.

"We didn't pray." She whispered the words about a forgotten ritual she used to do with her dancers and everyone that worked on her tour.

The same woman who had gotten her from her dressing room approached her again. "Your spot is there." She pointed to the center of the stage. "I understand why you couldn't do a run through earlier today." She patted Shauna's hand. "Sorry about your mom."

The sentiments crushed Shauna's heart. She covered her mouth, afraid of the tears she felt coming.

Craig pushed the woman away. "I told you not to mention that in front of her." He signaled for the makeup artist to touch up Shauna's face again.

Shauna didn't need to be dolled up. Before her cue, she walked out on stage while her dancers performed their routine. She noticed their surprised looks as she came out before her choreographed moment.

A wave of screams and applause hit her as she stumbled to the center. The strength of the clamorous crowd kept her upright for a moment, but she knew it wouldn't last. She couldn't see faces as she looked out into the sea of people.

The music around her sounded foreign, not like she had sung over it before, but she knew she had, a million times for millions of people. Nothing seemed real.

She kept looking out into the crowd until she could focus on some faces in the front row. Shauna walked toward the front of the stage. It occurred to her that she must have missed her mark in the song when the music stopped.

Shauna found her dancers and her band standing still and staring at her. She needed an ally. Someone who would understand her.

She crouched down to make eye contact with a young man who screamed and cried.

"I love you, Shauna Stellar!" He reached for her but the barrier wall and the group of buff security guards held him back.

"I don't know what love is." She spoke in the microphone out of habit. "Why do you love me?"

The screams in the arena quieted down a little. Then the flashes started. Everyone with a camera-phone snapped her picture, but no one asked her how she felt.

Shauna reached her hand out to touch someone, anyone. "My body feels like jelly. I can't feel anything. Today wasn't a good day. And I didn't pray before I came out here, and I always do that. Good girls pray. They're thankful for everything they have because it could be taken away." Tears streamed down her face. "Do you know what I did?" She scanned the immediate crowd. "Of course you do. You all know every move I make."

The fans looked around them as she spoke directly to them. They looked as confused as she felt.

"Gone. I'll never see her again. And you all want to hear me sing." Her breathing increased. "When people take from you, they don't know what it does to you." She shook her head. She ran her fingers through her hair and came across a clip hidden under her tresses and close to her scalp. Without thinking, she undid it and removed some of her fake hair and tossed it to the ground. "I'm nothing. I don't like myself. I hate what I've done." Tears streamed down her face.

From the depths of her soul, like she had been holding on to the pain for her full twenty-five years, Shauna screamed so loud and so long that her throat became scratchy and ached.

She heard footsteps. When she turned, she spotted Craig running toward her. "Sorry I let you down." She dropped the microphone, closed her eyes, and let gravity do its work, rolling off the stage and heading to the concrete floor below.

The darkness soothed her.

* * * *

Truman Woodley stared at his phone at a picture of himself with his son, Gage, as he waited to hit the stage with his band. Even as he sat in a trailer that he and his four friends had to share with a magician and an amateur yodeler, he knew he could be a success for his boy. He couldn't give up.

He checked the time. Nine at night went way beyond his five-year-old son's bedtime. Plus he didn't need to get into an argument with his ex-girlfriend if he called. She would ask him about money he didn't have. At least after two years, she stopped asking if they could be a couple again. That ship had long sailed away.

"Some of us can't keep doing this." Charlie leaned against the inside wall of the trailer, and it felt like the whole thing shifted under the big man's weight. The wall creaked and cracked as soon as he touched it. He must have felt the movement. He straightened up before he continued. "I promised my wife that I would play bass for the Sliders for a year. We're six months in and I don't see that pot at the end of the rainbow. I have five kids."

"We know." Sully propped his feet up on a counter as he cradled his guitar.

"I know you know." Charlie scanned the group. "You all know what we have going on outside of this group." He glared at Truman. "If something doesn't happen soon, I don't know if I can keep going with this. At some point, I need to get a real job with real benefits to take care of my family, who I love with all my heart. Being out here in Virginia is killing me." He snickered. "What country band thinks their career is going to be made in Virginia? We need to go back home to Tennessee."

Truman returned his phone to his pocket, and then glanced at Ervin who only shrugged his shoulders.

"I'm down for whatever." Ervin drummed his sticks over his thighs. "But it would be nice to catch a break. We've been at this since we were in high school. It's been ten years going from gig to gig as Truman Woodley and the Sliders. Something's got to give."

"I hear you all." Truman stood in the middle of his bandmates, his friends. "I've sent our demo to several record companies. Our videos are getting lots of views on YouTube. We have ten thousand followers on Facebook. We're so close."

"Close is not going to be good enough pretty soon." Charlie sat in the chair Truman had occupied.

When Truman's phone rang, he hoped it would be some good news. Instead he saw the name *Ashley* across the screen. He didn't bother to go somewhere private to take the call. His friends knew the issues he had with his ex-girlfriend. Since she watched his son, he worried that something had happened with Gage.

"Did you get paid?" Ashley hit him as soon as he answered.

Truman sighed in relief. He pressed his free hand on a counter. Had she said something about his son, he would have been out of Virginia, done with touring, and out of his mind.

"I'm fine, Ash. How are you?" He hoped she caught his sarcastic tone.

"Yeah. Like you'd care." She snorted. "I just want to know if your son gets to eat the rest of the month or not."

He prickled at the implication that the mother of his child would allow their son to starve because her lazy behind couldn't, or wouldn't, go out and get a job.

"I deposited money into your account this morning. Didn't you get my text?" Truman marched back and forth. "It's not a lot, but it's something until—"

Ashley cut him off. "Until what, Tru? Gage needs clothes. He's growing like a weed. And I need—"

"The money is not for you." He tightened his jaw.

"If I don't have money, then I can't pay rent. If I can't pay rent, then me and your son will be on the streets."

He heard Ashley popping gum. His skin crawled.

Why did he make a child with her? Wait. He had made the decision at the time with his head not located above his shoulders. Never again would he be led around by his dick.

"You live with your mother in an apartment. You're trying to tell me that between the two of you and my money you can't pay rent?" He kicked his boot against the wall.

The motion and noise startled the magician, an older man with a lot of sweat covering his vast forehead.

Ashley huffed. "Mama's on disability. You know that. And Gage's not in school yet and I can't afford a babysitter."

Before he could tell Ashley about her mother being able to watch their son, Ashley cut him off by reminding him that her mother, only in her late forties, couldn't run after their five-year-old handful.

He exhaled loud enough for Ashley to hear it through the phone. "We're about to go on soon."

"Oh, you're playing a show? A *paying* gig?" Not that Ashley cared that each show they played got them closer to their dream of making it big.

Truman glanced at his friends. "I'll send more money when I can."

"I need more than your word, Tru. You need to do better for your son." Her voice rose to an annoying screech that made Truman pull the phone away from his ear.

"I'm doing the best that I can." He spotted Charlie shaking his head and dropping his gaze to the floor.

Truman wondered how many times Charlie had had this conversation with his wife.

"Do better." Ashley damn near growled her request. "Or I'm going to have to move to North Carolina."

"What?"

Ashley hadn't pulled this Carolina stunt before. Actually, she'd never threatened to keep Gage away from him.

"My grandmother lives there." Ashley popped her gum three more times in quick succession like a popgun. "Her place is paid off. She can put us up."

"Don't take my son away from my family in Tennessee. I'll do what I can to get you some money to get you by." Truman leaned back on the counter. He felt like a ton of bricks had been dumped on his back and shoulders. Even though he couldn't be there, his parents lived close to Ashley and could check up on his son at any time.

"I know you'll get me the money. And don't tell me what to do with *my* son. I'll take him wherever I want." The shrieking returned, and so did Truman's headache.

He could almost see Ashley with her chin jutted out, her blond hair with its dark roots spiked up like a rooster and smoke swirling around her.

Tired of Ashley's self-centered nature, Truman decided to let her have it. "You are a piece of work, you know that? It's always me, me, me. Did you ever think that maybe you need to get in there and earn a living for yourself? What do you have to say?"

Silence.

Truman had never known Ashley to be tight-lipped about anything.

So he continued. "And I'm telling you now. If you ever threaten me with taking my boy to some trailer park in Charlotte, I'll—"

"Daddy, what's a trailer park?"

Silence.

This time Truman had to stop himself. Thank God he didn't forget his manners and call the mother of his son anything but a child of God. The woman always fought dirty like a female version of his lead guitarist, Sully. He should have known that she would use their son as leverage in their argument.

"Hey, big man." Truman took some deep breaths away from the phone to compose himself. "Aren't you up late?" He would have to talk to Ashley about keeping Gage on a regular bedtime schedule. "How are you doing?"

"Fine. I drawed you a picture of you and your guitar." Gage's voice sounded less babyish than Truman remembered.

Truman hated missing out on these important years in Gage's life. As his father, he wanted to be by him and teach him how to be a man. He heard rustling through the phone.

"See? Can you see it, Daddy?" Gage's excited tone pumped up Truman. He smiled. "I wish I could, big boy. We're not on Facetime right now. Are you being good to your mama and grandmama?"

"Yes, sir. Just like you told me to." Truman imagined Gage's big hazel eyes, a combination of his brown eyes and Ashley's green ones, sparkling as he talked to him.

Thanks to Ashley's daily social media posts, Truman noticed how his child's dirty blond hair had turned brown like his.

He loved hearing his son's voice. His heart pounded a solid rhythm. His shoulders relaxed. More than anything, he wanted his boy by his side.

"I wish I could be there to tuck you in at night." Truman saw Charlie wiping his hand under his nose before the big man stood and walked outside.

Truman should have taken the call somewhere else. Charlie missed his kids as much as Truman missed Gage. Yes, something needed to happen for them soon.

"Would you sing lullabies?" Gage's voice sounded jittery like he talked while jumping up and down.

"Yep. All the ones you like." Truman blinked and a tear almost escaped his eye. Only his son could draw out a reaction like that out of him.

"Daddy, can you sing me one now?"

Before he could sing a note, Truman heard Ashley in the background screaming. "Daddy will need to send more money before he can sing to you over the phone."

Truman gritted his teeth. "I love you."

"I love you, sugar." Ashley chuckled. "But you know we're no good for each other. I'll be waiting for more money."

Ashley disconnected the call. Truman slid his phone back into his pocket. So among everything else going on in his life, he had to find a job so that he could send more money to Ashley.

Screams from kids riding on a nearby Ferris wheel filtered through the trailer walls and broke his concentration. He adjusted his baseball cap on his head and took in a deep breath. Ordinarily, he liked the scent of freshly made popcorn and cotton candy. Now it all smelled like defeat.

"I thought we were done with gigs like these." Sully kicked his boot against Truman's.

"This gig is better than some." Truman picked up his guitar. "It's a county fair and not a dive bar." When he noticed his friends starting to get ready to argue about the types of shows they'd been playing, he barreled through with his statement. "We get an album out, I think we'll be done with shows like these. Consider this as us paying our dues."

"Are we ever going to record in a studio?" Tony, their fiddler, chewed on his lower lip.

Truman held up his hand. "We're a hard-working group. We're going to get picked up." At least he hoped they did. He understood the ruthlessness of the music business. It would be nothing for them to never get a deal.

His one hope rested with a recording studio in Virginia Beach with an owner who sounded like she cared about him, his band, and the music. Then he heard Fatima Evans had passed away six months ago. With his champion gone, what chance did they have?

"I need some air." Truman sat his guitar back down and walked out of the trailer.

As soon as Charlie spotted him, his friend went back inside the trailer. Great.

Truman paced to work out some anxiety. His cowboy boots sank into the lush green grass. As the leader, he didn't want to go on this music journey without the guys he considered to be like his brothers.

Truman's phone buzzed in his pocket. He fished it out and answered it when he saw that the number came from a Virginia phone. He crossed his fingers, hoping for something good to happen.

"Mr. Woodley?"

Truman heard an unfamiliar gruff voice. "Yeah?"

He looked toward the stage. It looked like the last band had finished their set. Truman Woodley and the Sliders would be next.

"My name is Craig George. I'm a music manager, and I'm helping with the transition of Charisma Music Studio. I believe you signed a contract with the late Fatima Evans."

Perfect. They had this guy call Truman to politely tell him that he and his friends wouldn't be able to record their album. He knew he had made the right decision not telling the guys that he had a development deal with Charisma.

"Why are you calling me now?" He didn't want to put words in the man's mouth by asking if he and his bandmates lost their contract.

Craig cleared his throat. "I need to discuss your record deal, but I want to do it in person. Are you in here in Virginia Beach?"

"Uh, no. We're doing a show in Roanoke, Virginia right now. We'll be back sometime tomorrow." Truman's back already ached when he thought about the rough ride in the van for the long trip back home.

"Okay, how about the day after tomorrow? Come to my office. I'll text you the address."

Patience had never been Truman's virtue. "Are we getting dropped?"

Craig laughed, and that made Truman bristle. He didn't see his career as a laughing matter.

After the laughter died down, Craig composed himself enough to explain his reaction. "I don't think Charisma plans on not honoring your contract."

Away from the phone receiver, Truman released a long sigh. At least he had something to tell the guys other than saying that everything will be fine. He had a meeting with a stranger who assured him that he had nothing to worry about as far as their first album. Now he worried again.

Craig gave Truman a time and location for the meeting before the call ended. A young volunteer jogged to the trailer and called for the group. Each of them filed out one by one, glaring at Truman as they headed toward the stage area.

"Hey, guys. Wait up." Truman ducked into the trailer long enough to get his guitar. He caught up with his friends.

"You all right to play?" Sully hung his guitar strap on his shoulder.

"Great now. I got some kick-ass news." Truman beamed. "I have a meeting about our album when we get home."

"Album? What album?" Tony scratched his head.

"We have a deal with a label and they want to meet with me on Friday to discuss our album."

Charlie grabbed Truman's arm first. "You're shitting me." He slapped Truman on his back. "That's awesome."

"I told you guys not to worry." Truman damn near skipped as he relayed the news.

"This is happening. It's really happening." Ervin pumped his fist in the air before releasing a loud howl.

"Wait. Before everyone gets too excited." Sully stopped his trek to the stage, which halted everyone else's journey. "Did you sign us to a label already without discussing it with us?"

Truman made sure to look each of his friends in their eyes. "Yes. Almost a year ago, I met up with a woman named Fatima Evans. She seemed excited about signing a country group. So she asked if I would take a chance on her and her label and sign with her. I got a good feeling and did it."

"Without telling us?" Sully slammed the butt of his guitar on the ground.

"And what did you mean by taking a chance on us? Why would we be a risk?" Charlie's excited demeanor started to fade.

Truman dropped his gaze for a moment. "Because she normally records R&B, pop, and rap."

"Rap?" Tony's eyes widened. "And she knows we're country?"

"Knew." Truman rested his hand on his stomach. "After I signed the contract, I didn't hear from her. Then I found out she passed away about six months ago. I waited about a month after her death to make some inquiries. I hadn't heard back from anyone until today."

"This is when having a lawyer would help, or at least a *real* manager." Sully picked up his guitar and headed to the stage again.

"So they called you and they want to still record us. That's good news." Charlie's smile started to firm up again. "What's the name of the label?"

"Charisma Music."

Ervin pulled out his phone and started typing something on it. "Holy shit." The group stopped again.

"What?" Tony approached Ervin first, not surprising.

"You know what they nickname this label? Ca-Razy Music. You know that singer Shauna Stellar?" Ervin flicked his finger over the phone screen.

"Can't say that I do." Sully shrugged.

"She does all of those love songs. She did that song 'Love Me, Love Me, Love Me.'" Ervin kept his attention on his phone during his mad search.

Charlie's eyes got wide. "She sang that one? I know that song. Two of my kids were conceived while I was listening to that." He released a low, long whistle. "What about her?"

"Her mother was Fatima Evans. The reason they call it Ca-Razy Music is because Shauna went a little wacko about six months ago and took a header off the stage. She was babbling about love and stuff. People think she was high or drunk. She committed herself after that. Either way, if she's involved with the studio, it might be a problem." Ervin flipped his phone around. "But it'll be a good problem to have. Look at that."

Truman stared at the screen. The woman on it had long, wavy dark brown hair, a slender frame with the exception of her round ass, and skin that looked like caramel covered her body. She had her head back, eyes closed, and the microphone poised above her full lips. He brought his gaze down to her pert breasts and had to hold his guitar in front of his body when his lower half reacted involuntarily.

This Shauna Stellar danced a delicate line between sexy vixen and elegant lady. Truman understood how she could drive men crazy, but he couldn't see her having a bad day in her life…with the exception of losing her mother.

"Go to that meeting and tell them we don't want any part of them or their studio." Sully shook his head. "We don't need to be mixed up with an outfit that doesn't do our music and with someone who may not be right in the head."

Truman had to stare at his friend like Sully had lost his mind. "Are you kidding? This could be our only chance to—"

Sully cut him off. "I mean it. Tear up the contract and walk away. We don't need to go to bed with this organization to make it."

Charlie and Tony followed Sully.

Ervin stopped in front of Truman. "I know you'll do the right thing by us. You always have. If you think signing this deal and recording with them is a good thing, I'll stand with you." He looked back at Sully. "To hell with him."

"No." Truman shook his head. "That's not how this works. We said we would do things together. I messed that up a year ago when I signed something behind you guys' backs. If I'm going to lead us, I need to respect your wishes." He glanced at the other three in the group who stepped up on stage. "I won't let you all down."

Now Truman had to convince himself that he didn't need to be concerned about this upcoming meeting.

Chapter 2

"Tell me again, Craig. What do you mean I have nothing?" Shauna paced in front of her manager's desk.

If she kept moving, the negative thoughts threatening to creep into her skull would stay away. Plus walking had helped her over the last few months.

She did stop long enough to glare at Craig. The back of her legs brushed against the red leather chair that sat in front of his desk. She remembered buying him this pricey showpiece for his fiftieth birthday along with a black leather couch, mink carpet, and mahogany desk with platinum fixtures.

Good to see that they all traveled well from the office building she used to own to Craig's new digs in this dump down at the Oceanfront in Virginia Beach.

Craig adjusted his glasses on his thick nose. "Your half-year stint in rehab hasn't done wonders for your career."

She pulled her floppy red hat down lower over her eyes. "It wasn't rehab." Another lesson she learned in Peaceful Acres: call things like she saw them. "I just needed some time away." She sat on her hands to prevent Craig from seeing them tremble. Her emotions simmered, nearly breaking the surface.

Get it together, girl. Don't break.

Craig gazed down at his computer. "It was a lot for you to perform the day of…well, you know."

Yes, Shauna knew. Attempting to do a full concert on the same day she buried her mother sounded crazy. If that statement went for an apology, she would take it.

After a deep breath, she did her own damage control with her manager. "The time away did help. I got to do something I hadn't done in a long time: focus on me. Now I'm ready to get back to work."

Craig grumbled in that manner that made Shauna cringe.

He stood from his desk. "Audiences are fickle. Stay out of the spotlight and they forget about you. I can only post so much on social media before they figure out that it's not you."

Even virtually, Craig spoke for her. Shauna released her hands and spoke her mind. "Are you saying the fans don't care about me?"

"I'm saying it's hard to keep them interested without new material." He sighed loud enough to be annoying.

"But I recorded so many songs. What happened to releasing my album?" She wouldn't have been able to promote it, but lots of popular artists released work without promotion and did well. She could have been one of those people.

Craig lowered, then shook his shaved head. Her heart slowed its beat and she felt a heavy pressure on her shoulders, the same pressure that had crippled her spirit.

Come on, girl. Breathe. You are not weak.

"It had been a while since you had a release before you committed yourself." His dark skin seemed murky now, especially the more Craig spoke to her.

"Stop saying I committed myself." She folded her arms. "Going to Peaceful Acres was the greatest thing for me."

His bushy eyebrows drew together.

"It was the first time I took time for myself where the paparazzi didn't follow me. It was a vacation without all of the sand and surf." Maybe if she said it enough, that line of trash would sound plausible.

"Thanks to your sabbatical, Universe Records dropped you. Radio stations stopped playing you. The only video of yours on YouTube that's getting a lot of play is the one from your last show." He wrung his hands together. "The memes alone will drive you crazy." As soon as he made the statement, he flinched. Like he needed to cover up his mistake, he kept talking. "The fans stopped writing." He tapped his fingers on the desk.

She shook her head hard enough that the back of her neck ached. "That's not true. I still got fan mail. They cared."

Her fan mail that used to be delivered by the truckloads could now be brought to her by one carrier from his satchel in a single trip.

Shauna exhaled and eased back into the chair. "Besides, I shouldn't have to explain anything to anyone. Rock stars do crazy stuff all the time and get a pass. Since middle school, I have been homeschooled and tutored, so I didn't do the typical rebellious teenager stuff. I have been working hard since I was fourteen. I don't do drugs. I don't drink. I don't go out to parties. I need to be cut some slack here."

Craig sighed, then lowered his head again. If Craig thought her sabbatical made her soft, he had another thing coming. Forget what the doctors had said about her making some significant changes in her life. No, Shauna needed to keep on track like she hadn't missed a beat.

He stood from his desk and planted himself in front of her. He brought his hands to his hips. From under the brim of her hat, she spied his knock-off Rolex watch and simple gold wedding band that glowed against his dark skin.

"What happened to all of your good jewelry?" She flicked his watch.

"This is part of what I wanted to tell you after your last show." He covered his watch with his hand as he regarded her. "Your accountant ran off with half of your money and fled the country. We tried to get your attorney to sue the bastard, but she was in on the scam too and took off with more of your dough. Then you had all of the other people in your employ." He brought his hand up and ticked off people on each finger. "Your personal chef, your masseuse, your stylist, your acupuncturist." He snickered. "The reason you got six months in that place was because each time they asked for money, I fired someone you employed until there was no one left."

"Not even my vocal coach?" The person who had been with her before she signed her first record deal would never leave her, right?

"He was the first to go." Craig shook his head. "I don't mean I fired him. He left on his own as soon as you, um, went away."

She rubbed the back of her neck to relieve the strain and to keep her hands occupied. When her fingers brushed against the coarse, balled hair underneath her braids, she brought her hand down.

"I can't even afford to hire someone to style you. You have no money. Nothing. Nada. Zippo." He made a circle using his index finger and thumb.

She gritted her teeth, snorted like a bull, then spoke. "What about you? You could have gone off and represented some other hot up-and-comer."

He put his hand on top of her shoulder. It was the first personal touch she'd had since being away. She relaxed, but kept her gaze on him.

"I'm still here, aren't I?" His already deep voice dipped down to a lower octave. "I gave up my pay months before you went in. I hired my own lawyer to go after the bastards but they made sure to have ironclad contracts. I saw the writing on the wall and I tried to tell you but, well, you know."

Yes, she knew she hadn't listened to anyone. As one of the hottest R&B artists out there, no one had bothered to give her any bad news except for one thing.

"I also sold my house, the cars, the jewelry. Delores and I don't mind the comparably smaller house. She says there's less to clean, especially since the maid stopped coming by three times a week." He chuckled again but this time it was meant to ease her mind.

She reached forward to pat his hand, but stopped herself. The old Shauna wouldn't have shown this much compassion. Chantel Evans threatened to come out, and she didn't need her old, insecure self with her overwhelming need to please rearing her timid head. Like Craig used to tell her, "Release your ghetto fabulousness."

If she showed a softer side, Craig would probably worry that she couldn't be that hit maker again. From everything he had done for her, she knew he expected her to do great things again. Shauna wondered if she could deliver.

"And the restaurant?" Shauna remembered when Craig had bought the place for his wife because it was Delores's dream to own her own Southern-cuisine restaurant.

He smiled. "I don't care if I have to dig ditches to keep that place going. Delores has more than earned her right to have Dee's House."

It was nice to see a man so supportive of his woman's goals. It would have been nice to have someone supporting Shauna instead of using her, like her record label.

She scanned Craig's much smaller space. Bright white paint covered the walls, and it didn't match the expensive items he'd brought into the room. As soon as her gaze settled on his shelves and she caught a glimpse of her Grammy awards, she raised herself from the chair and strolled to them like a magnetized pull.

When she stood in front of the gold trophies, she stared at them. They reminded her of her old self. Her confident self even if the confidence stemmed from a lie, a fake persona.

She put her hand on the plate and ran her fingertips over her engraved name. A shiver crept up her back as though she had touched a tombstone.

"With no money and a crooked accountant, your taxes hadn't been paid. When the IRS sold your house and all your possessions while you were resting, I couldn't bear to let them sell those." Craig stood behind her. "I didn't have enough money to buy anything else."

What world had Shauna returned to? She would have been better off staying at Peaceful Acres but the doctors there had convinced her to go, move on with her life. How the hell was she supposed to do that?

Shauna turned around. She didn't want to keep staring at her awards, painful reminders of a life she used to have, about a person she used to be.

"I'm going to sing." The statement made her blink. She'd thought about it during her time away but never verbally expressed her desires. Then again, what else did she have left to use?

"Good girl." Craig beamed, a smile spreading from ear to ear.

"But I haven't sung in a while." She cleared her throat. "I'm not ready."

She hadn't sung a note since finding out her mother had passed away. She didn't know if she could get up in front of a crowd of people and sing like she used to as a former diamond-selling artist. She had to bring that old Shauna Stellar back and make her bigger than ever.

"I figured you would say that." Craig rifled through some papers on his desk as she approached him.

"So if I have no money, if everything I own is gone, what do I do now? Where do I go?" Shauna reclaimed her seat. This time she pushed her hat back and stared at Craig.

"Since you have no more houses or apartments, you will stay with me and Delores. She's missed the kids since they've gone off to college and gotten lives of their own. You'll be good for her. She can lay off me for a change." Craig laughed. "And your cousins are in and out of the house all the time."

Shauna fell back in her seat. Even though she loved Delores's home cooking, and her cousins made great substitutes for a brother and sister she never had, she really wanted to branch out on her own once she came out of Peaceful Acres.

Craig clasped his hands together and sat them on his desk. With a grin as big as the Atlantic Ocean, he made an announcement. "You, my dear, are going to get back into the music biz by producing."

Shauna furrowed her eyebrows, which she knew needed a good waxing. "Producing what?"

"Music. You know. That thing you know about so well." He smiled.

Shauna couldn't help but to grin with him. That same reassuring expression got her through her first on-stage performance by herself. He'd given her that same radiant look when he convinced her that she would win her first Grammy the night she did. He'd smiled at her the day he'd dropped her off at the rehabilitation center and told her she would be fine. However, she didn't understand this new plan.

"Oh, no. I'm not about to help someone else jumpstart their career while I'm struggling to revive my own. Besides, who will want me to produce them? *You've* called me crazy. Don't you think other artists out there think the same thing? I want to work, Craig, but I don't think even my opinions will matter to anyone." She wiped her eyes to stop any impending tears.

Craig shook his head. "I don't want to hear that negative talk from you anymore. I've known you since you were fifteen." He held his hand about three feet above the floor like her five-foot-nine stature could have ever been that height at fifteen.

"Besides, it's all you have left." He plopped a file in front of her with Charisma Music in iridescent lettering across the top. The folder nearly knocked over his nameplate.

"This was my mother's studio." Shauna kept her stare on the words.

"The smartest thing your mother did before she died, besides raising a wonderful daughter, was to will this place over to you once you turned twenty-five. I didn't want to tell you this before because of everything that was going on with you. I mean with your mom and—"

She raised her hand to stop him. She didn't want to hear a replay of the last few months before she took her much-needed rest, especially not about Raheem, one of the reasons she couldn't handle being in the real world anymore.

Craig straightened his tie. "The studio is yours. The IRS didn't take it."

"So? If Universe dropped me, doesn't that mean my production deal with them is out, too?" Shauna didn't see the possibilities like Craig. From the way he flashed his megawatt smile, she knew he had something in mind.

"Universe dropped you. But they haven't said anything about their affiliation with Charisma. I plan on making a personal visit and selling them on retaining the studio so that you still have a distribution deal at least." Craig smiled like he knew his plan would work. "So, you do what I said. You produce. Get your name back out there. Then eventually when you're up to it, you'll sing again."

"I'm up to it now." Yeah, and if she repeated that enough, she would convince herself. "I want my music to have meaning." For her, that meant writing her own songs, which she had never done either. "I have nothing to sing about. The Princess of Love Ballads is dead."

At one time she hated that media nickname. As an R&B singer, she'd sung more than just ballads. The slow love songs did put her over the top as a multi-platinum artist. What did she have to show for it now except for some memories and awards bought at a yard sale?

"She doesn't have to be."

"Yes, she does. I need to come back doing something way different than before. If I come back still singing the same stuff, I'll just capture some of my old fans. But I come back doing hip hop or pop or something, I'll rake in new fans."

He flashed her a quizzical look.

"It'll work." She nodded. "But I still don't see how having a studio is a good thing except for recording *my* next album. What artist is going to want me to produce them?"

"The one artist your mother signed before she died. He's all we have left." Craig looped his thumbs around his black suspenders. His normally rounded belly appeared flatter. Shauna knew his new physique didn't come from exercise but rather an adjusted new diet that excluded the rich foods he'd enjoyed when money had rolled in steadily.

Craig continued. "Your mother gave him and his band a two-record deal and we have the funds in the operating budget to produce one album."

"Why not drop him and use the money for me?"

Shauna had to think about *her* career, not someone else's. She needed to work. She didn't care if she had to walk all over someone to reach her goal. Raheem had done it to her. Bastard.

Craig held up one finger. "One word, my dear. Lawsuit. We don't have the money to fight him, and he would definitely win."

"No loophole?" If nothing else, she knew that every contract had its loophole. Then again, had she been such an expert on contracts, her accountant and attorney wouldn't have stolen all her money.

Craig continued, interrupting her thoughts. "No loophole. Go in the studio with him and make sure he has some hits." He hunched his shoulders. "Sorry, baby girl. I hadn't expected you to get out so soon. I was hoping the money generated from this guy's album would bankroll your comeback album."

"So who is he?" Shauna tried to keep her inquiry sounding nonchalant. With her gaze fixed on the folder and a hand on her lap keeping her bouncing knee restrained, she knew her cover had been blown.

Craig pointed down to the folder. "Look inside."

She flapped open the cover and caught an eight-by-ten glossy colored picture of a white man in a cowboy hat, jeans, cowboy boots, and white button-down shirt opened to mid-chest. In the shot, the man with a goatee leaned against a wooden fence with a lasso in one hand and the reins of a horse in the other. The stereotypical country photo made Shauna laugh.

"You're kidding, right?" Shauna kept her gaze on the singing cowboy's mesmerizing brown eyes. She rubbed her stomach when she felt a tickling feeling crawling over it.

"Does it look like I'm laughing?" Craig's face had gone stone-cold serious.

"Please tell me he's the next white soul singer who happens to like wearing this Grand Ol' Opry getup." She couldn't help but stare at his chest and notice his broad shoulders and large hands. She even liked the way his jeans fit him.

Craig shook his head. "Nope. Country. Straight up and down."

"I sing R&B. All I know is R&B. How in the hell am I supposed to produce a country singer? I don't know anything about their music. I mean

I can even understand hip-hop or rap, but this…" With great reluctance, she closed the folder on the singing cowboy.

Craig's eyes lit up. "Sure you can do it. Whitney sang a country song."

"Yeah, she sang it in an R&B way and made it her own. This man is a country singer who wants to sing that way. I can't do this." She shoved the folder back with the *Dukes of Hazzard* cutie inside and brought her hat down over her eyes again. "Why would my mother have even signed him? I didn't know she knew anything outside of soul music."

"There was a lot about your mother that you didn't know."

Shauna glared at her manager, but knew he had assessed Shauna and Fatima's relationship perfectly. Once Shauna's career took off, their relationship became strained, not as close as they used to be. She couldn't even tell her mother why she felt the need to remove herself from everything she knew to get her life in order.

"She wanted to branch out. Try some new things. Why don't you take a page from her book and try producing?"

Shauna shook her head, nearly losing her hat in the motion. "Let's just cut our losses. I'll sell the studio, pay this guy off, and go on—"

Craig cut her off. "Go on what?" He pounded his fists on his desk. "This is it, little girl. Music is all you have. My life, my world, is wrapped up in this business, in you. I believe in you. If I didn't, you wouldn't have made it here into my office. Now I've been waiting patiently for you to come back. I have made plans and backup plans and backup plans to those backup plans for when you come out. And when I present you with an offer, you turn your nose up at it? I don't think so. You're going to go down to the studio every day with Truman Woodley."

Shauna felt her eyes go wide. "His name is Truman Woodley? What is he, a Boy Scout?"

"Maybe when you start working with him you two can decide on a suitable name change. It worked for you."

Adopting a new persona had helped Shauna in a way. She could delve into a character without revealing her true self while she performed. She doubted this guy wanted to do the same thing.

"You are going to produce this album. All of this is going to lead you back to one thing." Craig held up his index finger like God announcing her fate. "You're going to sing again and to packed houses."

The tickling feeling disappeared and Shauna's stomach churned. Although she'd said she wanted to sing, the idea of standing in front of a crowd hit her like a punch in her gut. She saw herself on stage again babbling like an idiot and fainting like before.

She swallowed, hoping to calm her tightened insides, but instead her insides went in reverse. She recalled this same feeling the first time she'd sung on stage by herself at the tender age of fourteen. She bolted from her chair and ran to his glass doorway.

Shauna's pounding footsteps on the hardwood floor echoed in her ears. She ran past an office worker who must have recognized the international sign of being nauseous. He directed her to the bathroom but she only caught "...door on the right."

Shauna burst into the bathroom, pushed open a stall door, and collapsed at the toilet, purging her insides into the white, automatic bowl. As soon as she lifted her head slightly, the murky water swirled down, offering her a clean bowl to continue vomiting. She inhaled and caught the putrid stench of her predigested food.

After her second heave and the toilet's second auto-flush, she felt something over her shoulder. Shauna turned her head to see a crumpled white paper towel by her.

"Thanks." She accepted it. "God, what a day." She said it to herself but also to the kind stranger behind her who had just offered her some compassion in the form of the gritty paper towel. She would have to put on her Shauna Stellar face to appease this fan.

"Do you ever get the feeling like the world is laughing at you and you're not in on the joke?" Shauna sat on her haunches for a moment before attempting to stand. "I get home today and I'm told to produce this country singer who I have never heard of. I don't even listen to country music. And I have that guy's career, my manager's career, and my own career riding on everything that I do. It's too much. Something's got to give and I think it's going to have to be Slim Pickens."

She heard a flush from a couple of stalls down from her and a creaky door opening and closing. When her stomach felt settled after she'd purged, both physically and emotionally, she sat up on her knees, still facing the toilet.

"I just don't think I can do all of this." When she heard the water in the sink turn off, Shauna raised herself up from the floor. "I don't know who you are, but thank you for listening to me make a fool of myself." She smiled and laughed until she turned around and came face to face with her Bo Duke-Slim Pickens singing cowboy.

Shauna peeked behind him briefly to catch the row of urinals. Among everything else, she'd run into the wrong bathroom. On top of that, she ended up confessing that she didn't want to produce Truman's album.

She swallowed uneasily and attempted a clumsy smile, one that twitched at the corner and didn't stop until she put her hand over her mouth.

Truman towered over her. The gaze from his tobacco brown eyes bore down on hers until she felt smaller than the brain of an ant. Had she had a brain in her own head she would have remembered her own first rule of being a celebrity: never speak your mind in public. The truth always got twisted into something distorted and ugly. However, this time her rule hadn't failed her. Her rude statements had stung her.

She took a step back into the stall. Truman, looking like he had stepped right off his photo in jeans and white button-down shirt, scratched his head. His short, brown hair barely moved in the motion. He put one hand on the doorframe of the stall. The other hand held his cream-colored Stetson.

He smelled like the great outdoors, which included a mixture of fresh cut grass, leaves, tree bark, and honeysuckle. When she spent summers with Craig and Delores in Virginia Beach, the outdoorsy scent used to calm her. Now she would always associate the scent with embarrassment, fear, and anger—Truman's anger.

He placed his hat on his head, tipped it back with one finger. "And I thought our first meeting would be awkward."

Even through his smooth country accent she caught his sarcasm. He walked out of the bathroom.

She let out her breath, leaned against the cool tiled wall, and slid back down to the floor. "Great. Just what I needed, someone else to hate me."

The door opened. She expected to see Truman, ready to formally curse her out for her stupidity. Instead a young, pimply face man entered. He did a double take when he found Shauna in one of the stalls. He stared at her, then the urinals while hopping from one foot to the other.

He opened his mouth to say something when she cut in.

"Don't worry. I'm out of here."

Chapter 3

Truman stomped his way toward the elevator as some bald-headed black guy tried to stop him. In his suspenders and with a fancy gold watch, the dude didn't look like security. Then again Truman never thought he would have seen a big star like Shauna Stellar on her hands and knees chucking her guts out in a men's bathroom toilet.

"Just wait, Mr. Woodley." The pleading tone in the man's voice sounded desperate.

Oh, so now he was *Mr. Woodley*. So this guy knew him. Couldn't have been from Truman's shows at county fairs or the dive bars. Hearing Shauna talk, Truman wouldn't have an album.

Damn it. He didn't want to go back home to Tennessee with his tail stuck between his legs. He wanted to prove he could make it, especially to his parents who would welcome him back with that I-told-you-so look and the keys to the family business he didn't want to run.

"I don't know who you are, man, but you're in my way." Truman didn't stop moving.

"I'm Craig George." He presented his hand. "I spoke to you on the phone a couple of days ago."

Truman had never turned down a man's handshake. He grabbed Craig's hand, gave him one solid hand pump, and marched toward the elevator.

Craig continued. "I don't know what just happened with you, but I would like to talk before you leave."

Truman stared into Craig's eyes. He seemed sincere. He didn't have that sleazy look most record execs had. Looking at him closely, Craig seemed anxious. No. More like scared.

Truman understood desperation. He wanted to sing more than anything else. Fatima Evans seemed to be on his side when she'd signed him a year ago. After she died, Truman felt like no one would be in his corner.

God, he needed this record to make his career. Kids half his age made careers for themselves by singing on YouTube. He didn't want to propel his music on a gimmick.

Truman punched the down button for the elevator. "There's nothing to talk about." He peered over Craig's shoulder and saw Shauna creeping to a set of glass double doors. Truman pointed to her. "She said enough."

Craig turned to her. She held the glass door open, staring through it at the two of them until she finally ducked inside. She couldn't mask the scared look on her face, the little bit he could see of it. She had on that ridiculous hat that looked cartoonish.

Truman had been nervous about meeting the infamous Shauna Stellar. Stories of her diva attitude and tough demeanor paled in comparison to the heap he found on the bathroom floor.

Maybe the other stories he'd heard about her held some merit. Charisma Music had been nicknamed Ca-Razy Music by some insiders. Truman understood why now.

"What did she say to you?" Craig turned back to Truman.

"She said exactly what I thought you called me up here for in the first place. Me and my boys won't get to do our album." He kept his stare on Craig's eyes to see if the man flinched.

The elevator dinged. Truman didn't know what he would do once he got on, but he knew his dignity mattered to him a lot more than some record deal. He'd lived on tuna fish and crackers before. He could do it again.

Hell, who was he kidding? He didn't want that life again. Not when he and his friends could see the finish line.

Stop being so irrational, man, and hear him out.

"Wait." Craig put his hand on Truman's shoulder. "Please listen. I only want a few minutes of your time. And if you decide after what I propose you still want to walk, then I'll be the first to wish you luck."

The doors opened. Truman remained in his spot. He'd never been known to walk away from a bad situation. If he couldn't see this thing through, what kind of man would he be?

"What would you have to lose?" Craig's tone started to border on a car salesman's, but still with a hint of desperation.

"Five minutes." Truman backed away from the doors.

The elevator descended without him on it. His chest tightened at his decision. He took a deep breath to relieve the pressure. To properly manage the group, he needed to weigh out all options, which meant he had to hear them.

Craig exhaled and put his hand on his chest. "Thanks, man. It's all I ask." He led Truman back down the hallway. "And don't listen to Shauna. Sometimes she speaks before she thinks."

"Nothing wrong with that. Means you're speaking from the heart. No barriers." Truman had to admit that although he didn't particularly care for what Shauna had said, he appreciated her honesty. That trait didn't come along so often in the music industry.

After opening the glass door for Truman, Craig followed him inside. His gentlemanly side took over and Truman took off his hat. He found Shauna sitting still in front of a large desk with her back to him.

She didn't move. Didn't flinch. For her impressive height, she seemed small. Her light brown hair in braids hung below the brim of her hat.

When he'd first seen her in the bathroom, he assumed the office intern had partied a bit too hard the night before. From the curve of her waist and roundness of her backside, he could tell a woman had made her way into the wrong bathroom. From the way she threw up, he knew she needed some help.

Truman took residence in the chair next to her, being sure to keep his gaze forward. He didn't know what would blurt from her mouth if he looked at her.

Craig stood in front of his desk, splitting his attention between the two of them as he leaned back.

"Everyone comfortable?" Craig kept smiling like a pleased preacher at a wedding. "Either one of you want something to drink? There's coffee or I could get you a soda from the machine, and there's juice in the refrigerator. I don't know who it belongs to but I'm sure they won't mind if you—"

"Your time is ticking, Mr. George." If Truman's dream ended here and now, he needed to start looking for a job.

"You don't have to be so snippy with him."

Hearing Shauna's voice drew Truman's attention to her. Her low, breathy tone commanded his interest. He also wanted to catch the quiet queen's expression.

"I'm not being snippy, as you call it." Truman sat up straighter. "You know it would be easier to talk to you if I can see your eyes."

Shauna turned to him. Instead of taking off her hat, she flipped up the brim. "Happy?"

Seeing her clear light brown eyes, her high cheekbones, and her full lips, he could honestly say that the sight didn't make him *un*happy.

He'd recalled seeing images of her in this glamorous way. Tons of makeup, glittery outfits, a seductive look in her eyes, skinny little stiletto heels that pumped her ass up like on a pedestal. Without her makeup and in a plain white T-shirt and long denim skirt that rested way below her exposed belly button, she didn't look like that same larger-than-life celebrity.

Still pretty. A pain, but pretty.

"It's better." Truman brushed a nonexistent piece of lint from his pant leg. "I want you to tell me to my face that me and my guys aren't recording our album."

"Whoa, whoa, whoa." Craig held up both hands. "Who said you wouldn't be recording?"

Truman said, "She did," the same time Shauna said, "I never said that."

"I said that I shouldn't be the one *producing* your album." She lowered her hand, and the brim of her hat remained in its spot, folded up and keeping her face exposed.

"Why would you want to produce our album?" Truman turned to Craig. "I wanted to produce it—that is if we get to record. I know what songs I want and what artists I want on it with me." He turned to Shauna. "And I don't think you would do my music justice."

"Why is that?" She folded her arms. She started to look a lot more like her celebrity self and less like that real, vulnerable woman who seemed tiny a second ago.

"Because you're—" Truman waved his hand to her, but cut himself off.

She raised her finger at him. "If the word *black* or *woman* comes from your mouth, I swear I'll—"

"How about this word: R&B?" He tilted his head. "What would you know about country, and I mean real *country*, not this pop country that's out there now."

"Music is music. It's all beats and rhythms." Shauna glared at him.

Truman sat up straighter, ready to bolt in seconds. "I'm here to talk about my music, not get into some argument with a temperamental diva."

She turned her full body and attention to him. "Oh, no you didn't."

"Stop it. Both of you." Craig stood between the two of them but Truman felt Shauna's heat even through Craig's mature voice of reason. He pointed to Truman first. "You and the Sliders are going to get your album." Then he pointed at the two of them. "You're both going to coproduce."

Truman's mouth dropped open and from the corner of his eye, he noticed that Shauna did the same, but then composed herself.

"If this is my studio, why does it feel like I'm not running it?"

"Have you ever run a music studio before?" Craig cocked his head as he regarded her.

"Have you?" She responded with the same look back at him.

"Are you kidding me with this?" Truman shook his head.

Maybe Sully had been right. Maybe Truman should ask them to tear up the contract and he should walk away.

"Unlike you, Shauna, I know how to manage talent. Until you get to that level, I'm going to be here to guide you." Craig flashed a grin. "And I have a surprise."

Truman didn't want or need any more surprises.

"We need to have the album done and a Shauna-produced song of yours on the air in a month." Craig volleyed his attention from Truman to Shauna.

Truman breathed a sigh of relief, afraid Craig's next request would be something outrageous like a duet or something. "That's something I can agree on." Truman put his hand to his chest. "All I want to do is sing and perform. Getting the album out there fast is fine with me. Doesn't leave us much time for promotions, but we'll do all we can."

"And one more thing." Craig made his way around to the other side of his desk, out of striking distance. "I want a duet on the album."

Truman's heart pounded. He still had a chance to control this. "Okay. There's a country artist I've been dying to work with."

"No." Craig pointed to Shauna. "You and Shauna."

The bottom of Truman's stomach felt like it fell to the floor along with his chin. He and his band had sung songs about staying away from women like Shauna, flashy women with no substance, heart, or morals. How could he go back to his band, his friends since childhood, and admit to them that he'd made a deal with the devil?

"Excuse me." Shauna leaped from her seat and ran from the office.

Truman felt an immediate pang in his stomach. Did Shauna get sick from the idea of singing with him? Was there anything about Truman that didn't make the woman ill?

Craig nodded and pointed in the direction where Shauna ran. "Don't worry about her. She'll be fine on recording day."

Chapter 4

Even at two in the morning, Truman had found his Utopia. At the end of a long winding road, he drove the group's trusty van to the white stucco building. Bright lights spotlighted the place where he and the guys would be recording their first album. Not a bad place to be. He hoped his voice wouldn't fail him.

He turned up the country radio station when the sounds of the creaking shocks and clanging brakes threatened to overpower the music.

A white Mercedes sat in front of the glass and chrome front door of the studio. Truman pulled the van behind the luxury car.

"Don't get too close to that." Like normal, a pinch of worry laced Tony's voice. "You don't want to be paying out our first paycheck if it gets a scratch."

"I thought Shauna was dead broke." Ervin poked his head between Truman and Sully from the backseat. "That's what I read online."

"You know how rich folks are." Truman cut off the van and waited for it to stop its shimmying before he finished speaking. "They aren't rich because they don't know how to hide their money."

Truman figured that Shauna's down-home look the first time he saw her had to have been an act. He'd read all about these stars in their five hundred-dollar T-shirts and thousand-dollar jeans. He knew her whole outfit the day before had to have been worth more than the band's van.

Truman hopped out of the van and slammed the door. "Let's unload."

"You'd think they would have people doing that for us." Charlie stretched out his back.

"Even if they did, we're still hauling our own gear." Truman picked up his guitar case and grabbed a part of Ervin's drum set. "We didn't get to this point by being pampered. Work hard. Stay that way."

As Truman led his group down a long narrow hallway, he noticed the framed gold, platinum, and diamond records on the walls, most were Shauna's. She'd reached diamond status. Ten million records sold. He brushed against the frame secretly hoping that some of her luck, her magic, would follow the group. When Truman reached the studio door, he took a deep breath before opening it.

"Let's make it good, gentlemen." He pulled the door open. The subtle scent of cigarette smoke, and other not-so-legal types of smoke, as well as warm candle wax and fresh paint swarmed around his face.

In the dimly lit control room, he found Shauna sitting at the colorful boards. She looked different from when he'd first seen her. She didn't have on that ridiculous hat. Her hair had been taken out of the braids and pulled back into a ponytail that cascaded down her back like a horse's mane.

He half expected her to be in a business suit or worse, in one of her trademark sequined gowns. With her foot sitting on the chair, her knee to her chest, she looked more like an intern. God help them.

Then Shauna turned around. Her wide eyes held a mixture of hope, sorrow, and maybe a flash of anticipation. He hoped.

He couldn't stop staring at her. The closer he got to her, the more entranced he became. His stare went from her soft gaze down to her cute nose and her luscious mouth. Shauna placed her hands with long, delicate fingers on her lap, and looked so elegant and sexy. She pulled him into her, seducing him without saying a word, singing a note, or even a smile... until Sully's nudge broke the stare.

Shauna stood. Her T-shirt hung right above her navel. He couldn't stop staring at her flat stomach and her dipped-in waist that topped her flared hips. Truman strained to bring his gaze back up to hers and control his rapid heartbeat. He had to show her he meant business even if his body begged for him to be sinful.

"You want to introduce me to your band?" Shauna took a step closer to Truman and his friends, but maintained a safe distance.

"What?" Truman seemed shocked that Shauna spoke.

Her melodic tone lulled him to a weakened state that he would have given up a kidney if she asked. This woman had no idea of her inherent power.

Ervin pushed past Truman and Sully. "Hi. I'm Ervin Willis. Drummer."

Truman watched Shauna connect hands with Ervin. A strange flash of red colored his vision and his stomach knotted. Truman caught the subtle way Ervin smiled at her and how his friend pulsed his hand twice when he held hers. He'd been friends with Ervin long enough to know what that meant.

"This is Tony Waters." Truman pulled his short friend forward and pushed Ervin back. "He plays the fiddle."

"Nice to meet you, ma'am." Tony presented a wide grin.

As though he wanted to skip the rough treatment, Charlie offered his hand to Shauna. "Charlie Vaughan. Bass. How are you doing?"

She nodded and smiled politely as she shook his hand.

Charlie's mouth hung open. "Your skin is so soft." He slid his free hand over hers. "Do you have kids?"

Truman pulled Charlie's hands from Shauna's. "We should get started."

He cleared his throat, adjusted his baseball cap, and glanced at Sully, the last member of the Sliders who hadn't introduced himself.

"Sully?" Truman elbowed his now tight-lipped buddy.

"Yeah, we should get started." Sully brushed past Truman, shot a harsh look to Shauna, and disappeared into the recording booth.

"That's Sully Parrish." Ervin spoke to Shauna as he strolled to the studio with his drum kit. "Don't pay him no mind. I think he was dropped on his head as a baby."

From the way Shauna's jaw flexed, Truman could tell it did bother her. She didn't have to be so sensitive. She didn't know Sully. She didn't know any of them.

When the rest of the band disappeared into the soundproof booth, Truman stepped closer to Shauna. With each step, his heart pounded harder and harder.

What the hell was going on with him? His mind needed to be on his son, his band, and his music, in that order. With the exception of his music, he needed to keep his emotions in check.

"Sully's just nervous." Truman sat his case on the floor.

Shauna spoke as though she didn't hear him. "Let's go over your song list."

"My what?"

Shauna sauntered to the couch and eased down on it, curling her legs under her and looking poised like a cat. His hand itched like he wanted to pet her, stroke her from her wavy hair down her long back and to that sweet ass.

As soon as that thought entered his mind, he snapped his attention back to her face. As long as he stared in her eyes, he would be fine.

"I want to see the list of songs you're planning for the album. Or do you and your band fly by the seat of your pants on these things?"

More like a ferocious cat. Forget petting. Maybe he needed to hold her down, pin her wrist back, and—Christ, he had to stop. He had been around sexy women before. Shauna had him thinking and feeling in a way he hadn't in a long time.

"I don't understand why I need to show you my set list." He maintained his position but kept his stare fixed on the woman who seemed a lot more confident and sure of herself than the last time he'd seen her.

"It's not a set list. This isn't a show." Shauna rolled her eyes like she didn't enjoy dealing with amateurs.

That notion boiled Truman's blood. He stomped closer to her.

"Your album should tell a story, set a stage." She ran her hand over her hair. "You should start off with a bang to get people interested, then ease them in with some mid-tempo tunes, then bring them down with some slower songs, then finish it even stronger. Think of your favorite albums that you love listening to from start to finish. Think about the stories they tell."

He didn't. Instead he wanted to question her experience. What made her such an expert when she had to be a few years younger than him?

"How long have you been producing?" Truman glared at her, daring for her to break.

"I've never produced an album or even a song. You guys would be my first." Shauna barreled on. "But let me tell you about my seven albums I've put out, in particular, my first one. I was given a list of songs to sing by the label. Since I was new with no hits, they wanted to make sure I had some winners on the CD. They got some hack songwriter with one or two big hits to his or her credit to write most of the songs. The rest were covers. My manager thought, at the time, that was the best way to introduce me. You do have a manager, right?"

Truman kept his mouth closed but gave her one solid nod in response.

His slow response must have answered some other questions in her head. "Are you the lead singer *and* the band's manager?"

He kept his stare on her but his mouth closed. When Shauna sighed, Truman felt his stomach twinge.

"I may be new at owning a studio, but this is not my first time recording. If you let me, I can help you avoid some of the pitfalls I experienced." She held up her hand to him.

"We're supposed to be partners in this, right?" He folded his arms. "Why don't you make sure we sound good, and I'll take care of everything else?"

She ran her tongue over her teeth. He could almost hear her counting to ten in her head. His mother would be so disappointed in his combative behavior.

"Fine. Don't listen to me. I'm not your manager." She stood. "I'm not even your friend."

Craig stepped into the tense room. "So how is my dream team working out?"

No one spoke until Truman broke the ice.

"No disrespect to either one of you, but I have to get in there with my band and we need to tune up and rehearse." He shook Craig's hand, tipped his hat to Shauna, and walked toward the recording booth. The drama wouldn't help him sing any better.

"Before you do that, I have an idea." Craig held up his phone and smiled.

* * * *

Shauna had a sinking suspicion what Craig wanted to do. She kept her stare on him until he approached the duo.

"I plan on going to New York tomorrow to the Universe office to personally play a song from you guys." Craig pointed to Truman and the band in the studio. "So you all need to do a great job on recording one song that's an example of your style."

Truman nodded. "Sounds doable. We've been playing our songs for years, so we have them down pat."

Shauna had no idea Craig had planned on going to the Universe office. She knew the reason. He would make a plea to keep Charisma so that they would have distribution. If Craig planned on going tomorrow, Shauna would have to make a trip later that day. Time to act like a boss.

"Truman, you were right about something when you were in my office. A month to get your album out does not give you a lot of time to promote yourselves. So I have a plan." He patted the couch seat cushion next to Shauna. "Have a seat."

Truman split his attention between Shauna and her manager. Even she didn't know what Craig had planned.

Truman attempted to lift his guitar case and make a speedy exit. "I don't want to waste time. I should get in there and start rehearsing."

"We have the studio until nine so we have some time. What I want to do won't take long at all, but it'll have mega impact on you and Shauna." He patted the back of the couch this time. "Sit. Please."

Truman huffed but finally sat down next to Shauna. Good to see that Truman didn't want to be a part of this dog and pony show either. The way he kept his gaze cast down, he made it obvious that he barely wanted to even look at her. Seeing that hurt her a lot more than she thought it would. She barely knew this man. Why should it concern her that he didn't want to look at her?

He leaned back, though, like he didn't want to get near her. The supple leather squeaked under his weight. That worked for her. He hadn't exactly been Mr. Charming.

"Shauna Stellar still has about two million followers on her Instagram account." Craig took a few steps back. "So what I'll do is snap some shots of you with her and caption it that Shauna is working hard in the studio with Truman Woodley and the Sliders. You guys do have an Instagram account, right?"

Before Truman could answer, Craig took a picture of him.

"Um, I don't know. Tony normally handles our social media accounts." Truman looked into the recording booth.

"How am I supposed to tag you if you—never mind." Craig snapped another picture. "No. This isn't good. Truman, hand Shauna something. Your music. Yeah. That'll look good."

Shauna tried hard not to smile at her manager's antics. The man knew the best ways to work around any obstacles.

When she peered at Truman, he glared at her for a moment, then turned to Craig before he finally pulled out his music and handed it to Shauna. When she reached for it, Craig took a series of pictures.

"Good. Really good. You two need to be a bit closer together." Craig waved his hand to them. "Scoot in closer."

Shauna felt heat licking her cheeks. "Craig, I think you have the pictures you need. We really should get back to work." She started to scoot to the edge to go to the boards next to the sound engineer.

"No." Craig shook his head. "This will be even better. Trust me."

"Famous last words, right?" Truman chuckled like he wanted to make Shauna feel better.

It didn't work. Shauna shifted. "If you want working shots, I think you have it. We're losing valuable studio time."

"Shauna."

The sternness in Craig's voice stiffened Shauna's spine. She couldn't believe after ten years, she still responded to Craig's disappointed tone. She felt childish, but still buckled to his demands.

With great reluctance, she curved her back to ease her backside closer to Truman while still leaving a comfortable distance between the two of them. She left her leg under her behind, which allowed her knee to jut forward, creating another barrier.

Shauna waited a beat before bringing her gaze up. When she found him staring back at her, her body flooded with emotions. Embarrassed heat filled her face and neck. Her hands trembled so much that she had to set his music down and press her palms onto her thighs. Her knee bounced and she wished it didn't.

"Truman, lean forward, drape your arm across the back of the couch, and act like you're asking Shauna a question." Craig crouched down, preparing to take this picture.

Truman cleared his throat first. When he placed his arm across the back of the couch, Shauna felt like she had stopped breathing. Since she caught his outdoorsy scent again, she knew that couldn't be true. With his long arm, his hand almost reached her shoulder.

Craig pointed to her first. "Shauna, pick up the music again." Then he directed his attention to Truman. "Move in closer."

Truman adjusted his baseball cap on his head first and exhaled before he finally moved. He sat so close to her now, his face a few feet away from hers; she noticed the brown, short hairs over his cheeks from not shaving. She also noticed a small scar by his lip, and immediately wanted to ask him about it.

Truman placed his other hand on his knee closest to Shauna. Even there, she felt the heat from his skin.

This had to end soon. If it didn't, she would be crawling out of her skin. Not since her disastrous relationship with Raheem had Shauna been this close to a man. Despite their disagreement earlier, none of that mattered now that Truman had her cornered, hot and bothered.

"I guess I should really ask you a question now that I'm here." Truman's low voice rumbled through her body. He waited until Shauna regained eye contact with him before he continued. "Is this going to work?"

Shauna blinked. "What?"

"Us. This arrangement. Will it work?"

Shauna didn't know how to answer. She came to the studio determined to set boundaries and be the boss of this situation. All of that changed as soon as Truman got close to her and she looked into his eyes.

"I think I got it." Craig peered over his glasses at his screen. "Now I'll change the filter. Do the picture in black and white." He admired his work. "Oh, that's perfect." He turned the phone around to show Shauna and Truman. "Look. The dynamic duo."

Shauna stared at the small screen. What she saw didn't look like a music producer and her artist. She saw a man and a woman in dark lighting trying to find each other.

Truman must have seen something different. Without a word, he got up from the couch and grabbed his guitar but left the music.

"Your fans are going to love this." Craig looked so satisfied as he posted the picture.

Shauna, finally able to breathe again, tried wrapping her head around what happened. If she planned on taking this job seriously, she needed to keep her distance from Truman Woodley.

"Why did you do that?" Shauna shook her head.

"What? You mean get you his music?" Craig winked.

She should have appreciated the gesture, but it reminded her very quickly that even as an adult, she needed someone to help her navigate through basic interactions. She wanted to solve this dilemma on her own.

"I had that handled." Now feeling her power, she managed to stand and go to the boards next to their sound engineer, Hank.

"Yes, that's what I saw. Not him walking away with the music, but him wanting to turn it over to you as soon as you asked." Craig shoved his phone into his pocket. "And that picture, my dear, is going to push doubt from people's minds."

"Doubts about what? Me wanting to get back in the studio and work again?" Shauna had hoped her fans understood that she would want to get back into the swing of things again after getting out of Peaceful Acres.

Craig leaned forward. "No, that you're still a desirable woman who still is the Princess of Love Ballads. The bad breakup with Raheem didn't kill your sex appeal."

The thought that Shauna had kept in the back of her mind now came forward. It became real with Craig's words. Not only had Raheem embarrassed her by the way he had broken up with her, but her image as a sexy yet untouchable siren became shattered. How could she sing about love when she couldn't hold on to a man?

Despite what Craig thought about his picture, she didn't see Truman fawning over her. He saw a man forced to interact with her, just like with Raheem. Would she never break that cycle?

Chapter 5

"You're right, Sull. Let's get out of here." Truman stomped back into the studio with his guitar case in his hand.

The confusion riddling his body had his head spinning. He hadn't felt this out of sorts since high school when he dated the head cheerleader. Shauna couldn't be described as a perky cheerleader. She hadn't encouraged him. If anything, she got him thinking about other things like how good she smelled when he sat close to her on the couch, and how he could feel the heat coming from her body. Was she actually staring at his mouth at one point? Did she want to kiss him? Did he want to kiss her?

Oh, hell.

He threw the case down and went over to Ervin's drum set to tear it down. He hadn't gone to a recording studio. He'd stepped into a circus complete with a ringleader. Craig pushed them together like a meddling mother. As much as Truman wanted to hate the treatment, the close proximity got them to stop bickering about music and actually look at each other. He had to admit, the stripped down and vulnerable version of Shauna looked as appealing as the glammed-up one.

"What's going on?" Confusion covered Charlie's face.

"She said something stupid, didn't she?" Sully rested his forearm on the neck of his guitar as he watched Truman pack his things together.

"Will you shut up, idiot?" Ervin threw his drumstick at the back of Sully's head. "What's the deal, Tru? Why you want to split?"

Truman couldn't explain his feelings. It didn't make sense. One moment, he came into this situation preparing to be professional and accommodating. Then he found himself bickering with the woman who could jumpstart his career. By the end, he became mesmerized by her eyes and floral scent. He still remembered how her lips parted as she stared at him. Those full lips.

"Do we have to pay for studio time? Is that coming out of our money?" Tony pulled his notepad from his back pocket and wrote some calculations in it. As long as it kept him quiet, Truman felt content to let the man scribble away.

"This is a joke, man." Truman scratched his head. He turned to the guys. "I said pack it up, fellas, and let's roll."

"You don't have to tell me twice." Sully unhooked his guitar from the amplifier.

When Truman heard the pop it made after Sully disconnected it, he equated the sound with quitting and failure. He'd never quit at anything, but staying there and working with Shauna had him nervous that he would do something foolish…like think with "Little Truman" again.

"Wait." Ervin held up his hands. "This is our dream, guys. I'm not sure what happened. You know I always have your back, Tru. But I'm not willing to pack it in over nothing."

Truman kept his face straight. "She——" He couldn't finish what he wanted to say.

What could he say? She looked incredible without a stitch of makeup on her face? Her body had his fingers tingling because he wanted to touch her? Or that he loved the idea that she stared at his lips for a while?

Ervin put his hand on Truman's shoulder. "Like coach said, walk it off." He smiled.

When Truman looked through the glass into the control room, he found Shauna sitting at the control board next to a large man he hadn't seen before.

Truman's stomach tied in a knot knowing how much valuable studio time they wasted because he couldn't control his emotions. Shauna Stellar was just a woman. He had to treat recording their album as a job. As Ervin suggested, he did need to cool down.

"Let's take five and regroup." Truman's suggestion should have been geared to himself instead of his band.

Once the guys left the studio, he went inside the control booth.

"Hey." He approached Shauna.

"Truman Woodley," she began, "this is Hank, the sound engineer. He'll be here with us while we record."

"Nice to meet you." Truman put out his hand, but Hank kept his attention on the boards for a while before he finally acknowledged him and shook his hand with his meaty one.

"The guys and I are going to take a quick five before we start, okay?" He jutted his thumb over his shoulder.

She nodded again.

He turned but then her statement stopped him. "I like your songs."
Truman returned his attention to her. "You looked at them already?"
Shauna spun in her seat to face him. "Did you write all of these?"

"Except for the one called 'Beer and More Beer.' Ervin wrote that after a hard night of partying." He snickered, distinctly remembering when Ervin sang the hook to him after vomiting his guts out.

"I have some suggestions on changes if you don't—"

Truman cut her off. "I do. I wrote every word for a reason. No changes are needed."

Before the situation turned sour again, Truman walked out. He needed some space and a second to figure out how this woman got into his head so quickly.

* * * *

How could a man who managed to penetrate her soul from one look get so defensive about words? In her career, Shauna tweaked words to songs she'd been given all the time. As long as people bought the songs, what did it matter that she changed some of the lyrics?

As Shauna read the lyrics to each of Truman's songs, she got an understanding of the man underneath the worn out baseball cap. One song talked about meeting that special woman. He had another song that detailed the perfect day, complete with an impromptu baseball game with his friends, drinking beer by a swimming hole, and ending it with his woman by his side. Then he had a song that talked about someone special to him.

After Raheem dumped her, and her public meltdown, men looked at her as damaged goods. Even Craig echoed those sentiments with his latest Instagram picture. The idea plagued her thoughts, even during her stay at Peaceful Acres. She could never get over that stigma. Truman probably thought the same thing when he bolted from her after taking the picture.

It used to offend her when she would be in the pages of men's magazine as a woman they saw as hot and sexy. She worked hard to be more than just a pretty face. Now she would pay any money she had left to be seen as desirable.

She shuffled the songs around, arranging them into an order she thought would work for the album. She had to admit that Truman had some great music. Maybe she could convince Craig to scrap the duet idea. At least not for this album, and especially not with her.

She took a deep breath and caught the strong cigarette scent coming from the control room. She found Hank sitting in a swirl of smoke.

"There's no smoking in here, ever." Shauna's breathing increased but she tried to keep that and her cool in control.

She would not be working in cigarette smoke. The scent smelled awful. Even if she never sung another note for the rest of her life, the smoke hurt her throat.

"I've always smoked." Hank managed to speak while keeping the cigarette pinched between his lips on the side. "It helps me work." The burly man with the bushy beard didn't bother looking her way when he spoke, just like how he treated Truman.

"It doesn't help me work and I own this business. Put it out." She didn't want to throw her trump card down but this man forced her to do it. If he didn't straighten up, she would boot his behind out of the whole production.

Hank snickered at her and dropped the lit cigarette into his cup of coffee.

"Now find some fans and clear out the stench in this room." She stood at the doorway. "It's bad enough the place smells like pot. I guess my mother just let anyone come in to record."

Hank walked by Shauna as he peered down at her. "You got that right."

No one would intimidate her. At least not in *her* studio. She sat outside of the control booth and waited for Hank to come back with a fan. Glancing at her watch, a staggered sigh forced its way from her mouth when it hit her how much studio time they'd lost. How in the world would she have a song ready for the record label in a few hours?

Her heart pounded. She blinked several times to regain clarity on her blurred vision.

Come on. Don't do this. Keep it together.

She exhaled, shook her head, and tried focusing on the lyrics to the song called "Reeling" she wanted the group to start working on once they finished their break. Looking at the music, it looked like a nice mid-tempo piece that would put the group on the map. She still couldn't hear the music.

After springing from the couch, she sauntered into the recording studio where the group left their instruments. She stared at the piano in the corner of the room. It looked more daunting than when she'd taken her first step outside of Peaceful Acres.

Why did the idea of playing the piano again scare her? She started playing at the age of four. Some days touching the keys gave her more comfort than talking to her mother. Being an only child, the piano often became the sibling she wished she had.

Shortly after taking a seat, Shauna put both hands on the keys, looked at the music, and started playing. Her fingers tripped over some of the notes. She cursed under her breath and tried the song again. Each time she got better and better.

Her shoulders relaxed as her fingers moved over the instrument. The knot that had formed in her stomach before she sat down disappeared the longer she played. She'd reach nirvana without chanting.

When she opened her mouth to sing, she saw Truman standing at the doorway into the recording studio. Her hands froze over the keys as she stared at him. She swallowed as she tried getting a handle on what must have been going through his mind to hear her butchering his song.

She cleared her throat as she stood. "I think this song should be the one we work on first." She attempted to sound professional as she handed him his original copies back. "This one has chart appeal and the right tempo."

Truman took the sheets from her as she walked by him.

"You sounded good over there." He spoke to her in a soothing voice as she made it to the doorway.

Shauna turned to him. She kept her face straight in case he didn't mean what he'd said.

"That's kind of how I envisioned the song sounding." He sat the music on a stand, crouched down, and picked up his guitar again. "Good to see we're on the same page." He cleared his throat. "At least for this song."

She would take that small step for now. "We've lost a lot of studio time." As much as she wanted to smile and thank him, she didn't want to get sucked into his nice-guy routine until she knew his angle.

He hung his guitar strap on his shoulder. "Break time is over. Are you ready?"

Her mouth went dry. She clasped her hands together to hide her fear. "Let's do this."

The rest of the band bounded back to the room, excited and exuberant at three in the morning. They must have gotten a lot of sleep.

"Let's rock 'n roll." Ervin retrieved his drumsticks from the floor and made his way behind his modest drum set.

"Guys, we're doing 'Reeling' first. Let's do a couple of practice runs before we lay the track." Truman's commanding nature had his band falling in line.

Shauna took that as her cue to go into the control room. To hear the music better, she turned off the loud fan as she sat with Hank at the boards.

"Let's take it from the top, boys." Truman nodded with each tap Ervin made on his drumsticks.

"Before you start, gentlemen, do you need anything in there?" Shauna hated to interrupt the flow, but she wanted to hear perfection. "Some artists like candles burning, pictures of loved ones, stuffed animals." She loved burning blackberry-scented candles.

"Lady, we're in a recording studio, not a slumber party." Sully sneered at her through the glass separating them.

She gritted her teeth. Sully wouldn't break her.

"You know, I've always wanted pictures of the kids in front of me when I played." Charlie reached into his pocket and pulled out his phone. He set it up on a nearby easel and smiled as he stared at it.

Truman patted his pocket but didn't retrieve anything. Maybe he had a picture of a girlfriend or wife he wanted to view but didn't in front of Shauna. Now she couldn't stop staring at his pants for a different reason.

"Fine. I don't care if you want the whole family in the recording studio. We need to play." Sully strummed an angry chord on his guitar.

"Then tell me about the song you're about to sing." She spread her hand over the lyrics.

"You've got to be kidding me." Sully groaned and leaned his head back.

She could feel his frustration rising through the control booth glass. She had a job to do and she knew what worked.

"Tell me what 'Reeling' is about." Shauna directed her attention to Truman.

"If it gets us recording faster." Truman slung his guitar behind him.

Even angry Truman looked good. His brown eyes narrowed, his chest pumped up, and his lips looked tight. Not exactly kissable but definitely interesting. He started to get a morning stubble around his goatee. That made him even hotter.

"The song is about when you first meet that special person. It's when you get the butterflies in your belly and loss of appetite. And when you finally get to kiss that person for the first time, you're just in heaven. You're reeling."

Shauna hadn't noticed her mouth had hung open as she listened to him until Hank coughed. "Is this song about someone in your life now?" She attempted to make the question sound as innocent but professional as possible, but below the layer of her query bubbled a hint of curiosity, maybe even jealousy.

Truman looked around at his band members. He faced forward and said, "No. Not anymore. It's an older song but a fan favorite."

She exhaled and smiled. "Ordinarily I would tell you to sing the song to that person. It helps gives soul to your lyrics."

"Hell, Tru, just sing it to her so we can get on with this." Sully pointed to Shauna.

She stared at Truman as he made his way to the microphone. As he sang she noticed he moved his head around a lot as though he sang on a stage.

Thank goodness they weren't recording yet. The recording would have been worthless only because of his constant movement.

The man sang with so much heart; Shauna felt it from her seat. Chills covered her body until she felt like one big goose bump. She rubbed her hand up and down her arm as she looked over the lyrics as he sang. It didn't help that the man oozed sex.

In his loose-fitting T-shirt and his worn jeans, Truman looked confident and strong, attractive qualities in any man.

She made some notes on the lyrics, some changes she thought would work better in the song. Then she thought about how she would present these changes to a very protective Truman. He'd nearly bitten her head off earlier when she'd tried altering his lyrics.

At the end of the song, Truman and his band talked among themselves. From their smiles, they must have liked the sound and arrangement. Now came the hard part.

She turned on the mic to talk to them in the booth.

"Good take, boys. Let's can it." Hank spoke before she could say a word.

She turned to the burly mess. "What did you just say to them?"

Hank snorted, not like he was being insolent but because he breathed that way normally. "It sounded good. Why have them play it over and over again?"

"For one thing, I'm producing. Point two, Truman said this was a rehearsal, and he wasn't near the mic for half the song. It'll sound amateurish." Shauna knew Craig had to have been watching this whole display, but she wouldn't back down. She would want someone to stand up and say something didn't sound right if she had been in the booth recording. Actually, she did have that person in her life.

She glanced at Craig who winked at her, his way of letting her know he backed her decision. She set in her jaw and kept her gaze on Hank. The big man finally turned away from her and tinkered with the knobs and controls on the boards.

She turned on the microphone again. "Let's hear that song one more time."

She saw Sully and Charlie's shoulders ease down. Ervin's eyes lit up like she'd given them a million dollars. Truman looked confused.

"Was there something wrong in there? I know I said this would be a practice run, but it sounds like the engineer liked it." Truman questioned her as though he'd failed her.

She bit the inside of her cheek and counted to ten before she spoke. "No. Everything's fine. I want to get different takes. We can mesh the best takes together."

Truman nodded but his confused expression contradicted his compliance.

"This time, Truman, I need for you to stand right at the microphone." Shauna held her palm up to her face to mimic how Truman should stand. "I want to hear your voice clearly."

Truman glanced at Hank who only shrugged.

She ignored their unspoken conversation and continued. "Also, what do you think about changing the line 'You're the right one for me' to 'You're the one I need'?"

Sully groaned so loud Shauna would have been able to hear it with the microphones off.

"She's doing it, Tru." Sully pointed to Shauna. "I thought you said she wasn't going to change our music."

"She's not." Truman looked over the lyrics.

His icy stare momentarily stunned Shauna.

Instead of buckling, she pressed on. "The flow will go better if you make that change. Why not try it for the next take." She tapped her fingers. Her nails clicked against the surface while he whispered something to Sully.

Without answering her, Truman started playing the song over again. The strong chords showed Truman's anger. He kept his mouth right at the microphone but kept his eyes closed. When the line she wanted him to change came up, he sang it...the same way he'd written it.

Shauna's shoulders tightened. Her neck felt stiff. If she felt this wound up this early in the production, she would be a complete mess by the end.

Truman attempted to show her who would be head dog in this process. He probably thought she should have been happy that he obliged her on one point. Nope. Not having it. She wanted it done the right way, her way.

At the end of the song, Shauna turned on her microphone again. "Thanks for staying close to the mic this time. You can hear the difference."

You catch more flies with honey.

Before speaking again, she took a breath first. "But I would still like you to try the song with the alternate line. If it doesn't work, you can tell me 'I told you so' and I'll agree."

Truman moved close to the mic. "No. Every word I've written means something to me. I don't want to change anything."

She found the passion in his eyes. That didn't mean she wouldn't press forward to get her point across. She had a stake in this. "Let's take a break." Shauna clicked off the microphone.

"Good." Hank lumbered to his feet. "I need a smoke."

She stood. Before Craig or anyone else could criticize her performance, she slipped on her shoes and made her way to the roof. It had always been her favorite spot in the studio. She used to go there to sing if she had a hard time getting over a difficult passage. She especially liked to think up there. Right now she needed breathing room.

She burst through the door and found her familiar spot on the edge of the roof. She looked over and watched the waves crash against the beach.

The waves. They always put her life in perspective. She would have to learn to go with the flow, which didn't fit her nature.

She needed to learn to flow with Truman. Learn to ride his waves. However, he needed to bend and for more than where to position his mouth.

Shauna gazed at the full moon. "Hey, Mom. I know it's been a while since we've talked. I had to get myself together after you—" She couldn't muster the strength to say the word. "I need help. I wish you were here. You made everything better, even when I took for granted that you would make my life easier." She wrapped her arms around her body when a strong breeze came off the ocean. "You know this guy I'm working with now. You signed him. Did he give you this much trouble? If not, what am I doing wrong?"

Stars twinkled as though giving her a silent response. Like with everything else, she would need to figure this out on her own.

She stood, wiped off her backside, and made her way back downstairs. As soon as she hit the bottom landing she glanced toward the back door and saw Hank. He coughed and sputtered when he made eye contact with her. He pulled the cloudy pipe from his mouth and turned his back.

Shauna didn't need to ask him what he had. Truman and his band didn't deserve to be a part of someone else's shortcomings. Shauna had been through that, and didn't want to see anyone else suffer like she had.

The matter needed to be dealt with, but couldn't right now. Shauna made her way to the studio and reclaimed her position. Hank arrived about ten minutes later smelling of soap, Lysol, and potpourri. He must have rolled in the crushed, dried flower products until he thought the stench had been covered. It didn't matter. Not to Shauna.

After the band had played the song at least ten more times, the last time being the slowest and the sloppiest of the set, she called it a day. Truman never changed the line in any of the dozen times. Stubborn, stubborn, stubborn.

"I'd say this went well, huh?" Craig nudged Shauna's shoulder.

"Yeah, sure." She gathered her things together. She wanted to go home, take a long bath, and crawl into bed. "Can't wait to do this again in a few hours."

"That's the spirit." Craig patted her back.

Shauna took a CD copy of the many takes. She would listen to them in her sleep.

"Did you make a copy of that for me?" Craig pointed to the jewel case she held. "I'll need that for the meeting with the studio heads in New York."

She smiled. "Let me find a really good version of the song and record that on a single disc for you." She patted her manager on the shoulder like he'd done to her earlier. Craig stared at her for a moment as though he didn't believe her. That might be a good reaction to have. For what Shauna had planned for her day today would surely piss him off.

"I want a copy by tonight, okay?"

She nodded. He would get his copy. If she had luck on her side, she would be bringing him back a lot more.

When Craig walked away from her, Shauna looked over at Hank. She had one thing to do before they left. She didn't need to leave any loose ends.

"Hank, don't leave yet. We need to talk."

Chapter 6

Shauna pinched her thigh to keep awake as she waited in the main office of Universe Records. The short nap she'd taken on the plane trip to New York didn't help, especially since her mind kept tripping over the idea that all of this could be a colossal mistake.

She'd listened to every take of "Reeling." Every time Truman had sung the line she wanted him to change, her stomach twitched. She wished she could have convinced him to change that one lyric. It would have worked better with the song. But who was she? Just a woman who used to have top selling songs and more money than God.

Looking around in the Universe Records office, it looked like they had forgotten her. Her CD cover used to be on every large-screen TV hanging in the hallway and in the main office. Now the monitors showed videos of other artists, younger artists. At twenty-five, she felt like a has-been.

Shauna clutched her purse that held Truman's CD inside. Her knee bounced. The magazine she'd been flipping through had fallen to the floor, signaling her jittery limbs. She wanted to run her fingers back through her hair, but she refrained so she wouldn't ruin her perfect upswept hairdo that took her forever to achieve on her own.

Shauna grumbled. "I should be resting. I should be taking it easy. I should—"

"Ms. Stellar?"

Shauna turned to the receptionist. When the woman told her she could go into the conference room for her meeting, Shauna's trembling hands became coated with sweat. Shauna walked past the receptionist's desk. As soon as Shauna saw the huge room, she felt small again. This test would be her ocean, and Mr. Zinner and his team of consultants matched the waves that would be crashing down on her.

She smoothed her hands down her skirt and caught the gaze of one man looking at her legs, probably eyeing her boots, well, Nikia's boots. They didn't fit her style, but they worked in a pinch.

"We don't have much time, Ms. Stellar." Mr. Zinner pointed to his watch. He made it obvious that she no longer mattered to Universe or him. "I have another meeting right after this."

She turned her head and caught sight of herself in Zinner's wall of mirrors. She looked fierce. She looked confident. As long as she could hide the fear in her eyes, she could do this. Lives depended on her. Today she would be the fierce Shauna Stellar and not the scared fifteen-year-old Chantel Evans who had stumbled into this same office ten years ago.

She took a deep breath. "Okay." She hung her head down as she made her way to the table. In an instant she felt like nothing. Like a nobody.

Mr. Zinner pointed to two chairs at the end of the long conference room table.

Without a word, she sat in one of the chairs. "I would hope after more than two hundred and fifty million records sold for you that you would at least call me Shauna." She crossed her long legs and sat her Hermés purse, another borrowed item, on the table.

"What can I do for you, Ms., uh, Shauna? I haven't spoken to you in such a long time." Mr. Zinner danced around the fact that she'd had a mental meltdown.

She wouldn't be so ginger with the topic. She wanted to see this short, fat, bald man sweat even more than his already drenched state.

"Yes, time off can do wonders for your spirit. I see things a lot more clearly now." She kept her stare on him. Maybe if she kept her focus on one thing, she wouldn't feel so overwhelmed.

"That's wonderful." Mr. Zinner interlaced his chubby fingers together and placed his hands on his desk.

"But I'm back and I'm ready to work." She beamed to show some sincerity.

"I know our offices should have informed you of our decision when we released you from your contract." Mr. Zinner wiped his forehead.

"Not your offices, Mr. Zinner. *You* should have done it." Shauna smiled. "But that's all water under the bridge. I'm here to make sure you don't make another monumental mistake. You dropped me from your label as an artist. I understand why. It's all about business."

Actually she didn't understand. How could this man who promised to be there for her when he signed her at fifteen years of age drop her like some one-night stand? Why couldn't he look at her now? Had she changed that much?

"I'm glad you understand, Shauna." Mr. Zinner smiled as though the meeting would be ending soon.

Shauna couldn't go until she made this deal. She hadn't done much for herself since working professionally. This would be her first big step. "The only thing I ask is that you don't drop the association with Charisma Music. I'm producing a great new act."

"Who is it?" Mr. Zinner leaned in closer.

Shauna reached into her purse and pulled out a silver CD encased in a clear jewel case. When she scanned the room to look for the equipment to play it, an associate stood and strolled to her.

"Hi, again, Ms. Stellar." The young man took the case from her. "I'm Laz. I spoke to you, um, at your last show. I'm not sure if you remember me."

Shauna blinked. A lot from that day she managed to block from her memory. She did remember someone from the label talking to her, but didn't remember the person's face.

"Good to see you again." To hide the fact that she couldn't recall him, she simply smiled.

"You're looking well." He looked her in her eyes.

Out of everyone there, Laz had enough integrity to give her eye contact at least. Shauna appreciated the gesture. She asked him to play the CD for the group.

"Just think of a male version of the Dixie Chicks." She smiled at herself, impressed at her country music reference. "They're country but with a broader appeal."

Laz played "Reeling." The song, despite not being tricked up with heavy editing, sounded good, really good.

Truman's voice came through strong and clear. He seemed to growl some of his lyrics so he came across as sexy. She squeezed her legs together and fought against the urge to scream, "Isn't he wonderful?"

She had to admit. Truman sang like a man should sing. Strong, assured, passionate. That didn't mean he made their working relationship a pleasant experience.

"Who is this?" Zinner kept his stare on the sound system like Truman would pop out and introduce himself.

She wrestled with the idea of calling him Tru Lee, one of the new stage names she'd been thinking about for him. Shauna didn't want to make too many leaps today. "Truman Woodley and the Sliders. The next big thing in country."

Zinner grimaced. "Truman Woodley. Country music you say?"

One of Zinner's associates leaned over and whispered to him.

Zinner straightened up. "I don't know." He smirked and leaned back.

"Country music isn't as popular as it used to be. Even Taylor Swift has jumped ship."

"That was because she didn't have me to produce her." She liked this confident feeling even if it pulled everything out of her. She wasn't herself. She was Shauna Stellar, superstar. "With me producing this group, they are going to be the next big thing." She held her hand out to the associate as a silent way to summon him to bring the CD back to her. "My question to you, Mr. Zinner, is do you want to be on the next big wave or standing on the beach wondering why you didn't snap up this opportunity when it was offered to you?"

She shoved the CD back into her purse and kept her hands in her lap. Her mouth felt like she ingested sand, and she couldn't swallow. She could barely keep her knees from bouncing.

She needed this deal, and she wanted to secure this on her own like an adult, like a boss.

"What would you like?" Zinner rubbed one of his three chins.

Shauna's shoulders relaxed. "Retain Charisma Music. The band will finish their album as promised. You will get a small percentage of their album sales, which I predict will be through the roof. You'll get a bigger payoff because my name will be attached." Shauna stood. "You'll also pay us extra for retaining our contract." She heard gasps as she turned to the door. "If you don't, then I can certainly take our company to another label. Diddy was very nice to me while I was away. Maybe I'll take him up on his offer to—"

"I wish you luck in your pursuits, Shauna." Zinner struggled to stand.

Shauna smiled but inside her stomach squeezed into a tight ball. She'd failed. How the hell could that happen? She was Shauna Stellar. How could anyone say no to her?

Staring at Zinner, the realization hit her that he had said no. He wanted no parts of her or her company. Instead of crumbling right there and then, she walked confidently back to Mr. Zinner and extended her hand.

"It was nice doing business with you. Good luck to you." She shook her former boss's hand. This was the same man who'd promised her the world when she was fifteen years old. Now he acted like he didn't know her, like some struggling singer off the street.

Just get me to a bathroom so I can cry in peace.

Shauna pressed the down button on the elevator. She wanted no one to talk to her, touch her, or bother her until she got back home.

Home. Damn. She would have to face Craig. She'd ruined his meeting with Zinner and the executives. She didn't want to see the disappointed look on his face. She stepped into the empty elevator car and rode it down.

How would she be able to tell him and Truman that they had no distribution deal? Maybe now she could convince Craig that selling the company would be a good thing.

The elevator doors opened at the lobby level. A few people asked Shauna for her autograph as she tried navigating her way through them, shielding her face with her hand.

As soon as she reached the front doors to get out to the street, a hand gripped her arm and pulled her back.

"Let go of me." She struggled to get out of the hold.

She knew the paparazzi could be crazy, but they never put a hand on her. When she turned to see who had grabbed her, she gazed up to the face of the last person she ever thought she would see.

"Raheem? What are you doing here?" She pressed her hands against his chest to push him back.

Her stomach lurched. For once, she wished she could have thrown up on the cretin who'd broken her heart.

He flexed his chest muscle as though giving her a treat. "Looks like I'm saving you again." He licked his full lips, a trademark move of his that turned her stomach now.

She wondered if he had perpetually dry lips. She also wondered if any truth ever came through them or did lying come as natural to him as breathing.

"Come on. Let's go somewhere to talk."

Before she could object, he pulled her outside to his private limousine. His driver closed the door behind them, then moved into slow moving New York City traffic.

"What brings you to the NYC?" Raheem stretched his arms across the back of the seat he occupied as he stared at Shauna, who sat across from him.

"Meeting with Zinner. You?" Shauna snapped her fingers in an exaggerated way. "Wait. You have my old apartment here now. I saw it on that TV show."

Raheem lowered his head and puffed out a couple of chuckles before regaining eye contact. "The place held so many good memories. I couldn't bear to see someone else buy it. Besides, I got it for a steal."

Shauna scooted her way to the partition that separated the driver from the passenger area. "Please take me to the airport."

"Hold up, shorty." Raheem held his hand up.

"I'm not your shorty. Besides, won't your girlfriend or your baby's mama or whoever you're stringing along right now be upset that we were together?"

"Not when I tell them that there might be a 'Dirty Loving' remix version."

Raheem smoothed his fingers down his pencil thin moustache that topped his manicured goatee.

"What are you talking about?"

"Business, Shaun. You want the fat cats to know that you're back? Show them with a hit."

"You must be crazy. It's bad enough I'm in this car with you." Shauna crossed her arms over her chest. "I'm not going to do another duet with you." She turned to give the driver instructions to take her directly to the airport when Raheem's chilling words stopped her.

"So you don't care about coming back bigger and better than ever? You don't care about your fans?" Raheem kicked his legs out with his ankles crossed, looking like a crucified Jesus.

A chill coursed through her body. "Of course I care about my fans. It's you I don't like."

In mock horror, Raheem widened his eyes and put his hand on his chest. "Coming from you, that actually hurt. Now me? People already see me as a player. A dog. I'm the dick who got the Princess of Love Ballads dirty. Am I right?"

Shauna didn't answer. She paid no attention to what the press had said about him. If the public also thought of him as a heartless bastard, they characterized him correctly.

He shrugged. "Fine. You don't have to say it. What I will say is this. What if Miss Goody-Two-Shoes was able to tame the beast?"

"What does that mean?" Shauna hated that he baited her into asking about his plan.

"You do the remix with me. We get the song out there. Fans will dig it. They'll see you have a big heart and are full of forgiveness. Everything goes back to normal." He smiled, showing off his gleaming white teeth.

Shauna didn't know sharks got their teeth cleaned. The more she thought about his idea, the more it turned her stomach. "I appreciate you helping me back there. And I thank you for the ride. But I don't want anything else to do with you."

Raheem let out a long breath. "Fine. It's a shame you won't do the song with me. Make sure you stay off the Internet for a while. Thanks to your Insta post this morning, folks are already calling you crazy for hooking up with some country singer." Raheem laughed. "Is it true? Are you going to yodel at your shows now? Or have you completely given up singing?"

Shauna put her hand to her stomach. Although she hated hearing this from anyone, let alone Raheem, he made her think about the public's perception. Even when she finished Truman's album, she would have to concentrate on her own career. If she did this song, it could help her, Craig, and even Truman and his band. The exposure could be a good thing all around.

Shauna had to look out for her friends and family. Could she make this deal with Raheem?

"Let me buy you lunch. You're looking a little hungry."

Chapter 7

Truman had had it up to the top of his head with Shauna's diva attitude. When he'd found out that she'd fired Hank after the first night of recording, Truman lost his cool.

No more. She wouldn't get away with treating people like they didn't matter. That type of attitude existed in her world, not his.

He'd called Craig's house all day only to be told that Shauna had disappeared somewhere that morning and no one had seen her. She did leave a message that she would be home after five that night. That time worked for Truman, who had managed to find a job working for a trucking company that paid him cash under the table. He would be off work by the time Shauna came home.

Truman had called Ervin to go with him. Sully seemed too hot under the collar to go. Charlie wanted to watch his sister's twins because they reminded him of his own babies. Tony wrapped himself up with calculating their potential earnings.

Truman had showered and changed, not into anything special. He didn't need to impress Shauna although it seemed to him that nothing he did had made an impact. Every time the woman stood two feet near him, he'd made her sick. When he confronted her this time, he would really turn her insides out.

"So she fired Hank?" Ervin drummed his hands on the dashboard as Truman squinted to read the address and directions to Craig's house he'd written on a napkin.

"He said for no reason either." He took a sharp turn as he coasted down the street of an affluent neighborhood. He had heard rumors that a local boxer lived in that same neighborhood. Rich folks. Truman shook his head.

"Aside from asking you to change the line in your song, I don't see where she's acted out of line. Maybe there's a good reason for her to fire the engineer." Ervin propped his foot up on the dashboard.

Truman tuned his friend out. For this trip, Truman brought Ervin along to make sure Truman behaved himself. As much as he didn't want to admit it, Sully may have been right about having Shauna's name associated with their album. As soon as the press heard that she fired the engineer on the first day of recording, the album will forever be tainted.

He finally found the house. The same white Mercedes sat in the middle of the circular driveway.

"Ready to go?" Ervin finished his impromptu drum solo and hopped out of the shaky van.

Truman leaped out of the van and marched to the front door. He rang the doorbell and paced on the porch.

"Relax, man. I'm sure there's a good reason for all of this." Ervin smiled as usual.

The door opened. On the other side stood a woman that reminded Truman of a great restored Camaro. A classic, beautiful, mature black woman stared at him and Ervin. Her long hair held big curls that hung around her face. Her dark chocolate eyes stared at the duo even as Truman stared down her blouse to peek at her cleavage.

He immediately removed his baseball cap and nudged Ervin to do the same. "Hi, ma'am. I'm Truman Woodley, and this is Ervin Willis."

"You're the guys in that group Shauna is working with, right?" Her velvety voice did things that Truman's first girlfriend hadn't done, and they had done *everything* two young, horny teenagers could possibly do.

"Yes, ma'am. Are you her sister?" Ervin stared at the woman as much as Truman did.

She laughed. "Cute. No, I'm Craig's wife, Delores." She shook the men's hands and ushered them into the house.

Craig's gorgeous house floored Truman, more than meeting his attractive wife.

"Craig is expecting you." Delores walked in front of them. She led them to an office with two couches, a flat-screen TV, an entertainment center, and a desk. "Would you like a drink or something to eat? We've just finished dinner, but I can heat up anything for you."

As Truman said, "No, thank you," Ervin said, "Sure. What do you have?"

Truman smacked his friend in his arm. "We're here for business."

"I'm starving, man." Ervin rubbed his flat belly.

Delores smiled. "It's okay. I love to cook and I have plenty."

For a tall, skinny man, Ervin could really eat.

"Delores, have you seen—" A young woman bounded into the office. Her smooth, dark skin looked like polished onyx. Her petite body frame appeared tight. In her small top, Truman spied her flat stomach. Her short skirt showed off her toned legs. Jewelry dripped from her ears, neck, and fingers.

"Hello." She sauntered into the room. "I know who you are." She held her hand up to Truman. "Tru Lee."

"What?" Truman cringed at the name. "No. Tru*man Wood*ley. And this is—"

She pulled her hand from Truman and turned to Ervin. "Vin Willis."

"Vin?" Ervin laughed. "I kind of like that. And who are you?"

"Nikia Evans, Shauna's cousin." She held on to Ervin's hand as she stared at his friend like no other man existed in the world. "So you are the guys that are giving my cousin all of her headaches?"

"Hush up your mouth, gal." Delores popped the woman on her backside. "Take Mr. Willis into the kitchen and fix him a plate."

Nikia rolled her eyes. "As much money as I make and you want me to serve some stranger." She smiled when she called him a stranger. With the electricity that flowed between the two of them, they wouldn't be strangers for much longer.

"How about this. You point to where the food is and I can serve myself." Ervin gazed into her eyes. He even gave her the standard handshake pulse but he gave her more than two.

Nikia nodded. "I like that, Vin."

"I'm liking the new name." As Nikia led him out of the office, Ervin turned to Truman. "Hey, on the album I want my name listed as Vin Willis. Sounds like an action hero, doesn't it?"

"I'll go get my husband for you." Delores sauntered from the room.

Luckily Nikia pulled Ervin out of the office before Truman could give his honest opinion. Ervin didn't resemble an action hero nor did Truman think he had been a pain to Shauna. Or had he? She'd asked him to change a line in his song, *his* song. Maybe if he didn't have such strong attachments to his lyrics, he wouldn't have taken it to heart.

He strolled around the office. He found pictures of Craig and his family. From the photos, it looked like Craig had three sons of his own. Truman looked through Craig's CD collection. He had lots of Shauna's CDs from her *Sweet Sixteen* CD to her last one, *You Have My Heart*. Comparing the covers, Shauna had certainly made a metamorphosis from sweet young thing to tempting seductress. Her eyes. Her mouth. Her backside. Those legs.

Truman put the CD back into its assigned spot and continued looking through the collection. He came across one CD that caught his attention.

Flye and the Skillz Squad. *Ghetto Spectacular*. A young black man without a shirt and a stomach rippling with muscles stood on the cover. He had a do-rag on his head and what had to be a million dollars' worth of diamonds around his neck.

He looked inside of the cover. He read down the names of each member and stopped when he got to Nikia Evans' name. She rapped in the group. So talent ran in Shauna's family.

"Sorry I'm late." Craig burst into the room and scared Truman half to death.

He nearly dropped the CD he held in his hand. He clumsily replaced it in its spot. "Just noticing your collection. Interesting."

"When you're in the biz, you pick up a little of everything." Craig shook Truman's hand and made his way to his desk chair. "Want something to drink or eat?"

"No. Your lovely wife offered when she let us in." He nodded back toward where he suspected the kitchen sat.

"Us?" Craig scanned the room.

"Ervin, the drummer. He went into the kitchen with Nikia." Truman would leave out the fact that the two of them generated tons of sexual heat between them.

Craig looked a little more casual than usual. He had on a white tunic with matching white shorts and flip-flops.

"Shauna and I had a rough day, and we haven't had much sleep. But we'll be fine for the recording session tonight." Craig took a seat behind his desk and grunted before he settled back into the chair.

"You actually brought up two things I wanted to talk about." Truman sat down in front of Craig's desk. "Shauna and the recording sessions."

"Sure. Let's talk." He leaned forward and kept a laser-like stare on Truman. He looked back at the doorway. "I wanted to also talk to Shauna, face to face."

"Oh, sure. I understand. She is the producer after all. Give me a sec and I'll get her." Craig rushed out of the room.

The time alone would give Truman a chance to map out his arguments. Shauna shouldn't have fired Hank. She shouldn't have made the suggestion about his song especially in front of his band members. To work with him, she needed to gain a heart.

After about fifteen minutes, Craig showed up with Shauna. Truman stood when she entered the room. She did look tired. Her body swam in the oversized shirt she wore. Truman's eyes moved down to her shapely legs. God, did she have anything on under that top?

"Craig said you wanted to see me." Shauna sat in a chair opposite Truman.

Craig and Truman sat at the same time.

"The studio." Truman cleared his throat before continuing. "I think we need to lay some ground rules."

"Rules? For *my* studio?" She crossed her legs. "This'll be interesting."

"I don't want my songs chopped up and changed to fit a pop market." He stared into Shauna's cold eyes. "I wrote every word for a reason."

"I'm sure you did." Shauna's voice came out even colder.

Truman sighed and relaxed back into the chair. "As long as we have that understanding we'll be fine." Maybe she could be reasoned with in the right atmosphere.

She blinked. "Did you hear me say I agree to any of this?"

"I'm sure we can work these details out." Craig nodded like he wanted this to be the end of the discussion.

Not hardly.

"Why don't you trust me that I'm not trying to play you?" Shauna's jaw twitched like she ground her teeth down to powder.

"I don't know you to trust you." To keep his cool, he gripped the arms of the chair as he kept his stare on her.

"What do you need to know?" In a move that seemed to copy his, she also clutched the arms of her chair and even leaned forward.

Uh, oh. She wouldn't be backing down anytime soon.

Truman also leaned forward, putting his face a foot away from hers. "I need to know why you fired a man for no reason."

She rutted her arched eyebrows.

"The man has a wife and kids. Maybe if you talked to him you would have known that." Truman folded his arms and leaned back.

No way could Shauna come out looking like a rose in this situation. Unless she had some hell of an excuse for what she did, Truman wouldn't let her near his album.

Shauna glared at him. He couldn't tell if she scanned her brain to come up with excuses to give him or if she couldn't talk due to biting her tongue so hard.

Truman turned to the doorway when he heard giggling coming down the hallway. Ervin showed up with Nikia at his side. She had her arms looped around his.

What ability did Ervin have that allowed him to walk into a room, spot a gorgeous woman, and get her to fall for him in a second flat? Truman worked with a beautiful woman like Shauna Stellar and she got sick around him, and couldn't talk to him for more than five minutes. Then again, he didn't leave himself open for relationships or even new friendships.

"Whoa." Nikia halted in her spot. "Why do I feel like I stepped into a warzone?"

Truman glanced at the woman sitting across from him who had yet to explain herself. "I was explaining how my coproducer is a heartless, selfish, self-centered bully who cuts off people's livelihoods when they don't do things her way."

The tension thickened in the room until the air became still. Before anyone could say a word, Craig's phone chirped. He checked the screen. Whatever he read made his eyes go wide. He mumbled a curse as he slammed it on his desk.

"Damn, Shauna." He rubbed the top of his bald head until Truman thought the man would rub off the skin.

Whatever Shauna had done made the whites of Craig's eyes transform into a blood red color. The man fumed.

Shauna broke her angry gaze from Truman to stare at her manager. Her face softened when she gave him her attention.

Craig punched the keys on his keyboard. Pretty soon a website homepage populated on the screen that showed a candid picture of Shauna sitting at a table at a restaurant with some guy.

To Truman, the man looked put together, but slick. The duo ate outside, but her dining companion kept himself busy eyeing women walking up and down the street by them. For Shauna's sake, Truman hoped this man wasn't her boyfriend... Not that he cared about her personal life.

Craig read bits from the article surrounding the picture. "Sources tell us that after getting dumped by her former label, Universe, Shauna Stellar's old flame, Raheem, was quick to scoop her up. Rumor has it the duo may be planning a remix version of 'Dirty Loving." Can business and romantic sparks ignite again for this hot couple? Only time will tell."

"Oh my God." Nikia covered her mouth. "Shauna, you actually had lunch with Raheem? I can't believe it."

"There are a lot of things she's done that can't be believed." Craig stood from his desk.

Shauna appeared small in her chair again, like the first time Truman had met her.

"Where the hell do you get off doing that meeting without me? I told you I had it covered, and now they sent me a text saying they don't want to see me." Craig glared at his client.

"And what's up with you and Raheem? Please don't tell me you're going to record with him again after all he did to you?" Nikia put her hand on Shauna's shoulder, but Shauna brushed it off.

She slammed a jewel case on Craig's desk in front of Truman. "That engineer named Hank was smoking crack in my studio. I'm not going to have that around me. You should want the same for yourself." Shauna bolted to her feet. "I'm tired of being the scapegoat for everything that goes wrong around me." She pointed to Truman. "You want out? You don't trust me? Fine. There's no label anyway." Shauna scanned the room. "We all have nothing." Then she turned to Craig. "And yes, I went behind your back and met with Zinner. I'm not fifteen anymore. I can do whatever I want." She directed her attention to her cousin. "Whatever I do with Raheem is strictly business, nothing else. I have to think about—" She paused, "—my career. I'm going to control my life this time." She left the room as Truman stood.

Now Truman felt like a jerk. Shauna had been looking out for him and his band.

She disappeared. He'd pushed the one woman away who looked out for him and only wanted good people around him.

"Who's Raheem?" Ervin asked Nikia.

"Ex man. He dogged her out four ways to Sunday." Nikia shook her head. "He cheated on her and got another woman pregnant."

"He cheated on *her*? Is he crazy?" Truman didn't mean to blurt the statement, but he couldn't imagine that a man could want anyone else after having Shauna. As annoying as she'd been to him, she did pique his interest.

The phone rang.

"Probably people wanting to talk about the article." Craig cleared his throat. "I knew this was coming." He answered the phone and turned his back on the group to gain some privacy.

"I need to apologize to her." Truman went toward the door.

Delores stopped him. "You will. Just not right now. Give her some space."

"Tru, does that mean we're not recording?" Ervin put his hand on Truman's shoulder to get his attention.

Craig slammed the phone down. "I got some news."

Truman hoped the smile meant something good would happen for a change.

Chapter 8

As requested by Craig, Truman and the band arrived at the studio at 2:00 a.m.. Truman didn't know what to expect. From what Craig had said earlier, they had lost their deal with Universe Records. Even if they finished the album, the group would have no distribution. So why did Craig seem so optimistic?

"Universe dropped Ca-Razy Music?" Sully chuckled.

"Don't call it that, dickhead." Ervin punched Sully in his shoulder.

"Craig said Charisma was dropped but he still wanted us to come here." Truman pulled his guitar from the case. "Even if we don't record, we can still use the practice."

"Practice for what? More clubs and fairs? I'm over that, Tru." Charlie shook his head. "Theresa is going to freak when she finds out. Have you talked to Ashley?"

"No, not yet." Truman tuned his guitar. "I haven't been home."

Sully made a lewd catcall.

"Me and Ervin have been at Craig's house. We heard about the story there." Since then Truman had been trying to get Shauna to talk to him or at least forgive him for his assumptions and for giving her grief since the first day they'd met.

He'd tried getting Delores to talk to her for him. He'd asked Nikia to help him out but she said she knew her cousin and knew that the best thing would be to leave Shauna alone.

God, how could Truman be so judgmental? He'd never been that way before. Then came Ashley. She made him doubt any woman, whether in a relationship or not, could be trusted. Outside of his immediate family, Fatima Evans had been the only exception. Fatima listened to him and had no desire for Truman to change.

Regaining Shauna's forgiveness would be difficult if not impossible. Truman wanted that more than recording now. He couldn't get her hurt expression out of his mind.

"So now what?" Charlie asked. "We have no engineer."

"Yeah. I smelled the weed smoke. Didn't know Hank was doing crack." Ervin grimaced.

The front door opened. Like a breeze, Craig and a man who looked strangely familiar blew into the room. Maybe he looked so familiar because the man defined an average man. He carried the average height and weight. He had his brown hair parted to the side. His clothes hung from his sinewy body. The muted colors of his button-down shirt and slacks blended in with the wall color. For all intents and purposes, the man could have substituted for a chair.

"Good evening, gentlemen." Craig raised his hands and looked like a sideshow barker. "This here's Clayton Reese. He'll be our new sound engineer."

"Clayton Reese." Ervin looked pensive. "Where do I know your name from?"

Clayton cleared his throat, kept his gaze down, and clasped his hands in front of him. "I've mixed albums for Dolly, Reba, Garth, and some other big names in country. I also used to write."

"Yeah." Ervin wagged his finger at the man who flinched at the gesture. "I know where I remember your name from. You co-wrote that song with the dance." Ervin stepped around the room in precise movements that resembled a waltz with a mix of stomping roaches on the floor.

"The Hayride Hop-A-Long? My kids love that." Charlie beamed.

The band introduced themselves to Clayton. Truman thought he'd broken the new engineer's hand when he grabbed a hold of it.

"Y'all ready to get started?" Craig rubbed his hands together.

"Where's Shauna?" Truman looked around for her. His heart pounded thinking she could be anywhere close to them.

"She won't be joining us this evening." Craig gave a knowing look to Truman. "Feeling a bit under the weather. Since Truman is the coproducer, we still have a vision for the music."

"But what about distribution? Do we have a label?" As usual, Tony raked his fingers through his hair.

Craig smiled so wide it hurt Truman's face. "As much as I hated Shauna's stunt, the story has gotten a lot of attention."

"What does that have to do with distribution?" Sully scowled, lately a standard expression.

"A company showed interest in picking you guys up."

The guys' mouths dropped open as they looked at each other. All at once, they jumped up and down in the studio. They screamed as they hopped around in a circle. The whole moment brought Truman back to their senior high school baseball game where Truman had hit a homerun and got Sully, Ervin, and Charlie to home base.

Craig had been right about everything. Almost everything. He'd said Shauna would be fine with working with Truman but she hadn't. Truman hadn't made it easy on her either.

"So now what?" Tony jumped in front of Truman. "Do we sign with them?"

"Whoa, whoa, whoa, guys." Sully stepped into the center of the circle of men. "Contractually we have to satisfy our commitment to Charisma Music first. Wished we didn't."

"Hey." Truman pounded his bandmate on his shoulder for the rude statement.

"Then we sign?" Tony took out his notepad and pen.

Craig cleared his throat and turned his gaze.

Truman felt a sinking feeling in his stomach. Something felt off. "What's up?"

"The company offering us the deal is Nanco Productions." Craig dropped his gaze to the floor.

"I've never heard of them." Charlie shrugged.

Sully's smile melted. "I'm surprised you haven't, Charlie. They mainly do children's albums."

A boulder dropped in Truman's belly.

Craig continued. "Hank has been very vocal since his firing. He's gone off and told his story to some gossip site. I did some damage control to counteract his claims that Shauna acted without reason. An exec with Nanco read the exchange and liked what they saw. They want you to do a children's album about staying away from drugs."

"Jesus, we *are* that joke band." Charlie smacked his forehead.

"No, you're not." Craig held his hands up to calm a potentially tumultuous situation.

"We can't do an album like that." Charlie shook his head.

"So we keep recording." Truman returned to the main studio and retrieved his guitar.

The group turned to him.

Truman tried to keep his voice steady. "We made a promise to Shauna. Charisma Music." He needed to make amends with Shauna Stellar as soon as possible, and keeping his obligations to her would help. He turned to

Craig. "You said we'll be okay. I believe him."

Sully grabbed Truman's arm and turned him around. "Fine. But if County Line Music offers a deal, I'm taking it for us."

Truman scanned the group but didn't immediately respond.

Sully didn't move from his spot. "Ever since we started this band, that has been our dream distributor. I say we throw our hat into the ring with them. Let them know we want to record for them as soon as our contract is up with Charisma."

Truman kept his gaze down before speaking. "Let's cross that bridge when we get to it."

Craig stepped closer to Truman. "Sure. I wish that y'all would—"

Truman cut Craig off. "Great." He adjusted his guitar around him and strummed out a riff from the song "Reeling." "We have work to do, men. We're losing valuable studio time."

Truman noticed the confused looks on his band members' faces. He turned his gaze away as he took his position. They didn't need to know how he felt about upsetting Shauna. He couldn't tell them either.

It hit him right before Clayton told him to start. Truman had become his own country song. He couldn't even get himself a beer either.

The group spent hours recording their second single, "Working For Your Love." Every time Truman sang it, he looked into the booth hoping that Shauna would show up. She didn't. Knowing her, she wouldn't either. How could he blame her? He had accused her of not having a heart or knowing her employees.

"Truman." Clayton adjusted controls on the boards as he spoke. "You're sounding a little flat again." He gazed down at his watch. "We only have a few more minutes of studio time left. Do you want to keep trying to get this song right or try again in the morning?"

As much as he didn't want to, Truman decided it would be better to try in the morning. Even Craig had thrown in the towel and left the session early. Truman's hoarse voice showed the hard work he'd put in that session. He felt wrung out of emotion. He had to admit that Shauna's philosophy of dissecting the song before singing it made sense.

"You doing all right?" Ervin tapped Truman with his drumstick.

As Truman started to answer, the front door slammed open. Raucous talking and noise hurled from that direction and down the hall. Each of the Sliders and Truman stopped in their tracks and looked outside of the studio. At the doorway stood about five black guys. Truman looked at each of them in the face.

One man who stood in front of the group approached Truman. The closer he got the more Truman realized that he recognized him from his album cover, Flye and the Skillz Squad.

"You Dudley Do-Right?" Flye rubbed his hands together like he wanted a fight.

The guys behind him snickered and slapped each other high fives for the remark.

"Truman Woodley." Truman extended his hand to the man in a white bandanna, leather pants and a white tank top.

Flye ignored his goodwill gesture and continued standing in front of him with a menacing scowl. Truman lowered his hand and went back to packing his guitar.

"Good to meet you too, Flye." Truman lifted his guitar case by its handle.

"Oh, so country boy knows who I am." Flye turned to the group behind him; his dreadlocks peeking under the bandanna swung with his movements. "Good. You'll know my name when I'm stomping my size thirteens in your ass."

"Hey." Sully stepped up to Flye and that in turn caused the Skillz Squad to move closer. Ervin hopped over his drum kit. Charlie forgot about being a family man, and Tony dropped his penny pincher ways to close in on the group.

"What's this?" Flye surveyed Truman and his friends. "You all going to stand us down?"

"We're not trying to fight either." Truman put his hand on Sully's chest to push his friend back. "I don't know what your problem is with us. We're leaving."

"Your problem, punk, is that you messed with my cousin." Flye took off his sunglasses that had to have been worth more than Truman's entire wardrobe, and he hung them on his T-shirt. Whenever Flye flexed his arms, the multitude of tattoos covering them wiggled and came to life.

"I don't know what you're talking about." Truman shrugged.

"Shauna Stellar. My sister says that you've been giving her a hard time."

"Is your sister Nikia?" Ervin moved forward.

Flye scrunched up his face as though he'd smelled something horrible. "How do you know my sister?"

"I met her last night at Craig's house." Ervin smiled and nodded his head. "That's a talented woman."

"What?" Flye charged after Ervin while Truman and Sully tried to keep him and members of his crew back.

"I mean she can sing." Ervin tried breaking through the barrier of Truman and Charlie's arms.

"You stay away from her." Flye pointed to Ervin.

"What's going on?" Through the sea of men, Nikia cut her way in until she reached Flye and Truman. "Who were you talking to?"

"Stretch over there." Flye jabbed his finger into Ervin's chest.

Ervin usually stayed quiet and calm…until you touched him the wrong way.

"Don't you touch me!" Ervin shoved Flye back into his boys.

Flye's crew shouted obscenities at Truman and his friends.

Tensions ran high in the room as the groups closed in on each other. Truman's breathing came out as pants and the back of his neck tensed. He widened his stance.

Nikia became sandwiched in the middle although Ervin did his best to keep her protected.

Truman stood in front of Nikia and Ervin since Flye had his back to his boys, and kept Sully covered. "Whoa. Let's just calm it down here." He held up his hand.

When Truman's face relaxed as soon as he saw an angel standing behind the Skillz Squad, the room got quiet. Shauna stood in the doorway watching the melee. Her eyes welled with tears as she scanned the room.

She shook her head. "No fighting. I told you I didn't want to see this." She pointed to the Skillz Squad. "You all make me sick." She ran from the studio.

"Shauna." Truman went after her.

The Skillz Squad let him through to get out the door. He saw her ducking into a gray Land Rover and locking the doors.

He stood by her window hoping to sway her. "Shauna, roll down the window. We need to talk."

She didn't say anything. When she wiped her eyes, she kept her face forward.

"Please." He tried the door handle, hoping she would have unlocked it.

"Go away." She wouldn't even face him. "Now you see why I didn't want to produce?"

She looked so fragile in the car. Shauna wrapped one arm around her body and the other hand she used to shield her face. Her hand shook.

Damn he felt like an asshole. He couldn't tell if her reaction came from fear or hatred. Whatever fueled her, she wouldn't be coming out of the car any time soon.

"Now is not the time." Nikia sauntered to the other side of the car. "I'm taking her back home."

"But—"

Nikia whispered over the car from the driver's side. "Talk to Vin. I told him what to do." Then she winked at Truman. Like a shot from a gun, she sped off down the road.

Truman had never seen Shauna looking so angry. One thing proved evident. After a day of recording without her, he needed her input in the studio.

* * * *

"Girl, are you sure you want to do this?" Nikia split her attention between the road and Shauna sitting next to her. "I've told you ever since you came home that I would be more than happy to give you some money. If it wasn't for you, I wouldn't have a career."

Shauna shook her head. "I didn't earn that money. You did. I'm not going to take any handouts." She smiled to calm her cousin. "I'll be fine."

"Does Craig know you're doing this?"

"No, and don't tell him either."

"Oh, hell. You know I can't keep a secret to save my life. And this one is a big one. Raheem? Really?"

"I'll be fine." Shauna needed to keep telling herself that.

Shauna had no plans of going back to the studio and seeing Truman and his band again. She needed a ride to the airport, and Nikia promised to take her straight there. She should have known her cousin would have stopped off to see Ervin. Nikia hadn't stopped talking about him since she met him only last night.

Shauna had seen Nikia go gaga for a man before, but something about Ervin seemed different. Too bad Shauna couldn't experience that same compatibility with Truman. He could make her heart race like no one else, both in excitement and frustration.

Seeing Truman and his band square off against Flye and the Skillz Squad reminded her of the fights she would see around her old neighborhood, some ending with someone being taken away by ambulance or police car. She hated to see that amount of animosity from anyone, especially from her family. She didn't like seeing Truman that worked up either.

Even though she questioned the reasoning for the trip, going away to New York right now for work seemed to be a perfect option. If she had no plans to go back to the studio to help Truman and his band, she needed to do something for herself. Even though it seemed like she had made a deal with the devil, doing this recording with Raheem would put her back in the swing of things. As it stood, Shauna still couldn't stand her own reflection.

Shauna had taken Raheem's private car to her old apartment and she waited for him. She sat in his living room, watching TV and flipping through a multitude of magazines he'd left on the coffee table, all with him as the feature story. Nothing changed. Raheem continued to be that selfish bastard she remembered. This time she would use his selfishness to her advantage.

When he saved her after her meeting with her old record company, Raheem had tried convincing her to stay to record the remix and not return home. Shauna had chalked up not staying on because she wasn't prepared. She took the night to think about her decision. Life passed her by the longer she waited. If she wanted her career back, she needed to do something now. She made the choice to accept his offer.

After about forty-five minutes, Raheem bounded down the stairs. "Sorry for the wait, love." He wore a black silk bathrobe and matching pants. "Just give me a few more minutes."

Shauna huffed. "I don't have a lot of time. I have to get back down to Virginia. Why aren't you ready? I thought you made the arrangement for the studio for this time." The sooner she could get through this ordeal, the better. If she sang this one song, he would leave her and her business alone... she hoped.

"Hey, when you're Raheem, the people will wait for you. We'll get there. If you need something to eat or drink, go help yourself. I believe you know where everything is." He winked at her and it turned her stomach.

How could she stoop so low? Did she desire to get back into the music biz so badly that she would record with a man who humiliated her? Then she thought about Truman. He treated her no better. Or maybe he had.

He did try to apologize to her this morning, but she refused to listen to him. How could she look the man in his eyes when all through the night she thought about nothing but him?

His brown eyes burned into her dreams in such a good way. She could stare into them forever. She remembered sitting next to him on the couch and how good he smelled. Shauna had been so close to his lips that she could have kissed him, wanted to kiss him.

To keep her mind off Truman, Shauna stood and peered around her old place. She hated seeing all the changes Raheem had done to it. He had all the cream-colored walls painted to a garish purple and orange. He had speakers everywhere around the room, not recessed in the walls, but sitting out for everyone to see. The place resembled a frat house.

The doorbell chimed this ostentatious ring. Knowing Raheem, he had some manservant to answer it.

She continued scanning the room until the bell rang again. This time Raheem asked Shauna from upstairs if she would answer the door for him.

She shook her head as she strolled to the door, and whipped it open. She saw another familiar face on the other side, one she hadn't seen since that infamous night when Raheem showed himself as the jerk she suspected.

Dressed in a barely there dress, the attractive black woman slinked into the apartment, staring at Shauna the entire time. The last time Shauna had seen this woman, she had a very pronounced baby bump.

"My man upstairs?" She cackled on the way up.

Shauna didn't answer her. She didn't have to. During the woman's trek, she slipped out of her dress, revealing her nude body by the time she turned to go where Shauna's old bedroom used to be.

After some laughter, Raheem called downstairs, "Uh, I'm going to be a little bit, babe. Make yourself at home."

Shauna felt the panic building inside her. Her stomach compressed like she wanted to vomit. To steady herself, she took a couple of deep breaths.

She couldn't break down, not here. Raheem wouldn't help her. She imagined him and his whore of a girlfriend would just laugh at her...again.

With tears stinging her eyes, Shauna darted to the couch, grabbed her purse, and hightailed it out of her old apartment.

What was she thinking hooking back up with Raheem? That man would never change. One thing she knew. *She* had to change.

Chapter 9

Truman's hands shook from exhaustion as he sat in front of Craig's house again, this time with a van full of his band members.

"Are you sure this is what Nikia wants us to do?" Truman directed the question to Ervin, who stared at the house like it resembled a steak and he hadn't had a meal in years.

"Positive." Ervin slapped Truman on his shoulder. "She said that Shauna doesn't know we're coming over and wouldn't want to hide out in her room."

"Great. A sneak attack. That's what I want to do to her." Truman shook his head. "Let's get out of here."

"Hell no, buddy. Drop me off. I'll get Nikia to take me back to the house." Ervin opened the door even as the van rolled.

It didn't take long for Truman to notice the number of high-priced vehicles in the driveway. Hummers, Escalades, Bentleys. It looked like a family get-together at Craig's house. More than likely Flye would be in there with his Skillz Squad. Truman wouldn't leave his friend in there alone.

"Let's go in." Truman parked the van.

"Are you serious?" Sully kicked the back of the driver's seat from his spot in the backseat. "You know what's going to happen in there."

"No, I don't. Y'all just keep cool." Truman opened his door. He waited at the door for the entire group before he rang the bell.

Seeing Nikia answer the door wearing the tiniest black two-piece bikini Truman had ever seen made the group gasp. Her smile brightened the darkened foyer. She kept her stare directly on Ervin.

"Glad you could make it." She reached her hand out to Ervin. "Aren't you going to introduce me to the rest of your band?"

"Who?" Ervin let her pull him into the house.

She giggled when he seemed thrown off by her question. So Truman stepped in and introduced Sully, Charlie, and Tony to her.

"We're having a little party out back by the pool." Nikia peeked over to Truman. "Shauna should be there."

Truman's mind tripped over what kind of outfit she would be wearing. Would it be a bikini like Nikia? Or maybe a short sundress.

He shook his head. He had come there on business. Nothing else.

Nikia led the group to the enclosed pool in the back of the house. The June weather had warmed up considerably and made it the perfect condition for a pool party. Stone tiles surrounded the patio area.

When the group stepped out on the patio, Craig, Delores, Flye, and the Skillz Squad turned to them.

Charlie leaned over to Truman to whisper. "Is it me or do you hear the whistling theme from *The Good, The Bad and The Ugly* right now?"

Truman jabbed his friend with his elbow.

Delores smiled as she approached the group. In shorts and a T-shirt, Delores looked as lethal as Nikia in her bikini.

"Nikia said she'd invited you all." She took Truman's hand. "I'm so glad you made it. My sons couldn't make it but I guess that's what happens when you get older. You forget your parents."

Truman smiled at her but he felt her pain from the way she turned away. "Thank you for allowing us in your home." He squeezed her hand gently to let her know he at least appreciated the gesture. He introduced the rest of the group to her.

Delores directed the guys to the food and drinks and begged them to help themselves.

Truman looked around to do a head count of his members. Charlie huddled over to a side table with Delores as he flipped through different pictures of his babies. Ervin disappeared although Truman had full confidence that he had to be nestled up under Nikia. Tony made his way over to the food table.

"What the hell are we doing here?" Sully's red face couldn't mask his frustration. "We should be practicing on our spare time, especially since you're Mr. No-Show during the day. Where are you all day anyway?"

"Don't worry about it." Truman couldn't tell Sully about the job. How would that look that a contracted recording artist still needed to work to make ends meet?

"Why don't you get something to eat and chill out?" Truman scanned the party again this time looking for Shauna.

"I'm sure they won't have anything I like." Sully made his way to the food tent.

When Truman made another pass around the party, his gaze settled on Flye. It didn't take the muscled man long to saunter over to him. Like his father had taught him as a kid, Truman stood his ground and kept his stare on the man.

"I guess you didn't heed my warning." Like before, Flye started flexing his muscles.

"We were invited here." Truman squared off against him.

The two stood eye to eye with each other until Flye smirked.

"Watch yourself with Shauna. That girl's like my little sister. If she's upset, then I get upset. Right now, she's not too happy." Flye shook his head, which made his dreadlocks swing back and forth.

"And that's my fault?" Truman didn't want to be antagonistic. He wanted to hear her side.

"Your name seems to come up a lot when she's complaining." Flye looked over his shoulder. "Wanna sit?"

Truman nodded. On their way to a table, Flye snagged a Heineken from a cooler. Truman picked up a long-neck Budweiser and twisted off the lid. Like heads of state, they sat at a table at the side of the pool.

"So what's your deal with Shauna?" Flye took a swig of beer and set the bottle on the glass-top table.

Truman shook his head. "Just like with any new working relationship, we're feeling each other out."

Flye raised his eyebrows.

So Truman clarified himself. "We're trying to get used to each other's work habits."

"Do you have a problem with her because she used to be rich?"

"No." Truman didn't think about money when he thought of Shauna, not lately. From her work in the studio, he now regarded her as an expert, one who cared about the end product.

Flye continued. "Do you have a problem because she's black?"

"No. Of course not." Truman didn't see color when he looked at Shauna. Never had, not even from the beginning.

"Do you have a problem with her because she's a woman?"

Though her sex and her sexiness couldn't be denied, Truman thought a while before he answered. "I don't think so."

Flye snickered. "I wouldn't have had my sister in the group if Mama Dee didn't tell me to give her a chance." He nodded toward Delores who still looked interested in seeing pictures of Charlie's children. "I mean how am I supposed to come off hard-core with my baby sister backing me up? But to be honest, Lil' Bit comes off harder than me sometimes."

Truman glanced over to the pool where he watched Nikia swimming to the edge toward Ervin. When he crouched down to talk to her, she reached up, grabbed his shirt, and pulled him into the pool. He, in turn, pulled her down under the water with him.

"Shauna's special, dog." Flye finished off his beer.

"I know. Hit records since she was a teenager."

Flye cut him off. "No. I mean more than that. Even when we were little she made everything all right. She wouldn't have to say a word and people wanted to be around her, you know."

Truman knew what he meant. He thought about the moment he'd seen her getting sick in the bathroom and how he'd wanted to help her.

"And honey dip hates guns and violence and shit. She's like an angel. Probably why she cracked when all that stuff happened to her. She's stronger than she thinks."

Truman nodded. "So did she get you into the music biz?"

"Yeah. But I ain't got the pipes that she has." Flye laughed. "I could talk my way out of anything. That's what Auntie Fatima used to tell me all the time. So I started rapping."

"Fatima. Yeah, she was great." She'd been Truman's angel. She had given him a chance when no one else would. At hearing her name, his heart drummed.

As Truman thought about his former mentor, he mentally compared her face and features with Shauna's. Both had the same almond-shaped eyes. Both had heart-shaped lips, although Shauna's lips looked fuller, juicier. He never noticed Fatima's ass, but he couldn't stop looking at Shauna's.

"Family means everything to her. Couldn't believe it when her mom died. Cancer. Shauna tried going on without her, but, you probably know how that went." Flye bowed his head.

"Is that when she—"

Flye didn't say anything. He dove his hand down to the tabletop while making a whistling sound that resembled a bomb crashing down to earth. "She shouldn't have done the show, man, not on the day of her mom's funeral."

Truman slammed his beer bottle down on the table, surprised he didn't crack the glass. "She attempted to do a show after burying her mother?" He now had another assessment of her.

Did Shauna hate her mother? Did she do it to help get over the pain? Or did she do the show out of obligation? His stare went directly to Craig.

"No wonder. I wouldn't be able to talk, let alone sing if my mother died and I had attended her funeral." Truman shook his head.

"How did you know Auntie Fatima?" Flye asked.

"She was the one who signed us to Charisma. She saw me and my band playing a show in some dive bar. I couldn't believe it when she talked to me about signing us."

"Country, huh?" Flye laughed. "That's some shit. I wonder why she decided to go that way. Doesn't sound like Auntie Fatima."

"I don't know. But I'm glad she did." Truman finished off his beer.

Ervin and Nikia ran over to Truman and Flye.

"I'm going to get Vin a swimsuit and get him out of these wet clothes." She took Ervin's hand.

They looked so natural together. Truman noticed how Flye shifted in his seat as soon as they touched each other. Truman stared at the union of their hands, then watched their expressions. Both seemed happy to be with each other. Made him wonder why he couldn't be as lucky.

"So what's up with your name?" Flye asked.

Truman stared at him for a while and wondered what the man called Flye meant. No way his mother named him that at birth. If she did, then she must not have liked him very much.

"What do you mean?" Truman asked.

"Truman. That's like a president's name, right?" Flye scratched the back of his head. His dreads wiggled around like snakes on hot pavement.

Truman twirled his beer bottle in between his hands. "Yeah. But my mama liked it because she looked in a book of names and saw it meant 'true man.' My friends call me Tru."

Flye nodded.

"So what's up with Flye?" Truman smiled.

"Thought it was cool. Anything's better than Sherman." He shrugged. "You should do something with your name. Nikia said something about you changing it to Tru Lee. That's tight."

Truman shook his head. "No. I'm not changing my name. I have a son. I want him to see that he can be proud of his name."

"I can dig it. So you're married?"

Truman shook his head. "No. My ex has him right now while I record."

"I know what you mean. I have two of my own. Two different women." Flye grumbled. "Baby mama drama right there. 'Give me this. Give me that. Where's the money?' Take my advice. Get you a good lawyer and make up an agreement to what you're going to pay her before you hit it big. She'll try to take you for all you're worth."

Ashley did her level best to drain Truman of his funds now before he made real money at his music. At least he and Flye had something in common.

"Speaking of money…"

Flye cocked his head. "I know you're not trying to hit me up for a loan." Truman waved his hand at him. "Not for me. I know Shauna is going through some financial problems now. Has she come to you for—"

Truman couldn't finish his question before Flye answered. "I tried, man. I straight up gave her dough, and she turned it down. I offered to put her on one of my tracks to get her back out there. She wasn't feeling it. Even sis tried. The best way I could help her is by getting studio time at Charisma and paying her that way. She would accept my money for that. But cuz is headstrong and wants to do this rebirth of hers on her own terms. I can respect that."

"Are we trucing?" One of Flye's crew members approached the table.

"We weren't really beefing." Flye settled back into his chair. "Just had to get some things straight."

Craig slipped over to the group and stood by Truman. "Having a good time?"

"Yeah. Flye's pretty cool." Truman nodded his head toward Shauna's cousin.

Craig pulled Truman from the group. "Good. Now it's time to get to work." He faced Truman toward the door that led to the house. He saw Shauna standing in the doorway.

Chapter 10

Shauna's smile dropped when she scanned the pool area and found Truman and his band members there. Couldn't the guy get the hint? She wanted to stay as far away from him as possible. He'd said enough the night before when he'd accused her of not knowing her employees.

When she saw him approaching her, Shauna retreated into the house. She didn't need to hear Truman yelling at her again. Between her label turning her down to her face, and then her humiliating trip to see Raheem, this had been a taxing day.

"Shauna, wait a minute," Craig called after her.

Shauna peered over her shoulder before disappearing into the house. She went to the den to seek some solace. Until she turned around, she didn't realize Truman had been following her.

"Nikia invited us over." Truman held up his hands to her like he needed to defuse a potential blowup.

"She's the only one I didn't see out there." Shauna looked behind him. "Where did she go?"

"She was supposed to be finding a swimsuit for Ervin. Knowing Ervin, they may have gotten detoured." In a gentlemanly gesture, Truman took off his baseball cap.

Her heartbeat sounded in her ears and her palms felt sweaty. Right now, though, she couldn't tell if her reaction had to do with her anxiety or Truman's proximity.

"If Nikia invited you, then maybe you should be out there with Flye and them." Shauna stepped back farther in the room.

"She invited me here to see you since you won't talk to me."

"I think you said enough." She turned her back on him. "I told Craig that I couldn't do this. I knew this would be a mistake." She pivoted and returned her gaze to Truman. "You have a new engineer. And he's done country music. Most importantly, he doesn't do drugs."

"He's fine. I guess."

Shauna stared at Truman who made his way to the entertainment center. He turned it on and popped in a disc.

"Listen to this." He clicked a couple of buttons.

She raced to him and pushed the eject button before the disc could slip its way inside. "No. I don't want to hear any music right now. I don't want to help you." She wrapped her arms around her body and backed from him. "I can't help you."

"What do you mean, can't? Ever since the first day in the studio, you've told me how great and special that you are. I'm telling you here and now—" He paused.

Shauna swallowed, knowing the next words out of his mouth would be something hurtful, something to knock her down another peg or two. She couldn't take it. She started toward the door until his words froze her to her spot.

"You're right." He wrung his hat in his hands. "You're special."

His kind words drew a smile from her.

"I can also tell you without a shadow of a doubt that you're no superstar either."

Those cutting words drove Shauna to turn and leave. Men were all alike. They were all out to use and hurt her. Here she almost thought she'd found a different type of man in Truman.

"No, wait." He held her arm and pulled her so that she stood directly in front of him. "What I meant to say is that you're more than just some superstar diva. You're a talented musician. You're one hell of a singer. You need to realize those things and forget about this fame stuff. You should be famous for putting out amazing music and not for who you associate with or some damn remix." Truman swept his fingertips over her face to tuck strands of her hair behind her ear.

The intimate touch ignited an unfamiliar heat inside her. She stepped back from him again and kept her gaze to the floor until he spoke again.

"I apologize for what I said earlier, and yesterday, and, hell, every day I've been with you." He smiled a genuine smile that melted her resolve. "I should have gotten the whole story before accusing you of being selfish and heartless. I'm sorry."

She shook her head. "Don't. It's the first honest thing anyone has ever told me in a long, long time. I appreciate it." She also appreciated the intimate touch.

"Now what did you mean by you can't produce me?"

Shauna stared at him. "I'm not making good decisions right now for myself. I definitely don't want to mess anything up for you."

Truman snickered. "I don't believe that." He returned his attention back to the disc player. "Care to hear something with me? I know we're not working right now."

She touched his arm. The warmth of his skin seared her fingertips, fusing her to him until she didn't want to let him go, even if she could.

Facing the entertainment center, she kept her gaze forward. She watched the lights on the stereo display jump up and down. Then "Reeling" played.

Shauna listened to the rough cut. Overall she liked the sound of the band. They played seamlessly as a unit, each complementing the other. Truman's voice tied it all together.

"I've heard this." Shauna attempted to walk away but Truman blocked her with his body. The scent of grass and honeysuckle surrounded her. If she didn't get away from him soon, she would embarrass herself again by flinging herself into his arms and kissing him.

She hadn't felt a desire like that since…never. Not even with Raheem, who defined reckless. No one had ever made her feel this primal.

"Please. There's something else I want you to hear." His low voice felt like it held her and turned her back around to the stereo.

Shauna pivoted. A different song played. When she listened to lyrics, she knew it was the song "Working For Your Love." Shauna listened to the song and winced when she heard Truman not hit a note she knew he could sing. She'd heard him hit it in "Reeling."

Shauna took a step closer to the stereo and listened intently. Truman didn't sound the same. He'd lost that passion he'd had before. At the end of the song, she reached for the stereo to play the song again.

"So you hear it?" He moved in closer to her.

She didn't answer. With a musician's ear, she listened to the song again. The lyrics worked. The arrangement fit. She would have had the guitar riff shortened and maybe make Tony's fiddle solo longer. Truman didn't quite work.

"You can fix it, can't you?" Anticipation filled Truman's voice. "You're probably working out solutions in your head right now."

She glanced at him. He had so much hope in his eyes. She should have told him to stop. She couldn't deny that nagging musician's voice in her head that propelled her to keep listening. As much as she wanted to ignore her heart, it prompted her to keep this man close.

"I can write my suggestions down and give them to your engineer."

She turned away from him to get a pad and pencil from the coffee table. "It's not the same." He cleared his throat. "I'm not the same."

"What's that supposed to mean? You're the producer now. You know how you want this to sound." She turned to him.

When Truman didn't respond, she brought her attention back to the paper.

As she wrote, "Working For Your Love" ended. Another song started that made Shauna's hand freeze over the pad. It was an acoustic version of "Reeling" with just Truman, his guitar and that one line she wanted changed, changed.

She gazed up at Truman.

"You're the one I need." His voice lowered so that only she could hear him. Shauna gasped.

He continued. "You're right. That lyric does work better that way."

Her throat closed. She had to bite the inside of her lower lip to keep from smiling. He had changed. However, she had to be sure.

"If I come back as your producer, I need to be treated differently. This won't be my only suggestion on your album. I'll want to make other changes that I need you to be open to."

He eased into her space. "I may not do every one of them but I'll at least try."

She swallowed, then jutted her chin to keep up her business countenance. "That's all I'm asking."

"So I guess I had better ask you this the right way." He took a deep breath. "Will you be my coproducer? Gosh, it feels like I should be dropping down to one knee or something."

She smiled. "Yes. But if you try that prima donna stuff on me again, I'll walk."

He laughed. "Me? A prima donna? That's a new one. What about you?"

"I'm really harmless."

Truman shook his head. "Oh, no. You're definitely lethal." He stared at her for a moment. "Yes, definitely lethal."

She nodded. Then she caught something in Truman's song that sounded odd. She'd heard it in the first song and it got stronger in the second. In this last song, the sound seemed out of place.

"Why did you add a backup moaning vocal?" She moved closer to the speaker.

"I didn't." He stepped closer to the speakers, too, and listened closely. "I thought the noise was coming from outside."

She stepped slowly toward where she thought she heard the offending sound. The closet. She put her hand on the knob and twisted it. Yanking it open, she shrieked and fell backward. She hadn't expected to see her cousin and Ervin both completely naked in Craig's closet.

"We're still looking for a suit that fits him." Nikia looped her arms around Ervin's neck.

Ervin reached for the doorknob while trying to keep himself covered. "Nikia will give me a ride home, man." He slammed the door.

Shauna felt the heat flush in her cheeks. Nikia might not have been embarrassed by her actions, but Shauna would have to be for the two of them.

The image of Nikia's leg wrapped around Ervin's pale body would never leave Shauna's thoughts. As lewd and tasteless as it all looked, she felt jealous that Nikia could be that free with her body, with her sexuality. In her jeans and crop top, she felt almost prim and proper next to Nikia.

"Let's go back out to the party." Truman took the CD from the player. With his face looking suddenly red, he seemed more embarrassed by his friend's actions than Shauna had been of her cousin's.

Shauna allowed Truman to put his hand on the small of her back as he guided her back to the pool area. The intimate touch felt right, which should have scared her out of her mind. Yet with Truman, a sense of security washed over her.

"Where's Nikia?" Flye peered around the duo.

"She's busy trying to find the right suit for Ervin." Shauna kept her gaze from Flye. He always knew when she lied. "May I?" She reached for the CD from Truman's hand.

He stared at her for a second before letting it go. "Hey, I want you all to listen to this." She popped in the disc and turned up the volume.

When "Reeling" came on, the Sliders cheered. Flye and the Skillz Squad tilted their heads like confused puppies.

"This ain't bad." Flye nodded his head. "I can feel a phat collabo in this. Country and rap. Worked for Nelly and Tim McGraw."

Off the top of his head, Flye started a rap about a woman who wouldn't give him the time of day. Some of his lyrics seemed geared toward the rocky working relationship between Shauna and Truman. She glanced at Truman while the song played. When he smiled, her stomach flittered.

At the end of the song, Dice gave Flye a high five. "That was tight." He turned to Truman. "Come on, man. You have to do a remix of this. Fans would go bananas to hear Flye on a country track."

"I don't think we can afford to pay Flye what he's worth." Truman stared at all his jewels.

Flye nodded. "You got that right."

"What about not wanting to change our music?" Sully stepped up to Truman.

"We're not." Truman turned to his friend.

Sully sulked to a table and plopped himself down.

When Truman's solo version of "Reeling" came on, the band members all had different reactions. Charlie stood from the table as he listened to the newer version. Tony's lips pressed so hard together that it made a thin line. Sully's eyes were wide and his bottom lip dropped down.

"Are you trying to cut us out?" Tony wrung his hands together.

"No." Truman waved his hand in front of his friend. "I was just trying something."

As soon as Truman sang the new lyric, their expressions changed again. Both Charlie and Tony looked at each other and nodded.

Sully shook his head. "Sellout."

From Truman's pained expression, Shauna knew he didn't expect that type of response from his friend.

"Don't worry about him, man." Flye slapped Truman on the back of his shoulder. "We all sell a little of ourselves for this business, don't we?" Flye clapped his hands together, then rubbed them. "So when are you two going to do a collabo?"

First she had caught her cousin in a compromising position with Ervin, and now this. Shauna's face flamed hot with embarrassment.

"Flye, we're not even thinking about doing a duet." She stopped the CD and pulled it out.

"Maybe you should." Flye nudged his cousin's shoulder. "Now, is this a party or is this a party?" He slipped his iPod into the player and blasted some hot tunes. "Let's dance."

It had been over a year since Shauna shook her behind on a dance floor, which seemed strange for her. For as long as she could remember, she danced. She always had a dance routine in every one of her videos.

After three or four up-tempo songs, a slower song came through the speakers.

"Come on." Nikia giggled and pulled Ervin onto the makeshift dance area.

The lanky man nearly towered over the petite woman as she clasped her arms around his neck and hung on to him like a Christmas ornament.

Shauna had kept herself content watching the action from a bench by the fire pit until she heard a deep voice from behind her.

"Want to dance?"

Shauna gasped and turned around to see Truman with his hat off and his hand extended. She smiled and shook her head. "No, I just want to watch them."

"Funny. I never pictured you as a sideline-type of woman." He moved in front of her. "Besides, maybe this will help us get along better...

in the studio."

"Ah, so if we can dance together—"

"We should be able to work together, don't you think?" He grabbed her hands and helped her onto her feet.

Truman held one hand out and slipped his other hand around her waist. He made sure to leave room in between their bodies. That didn't prevent Shauna from feeling the heat from him.

"Truth be told, I couldn't have danced to those faster songs." He laughed. "I'm not coordinated."

"I could teach you." The statement came as a surprise to her.

From the woman who had been determined not to help another man again, Truman got her to break down some of her walls slowly but surely.

"That's okay. As long as I can do some line dances, I'm fine." He swayed her back and forth.

The music sounded muted in her head. His simple touch warmed her flesh and it reminded her of her reaction when he simply looked at her while Craig took a picture of them sitting on the couch in the studio. If he moved her body close to his, no way could he not feel her pounding heart.

Shauna swallowed hard. She had to get her mind off Truman, his body, and his incredible mouth. "Will you teach me some of those line dances?" Her voice cracked when she made the request.

"Really? You want to learn how to boot scoot boogie?" His hand moved down to the small of her back again, right above her ass.

She trembled. "Only if that's a real dance."

"Oh, it's real." He twirled her around.

When she resumed her position in his arms again, she moved her body in closer. The new body position allowed her to wrap her hand around the back of his neck. She closed her eyes and rested her head on his chest. As soon as she did that she heard something that sounded like a growl. Had Truman just moaned?

Shauna smiled. She didn't know if he saw her expression. He pulled her body in closer to his. He swayed his hips like a man with confidence. Again, her mind raced to ideas of what he would be like in bed as a lover. Would he be just as tender and generous there as he seemed on the dance floor?

When the song ended, Shauna took in a deep breath and rubbed her cheek against his chest. Her fingertips brushed the back of his hair. With her ear pressed against his chest, she heard his heart pounding. It drummed as hard as hers.

For someone who seemed as excited as her, she never expected to feel Truman break the hold and move away from her like she had a disease.

"Excuse me. I have to—" Truman didn't finish his statement. He retreated to the back corner of the yard and covered himself in the darkness.

Shauna crossed her arms over her chest. For as long as she lived, she would never understand men. She thought they finally broke down a wall.

Nikia and Ervin sauntered up to Shauna.

"I don't know what's wrong with your friend." Shauna shook her head. "One minute he's nice to me. The next, he's pushing me away and running off into the woods."

Nikia laughed. "Oh, honey, you cannot be that naïve."

"He ran. But it wasn't because he didn't like you." Ervin winked. "He likes you *a lot.*"

When Shauna didn't respond right away, Nikia happily filled in the blanks for her. "Your boy was getting too excited during the dance and had to cool off."

Shauna stared at her cousin and Ervin. "No. Are you saying—"

"You brought him to attention." Ervin gave her a sloppy salute, which made Nikia laugh.

If Ervin and Nikia nailed their assessment, Shauna had one question answered. Truman did find her attractive; at least he desired her body. Now the real question and predicament: How would she react to him now in the recording studio?

Chapter 11

After two weeks of recording and, finally, a couple days of rest, the return to the studio seemed a little lackluster.

Truman finished singing "Working for Your Love" and bowed his head as though he had fallen asleep on his feet.

"Let's take a break." Shauna sat back and rubbed her eyes.

She gazed at the engineer, a quiet man with incredibly impossible posture. Clayton had a shiny green Granny Smith apple on top of the boards.

"Clayton, you can eat whenever you want." Shauna stood and stretched out her back. "Just no juice or food on the boards."

Clayton's face masked in confusion until he looked at his apple. "Oh, no, ma'am. The apple is not for eating. It's my timepiece."

Now Shauna looked confused. "Excuse me?"

"I time how long it takes for a record to be made by the length of time it takes for this apple to spoil." He pulled a white handkerchief from his pocket and shined the fruit. "If the fruit is still good by the end of the recording session, then the album will be good. If not, well, the apple doesn't lie." Clayton smiled, stood, and strolled out of the control room, his back as stiff as a board.

Shauna sighed as she made her way to the couch. She curled her legs up and closed her eyes. As soon as she did that, the same images flooded her thoughts: Truman's body, the dance, and his hasty retreat. Her pulse raced.

Shauna glanced at Truman as soon as he sauntered out of the recording studio. He stretched his arms over his head. Her gaze caressed his body, and what a body. Wide chest, flat stomach, long legs.

When he brought his arms down, she directed her gaze to his. "You want to have a seat?"

"I would, but I think if I did I would zonk right out." He smiled and rubbed the back of his neck.

"You didn't get any rest on your days off?" What she really wanted to ask was, "Who kept you up all day long so that you're this tired now?"

"Too much stuff to do. You know how it is." His pacing resumed.

She hadn't noticed her neck stiffening until he touched his. Her shoulders felt tight like if she received another piece of bad news, it would break her.

"So what do you think?" This time his inquiry sounded sincere.

"About what?" She hoped his curiosity had nothing to do with Nikia and Ervin or the dance.

If she didn't want to talk about the situation with her own flesh and blood, then she wouldn't be talking about it with this man.

"The song."

"Oh." She smiled. "Better than before. It seems like it's still missing something." She rubbed the back of her neck. "I don't know if it's in the arrangement or if it's—"

He butted in. "Me?"

She didn't want to look into his eyes but she looked up. Truman's eyes were full of honesty. He wanted critical feedback.

She rubbed the back of her neck again before answering. "I don't know what it is. You're not really here tonight. I can feel it."

"Kind of like the way you can feel that crimp in your neck?" He pointed at her.

She brought her hand down. "It's nothing. Just stress I'm sure."

He made his way behind her. She pivoted to him but he whispered for her to keep looking straight.

"I need to do something or I'm going to fall flat on my face." His hands touched her shoulders with his thumbs resting on the back of her neck.

"You don't have to do this." She tried getting away from him.

"Relax."

A jolt of electricity bolted through her body as soon as his magic fingers began their caress. She sat up straighter. The first rub and she collapsed into a pool of jelly. She didn't want to give in to his gesture but his hands felt wonderful on her.

She closed her eyes. She reached for one of the oversized pillows on the couch and held it close to her body. Truman didn't need to see her hard nipples through her shirt.

"So tell me what I'm doing wrong."

He was massaging her clothed and in public, she thought.

"What?" She concentrated on his hands and how she'd gotten to this position.

"Why is the song not working? Is it the lyrics?"

Shauna shook her head. "They're fine."

"I didn't tell you the whole background of the song like I did with the first one." He dug his fingers deeper into her flesh until she moaned.

She covered the moan by immediately clearing her throat. "So tell me how it was that you came to write this one."

And why is it that you got me thinking about you naked?

"'Working For Your Love.' I wrote it when I was dating a woman. She put me through my paces. She defined hard-to-get." He laughed. "So I wrote the song for her. She heard me play it in a club one night. The rest was history."

Shauna snapped her eyes open. "So you're married?"

"No. It was an old relationship. It's hard to have a relationship in a crazy biz like this."

She tilted her head. "Yeah. I know what you mean."

"Like with Ervin and Nikia."

She wanted to hear his theory on them. His perspective on their union might shed light on any potential romantic prospect between the two of them...not that she thought about it.

"What about them?" She twisted her head from side to side the more he relieved the tension.

"I told him not to get anything started with her." He moved his hands down her back to rub between her shoulder blades. She instinctively sat up forward to give him better access.

"Why shouldn't he start anything with Nikia?" Shauna chewed her lower lip in anticipation of his answer.

"Because she's a lot more successful than him and when push comes to shove, she'll pick the career over him. What do you think?"

His answer, though not romantic, sounded plausible. She'd hoped he would have seen the potential and would have argued for Ervin to fight for the relationship. Or maybe she wished that for herself.

"I think you're right. I mean I personally would never date anyone in the business."

Truman's hands stopped briefly before he continued kneading. "You wouldn't?"

Shauna sat erect. "No. Too many problems. Like you said, one person is usually more successful than the other so you have the whole competition thing going on. And then there's touring separately. Just too many problems."

"I see." Truman's voice lowered. "So you would never entertain the idea of going out with another musician no matter the connection?"

She looked up to him. The energy between them buzzed in the air. If his hands got any lower on her back, then his face would be right over hers and he could…no. She couldn't put her heart out on the line like that.

"I already dated one person in the business, and that didn't work out. So—"

"So that just leaves a whole lot of men up the creek."

Shauna turned her head. She had to look at him in his eyes. Did he really want her or had she imagined their bond?

As soon as her gaze connected to his, Shauna felt a strong pull. She moistened her lips. She watched his gaze drop down to her lips and back up to her eyes. Her rational side begged her to pull away, to not kiss this man at all. Her body screamed for her to take this man up to the roof, find a quiet spot, and devour him.

"Are we ready to get back to work?" Clayton padded into the room, oblivious of the action between Truman and Shauna.

Shauna jumped to her feet. She pulled her shirt down and smoothed her hair back.

"Nothing was going on here." As though her excited feelings clung to the outside of her body, she vigorously brushed down the front of her shirt. "Truman was just rubbing my back. Tension."

"What?" Clayton screwed up his face as he stared at her.

"Never mind. Maybe we should get back to work." She resumed her place at the control boards and tried to control her fluttering heart by taking several deep breaths and counting to ten.

When Truman and the band started playing again, Clayton leaned close to Shauna. "He has a good voice." He nodded as well.

"Yes, he does." This time Shauna did bite her tongue to keep from blurting that Truman also looked and smelled good, too.

"If the rumors are true, you could be sitting on a gold mine." Clayton cleared his throat. "I heard through the grapevine that Craig has one woman in mind for Truman to sing a duet with, and he said Truman was excited about it."

Shauna's heart actually fluttered. She tried not to smile but the idea that Truman thought of her singing with him flattered her.

"And who is she?" She already knew the answer.

"Laura Smalls."

The earth stopped spinning. Her mouth hung open. She felt like Clayton had just named the woman sleeping with the man she loved.

"Who is she?" She had to know about this stranger.

"Next big thing in country music. Has a few hits under her belt and looks like a Barbie doll." Clayton made some volume adjustments.

Shauna forced a smile. "Thanks for telling me. I'll make some calls and see if she'll consider doing the duet."

"You don't have to worry about that. I heard Craig say she'll be here in a couple of days."

Great. That doesn't give Shauna much time to get adjusted to this idea.

Shauna held up her thumb. "Good news all around."

Maybe to keep sane, she needed to only think about the music.

Chapter 12

Truman wiped his brow after tossing the last shovel in the back of a work truck. Such a glamorous life for a country singer.

"Quitting time, Truman." One of his coworkers pulled off his hard hat and carried it under his arm.

Truman nodded and took off his hardhat. It felt good to work with his hands again. Even if he got rich and famous, he would help build his new house. He would design it, lay down the foundation, and add special touches inside. He would be hands on in everything that he did.

Truman prayed before starting the van. Some days she started up without trouble. Other days, she didn't want to be bothered. The stars must have lined up for him. Not only did the van start up on the first try, but it didn't shimmy and sputter nearly half as much as usual.

He patted the dashboard. "Good girl." He turned on the radio and amplified his favorite country station.

"What a great summer day," the DJ began. "It's five o'clock, folks, and you know what that means. It's 'Rising Star at Five' and today is no exception."

He drove the truck toward the main road behind a row of other employees looking to get their tired butts home. He rolled down his window, hoping the cool breeze would relieve him. Even with four hundred dollars in his pocket, he felt spent. He would put half the cash in his checking account and deposit the rest into Ashley's. It should get her off his back for a week at least.

"Today's Rising Star isn't really new to the country scene. Not the local one anyway," the DJ said.

"Yeah, probably some bar band like us who's been doing this for years." Truman yawned and inched up closer to the car in front of him.

"I've seen them play live, and my favorite song of theirs is 'Beer and More Beer.'"

Truman's eyes widened as he stared at the radio. The DJ couldn't be talking about Truman and the Sliders. They hadn't released their album. "We got handed this CD today. Now, we haven't even heard it yet, folks, so you're going to have to call in and tell us what you think." The DJ gave his phone number and then played "Reeling."

Truman listened to the first few notes, then screamed and laid his hand on the van's horn. He poked his head out of the window and hollered loud enough for the people driving by to hear him.

The song sounded good. He didn't know Shauna had cleaned it up and made a radio-ready version.

Sully's solo made the tune stand out. Tony's fiddle gave the song a nice smooth tone. Ervin kept them all in check with his steady beat.

Truman and the band had made it. News like this couldn't be contained. He wanted to tell someone. He could get to Craig's house faster than getting to the guys. He would go to Craig's and then call his guys from there.

Nothing could spoil this great moment. Not even Ashley. He would have to call her and share the news. Even if she asked for money, it still wouldn't bring him down. He had a song from his upcoming album on the radio. It couldn't get any better than that.

* * * *

Shauna crept downstairs, then peeked around a wall to see what giant pounded on the front door. She could have used Nikia's ballsy strength right about now. Too bad Nikia slept like the dead, so she had to greet this unknown visitor.

After the third pounding, she saw Truman's van through the front window. She took two deep breaths to try to slow her drumming heart. Nerves would have wreaked havoc on her stomach had she known he'd planned on a surprise visit. Now she didn't have time to think about getting sick.

With it being a little after five o'clock, she wondered why he paid her a visit this early.

She opened the door. His excitement, along with dirt on his T-shirt and jeans, covered him from head to toe. He had on work boots instead of his usual cowboy boots. He had a five o'clock shadow around his goatee. He looked sexy as hell.

"What are you doing here?" She rubbed her eyes and remembered that she opened the door in her normal sleep attire of shorts and a cutoff T-shirt.

"I just heard me on the radio." His brown eyes sparkled. "'Reeling' was just on the radio."

"It was?" She'd mixed the final copy but didn't know Craig had gotten it. She stepped aside and Truman bounded into the house. "I'm sorry. You should have been told before the song was released so you could have been prepared."

"No, it was perfect. Had I known beforehand that the song was going to be played today I wouldn't be any good at work."

"Work?"

Truman cut his eyes away from her. "You know. Practice."

If she were a superhero, her Spidey senses would be tingling.

"I had to tell someone." He looked at her. "I wanted to tell you."

She couldn't stop the smile that formed. Her chest swelled with pride. He turned on her radio and searched for the station.

"The DJ asked people to call in. I want to hear the responses."

The song ended. The DJ summed up his feeling. "So that was 'Reeling' by Truman Woodley and the Sliders. I don't know about you, folks, but I smell a hit."

Truman screamed, which shocked Shauna. Laughing seemed like an appropriate response. She certainly didn't fear him even as he pumped his fist into the air.

"First caller. You're on the air."

"Yeah, I heard the song. I like it. What did you say that guy's name is?" a female caller asked.

"It's Truman, baby," Truman said to the radio. He turned to Shauna who marveled at the sight. "They love it. Can you believe it?"

"Yes, I can." She knew he had talent. He just had to be packaged in the right way.

"Next caller."

"Hey, heard that tune. That's different from 'Beer and More Beer,' but it's still good. When's his album coming out?" a male caller asked.

Truman looked at Shauna. "When?"

"I don't know. The plan was to release the single and get some buzz off that first. Without a distributor, at this point we're hoping to get some nibbles from some record companies. But it sounds good so far." She tried to act as professional as possible. Seeing him look so excited got her pumped. "We need to talk to Craig and find out—"

He snatched her off her feet and hugged her hard. Her breath escaped her but she didn't mind. She felt safe in Truman's arms. To keep herself steady, she wrapped her arms around his neck as he jumped around the room with her.

"Thank you, thank you, thank you." He danced around with her.

"No problem. It's my job." She brought her face up to look at him eye to eye. Before she knew it, he sat her back on her feet, brought her face forward, and kissed her.

The light kiss popped against her lips. Seemingly harmless and full of gratitude. Then he leaned in for another kiss, a longer one.

This time she closed her eyes. Her breath caught when the realization hit her that he had his lips on hers... And she liked it.

He pulled back again. Searching his eyes, she found confusion, fear, longing but overall he looked satisfied.

"Oh, hell." He dove in for a third kiss.

She felt his heart beating hard against his chest. Or was that her heart beating? Her insides felt like mush and her arms dangled at her sides, powerless to do anything.

She closed her eyes. His lips felt smooth on hers. In between breaths, she caught his manly scent. He smelled of hard work. Coming from an environment where men smelled more perfumed than women, she welcomed the change.

He pulled back from her slowly. He blinked several times before speaking.

"I'm happy." He stroked her cheek with his thumb.

"Happy that your song is on the air? Happy that you kissed me? Or happy that I didn't slap you?" She stared at Truman.

"All of it." His hands settled on her waist. "Are you going to slap me?"

Slap him? Never. As much as her body ached to kiss and touch him again, Shauna had to be grounded in reality. She couldn't open herself up to another man, another potential heartbreak, another loss.

She shook her head as she gazed down at her feet. "Truman, we can't—"

"What's all the noise down here?"

Shauna saw her cousin galloping down the stairs and wearing a long T-shirt that had the band logo for the group Alabama on it. Must have been a souvenir from Ervin.

"Truman's on the radio." Shauna walked away from him. Nikia's infamous bad timing came at the right moment.

Nikia nodded. "That's tight. My Vin is on the radio. Let me give him a call. Maybe he'll want some celebration sex."

Shauna's cheeks felt hot as she kept her back to Truman. Did Truman think about having sex with her when he'd kissed her? Lord knows she'd thought about making love to him.

Shauna put her hand to her chest to slow down her thrumming heart. The trick didn't work before, but it still comforted her.

She would have to tell him that their relationship would stay strictly professional. She wouldn't delve into his personal life.

The ringing of Truman's phone interrupted her thoughts.

"Excuse me." He answered it and simply turned his back on her instead of leaving the room.

Although he didn't ask for it, Shauna decided to give him some privacy by excusing herself to go to the kitchen. Before she could cross into the other room, Truman disconnected the call and cursed.

The gleam he'd had in his eyes disappeared. He balled his hands into fists like he wanted to punch a wall or worse yet, another person.

Shauna should have found a barrier to put between them, but she couldn't. He looked like he needed a friend. Her heart pulled for her to be there for him.

"What's wrong?" She tried to get eye contact from him, but he looked down at the floor as he muttered curses under his breath.

"Truman, talk to me." Touching his hand seemed to help.

He finally took a deep breath before connecting his stare to hers. "Ashley."

"What?" Hearing him say another woman's name cut Shauna in her heart. How could the man kiss her, then bring up someone else? He had some nerve.

"The mother of my son." He took off his hat and scratched his head.

The fact that Truman had a son hit Shauna hard. She didn't know that information from any of her Google searches. She blinked and backed away from him like a stranger had invaded her home.

"She took him." He started marching back and forth. "I sent her money every week and she still took him." He shook his head. "I have to get him back. She won't get away with this."

"Took him where?"

"I have to go." He made his way to the front door.

"Go where?" She went after him.

"North Carolina."

Shauna's throat went dry. She had to process so much in a short amount of time.

Breathe, girl. Don't panic. Don't freak out.

"I'm sorry. You're going to have to put off recording or record without me. I have to get my son." He opened the door and took a step outside before Shauna grabbed his hand and stopped him.

She squeezed his hand so that he wouldn't feel her shaking. "How do you expect to go down there?"

She felt him slipping away from her. Even if nothing else outside of work started between the two of them, she still wanted to talk about what had happened, about her new feelings toward him. He couldn't go away yet. She couldn't let him.

He shook his head. "I don't know. I'll catch a plane, get on a bus, take a train. I'll walk if I have to. But I'm going."

In front of her stood two choices: She could let him go and risk not knowing when she would see or hear from him again, which would delay the release of the album, or she could be a woman and go with him to discuss the kiss and how she felt about him while keeping the project on track.

Realizing her little-girl days had been over a long time ago, she took a deep breath and said, "Then I'm going with you." The words surprised her. In this tense moment, she felt a need to protect him. It went beyond the kiss. To see him so passionate about his son warmed her soul.

"No. I don't know what I'll find in Charlotte when I get there. I don't want you to get involved in the middle of my personal drama." He lowered his voice and stroked the side of her face with his fingertips.

She started to like the feeling. As soon as his hand touched her flesh she knew. "I'm going with you and that's final." She pulled him back into the house. "As owner of Charisma and coproducer, I have an obligation to keep an eye on the talent."

Yeah, that sounded good. If it convinced him, she would be happy.

"We can take a plane but last minute tickets can be expensive." Shauna paced.

"I have four hundred dollars cash on me." Truman took the wad out of his pocket.

"It won't be enough for the two of us to fly down and get back."

Currently she had no liquid assets. She had taken money from Nikia the first time she went to New York. For her second trip, Raheem footed the bill. She doubted if even her name could get her by anymore. It certainly hadn't with the record company.

"Then I'll go without you."

With the fate of his son on the line, she couldn't take his words personally. Fear had to fill him at the moment.

"And it won't be enough for you *and* your son to fly back." She still had to be the voice of reason.

Nikia sauntered downstairs wearing a silk robe this time. "Ervin was really excited to hear about the song." She lifted her eyebrows.

"Nikia, Truman and I have to go to North Carolina. Can I borrow your car?" Shauna turned to Truman. "Your van won't make it there and back."

"Sure. Take the Mercedes. I'm having a Hummer delivered to me tomorrow anyway."

Shauna turned back to Truman. "Wait down here while I change and pack, and I'll be right back." She stroked the side of his face. She felt the sandpaper grit covering his cheeks. "Don't worry. We'll get your son."

Nikia followed Shauna upstairs.

In her room, Shauna switched her sleep attire to jeans and a T-shirt. Then she threw clothing into an overnight bag. "Will you tell Craig what's going on?"

"*I* don't even know what's going on." Nikia leaned against the doorframe as she watched her cousin bounce from one side of the room to the other.

"Truman has a son."

"Uh, oh. Red flag."

"His ex took him to North Carolina without telling him."

"Another red flag."

"I offered to go down with him to get him back."

"Penalty in the end zone." Nikia shook her head. "Girl, you were supposed to do him, not get involved. Why are you doing this?"

Shauna stopped and stared at her cousin. "Because I know if it were me, Truman would do this for me."

"I like Ervin. He has a big—"

"Not now, Nikia."

"—heart. I wasn't going to get dirty."

It would be the first time she didn't.

Nikia sat on Shauna's bed next to her open bag. "Anyway, I know he would do the same for me. But I wouldn't want him to. I don't want to get all up in his business and he shouldn't want to get in mine. Do yourself a favor and give that man some money for a plane ticket and set him on his way. You do not need to get in the middle of some baby-mama drama."

Shauna had told herself the same thing before Truman announced his plans to go down to North Carolina. She couldn't let him go. Not when they hit a milestone. That kiss.

"I can't. I have to go. I have to help him." Shauna stopped at her opened bag. Without looking at Nikia and seeing her judgmental expression, she made a confession. "He kissed me. I mean we kissed. There was, um, a kiss."

"Oh, no."

From Shauna's peripheral vision, she caught Nikia shaking her head in shame. She would have thought of all people Nikia would have been happy for her.

"What?" Shauna ducked in her bathroom and gathered up her toiletries.

"Your nose is so wide open for this man and you don't even see it."

She dumped the supplies into the case. "It is not." She tried laughing off the assumption.

"You wouldn't even pull a splinter out of Raheem's finger but you're willing to drive down to North Carolina to save some man's kid?"

"It's not some man. It's Truman."

Nikia put her hand on Shauna's shoulder. "And you're not some flunky. You're Shauna Stellar. Do you want to be caught driving down with a country singer in search of his son? That's no way to get your career back."

Shauna zipped up the bag. Since she started working as a singer, she'd been selfish, only thinking of how to get herself to the top. This time she felt different. Helping Truman would be helping herself because she wanted to help him. She needed to be with him.

"This isn't about me or my career. It's about Truman and his son."

Nikia stopped her before she could leave the room. "Wait." Nikia darted down the hall to her room, knocked some things around, and then ran back to Shauna like a gazelle.

"Here." Nikia pressed a thick wad of cash into Shauna's hand. "Are you sure you don't want to fly?"

Shauna held the cash in her hand. She didn't have to count it to know it would have been enough to fly her and Truman around the world and back.

"I can't take this." Shauna tried shoving the money back to Nikia. "I don't know when I'll be able to pay you back."

"Don't worry about it. It's Flye's money anyway. He told me to hold it for him when we went to a club the other night. He won't miss it." Nikia pushed Shauna's handful of cash to Shauna's chest. "Oh, wait. One other thing." She ran to her room again and came back with a handful of condoms.

"Nikia." She tried stopping her cousin from loading the colorful packages in her bag.

"If anything happens, I want you to be protected." She stopped and looked serious. "You want my gun?"

"No." Shauna shook her head and hung the bag strap on her shoulder.

"Get plenty of gas. Stay at nice hotels. And eat at good restaurants. If I hear he took you to some no-name motel and you ate some Stuckey's, I'll cut him. Maybe the drive will be good for you two. You can clear the air about what's going on with you. Several hours in a car will do it."

Shauna shoved the cash into her pocket. "Two days at the most."

"Go. I'll tell Craig." Nikia nodded toward the door.

Shauna made it downstairs where she found Truman pacing the floor. "I'll follow you to your place. You pack and we'll hit the road."

"Are you sure you want to do this?" He stood in front of her, searching for the truth.

Shauna nodded, ready for the trip of a lifetime.

* * * *

"You're leaving? Are you fucking crazy?" Sully grabbed Truman's shoulders.

Truman wriggled out of his friend's grip and continued packing. "It's Gage. She took him to North Carolina." He pushed his clothes and toiletries down into a duffel bag.

"Good. Carolina is close to Virginia, closer than Tennessee. On your day off, you can go visit. But now is not the time to cut out. You know she's not going to hurt your son."

Sully didn't understand. Ashley took Gage when he'd asked her to stay in Tennessee. If she wanted Truman to react, she won.

"I know what you're going through, man." Charlie patted Truman on his back. "Go get your kid."

Sully shook his head. "Fine. Let me pack some stuff."

"No." Truman threw the bag over his shoulder. "I'm not going alone."

"Oh. Who's going with you? Ervin? I haven't seen him." Tony scanned their tiny shared room.

"He's probably laid up under that black bitch again." Sully laughed, but Truman fumed.

He dropped his bag to the floor, grabbed his friend by the front of his shirt, and pulled him up off the floor about a foot. "Don't you ever talk about Shauna or her family like that again, you hear? They're good people. You would recognize that if you weren't being so damn selfish."

"Me be selfish?" Sully struggled from Truman's grip and backed away from him. "You're going off to North Carolina for God knows how long to get your son. We just had a song on the radio. We got people interested in us. But all you care about is your boy who is with his *mother*. He's not missing. He's not hurt. This is all about you and your power struggle over Ashley. Call it fatherly devotion if you want. You know I'm saying the truth."

Truman snatched his bag from the floor. He didn't want to look at Sully anymore. His friend had shown his true colors at a time when he needed support. As soon as he got to the front door, Truman heard Sully snickering.

"You're going to North Carolina with Shauna?" Sully pointed out of the front door to the white Mercedes at the end of the driveway. "This isn't some mission to save your son. It's a spur-of-the-moment getaway with you and your hot new producer. Your dick gets hard for her and you forget about everything else. Damn, Tru, so much for not thinking with

Little Truman anymore."

"Fuck you, Sull." Truman stormed through the front door.

Behind him, he heard Sully scream, "I'm sure she'll do that for you."

Truman threw his bag in the trunk and hopped in on the passenger side. "Ready?"

Shauna nodded and took off before either one could change their minds. After the initial few minutes of silence, Shauna spoke.

"Gas is topped off." Shauna kept her stare on the road. "I have my toothbrush, toothpaste, floss, comb, brush, mouthwash—"

"What are you doing?" He stared at her.

The car still smelled new. The black suede seats hugged his body. He should have showered at least.

"I always do this. Ever since I was a little girl." She split her attention between him and the road. "I do an inventory of the things I packed out loud. I'm afraid I'll forget something."

"I guess from all the traveling you've done, it's not hard to forget something here and there." The smooth, quiet ride relaxed Truman too much. He settled into the seat, then slid it back as far as he could.

"You can go to sleep, you know." She cut him quick glances. "You look exhausted."

"I'm fine." He stretched his arms over his head. "Besides, you don't know where we're going."

She had been so caught up in not letting Truman go Shauna had forgotten to ask. "You're right. Where are we going?"

Truman rubbed his eyes. "Charlotte."

"One of my favorite towns. I know how to get there." She waited a beat, then continued. "I could never sleep on the tour bus so I would stay awake and watch how we got to different places. It helps to have a photographic memory."

Truman tapped the built-in GPS in the console. "This will help us." He smiled and closed his eyes. He needed to rest them.

"Oh, no." She slammed her hand against the steering wheel.

He bolted straight up. "What's wrong?"

"I forgot to pack pajamas."

He wouldn't be sleeping now. He couldn't get the image of her naked body lying in the hotel room bed out of his head.

Chapter 13

If Truman's stomach hadn't growled, he could have slept comfortably in Nikia's luxury sedan. He couldn't imagine making this trip in the old van. Shauna handled the car like an expert.

After stretching his aching limbs over his head, he sat up and rubbed his eyes to help him focus. The clock on the dashboard read 1:15. They'd driven almost seven hours straight. He'd slept for that long.

"Hey, sleepyhead." Shauna barely sounded awake herself. "I knew you were tired."

"What was the tip off? The bags under the eyes?" He brought his chair erect and scanned the signs for where they were.

"No. Your voice. Your singing voice actually." She cleared her throat. "The last few times in the studio you've been sounding a little exhausted. Your voice has not been as powerful as it was before."

"I didn't know it was that obvious." He had to smile at the fact that Shauna recognized small quirks within him.

What else was obvious to her? Did she know that he was so attracted to her that she consumed most of his thoughts? Did she know that he thought about making love to her? She probably did now after the kiss and his embarrassing exit after their intimate dance.

"A good producer can hear that if she's paying attention." She split her attention between the road and glancing at him.

He stared at her until the interstate light illuminated her face. Her skin glowed and she looked like an angel. "When I leave the studio in the mornings, I work a construction job all day."

Shauna looked at him with her mouth agape, not saying a word.

"When I get home, I practice with the guys before we hit the studio. I'm lucky if I get three hours of sleep before recording." He rubbed his eyes, thankful for the hours of sleep he got on this ride.

"No wonder you've been looking exhausted. Why would you do that?" Shauna barely acknowledged the car's GPS system when it advised her to take an exit in the next two miles.

"The mother of my son demands money from me almost every day. I'm not making anything from my music right now while I record. I have to work. I have to support Gage." He rested his hands on his thighs.

The dried plaster and mud caked on him scratched the underside of his fingers. He should have changed clothes.

"You've been driving for hours. Have you even stopped to get gas or go to the bathroom?" He glanced at the gauges. Gas gauge rested one notch above empty. If she didn't have to go, then he surely did.

"I just really wanted to get you to your son." She smiled but kept her attention on the road. "I know how important it is for a parent to be with their child."

A pensive look crossed her face.

"Miss your mom?"

A tear managed to escape and roll down her cheek as she nodded. "People keep telling me it'll get better, like as the days go on, I won't miss her as much or something. I hate that."

"You should. I miss her all the time." He patted her leg. "She was a great lady."

Shauna glanced at him. "I keep forgetting she signed you. If I were a good daughter, I would have met you long before now. The last year of her life, I was too busy in my own world to sit down and have a simple conversation with my mother. I feel so stupid."

"Hey, don't beat yourself up. I'm sure your mother was very proud of you and all your achievements. I mean, come on. You're Shauna Stellar."

She wiped her face. "She didn't like who I'd become."

"Your mom loved you." He put his hand on her shoulder.

"I know that." Shauna glanced at him. "I just don't think she *liked* my new attitude. I think taking on a country act was her way of thumbing her nose to me and R&B and everything I was about." She sniffed and kept her stare on the road.

"Maybe Fatima just wanted to try something new. Nothing wrong with that." He started to feel the itch to delve into new territory himself. "You know, when I met Fatima, she talked about two important things in her life. One was her family. The other was the music. We talked about music like guys talk about sports. I couldn't believe the songs and artists that we both liked. But when she talked about her family, I had no idea you were her daughter."

Shauna shook her head. "That's good to hear."

"It should be." Truman rested his hand on Shauna's thigh. "She didn't tell me about Shauna Stellar. She told me about her amazing daughter who works hard and is smart and beautiful. The one picture of you that she showed me was a baby picture. She was wearing some dress with purple flowers over it and she was holding this gorgeous little baby. When she showed me the picture, she said, 'This is perfection. Everything I do, I do for her.' I totally understood that. It was something else that united us. Make no mistake. Your mother adored you and was very proud of everything you did. For the short time I knew her, she never said an unkind word about you."

Shauna's tears flowed before she released a small sob.

Truman didn't mean to upset her, especially during her drive. Up ahead, he spied a gas station next to a diner. "Pull in to the station."

Shauna did and as soon as she put the car in park, Truman pulled her into his arms and held her. In that moment, he felt her body relax as she released a torrent of tears.

Truman didn't say a word. He wanted to be there for her without her feeling judged or that she needed to explain herself. He rubbed his hand over her back, making small circles that he hoped soothed her.

"I talk to her all the time." Shauna wiped her face as she pulled back from Truman. "I'm always asking her for advice. I miss her so much."

Truman kept quiet and simply nodded.

"Can we get something to eat, please? I'm starving."

He smiled. "Yes. I'll fill the car with gas, and then we can go to that all-night diner next door. Sound good?"

Shauna nodded.

After breakfast, Truman took over driving duties. He knew Shauna had a great heart. She'd made the decision to go several hundred miles for him to get his son. To see her now, she'd changed to a different person. The farther south they got, the more open she'd become as though getting away from home freed her.

"So tell me about your son." Shauna turned her body to face him.

He split his attention between her and the road like she had done. When he caught her smiling, he couldn't help but smile with her. Her interest in him and his son felt genuine.

"He's five." As though he needed to illustrate it, he held up his hand with his fingers splayed.

"What's his full name?" she asked.

"Gage Grant Woodley." Truman glanced at Shauna and spoke

before she could ask. "I know. My family seems to have a thing for presidents' names, right?"

She nodded.

"We're more into meaning. Grant means great." When Truman thought of his shining star, his smile widened. "He's the best thing that ever happened to me. Most guys get all panicked when the girl they're seeing suddenly says she's pregnant. I didn't." He wanted to be sure to look Shauna in the eyes when he said that. He wanted her to know his true feelings.

"Did you feel that way because you were in love with Ashley?" She dropped her gaze when she asked the question.

His smile fell. "No. I thought I was in love with her. And she thought, because she liked looking at me perform on stage, that she was in love with me. Basically we enjoyed each other's company, if you know what I mean."

Shauna nodded and looked away.

Telling her about his young, dumb ways made him feel like a jerk. His irresponsible behavior from six or seven years ago no longer existed.

"But I realized I could be an amazing dad. Boy or girl. It didn't matter. I wanted to have that child." His eyes widened when he caught some familiar street signs and landmarks. He felt close to his son already.

"Gage's a great kid." Truman drummed his thumbs on the steering wheel. "Smart. Funny. Always smiling. He can name every president that ever was and when they were in office. Grandpa Woodley taught him that."

"He sounds like a wonderful child." Her voice warmed him like being wrapped in his grandma's quilt. "Why did you decide to pursue your career instead of staying home with him?"

"It wasn't that simple." If he could give Gage nothing else in life, he had to give his boy pride to be a Woodley, something Truman had been robbed of most of his years.

"I just know how hard it was to be separated from my family when I was growing up. I was always on the road with Craig and Delores when she used to tour with us. Once I have children of my own, I won't do that to them. They'll always be with me. Always."

A sudden pang of guilt struck him as he turned into the trailer park where he knew Ashley's grandmother lived. When his eyes settled on the white and blue-trimmed trailer set off in the back corner of the park, his hands gripped the steering wheel. Every vein and artery throbbed until his head filled with the sounds of the constant drumming. He turned to Shauna.

She spoke. He saw her lips moving, forming words, as she looked right at him. He couldn't hear her.

He stared at the mobile home. A toppled bicycle decorated the front yard. His mind raced with thoughts that Gage might have fallen and he had to be rushed to the hospital. The empty driveway worried him. Where could Ashley be with his son?

"Are we here?" Shauna scanned the area.

The question snapped him from his trance.

Instead of answering, he threw the car in park and hopped out.

"Truman. It's three in the morning. Wait." She followed him up the stairs.

He didn't want to wait. He wanted to tear the door down, go inside, and snatch up his son.

He pounded on the aluminum screen door. "Ashley." He glanced at the windows to see if he noticed any movement. Nothing. No lights. No sound. No motion.

"Stop." Shauna put her hand on his arm. "You want to be calm when you do this otherwise you're going to scare Gage. You don't want to do that, do you?"

Her touch felt like an angel had consoled him. He hated to admit that his hot-headed nature would frighten his child. If he blasted through the trailer and yelled at Ashley like he wanted to, Gage would have been terrified.

"Hey," a voice said from behind them.

Truman turned to find an older man standing at the bottom of the steps that led to the door.

"Looking for Mrs. Boyd and that gal she took in?" he asked.

"Yes, sir. We came in from out of town to see them." Truman slowly descended the steps.

"They ain't here. They went to the state fair out of town. They'll be back tomorrow. Mrs. Boyd don't ever miss church." The man spat out some tobacco and wiped his wrinkled lips with a blue-and-white handkerchief.

Truman put out his hand. "Thank you, sir. 'Preciate the information." He shook the man's hand, careful not to squeeze too hard. "Could you do me a favor, though? Don't let Mrs. Boyd or her granddaughter know that someone came around to find her. I want it to be a surprise." If Ashley knew Truman made the trip, she would have hightailed it back to Tennessee, which wouldn't have been a bad thing. At this point, he desperately wanted to see Gage.

"Will do." The man looked at Shauna and tipped his baseball cap. "Ma'am."

She nodded to him, then followed Truman to the car. Truman opened the door for her and slammed it shut when she got inside. He hadn't expected this. He wanted to whisk into town, get his son, and go. Not that it would be that easy. Ashley would fight. He knew that.

Shauna put her hand on his shoulder when he got into the car. "We can't wait out here all day."

"Why not?" Seemed like a reasonable question. "That way if they come home early, we can get a jump on them."

This time she put her hand on his knee. Her delicate touch made him jump. How could a hand so dainty shoot sparks into his body like that?

"I don't know about you, but I would like to get cleaned up. Sleep in a real bed would be great." She slid her hand from his leg. "Besides, the idea of getting a jump on a five-year-old doesn't sound too hip to me."

"I didn't mean it that way. I just meant..." He rubbed his eyes. "I don't want to miss him."

"You won't. We won't. It's now Saturday. We can both get hot showers and get some well-needed sleep. On Sunday, we'll get up bright and early and meet them here. Maybe you all can go to church together."

Truman didn't want to leave. He felt too close to just walk away. What if they came home early? What if the old man had lied and Ashley had gone again? Truman's heart already felt strained. When he looked at Shauna, he could almost hear his heart snapping. To be in a hotel so close to her would be a test of his will.

Shauna licked her lips.

Oh, yeah. A true test.

"So what do you say?" Shauna stretched her arms over her head showing off her toned tummy.

Truman sighed. "I think I saw a motel up the street. It looked clean and—"

"Uh, I don't want to stay in some motel." She shook her head.

Great. She picked now to release her inner diva?

"I don't have the cash needed to stay at a five-star hotel, Shauna."

She reached into her front jeans pocket by raising her hips off the seat. The hairs raised on his arms and the back of his neck. Thank the Lord that nothing else stood up on his body.

She pulled something from her jeans and settled back into her seat.

"I have money. See." She held up a wad of cash, more than he'd ever seen in one place in his entire life.

His eyes widened as he stared at the roll. "Where did you get this?"

"Nikia. She gave it to me before we left. She wanted to make sure we stayed in nice places and ate really well." She beamed but he didn't share in her glee.

"You mean we could have flown here and you didn't tell me?" He glared at her until she lowered her hands.

Her smile dropped from her face. "I thought it would be better for us to—"

"To what? For you to make a fool of me? Make me jump through your hoops again? God, lady, what kind of power trip are you on? Does everything have to be about you?" He started the car. "I could have flown down here faster than us driving half a day."

She held the money in her hands and hung her head down. He felt the hairs on the back of his neck settle down as he drove down the street. Why would she do something like this? They'd even discussed flying and she'd talked him out of it.

He pulled into the motel parking lot and stopped at the registration window. The letter C in "check-in" had blown out in the red neon sign. An older woman with bright red hair sat behind the windows covered in iron bars. She chewed on some gum. Truman could almost hear her popping it from inside of the car.

"I'll stay here." He put the car in park. "You can go to whatever hotel you want. I'll see you in the morning."

Shauna grabbed his arm as soon as his hand hit the door handle. When he looked back at her, he found hurt and confusion in her eyes.

"Please don't leave." Desperation filled her voice. "I only wanted us to get to know each other. I thought we could talk on the way."

"Talk? What do we need to talk about?"

She swallowed, sat back, held her head up like the Queen of England, and said, "The kiss."

* * * *

Shauna certainly didn't want to talk about that kiss, that earth-shattering, mouth-watering, knee-buckling, spine-tingling kiss that she longed to have again. She couldn't think of anything else to keep Truman in the car but the truth.

"I need a drink." He scanned around the hotel until his gaze settled on a dirty convenience store nearby. "Beer and bed. Sounds like a winning combination."

She'd known she and Truman could have flown to North Carolina with the money she held in her pocket. The lure of being in a confined space with him and get him to talk about Ashley, his son, that kiss, and his music proved too appealing for her.

Now that he knew, he looked at her like he couldn't trust her.

He popped open the trunk with the lever. "I can afford this place. I'm staying here."

Her heart stopped. She wanted so much to scream at him, shake him and convince him that she had good intentions, the very best intentions.

He slid out of the car before she could argue her point. Once he pulled his duffel bag from the trunk, he slammed it with such force she thought he would put his hand through it. This time, her looks or talent or connections wouldn't get her out of this dilemma. She had to do some fast talking.

She jumped from her side of the car and started to approach him. When he shot her a hate-filled look, she backed away. He didn't look to be in the talking mood.

Fine. Two could play that game.

"I'll come by to pick you up at seven." She ducked into the driver's side.

"Six," he shot back.

She didn't turn to him.

He kept talking. "And if you don't show, I'll walk there and walk home."

She slammed the door before she could hear him say anything else. Cranking up the music, she drowned out any outside noise. If Truman wanted to be pigheaded, then she would be too. If he wanted to stay in this filthy dive, she would let him wallow on the stained sheets.

Thank goodness she'd seen a nice hotel on the way. She kept her stare on Truman standing at the front window to register for a room as she backed from the building.

He glanced at her. The bill of his cap shadowed his eyes and added to his mysterious nature.

She sped from the parking lot, screeching the tires by mistake, but she smiled from the effect anyway. Once she got on the main highway, she turned down the music. Now she wanted to hear Truman calling after her, maybe even see him running down the street. Someone had to need her for other reasons than just her face and her voice.

When she parked in front of the hotel she would be staying at, she drummed her fingers on the steering wheel. She chewed on her lower lip until she bit down too hard.

"Calm down, girl," she said to herself. "So you've never actually stayed in a hotel by yourself. You've never driven several hours with a strange man either, and you did that."

She took a deep breath, closed her eyes for a moment, and waited until her heart slowed to a reasonable beat. She could do this. If nothing else, Truman had brought out her inner diva.

She hopped from the car and sauntered to the hotel. The closer she got to the counter, the more confident she felt. She walked with a purpose, head held high, shoulders straight. The idea of having a hotel room alone away from all her obligations appealed to her...until she put her hands on the counter and stared at the young man behind it.

Normally Craig would have handled getting her hotel room. All she had to do would be walk in and go straight to her room. Someone else would bring in her bags. The new Shauna wouldn't be that sheltered.

"Yes, ma'am?" The man looked at her calmly at first; then his eyes flashed and he covered his mouth.

She looked over her shoulder to see if she could find what had offended this man. Was there some masked gunman in the lobby? Was Beyoncé staying here?

"You're Shauna Stellar." He pointed at her like she couldn't figure out who he meant. "I can't believe you're here and standing in front of me."

She forced a smile. For a brief moment she'd almost forgotten that she used to be Shauna Stellar instead of Chantel Evans, only child of Fatima Evans.

"Hi." She extended her hand to shake his.

The man grabbed her hand and cranked it hard enough so that her body shook as well.

"Pleased to meet you. Damn hotel policy. I wish I had my phone."

Thank God for small favors. She didn't need candid shots of her leaking out.

"Do you have any available rooms?" She offered a smile as prepayment. "I just need to crash until Sunday."

He nodded. "For you? Anything." He flashed a wide smile. "I'm Travis, by the way."

She smiled in response. Keep the replies short and to the point and maybe she could get to her room faster.

"Got a nice suite." Travis leaned over the counter and whispered. "We're only supposed to give it to local VIPs but how often does a celebrity just walk in our door?"

"I guess not often?" She produced her cash to pay for the room up front, which made Travis's eyes glaze over. She couldn't be bothered by what other people thought of her, especially not now.

"We have twenty-four-hour room service." Travis handed the card key to her.

She smiled and tried hard not to keep herself controlled. "Good to know after I get some sleep."

A door behind the registration desk flew open and another young man in the same white button-down shirt and red vest stumbled out. He laughed until he looked at Shauna.

"Whoa." He pointed to her.

She turned away. Her head throbbed as she reached down for her bag. She hated being viewed as a product and not a person.

"What a fine woman." The man licked his lips.

Travis rewarded his colleague's comment with a punch in his stomach. "Are you stupid? Don't you know who she is?"

"You mean besides the hottest looking woman to walk in here since—"

Travis cut him off. "Shauna Stellar. The singer."

The man nodded. "Guess you're going in disguise. I mean you're hot now. But I've seen you hotter."

So a ponytail, jeans, and sandals qualified as dressing down. Had she known that she would have saved her money on all those wigs and sunglasses.

"Good thing you made it here before you got caught up in the swarm of cop cars down the street." The other man winked at her.

She accepted her room key from Travis. "What are you talking about?"

"I was listening to the CB radio scanner back there and heard that the motel up the street is getting busted again for drugs. They're sweeping the whole place."

"What?" Her heart raced. Was Truman at the motel they were talking about? She couldn't sit by and see him get arrested.

"Yeah. There's some place up the street called the Magnolia Motel. They're always getting busted for drugs and prostitution, sometimes the occasional murder. You want to see a real life *Cops*? Go there and watch from across the street."

She swallowed. Magnolia Motel. Truman.

She headed to the elevator. He'd said he didn't need her so she wouldn't be there for him.

Then she stopped. What was she doing? She was never this uncaring no matter how diva-like she could be.

Shauna turned and ran to the door.

"Do you want us to get your bags, Ms. Stellar?" Travis asked.

"No. Um, no." She burst through the door. If she couldn't explain to the desk guy why she had to go save a man she hardly knew, then what in the world would she say to Truman? She didn't know. She would figure it out on the way.

Chapter 14

Truman let out his breath in the shower long enough to take in another deep breath and hold it. He thought he could muster the stench in his room. He'd worked on a pig farm as a teenager. He'd been in locker rooms with his friends after long games. This disgusting odor surpassed both of those.

The room smelled of must, cigarettes, cigars, bad cheese, and probably a dead body. He had to look under the bed and in the closet to make sure a corpse didn't share his room. He didn't bother unpacking his belongings. He didn't know what had been in the dresser drawers but they stunk worse than the room.

He needed the shower. He had to wash away the day-long drive and try to drown out the thoughts that Shauna had kept all that money from him. Not that he would have asked for her money anyway. A man did what he had to do on his own without any handouts. Besides, how could he trust her? What else was Shauna keeping from him?

After the shower spat a blob of rusted water at him, Truman decided he'd had enough of this American water-torture treatment. He cranked the wobbly knobs to turn off the water but the showerhead and faucet both dripped.

When he pulled the curtain open, he heard someone banging at his door. Great. Probably some teenagers looking for something to do. He remembered knocking on hotel room doors and running when he had too much time on his hands as a kid. He ignored it.

He rubbed the off-white towel over his hair until he dried it enough to not bother him while he slept. Then he worked on his body. By the time he dried his feet, the pounding on his door stopped him short.

No prank. Whoever wanted his attention will wish they had never messed with him.

He wrapped the towel around his waist and had to hold it on the side to keep it closed. He stomped toward the door. When he put his foot down at the doorway, a sharp tack pierced his sole.

"Damn it." Truman turned his foot over to spy the two bloody pin pricks.

"Truman? Are you okay?"

He furrowed his eyebrows, then looked at the door. Shauna? She'd come back?

He opened the door. He tried hiding his shocked expression when he saw her. Hopefully he'd done a better job than she had when she saw him.

Her eyes went wide and she scanned him from his head to his feet with her eyes stopping about midway for more than three seconds. He kept his face stoic but inside his stomach flipped. Then she covered her nose. So much for a magical moment.

"What are you doing here?" He put his hand on the doorframe.

"Get your things. You have to get out of here. Now." She tried going into his room but he blocked her passage.

"I don't think so." He started to shut the door. "I've paid for it for the day. I'm going to get some sleep and head out in the morning by six. Now if you'll excuse me."

He attempted to shut the door but Shauna blocked it with her hand. He didn't know what had happened to that shrinking violet that had driven away earlier, but she no longer existed. She wanted to be there and, most importantly, wanted to be heard.

"I said move." She looked over her shoulder. "We don't have much time."

"Time for what?"

She gazed down at him again. "Could you please put some pants on?"

"Look here. I didn't come to the door like this to impress you or make you nervous. I just got—"

"I don't care. If we don't get out of here soon, we'll…" She looked over her shoulder again.

This time he caught what she must have been listening out for…police sirens, lots of them.

Without a word, he turned into his room, pivoting on the ball of his foot with the small wound. He winced and hopped as he made his way to his duffel bag that he'd sat on the bed.

With no time for modesty, he dropped his towel, pulled out a clean pair of jeans and slid them on. He kept his back to Shauna, afraid to catch her expression to his bare behind. He normally didn't prance around naked in front of women, but this situation called for him to lose all modesty.

When he turned back to her, she stood frozen to her spot, her mouth hung open.

"The car is running." She backed up from the doorway. "We have to go now."

He snatched his bag and grabbed his shoes from the floor. Anything else he might have left in the room they could keep. He had his wallet and identification. He left the room key on the nightstand next to the bed. No need to check out.

"Come on. Let's go." Shauna jumped in on the driver's side.

Truman threw his bag in the backseat and barely got himself into the car before she started backing up from the spot. Before she could drive out of the lot, five cop cars blocked her.

"Great." Then Shauna cursed. "This is what you need to start your career. A rap sheet."

He stared at her as she covered her eyes with her hand and shook her head. She'd thought about his career. No woman in his life had ever taken such a serious interest in his music or his career. Not his mama. Certainly not Ashley. Shauna had her own self to think about.

She could have let him get in trouble all on his own and saved her own neck. That's the way the music world had treated him. They were all behind him until something bad happened; then they scattered like roaches. Not Shauna. In the glow of the blue and red police lights, she looked absolutely gorgeous.

Truman saw a couple of officers emerge from their vehicles. One went to the registration window. The other approached them.

"I'll talk to them," he said. "It's because of me that we're here in the first place." He reached behind and pulled out a T-shirt from his bag. He couldn't talk to the officers with a bare chest.

"No." Shauna sounded more fierce and determined than he'd ever heard her. "I'm handling this."

She powered the window down and waited for the officer to approach her.

The cop leaned down and peered into the window. His leathery face looked like a catcher's mitt as he split his attention between the two of them.

"License and registration," he said almost robotically.

She leaned over Truman's lap to get the document from the glove box. Her exotic perfumed scent swarmed around his head. He couldn't help but to take in a deep breath. Her wonderful aroma reminded him of when he used to go up to the mall to check out a girl who worked the perfume counter. That girl had never smelled of flowers. She smelled like a woman. Every time he caught her scent the hairs would stand up on the back of his neck and over his arms.

His body tingled when Shauna put her hand on his knee to steady herself.

Forget about the cops. Truman was in way over his head with Shauna.

She handed the two items to the officer and sat back, her arms crossed over her chest.

The officer stared at the two items. "You were in a bit of hurry, weren't you, miss?"

"Yes." Shauna remained cool and calm. "I don't like to be near this place. When my friend called to let me know he was staying here, I wasted no time in coming here to get him."

Friend? She thought of him as a friend or did she say that for the police? Either way, to see Shauna this bold and confident made his heart swell with pride.

"Are you originally from here, ma'am?" The officer stared at her identification.

"No. I've been through here once or twice before."

"For business or pleasure?"

Truman couldn't tell if the officer tried to flirt with Shauna or dig for information. He chewed on the inside of his cheek to keep from opening his big mouth and getting the duo into more trouble. He didn't want this man or any other making passes at Shauna.

"Always business." She glared at the cop. "There's nothing for me here."

Truman smiled. If the officer tried reeling her in, she hadn't accepted the bait.

The cop tipped his hat back. "You park right here on the side. I'm going to run your ID"

When he walked away, Truman wasted no time in getting some answers.

"How did you know the cops were coming?" He slipped on his shoes.

She stared at the officer as he punched some information into his computer and compared the information on the documents she'd given him.

"The desk guy at the hotel where I registered heard it on his CB radio." She didn't take her gaze off the officer.

"And you came here to help me?"

She finally turned her head. Her brown eyes held his stare. Her lips parted slightly before she answered. "Yes."

He heard his heart beating in his head. "Because you didn't want to see me get in trouble?"

She nodded. "Yes."

He leaned in close to her. "Because you like me?"

She ran her tongue over her lip, then nodded again.

That answer gave him everything he needed. His body went into autopilot as he leaned in closer to her. She sat still. The heat from her body pulled him in like a magnet. When she closed her eyes, he took that as a sign.

He brushed his lips against hers. Her body jumped, and he heard her gasp but she didn't move away. He had truly taken her breath away and the thought of that enticed him even more. He pressed his lips against hers. Placing his hand on the side of her face, he brushed her smooth cheek with his thumb.

When she put her hand on his thigh, he thought he would leap right out of his skin. Her soft lips formed perfectly on his as though she had been born to kiss him.

Unfortunately, when he heard a throat clearing, he took that as his cue to stop. He glanced up and found the officer standing outside of Shauna's window.

Shauna straightened herself and smoothed back her hair. She wiped her lips and flashed Truman a smile before turning to the policeman.

The cop leaned down. "I didn't realize we had a celebrity in our midst." He handed the items back to Shauna. He didn't let them go right away. Instead he added, "Had I known I was with the 'Love Me, Love Me, Love Me' woman I would have asked for your autograph. Although I must admit that I like Carrie Underwood's version of that song better than yours."

The dig at Shauna felt like a mallet to Truman's head. How dare he talk to her that way. He sat up ready to tell the cop off when she patted him on his knee to calm him. He settled back into his seat but kept an eye on the officer.

"That's fine. Some people liked Whitney's version of Dolly's song better than when Dolly sang it. Music is music." She snatched the ID and registration from the stunned officer.

Truman put his hand on her back.

"You two are free to go." The officer stood up straight. "Except for your little stay in rehab, your record is clean."

She bristled. Truman felt her tension as his own stomach knotted at hearing the crass cop's statement.

"Was that on my DMV record?" Shauna remained cool as a May breeze.

"No. My dispatcher told me about it. Said she'd read it in a magazine or something."

"Tell your dispatcher to get her facts straight. I was never in rehab." She started the car and glared at the officer. "Didn't you hear? I was in the nut house."

The officer's eyes widened as she took off.

Truman slid on his sneakers as she made it to a grand hotel in breakneck speed. The palatial building had a large fountain in front of its circular drive at the front door. He didn't know Charlotte, North Carolina had a hotel like this with a revolving front door and mirrored windows. Looking at her now, she deserved to be in a place like this and not like that horse dump of a dive he'd picked.

"Before we go any further, I need to say something." Shauna parked the car and waited a moment before she turned to Truman. "I'm so, so sorry. You were absolutely right."

Truman cocked his head. "About what?"

"I was selfish. I came with you to support you. That's true. But I didn't tell you about the cash because I wanted to spend time with you. I wanted to get to know you more." She shook her head. "I know that's wrong, especially now because you're here for your son, and because of me, I probably delayed you a day from seeing him." She put her hand over her heart. "That was not my intention."

"What do you want?" He had to hear it from her.

Shauna started to open her mouth, but stopped herself. Her stare alone screamed so many things. Regret, sorrow, and maybe a bit of desire. Or maybe Truman wanted to see that. He saw her plump bottom lip tremble out of nervousness before she drew it in her mouth and chewed it a little. It took every bit of willpower he had not to reach forward and release her precious lip from its prison.

"You can tell me anything you want." He meant that.

He held honesty up there with having a great appreciation for baseball.

"I'm sorry." She got out of the car and waited for him to get out before she continued. "I got a suite so you are more than welcome to stay with me. I mean you'll have your own room. Your own bed."

"I can't accept that." He shook his head. "I'll pay for my own room." Plus he didn't think he could remain a gentleman in the same suite as her.

"I don't think you'll want to do that." She smiled sweetly.

He followed her to the trunk. "Why is that? You think I owe you now because you swooped in and rescued me back there."

"No." She picked up her suitcase from the trunk. "The money I spent on the room is more than what you brought all together for this trip." She slammed the trunk lid down. "The room is on me."

"No." He got his duffel bag from the backseat, then met her around to her side of the car. As he took her bag and stared directly into her eyes, he said, "I'll pay my share."

"Sing me a hit and you'll pay me back plenty." She attempted to take her bag, but he wouldn't allow her to touch it.

He opened the front door for her. Part of the reason he performed the

Southern gentlemanly gesture had everything to do with getting another whiff of her heavenly scent.

"Thank you." Her genuine smile broke him.

Her aroma and smile paid him enough. Another kiss like the one they had in the car moments before would have set him for life.

On the ride up the elevator, he wanted to talk about their kisses. If they talked about them once they got into the hotel room, he knew it would lead to something else.

"So, Shauna, back in the car," he began after the doors closed.

She cut him off. "I think I have to use my card key to get up on our floor." She dove into her pocket to fish out her card.

"Oh, okay. We should talk about—"

"Found it." She smiled but kept her gaze from his.

"Will you quit interrupting me?" He craned his head around to gain eye contact. She stumbled back.

"No." She pushed past him. "If I let you talk, then we'll talk about that kiss."

"Those kisses. Remember, you wanted to talk about it before." He lowered his voice.

She swiped the white card through the reader so many times he thought she would whittle the plastic down to a sliver.

"You like confrontation, don't you? The cop back there, me."

He blinked at her statement. How could a woman who just stared down a cop refuse to look him in the eyes? He reached for her face again but the doors opened, and she ducked out before she could explain herself. He followed her, not for the room. He honestly wanted to get deep into her thoughts.

She opened the door and held it for him. This hotel room made his look like a doghouse. He couldn't smell smoke. Instead he inhaled a flowery scent. Stains didn't spot the carpet or walls or curtains. The vibrant flowered curtains made it seem like the aroma came from them. And there were rooms. Not just a bedroom and a bathroom. Between the large kitchen, the dining room, the living room, and two doors on either ends of the living room, he felt like he'd stepped into someone's apartment than in a hotel room.

She bounded from one door to the other. "These are the bedrooms." She pointed to the two doors across from each other. "Does it matter which one you want?"

"I just want a place to lay my head." He lifted his arm and took a whiff. "And maybe another real shower with clean water."

She nodded. "Then I'll take this one." She pointed to the room on the left side. She approached him and slid her hand over his to get her bag from him. Her touch shot sparks through his skin. Her soft flesh made him want more.

He moved closer to her. "I'll take it to your room."

She clutched the handle with both hands. "No. I have it."

"I'm trying to do the right thing and take this for you. Why won't you let me be a gentleman?" He kept his stare on her when he noticed she wouldn't look at him.

"Because I'm afraid I wouldn't act like a lady." Shauna released a long, haggard breath. She brought her gaze up. "I'm feeling a little dirty, you know, after the long drive."

Truman's heart pumped hard.

She took a step back into her room. "I'm going to take a shower." She stepped out of her shoes. "Will you put out the 'Do Not Disturb' sign on the door?"

"Sure." Truman took a step closer to her.

"See you later." She slammed her door.

He heard her locking it.

Damn. Talk about mixed signals.

Chapter 15

Shauna hadn't felt this out of control in a long time. In her bare feet, she paced in her room, letting her feet sink into the plush carpeting as she thought about her situation. She had Truman in her hotel room. She had seen his naked ass only minutes ago. Now he would be hot and wet and in a shower stall a few feet from her.

"Jesus." She stripped out of her clothing and threw them on the floor.

Shauna ran to the bathroom and started her shower. She needed to cool off her teenage lust. It had to be that. Lust and nothing else. So the man had dreamy eyes. So he had large, powerful hands. So he kissed her and made her knees buckle.

Shauna made the shower colder hoping it would cool off her overheated flesh. Standing under the pelting water, she closed her eyes, and thought about Truman. Did he want her as much as she desired him? Would he want to touch her? Caress her? Take care of her?

By the time Shauna opened her eyes, she noticed she had one hand cupping her breast, now heavy and sensitive, and the other heading down between her legs. To occupy them with something less wanton, she pumped some liquid soap into her hands and covered her body, sliding her hands over her arms, stomach, and legs. Touching herself made her think about Truman. What did he look like all wet?

Shauna slammed her hand against the faucet to turn off the water. As the water drained, she jumped from the stall and grabbed a white towel from a wire shelf next to the commode. With her hair slightly wet, and her body just as slick, she wrapped the towel around herself, went to her bedroom door, and opened it with such force she thought she had pulled it off the hinges.

She marched over to Truman's closed door. Through it, she heard his shower going. When she heard him singing, she melted even more.

Not sure what to do, but afraid of not doing anything, she softly knocked on the door. Even a mouse wouldn't have been able to hear it, but she started in the right direction. She couldn't stop now. Couldn't back away.

Shauna knocked on his door again, a little harder but still not hard enough for him to hear it.

"Come on, Shauna. You can do this." With her fist, she pounded three times on the door and listened.

The singing stopped for a moment, but the shower continued. After a beat, the singing started again.

"Damn." She beat on the door again, not caring if she would wake up the other guests in the rooms around them.

At this point, she couldn't stop herself. Her body propelled her to action. She heard the water stop this time, but that didn't keep her from pummeling the door. She only stopped when it opened and Truman stood on the other side dripping wet with a towel around his waist.

"What? What's wrong?" Truman ran his hand over his face and scanned the room behind her. "Is someone trying to break into the room?"

Shauna took a step back and swallowed hard. She opened her mouth to talk, but nothing came out.

"What is it, Shauna?" He lowered his voice to something probably meant to be soothing, but she caught a seductive tone in it.

"I don't know how to do this." Her statement came out in a whisper.

Be direct. Say what you want.

She heard her counselor's voice in her head, but she knew his advice had nothing to do with this situation.

"Take your time." He fisted the towel around his waist.

"I didn't grow up with sisters." She shook her head. "Or even girlfriends. I sang songs about love and romance, and I have no idea about any of it." She looked at him. "I've been sheltered from a lot. Right now, I feel... This is crazy. You think I'm crazy." She started to turn away when Truman grabbed her hand.

When she reconnected her gaze to his, he spoke. "Don't talk for me. I never thought you were crazy. Didn't then. Don't now. You have something to say. Say it." He let her hand go but moved in closer to her.

"Before each of my shows, Craig doesn't allow me to talk." Shauna put her hand to her throat. "Preserve the voice, he would say. I've never gotten a hotel room on my own or handled my own money. I've felt like a muted child all my life...until now."

"And now?" Truman's voice became guttural.

"I feel like a woman." She raised her head. "I want you, Truman. I don't know if this is what normal women do. Do they make proclamations like this?" She didn't allow him to react. "They don't, do they?"

"Not so much. But I like this. I like you. No woman has ever gone through so much trouble to get my attention and keep me safe and happy."

Shauna took a few steps back toward her bedroom while she fixated on droplets of water cascading down his perfect form.

"I want you." He ran his hand back through his soaked hair, flicking water on her face.

When she made it back to her bedroom with Truman now standing in it with her, she sobered to her situation. She stood naked in a bedroom wearing only a towel in front of a handsome, sexy man who also had a towel around his waist that steadily rose up in the front.

Truman reached for her.

"Wait." She held her hand up to stop him. To ease his confusion, she explained why she halted the action. "This is going to sound strange but—" She paused, not sure how to phrase the request. Then she looked in his eyes. "Can I touch you?"

He didn't question her. He didn't laugh at her request. As though he thought speaking would frighten her, he simply nodded.

Shauna swallowed and scanned him first from head to toe. While keeping the towel around her body with one hand, she raised her free hand up and touched a few strands of his still wet hair. As soon as she allowed her fingers to rustle through his silky tresses, he moaned.

The sound alone made her wet. She dove her fingers in deeper, gripping his hair before trailing her fingers down the sides of his face, over his nose and the little divot under his nose. He smiled when her fingertips danced over his full lips.

She took a deep breath before exploring further, venturing her hand down his thick neck and over his collar bone to his broad shoulder. Shauna didn't know what to expect when she put her hands on him, but she liked the feeling. His skin felt supple under her touch, substantial but smooth and hard where it needed to be.

As soon as she moved her fingers down his arms, his muscles flexed. She didn't know if the reaction came involuntarily or if he did it to impress her. From the way Truman closed his eyes and leaned his head back, she suspected the response came naturally.

She brought her hands down to his. Instead of simply touching his fingers and moving on, she interlaced her fingers with his. Then she moved closer to him and pressed the side of her face against his chest, allowing the heat of his body and the water to fuse them together.

"I only had sex one time, and that was with Raheem." Shauna felt the need to explain her actions and hoped he would understand. "It was fast. It hurt." She exhaled. "And he wouldn't let me touch him."

Truman removed his hand from her grasp to cradle her chin and bring her head up to look at him. "I am not like other men." His deep voice vibrated the floor. "We have time. Touch me all you want." He took a step back. "Do you want to explore my whole body?"

She didn't answer verbally. Shauna reached out and touched his chest first. The wide planes of his chest had her drooling. She brought her fingers down to his nipple and circled it lightly. It amazed her how hard it became, like a pebble.

When she looked up, she noticed the way Truman stared at her. His breathing became ragged. Was he growing impatient with her?

"You think this is weird." She drew her hand back.

He captured it. "I think this is the sexiest thing a woman has ever done to me." He glanced behind her. "Maybe it's time we take this to the bed. Is that okay?"

Feeling the need to explain herself, she took several steps back in case he wanted to run. "Would you be okay if all I wanted to do was touch you?"

"I'd be fine." Maybe to calm her nervousness, he stood on the other side of the bed away from her. "Would you be okay with only feeling me?"

She didn't know how to answer. Fear filled Shauna, and she didn't understand why. She wanted to be with Truman. Everything about the connection felt natural and real.

"Wait right there." He went to the window first and drew the blinds to cloak the room in as much darkness as he could.

With it being early in the morning, she knew it wouldn't be possible to put them completely in the dark, but he did a great job. The dim lighting did calm her a little.

Then he walked behind her to her bathroom and extinguished that light. He stood behind her. She felt the heat from his body warming hers, although he didn't touch her.

"Better?"

She trembled when he spoke. "Yes. Thank you."

She heard him padding back to the other side of the bed.

"Do you want me to lie down?" Truman could have done whatever he wanted, but he gave the power to Shauna.

She started to answer but stopped. "Do you want me to get undressed?"

"Ever since the first moment I saw you." He didn't hesitate.

That response made her smile. "Will you lie down with the towel?"

Truman obliged, positioning himself in the center of the bed and placing a couple of pillows behind his head.

Shauna took a moment before her need overtook her senses. She dropped her towel and climbed in the bed. No makeup to hide behind. No glittery gown. No extensions. Truman got the real her. She had to thank her lucky stars that Truman darkened the room.

"Jesus, Mary, and Joseph. You are beautiful." He cupped her face.

"You can't see me in the dark." She held his hand against her cheek.

"I can see you."

With her breasts exposed, she felt both free and vulnerable. She slid her hands down his arm to his chest again. Feeling his flesh became an addiction. Touching him would only satisfy one need. She wanted more.

Shauna danced her fingers over his rippled abdomen. Truman flinched under her touch. The sudden, jerking motion jiggled the towel he still had around his waist.

Like opening up a Christmas present, she undid the bunched section of towel on his side and flopped it open, exposing his erection.

She uttered the only word that came to her mind. "Magnificent."

"Same applies to you." He brought his hand down from her face and rested it on her thigh.

"Is it okay to touch you now?" Truman stacked the deck in his favor by brushing his thumb over her leg.

"Yes." Shauna had to catch her breath before she continued. "Please."

He moved his hand over her legs so slowly like an artist moving his brush over a canvas. He didn't move his hand to her obvious erogenous zones. She wouldn't have minded if he moved his hand between her legs or cupped her breast.

Truman treated her with respect. "You can keep exploring my body." Like she needed help, he placed her hand low on his midsection.

Shauna swept her fingers back and forth over his stomach, then brushed them down one leg and then the other. She felt him trembling under her touch.

"You can touch me more." Feeling brave and needing him more, she placed his hand on her breast.

As soon as he massaged her tit, she sighed. He kneaded her, slowly at first, like manipulating precious dough. Then his large thumbs circled her nipple.

It hardened to a painful extent to where she loved the ache. She pressed his hand against her body harder. She wanted the feel of him imprinted into her mind.

It took her no time to bring her hands down to his long, hard shaft. As soon as she wrapped her fingers around it, Truman sucked air between his teeth. She brought her hands up to the tip, squeezed it, then eased them back down to the base.

"You know how to drive a man wild." He smiled. "You tell me what you want. I want to hear you."

Before she could make a request, Shauna slipped a hand behind Truman's head and pressed her lips against his. He eased his hand behind her as he slid his tongue into her mouth. God, she loved this experience.

She broke from the kiss long enough to tell him what she wanted. "Don't stop needing me." She let him go long enough to lie on top of him. "Want me. Please want me."

Truman lifted his head. "I want you." He kissed down her neck. "I need you so much." He turned her over onto her back and continued down to her breasts.

He palmed one while licking her other nipple. Shauna wrapped her legs around his wet and warm body. Every cell in her tingled. She couldn't imagine feeling anything better. Here she had a man who desired her and paid attention to her and listened to her. The thought of that alone made her even wetter.

As though he sensed her increased desire, Truman kissed down her body until he positioned his head between her legs.

"What are you doing?" Shauna peered down.

Truman let his actions speak for him. He parted her labia. Before she could say anything, he gave her one long, slow swipe of his tongue, making sure to press the tip against her clit.

Shauna arched her back from the bed and gripped the comforter. Her heart pounded so hard she thought it would burst from her chest. She didn't want to die yet. Not when he had her so close to her first real climax.

He continued licking and teasing her. If that didn't curl her toes enough, he massaged her inner thighs, and then he hummed. That vibrating feeling alone made her arch her back.

Beyond her control, she reached down and gripped a handful of his hair. Never had Shauna been this demanding about her needs. She had never had a man be so attentive. It felt like Truman licked her for hours, only coming up for air once or twice.

His skilled tongue swirled around her clit before he moved down and slipped it inside her.

"Stop. Stop. Please." Shauna raised her hand.

Truman halted his oral action. "You don't like it?"

She waited until she could catch her breath before speaking. "I love it."

She sat up. "I want my first orgasm to come from when you're inside of me."

He looked around the room. "Please tell me you have condoms. I don't have any."

She thought about teasing him, but delaying him would also mean holding off on her fun. "My bag."

Truman leaped from the bed to retrieve it.

"Inside."

He didn't need any other direction than that. He zipped open the bag and rifled his hand through an interior pocket. She didn't even have to tell him where she had them hidden. Shauna would have to thank Nikia for her quick thinking.

Truman placed a pile on a nightstand and tore open a package with his teeth. "Please tell me this isn't a dream." He rolled the rubber onto his erection.

"You have me here in a hotel room all day and all wet."

"Thank God you don't know." Truman climbed in bed.

"Don't know what?" Should Shauna be worried? Did he have a disease or a wife or a bunch of other kids he hadn't told her about?

He hovered his body over hers and stared into her eyes. "Thank God you don't know how unbelievably sexy you are and how *I* would have killed for this moment."

Shauna laughed. "You don't know that I feel the exact same way. Lucky woman."

He took her hand and brought it down to his hard shaft. He made her hold it. Even through the thin rubber, she felt him throbbing.

"Position it." He nodded his head as she slowly moved the tip up and down between her slick lips.

When she had it at her opening, Truman eased himself in her so slowly time stopped. Shauna dug her heels into his calves and clawed his back. Feeling every bit of him as he delved deeper and deeper in her made her appreciate the intimate connection.

Down to the hilt, Shauna held her breath and constricted her arms around him.

"Breathe. Come on, baby." Truman kissed her forehead.

She felt her stomach compress into a tight ball while a full-on fireworks show shot off behind her eyes and in her head.

"That's it. That's it." Shauna felt tears running down her face and hoped it didn't freak Truman out. To calm him, she laughed. "That's an orgasm." She kissed his lips, his chin, his nose, the side of his face, and any part of him she could reach. "Don't stop."

He shook his head. "I don't plan on it."

Truman took his time with her, making slow, easy thrusts between her slick walls as he stared at her. She loved his body and the way he used it. Out of his clothes, he carried defined muscles. Maybe not eating that much and working all the time did it. Either way, she loved it. She loved feeling his abs on her. Shauna moved her hands down to his ass and squeezed his hard cheeks.

When he increased his speed, Shauna gripped him harder like she wanted to last longer than eight seconds on this bucking bull. She licked the side of his neck and tasted his salty sweat. Even that turned her on.

Truman surprised her by rolling over on his back and making her be on top of him. As though people could see her, she covered her chest and shook her head.

"I've never done this." She hated to fail at anything. "I don't know what to do."

Instead of going back to the missionary position, Truman smiled. "Do what feels right." He took her hands and placed them on his chest. "What does your body tell you to do?"

Shauna did nothing at first, or at least she didn't think she did. She felt her vaginal walls tighten and contract, and assumed it did it because of her nervousness. Either way, Truman loved the feeling, evident from the way he squeezed his eyes closed and moaned.

"What are you—oh, yeah. Never felt that—don't stop." He held on to her waist and lifted his hips to thrust in her.

Although she had never been in that sexual position before, her body responded. She gyrated her hips back and forth, moving him in and out of her.

"Deep. So deep." She leaned her head back. "Again. Again. Again." She held his hands while another orgasmic wave crashed over her.

Truman gripped her thighs. She liked the way he captured her, made her feel he wanted her.

She leaned forward and pressed her breasts against his chest. In that position, she still rocked her hips while she kissed him.

In between kisses, she spoke. "More. More."

"More sex?"

She shook her head. "Positions. Are there other positions?"

Truman laughed. "How dirty do you want to get?"

Shauna smiled. "I want to try it all."

"We can't do them all right now, but we can do more." He patted her backside. "On your stomach."

"On top of you?" She stayed in her position and propped her upper body on her hands but stayed on top of his dick.

He shook his head and patted the mattress next to him. "Here."

She slid him out of her, a task considering how much she loved him being inside of her. Then she faced the headboard and got on her stomach as he requested.

Truman got up and moved on top of her. "Tell me if I'm too heavy." He aimed for her core and slipped in with one easy motion. "So damn tight."

"Bad?"

"Good. Excellent." He interlaced his fingers in hers as he made long, slow strokes. "You like it?"

She nodded.

"Say it."

She could hear him talking between gritted teeth. "Yes. Feels good. So...so..."

"Not yet. Don't come yet."

The request seemed impossible. The orgasms came and she couldn't control them. As much as she loved touching him and feeling him inside her, she couldn't get enough of feeling his weight on her body. She didn't feel trapped or constricted. She tightened the hold on his hands and drew them close to her mouth to kiss them.

"Beautiful." Truman kissed the side of her face. "Sexy." His thrusting accelerated. "Best. Body. Ever."

Again, her body reacted in a way she didn't expect nor could control. She curved her back, which brought her ass up higher. Truman grunted. She felt his body shake.

When he slipped his hand underneath her and played with her clit, she broke.

"I can't hold out. I'm coming." Her body trembled.

Truman pulled out of her quickly and turned her over onto her back in a blink of an eye. "Need to see you." He entered her again and hooked his arm under her leg. "Come with me."

She couldn't tell if shower water or sweat covered his face. Either way, he looked intense and sexy. Shauna felt her body tense up again.

"Yes." He nodded. "Yes." He gritted his teeth and growled as he held himself inside her.

Shauna didn't know if she could come down off this high. As soon as she took a breath, Truman eased down, resting his body on top of hers.

"That was fucking amazing." Shauna covered her mouth.

Truman laughed. "You cursing is so cute." He kissed her. "Be right back."

As soon as he hopped out of bed, Shauna crawled under the covers, suddenly feeling chilly without his warm body.

Truman came out of the bathroom and stood next to the bed. Even flaccid, he looked impressive. "Have you really only had sex one time before this?"

Shauna couldn't believe she admitted that but it had been true. She nodded as Truman got into bed.

"It was toward the tail end of the relationship with Raheem. He started saying that there was something wrong with me because we had been going out for almost a year and never had sex." She paused before continuing her story. "Our relationship was arranged. Because I started in the business so young, I became the reluctant poster child for virginity."

"You say that like it's a bad thing." He pulled Shauna close to him and let her lay on his chest as he held her.

"I know. But starting out, I wanted to be known for my talent, not that I was raised right. As soon as I turned twenty-one, Craig pushed me to be sexier, edgier. I was now competing with other female artists who seemed to love flaunting their sexuality. One female rapper admits happily that she's a proud bisexual."

"That's not Nikia, is it?"

Shauna laughed. "Nikia is a lot of things. Bisexual isn't one of them." She patted Truman's forearm. "Another female artist is famous for her extensive dating. And another one is practically nude when she performs on stage or does a music video. Pretty soon, my talent wasn't enough. And I wasn't a social media hound either. That's Craig."

"I could tell." He kissed her temple.

"Anyway, after a year of wearing low-cut gowns with high slits, Craig decided that I needed to have someone on my arm so people would stop wondering about my sexuality. Apparently, because I didn't go out in public with my dates, I was seen as either a spinster or a prude. And yet recently a boy band proudly wears purity rings and that was seen as noble. It's crazy the double standard that exists."

Shauna felt Truman moving like he had shaken his head.

"So Craig did a little research and decided that Raheem and I would be a great match. First, he had us do a duet. That was 'Dirty Loving.' It did sell very well. He already had a couple of hits on the R&B charts under his belt before then. But our duet put him in with a pop crowd thanks to me. He also had a slight scandal when he was caught skinny dipping in some stranger's pool while he was at a party, so he had a bad-boy reputation."

"Your definition of bad boy and mine differ tremendously." He chuckled.

"I guess I should say he was considered a bad boy in our industry, and it was a reputation that would work for me. It was a sexual scandal but not one that was so bad that I should be turned off by it. At least, that's how Craig had explained it to me. Our labels thought we would look good together. They saw us as a younger version of Jay Z and Beyoncé. That kind of power couple." She craned her head around to look at Truman. "Do you know who they are?"

He snickered. "Yes. I'm with it enough to know that couple."

She smiled. "Sorry. We got together. It was awkward at first because it felt like a business arrangement, like we had to be together. They sent us to restaurants where they knew paparazzi would be to capture and document our relationship. Raheem was a gentleman at first. He was dating the Queen Virgin. He had to be." Shauna tried keeping the bitterness from her tone, but talking about her past relationship made her feel heated. "Anyway, my career was hot. His career was taking off. Our schedules didn't mesh. At first, it was easy to put off any kind of intimacy. I would be on tour or he would be touring. We would see each other at award shows and prearranged date nights. As soon as the event was over, I was taken back to my home or hotel, which was fine with me." Shauna brought the comforter up over her breasts and covered herself tightly. "The press nicknamed us Shaheen, which I hated. It took away my identity and fused me with him, when I wasn't even sure what we were or what we had. As I became older, I wanted to explore more of my sexuality and I started wearing more risqué fashions because designers liked sending me clothes. They would see me looking sexy and people automatically assumed I was this promiscuous woman with an insatiable appetite, especially because I was with Raheem who sang songs about having sex and being reckless. They bought into the sexy image. I think in a way, I did, too. I was an adult. I did want to explore my sexuality more. So one night, I told Raheem I was ready. He, um—"

Shauna didn't want to tell the story. She'd lived it once. It hurt her to recall it again.

"You don't have to tell me if it bothers you." Truman wrapped his arm around her waist.

"No. It's okay." She nodded. "It was quick. Very quick. We were coming back from dinner in a limo. Raheem didn't even wait to get to the apartment. He ripped my panties off and took me. He thought it was funny that he took my virginity in a car." She took a deep, cleansing breath. "I had a vision in my head of how my first time should be before that moment. Raheem and I are the same age. I guess I thought he would have been just as green as I was. I thought he would want to take his time. I should have waited for the right one. I am glad I didn't do it again with him. So many regrets." She settled back against Truman. "After that, we were never the same. We argued all the time. I stayed away from him as much as I could.

I also became way more popular than him because I worked nonstop. I had been nominated for an Oscar for singing a song in a movie about Pearl Bailey. As I was getting ready to go to the Oscars, he called me a stuck-up, um, not a nice person. He stormed out. Later, though, he was on camera with another woman who was pregnant with his child. He admitted on live TV that our relationship wasn't real and he was now with the real love of his life. It was humiliating, and I felt used. I never want to feel anything like that again."

As soon as she closed her eyes to get comfortable with him, he shifted and positioned her off him and against the pillows.

Truman slipped out of bed and picked up the towel he'd used to cover his body. This time he draped it over his genitals. "I don't want to disturb your sleep. I'll let you get your rest and I'll go back to my room." He leaned down and kissed her forehead, not even on her lips. "Good night."

Shauna sat up with her mouth agape. What just happened? No way would she let this moment end this way. She leaped out of bed to go after the man who'd just rocked her world.

Chapter 16

Making love to Shauna came as a dream to Truman. A sexy woman like Shauna Stellar, with her long brown hair, endless legs, juicy apple bottom, and the face of a goddess, wanted him. Maybe she should remain that for him. A dream. A fantasy. Nothing more. She had already told him that relationships with people in the industry wouldn't work. Why get comfortable? Why try to get cozy?

The more Shauna talked about her ex, the more Truman's blood boiled thinking about that weasel, Raheem. Even though their relationship had been a setup, Raheem didn't have the right to treat her that way. Then again, Truman had been set up with Shauna, not in a romantic setting. She had a job. He had a job. For a brief moment, he forgot about his goal. For that reason, Truman had to make a hasty retreat from Shauna.

"Hey, wait." Shauna managed to catch up with Truman before he could get to his bedroom. "Did I miss something?"

He turned and found her standing naked and looking incredibly sexy, even with her arms folded and her hip cocked.

"I didn't want to mess up your sleep. You did almost all the driving to get us here. You must be exhausted." He tried smiling to mask his true feelings.

"I'm tired of people sugarcoating the truth." She moved in closer to him. "We had a really wonderful moment. I shared with you something I hadn't even told Nikia, and we're close. I thought we finally gotten through our issues. And you bolt and think I would be fine with it?"

When Shauna laid out the situation that way, he felt like an absolute heel. "I was trying to be a gentleman." He would leave out the part about also trying to protect his heart.

"By leaving me alone to come to my own conclusions?" She shook her head. "I'm not budging from this spot until you tell me what's going on.

Why didn't you stay in bed with me?"

Truman regarded her for a moment while he assessed himself in his head. "You know it's going to be hard to explain with you standing here naked."

Shauna exhaled hard through her nose. "Talk."

Before he did, he tied his towel around his waist first. He planted his feet firmly on the carpeted floor. "Right after Ashley and I broke up a couple of years ago, I swore I wouldn't be led around by my, um, libido." He dropped his gaze for a second like he needed to illustrate his point. "Every time I did that, the consequences weren't great for me. I came into this recording situation with business on my mind. Nothing else. I was going to go in, record, go home, write, and do it all over again. Keeping focused." He stared at Shauna and couldn't help the smile that sprang to his face. "Then I saw you. And, yeah, we fought a little. We're both passionate. Since that day Craig made us pose for that picture, I haven't been able to get you out of my head, which is not a good thing. I get off track. I make impulsive decisions. After what you told me happened between you and Raheem, I didn't want you thinking that I would ever use you in any way. Not in my career, not financially, nothing. I like you." He held her shoulders and truly focused his full attention on her. "I really like you. And what we did in there and what you told me, I will treasure always. I would much rather you feel like you had this great experience and move on than think that I had some other motivation behind it other than wanting you so badly that my body hurts when I see you." He cupped her cheek. "I respect you as a singer, as an artist, as a producer, and as a woman."

Shauna held his hand and brought it down. "If you truly respected me as a woman, you would have been a man and told me all this."

He nodded at her honesty, although it stung.

She continued. "I appreciate you thinking of my feelings. Never once did I think that our sexual experience was anything other than a mutual desire. I wanted you. You wanted me, right?"

He smiled. "No doubt."

"Promise me this. The next time you have any kind of issue, whether it involves me or not, you talk to me." She continued holding his hand.

"I will if you promise me this. Stop trying these quick-fix schemes to get back your status. This Insta-snap or Face-tweet or whatever they are, stop doing them. And for God's sake, don't deal with Raheem anymore. Your dignity is worth a whole lot more than anything he could do for you." He brought her face up so he could look into her eyes. "Superwoman, stop trying to save the world. It's no wonder you snapped. You try to take on everyone's burdens on top of managing your art. I'm a grown man. If this record deal doesn't work out, I'll be okay."

Her tough demeanor faded and her body softened. "But Craig and your band and—"

Truman pressed his lips to hers. When he broke from the kiss he said, "We'll be okay." He put his hand to her chest over her heart. "Heal yourself. Take care of you. Most importantly, ask for help. I promise you from here on out, I'll do the same."

The more they talked, the more relaxed Shauna looked until she slowly eased her body against his and allowed him to hold her.

"You are so good for me." She moaned.

Truman's body tingled. "Yeah?"

She nodded. "You're the first person who allowed me to have fun. You're having a good time with me, right?"

When Shauna peered up at him, Truman struggled to respond. Should he tell her that having amazing sex with her meant more than a fun romp in the sack? He now wanted more. In looking at her, she didn't look like she desired anything serious. Why should she? She had worked hard since she was fifteen. She dated a supreme asshole. She had an opportunity to put her life back together. No way should Truman pressure her for more. So he simply nodded.

"You're a woman who is committed to your career, committed to doing good work and committed to being a good person. You go into everything you do with your full heart. You have to respect that." He meant every word.

She smiled. "You have a way with words."

"That's why I'm a better songwriter than you."

She peered up at him. "That's not hard to be. I've never written a song."

"You haven't? We are going to have to change that. And you will be successful because I'm the best." Truman dug his fingers into her sides and wiggled them. "Tell me I'm the best. Come on. Admit I'm a great songwriter."

She laughed, which meant that he had made his goal. "I'm not going to say it." She squealed and attempted to pull his hands away from her. "Please stop. You're killing me."

"All you have to do is say it." He pulled her in next to him while continuing to tickle her with his free hand. "Just say that Truman Woodley is the best songwriter in the whole world."

Shauna couldn't stop laughing. When he eased up a little, she managed to say something. "Truman Woodley is the best."

He smiled. "Come on. Finish it."

She held his arms. "I did."

He nodded and stopped the tickle torture. "The more I get to know you the more I want you. I want to keep peeling layers to you, Shauna Stellar."

Shauna waited a beat before she said, "Chantel."

"Excuse me?"

"My real name is Chantel Evans. Shauna Stellar was a name Craig made up because it sounded better, more marketable."

Truman leaned forward and kissed her. "It's nice to meet you, Chantel." Then he put his finger to his lips and tried to look pensive. "You know what that means."

The smile dropped from her face. "What?"

Truman looped his arms around her waist and walked backward to the other bedroom. "We're going to have to have sex again so that I can call you by your real name. And since I had Shauna in there," he pointed to the first bedroom, "I'll have to have Chantel in here."

She held his shoulders. "Only if you insist. But we'll need the condoms."

"That's the easy part." He ran to the other bedroom, allowing the towel to fall from his body, and grabbed the remaining condoms he left on the nightstand.

Truman returned to find Shauna, or rather Chantel, standing in the doorway with her arms over her head holding on the doorframe. He became somber for a moment as he studied her. It hit him that after completing the album, this arrangement would be over. No way would Chantel want to continue this light-and-breezy relationship. For now, he would have to enjoy what he had.

"What?" Her smile melted.

"I'm a pretty lucky man to have a woman as great as you want to spend time with me and willing to put up with my drama." He pressed his lips against her forehead when he got in front of her. "I appreciate every part of you."

He meant that. Except for the fact that she belonged to the masses, Truman fell hard for Shauna Stellar. He had Chantel Evans in his arms. The warm, trusting, open woman also managed to capture his heart. So much for keeping his focus.

* * * *

Revealing her true self to Truman lifted a weight from Shauna's shoulders. She no longer saw herself as a stage act, a star. Shauna Stellar found a country singer. Chantel Evans found herself a man. She reconnected to her old self.

She also realized that despite their amazing physical connection, Truman remained loyal to his career and family. He wouldn't have time for her, especially after getting his son. To save herself, she had to act like keeping their arrangement light and fun worked for her. When the album wrapped, he would be on a promotional tour, a concert tour, and on to bigger and better things without her. Being honest with him and herself would keep her grounded and protected. If after the completion of the album Truman said good-bye, she would be fine. She would have to keep telling herself that.

For the rest of the day and night, Chantel and Truman spent it talking, sleeping, eating, and making love. Her body ached in the best way. When Chantel woke up the next morning, she found Truman gone from her bed. She scanned her bedroom until her eyes settled on the digital clock next to her. A quarter to six. Damnit, why didn't she set her alarm? She knew Truman wanted to go get his son.

She stumbled from the bed and over to the bathroom. She didn't see his duffel bag. Did Truman leave her? Had he taken Nikia's car and gone to get Gage on his own?

Just as she reached for the phone to call down to the front desk, she heard someone fiddling with the doorknob and key card entry at the door. Truman came through with an armful of bags and cardboard tray of drinks.

"Good morning." He still beamed from yesterday. "I wasn't sure what you wanted for breakfast so I got a little of everything. I bought doughnuts, coffee, orange juice, biscuits, eggs, pancakes. You name it, I have it."

Chantel smiled. "Why don't you set up what you have and I'll go take a shower and get changed."

Truman started to take off his shirt. "Why don't I join you?"

Chantel held up her hand. "We don't have a lot of time to play around. We have to get Gage."

"Come on. You greet me naked and then you don't want to play? Not fair."

"Later. I promise." It didn't take her long to shower, get dressed, and repack. She knew the importance of Truman seeing his son. She didn't want to be the reason he missed him again.

When she emerged from the bedroom, she had her bag in hand. She placed it next to the door, then turned to the small dining area where he had two plates set along with the food in an organized display.

"Everything looks good." She approached the table.

"There's just one thing that's missing." He scanned the food.

"What?"

Before she could respond, he pulled her into his arms and he planted a full good morning kiss on her that weakened her knees.

He pulled back and stared at her. "I just want to make sure that what happened yesterday was real."

She kept her gaze fixed on his and finally had enough sense to smile and nod. "Very real."

"Good." He turned to the table. "Let's eat."

Eat they did. His appetite seemed ravenous as he shoveled down as much food into his mouth as he could. She loved seeing him smile.

After they ate, he packed whatever food that would travel well into a bag and carried her suitcase downstairs. Shauna checked out of the hotel and had to endure the stares from the man behind the counter who bounced his attention from her to Truman.

She didn't know if his reaction stemmed from her celebrity status or the fact that she was in the hotel with a strange man. No matter. She couldn't change everyone's perception of her. She had to be the best person she could be.

She snatched the receipt from him and went with Truman to the car. He drove back to the trailer park. Creeping along, she felt knots forming in her stomach with each crunch of gravel under the tires as they rolled up to the small trailer home. He parked in front of the place and looked around before getting out of the car.

She hoped the fact the driveway still didn't have a car in it didn't bother Truman as much as it did her. Maybe Ashley and her grandmother hadn't gotten home yet.

He turned off the car. Before getting out he turned to Shauna. "You can stay in here if you don't feel comfortable going inside."

She jutted out her chin in a show of strength...even if her insides quivered. "No. I'm going with you."

They exited the car together and stood in front of the steps. The toppled bike that had been left in front of the house had been moved. Someone had to have been here.

Truman knocked on the screen door and waited.

After a long wait, Chantel squeezed his hand. "Maybe they've gone to church already."

He didn't respond. He knocked on the door again and this time called Ashley's name.

After another long wait, Shauna put her hand on his shoulder. "Let's just wait in the car for them to show up."

Then the door opened. Truman returned his attention to the screen door. When Shauna saw a pair of wide brownish-green eyes staring up at her and Truman, her heart swelled. The child opened the door all the way and smiled.

"Daddy!" Gage unlocked the screen door. Thank goodness the boy did it in a timely fashion otherwise she thought Truman would have ripped the door from its hinges.

He lifted his son into his arms and twirled him around. "My boy. My baby boy."

To see Truman's love, up front and personal, touched Chantel. She fought hard not to weep in front of this child and his father.

"It's so good to see you." Truman kissed Gage on the side of his face. "I missed you so much I had to come down and see you."

"I missed you, Daddy." Gage looked up over his father's shoulder at Chantel. "Who are you?"

"I'm sorry, Son. Where are my manners?" He sat the boy down. "Gage, this is a friend of mine. Chantel Evans," he said with a wink, "meet my son, Gage Woodley."

Gage buried his face in his father's neck to keep from looking at her.

"He used to be really open with people." Truman patted his back. "Guess age has made him funny with strangers."

"It's okay." Chantel wanted so much for Gage to like her but he didn't know her.

"So what did you have for breakfast this morning, champ?" Truman set his son down.

"Y'all ate breakfast already?" Gage screwed up lips.

Truman's smile dropped. "Son, it's almost seven o'clock. We always eat before going to church."

Gage shrugged. "Sometimes Mama forgets to get up early so we miss breakfast."

Chantel saw Truman's face becoming red.

"Where's your mama now?" Truman tried maintaining a smile.

"She had to go out for a bit. But she said she'll be back and to not let nobody in." The boy covered his mouth. "Don't tell Mama I opened the door for you, Daddy. She'll give me a beating. I knew it was you because I heard your voice through the door."

Truman's hands balled into fists. "Gage, honey, let's go pack you a bag and take a trip. I think it's time for you to spend some time with me. Would you like that?"

Gage smiled and nodded. "Can I take my bike?"

"Sure." Truman darted into the trailer with the boy behind him. Chantel followed to make sure he didn't trash the place in anger.

The small trailer already looked like a dump. Toys littered the floor and clothes covered the furniture.

"Do you have a suitcase?" Truman asked as he surveyed the mess.

"Suitcase? What's that, Daddy?"

"It's what you put your clothes in when you travel." He snatched up clothes from the floor and couch, and organized them in a pile.

"Oh, Mama uses Walmart bags like we did when we came down here." The child sat on the floor and chugged a toy tractor around his body.

"Go get me some bags so we can pack up your stuff."

"Now, Daddy?" The boy kept playing.

"Yes." Truman's voice rose. When Gage jumped, Truman adjusted his tone. "Get me a couple of bags and we'll get you some breakfast."

"French toast sticks with syrup?" Gage hopped around.

But he said syrup as though it had three syllables like *sear-ree-up.*

"You bet."

Gage cheered and disappeared into another room. Truman spun on his heels and looked fit to be tied.

"I can't believe she lives like this." Truman adjusted his ball cap on his head. "She left a five-year-old boy alone."

Gage returned to the room and Truman slapped a smile on his face to keep up his happy countenance.

"Put all of your clothes in these bags and get all your toys."

"I'll help you." Chantel bent over to assist him.

"I can do it by myself." Gage grimaced, and with his angry expression, he looked exactly like his father, except the child's brown hair had a little more curl than Truman's, and he had flecks of green in his eyes.

"Don't be rude, boy. If Miss Evans is offering you help, you accept it." Truman lowered his voice to a growl.

"I don't mind helping you, Gage." She smiled at the child, then glanced at Truman. "Give me the keys to the car and I'll start packing his things."

Truman handed her the keys and turned to Gage. "Where do you and your mama sleep?"

The child stood at the end of a short hallway. "Go down and turn that way." He motioned to the right.

"I'll be right back." Truman stomped down the hall as Chantel scooped up as many of Gage's clothes and toys as she could. She loaded the items in the trunk until it seemed like they had cleaned the living room.

When she returned to the trailer, Truman stormed into the room. His eyes held a rage she'd never seen before, small and red like a rabid dog.

"We have to get out of here."

"Wait. I have to go potty." Gage dashed down the hallway to the bathroom.

Truman leaned close to Chantel. "I found pot on the nightstand and something that may be crack. I've never seen it before, but I think that's what it is. I can't believe she let that crap in this house with my son. I could kill her."

"Let's just be glad we got here in time before something awful happened." She held his hand to keep him calm.

Gage returned to the room with sneakers that lit up whenever he walked. "I'm ready." His smile widened. "Hi, Mama!"

Chantel turned to the door and saw a petite woman on the porch. The gray screen in front of her made her skin look pale. Once she opened the door and stepped into the trailer, Shauna saw that Ashley's real skin looked no better.

Her hair had dark roots, white shaft, and yellow ends. She had it pulled back in a tight ponytail and her green eyes looked clouded.

"What the fuck is going on here?" Ashley flicked her lit cigarette out the door. "Gage, baby, I told you not to open the door for nobody, right?"

The boy hid behind his father. "But I just let Daddy and his friend in. That's all."

"I can't believe you brought him down here to North Carolina after I asked you not to." Truman put his hand on his son's shoulder. "You said you would only do that if I didn't send you money and I have been."

"It ain't enough. I told you that before." Ashley put her hands to her hips. "Besides, Mama said she needed her space, and Grandma said she didn't mind me coming here."

"Yeah, but I minded. You're close to my family in Tennessee. They can help you if you need it." He patted his son on his head.

"Yeah, but I'm not close to *my* family. They will actually watch out for me." Ashley pounded her chest.

Truman stroked his son's head and rested his hand by his ear while he pressed his head against his leg. "And I saw what's in your bedroom."

Ashley's eyes went wide. "What right do you think you have to go into my bedroom? You ain't my husband."

Truman looked at Chantel. "Take Gage to the car for me, please."

"The hell you are. You're not taking my child from me." Ashley blocked Gage from going over to Chantel.

"Why don't we all sit down and talk about this?" Chantel tried to talk in a soothing tone to keep everyone calm.

"Why don't you mind your own fucking business?" Ashley stared at her, then pointed to her. "Why do you look so familiar to me? Where have I seen you before?"

"Don't worry about it, Ashley." Truman lifted Gage into his arms. "Get yourself straight." He grabbed Chantel's hand with his free hand and the three walked out of the trailer.

"You can't take my son. I won't let you." Ashley beat on Truman's back as Chantel got into the backseat. Truman handed Gage to her.

"Lock the doors." Truman closed the door behind her.

Chantel locked the back doors and the passenger side front door.

"Wow. Is this a lemonsine?" Gage looked around.

"Limousine, baby. No. Just a Mercedes." She leaned over into the front seat and put the key into the ignition. She started the car only when Truman opened the door and put himself in between the car and Ashley.

"You can't do this, Tru." Ashley sniffed. "This is kidnapping."

"You can't kidnap your own child. We have joint custody. It was just convenient for you to have Gage while I'm recording. But I'm not going to have him waiting to eat and sleeping in the same bedroom where you smoke pot and crack."

Chantel strapped Gage into his seat and looked out of the window to see Ashley's eyes widen. She reared her hand back and slapped Truman in his face, then spat on him. Until Truman spoke, time stood still.

"You're a regular mother of the year." Truman wiped his face.

"If you take him, I won't get any money from you."

Truman charged toward Ashley who squealed and ran up the steps to the trailer.

"Our child is not your meal ticket to extort money from me."

When he returned to the car, Ashley became brave again and climbed back down the steps. "I'll call the police on you."

"Fine. I'm sure they'll be interested in hearing that you left a five-year-old by himself and that you have drugs in your house." Truman looked around at the onlookers in the trailer park watching this Sunday morning spectacle. "That's right, folks. She has drugs in her house so if she calls the police, you be sure to tell them that."

He got into the car and sped off down the road.

"Are we on an adventure?" Gage asked Chantel.

"Something like that, sweetie." She looked behind her to see Ashley stomping in the middle of the street.

Chapter 17

Truman drummed his fingers on the steering wheel. He gritted his teeth until his head ached. It took everything he had inside of him not to drive back to that damn trailer and curse the day that he'd met Ashley.

He looked into the rearview mirror for the seventy-seventh time to look at Gage's reflection. Now that the sun had set and Truman filled his son's belly with a burger, fries, and a shake the boy had begged to have, he couldn't see Gage's slumped position.

Truman felt his phone vibrating in his pocket. He removed it and looked at the screen. As soon as he saw Ashley's name, he put the phone on silent and tossed it in a cup holder by his seat. No way would he talk to her while driving at a high speed. He would definitely get involved in a wreck, and he had precious cargo in the vehicle with him.

His seat jerked back slightly and Chantel popped her head between the two front seats.

"He's sleeping." She kept her voice low.

"Does he need a blanket or something?" He turned his head to get a glimpse of his baby boy and almost landed another kiss on Chantel. As much as he wanted to do that, now wouldn't be the time.

"I put his favorite blanket on him. He went out like a light." She patted Truman's arm to reassure him. "You can slow down now. We've made it to Virginia." She pointed to the Welcome to Virginia sign before he whizzed by it.

He slowed to about five miles per hour above the regular speed limit, which seemed to satisfy Chantel by the way she sighed.

Chantel stroked the back of his head. "You're a great father. Not many men would move Heaven and earth to get their children from what they think is a bad situation."

"Yeah, but what if he blames me for leaving him in the first place." He couldn't look at Chantel.

"You didn't leave him. You put him in the care of his mother and she got careless and stupid. The good thing about your son is that he still loves both his parents so to him there's nothing wrong. Someone raised him right." She kissed the side of his face.

A warm feeling covered his body before a chilling thought struck him. "The drugs. What if he blames me for exposing him to—"

Chantel placed her hand over Truman's heart. "Stop it. He loves you. You're a great father."

Truman exhaled and scratched his head. "If you weren't there—"

"You would have been strong enough to do the right thing for your son. Unfortunately, I don't know many men who could get spit in the face and not hit the woman back. I grew up in a time where women are called bitches and hoes." She draped one arm around the front of his body and held his shoulder. "I admire a man who is able to be a man and walk away."

He patted her arm. "I don't walk away from many fights. But I would never put my hands on a woman in anger. Doesn't take a man to do that."

"I guess Ashley was a different woman when you first met her."

Truman understood the underlying question Chantel didn't ask out loud. "She wasn't on drugs when we dated. Sure, she drank. I was twenty-two and she had just turned twenty-one. I thought once we had a kid, she would sober up." He shook his head. "I wish she would realize what a great thing we have. We made a child."

She laid her head on his shoulder. For the first time in several hours he breathed easier. He couldn't hear his heart pounding in his head. When he caught a whiff of Chantel's perfume, his body relaxed as though he'd been drugged.

"Maybe we should listen to some music. The car is way too quiet, and I think you're in your head too much." She reached for the radio.

"Better yet, why don't we do a little singing? I could use something to relax me. Singing always does that. What about you?" He glanced at her when she didn't immediately answer.

"No, let's just listen to some music. I don't want to sing." When she reached for the radio again, Truman held her hand to stop her.

"So why don't you sing anymore?" Truman figured he couldn't be the only one exposed here.

"Come on. You can't know all of my secrets in one day." She tried laughing but Truman could hear her nervousness underneath.

This time, he lowered his voice. "I've heard your songs. You have an amazing voice."

"Thank you." As a reward for his compliment, she nuzzled her nose in his ear before kissing the side of his face.

"You should sing again. I know it's in you. I see you writing song lyrics all of the time."

She started to pull away from him. "No, you haven't."

Truman held her hand tighter, not willing to let this one go. "The McDonald's napkin. When Gage was playing in the play area you were writing on a napkin with a crayon." He'd seen her looking so intense and mouthing the lyrics. When he'd thought she would look up and catch him watching her, he'd looked away. Watching her proved to him how much she loved music.

"So now you're watching me?" She pulled her hand away from his grip. "You saw me *trying* to write. I've never written a song before."

He felt like he had lost one of his appendages when she took her hand out of his. "I want to know how the greatest voice in music could abandon her gift like that."

"I didn't abandon my gift. I'm producing you, right?"

"But it's not the same as you—"

"Just drop it, okay. I sing."

The atmosphere in the car changed. The heaviness returned and it made Truman shift uncomfortably in his seat. He had to do something to lighten the mood. "Will you at least read me the lyrics you wrote?"

Song lyrics revealed a lot about the person writing them. He wanted to know what was in Chantel's head.

"No. Do I ask you to show me your newest songs?"

"Yeah. You changed the lyric in one of my songs."

"That's not the same." She shook her head.

"Of course. I forgot. There are your rules and there are my rules." He laughed.

"Okay. Tell me what you're working on right now then." She crossed her arms over her chest.

"It's a work in progress. I think you'll like it." He turned to her. "It's called 'Let's Figure Out How To Make You Love Me.' It's a song about a woman who is reluctant to reveal her true self to a man who is crazy about her."

"You are not." She returned to her original position close to him. "Writing that song I mean."

He smiled even wider. He sure could see himself falling hard if he wasn't careful.

"Sure I am. I think it should be on the album."

When she leaned in closer to him, he knew he had her. He smiled and whistled, waiting for her to go in for the bait.

"So how does it go?" She interlaced her fingers with his free hand.

He had her. Hook, line, sinker.

"I think the first line should go 'You like my personality and my crazy ways.' And the next line can be 'You think I'm funny and you dig my name.'"

Chantel laughed.

"'You say my kisses make you weak in the knees.'" He glanced at her. "Then comes the hook. 'So let's figure out how to make you love me.'" He returned his attention to the road. "So what do you think?"

"Good. But I never said your kisses made me weak in the knees."

"Baby, you didn't have to. Besides, what makes you think the song is about you?" He raised his eyebrows at her.

Chantel covered her eyes. "Did I just let you play me?"

"Like Monopoly. 'Do not pass Go. Do not collect two hundred dollars.'" He drummed on the steering wheel and laughed.

"Very funny. Actually I liked the way you started the song. I think it would have been a hit with the right melody." She wrapped her fingers around his hand again.

Heat surged through his body from her gentle touch. "Really?"

She patted his shoulder. "Sure. Maybe that could be the duet on the album. I'll let that be the first song I'll sing since going away."

"Are you serious?" He turned to her. When he noticed her sly smile, he rolled his eyes. "What an idiot I am."

"Take that, Mr. Monopoly."

Her sweet laugh made him feel light inside. "Very funny."

"Seriously, though, we should talk about the duet Craig wants." She tried moving closer to him. "Of the songs you have, you don't have one that would work for a duet."

"I did start something." He lifted his butt high enough to retrieve a piece of paper from his back pocket. "I started this after our first recording session." Truman didn't know how to finish it.

Chantel accepted the paper and turned on an overhead light. "'Meet Me Halfway.' I like the title."

"Thanks. Read it and tell me what you think." A nervous tickle crawled through his belly as she read it.

Without a word, she leaned back into the backseat. He spied her in the rearview mirror and caught her writing. This time, he smiled.

After a few minutes, she sprang forward. "What do you think of this?" She read the words that fit perfectly with how he opened the song.

"Yes. That's it. Will you write this for me?" Truman spouted the next lyrics, nice and slow so that Chantel could get every word.

"Great. What do you think about this for the hook?" She talked him through her thoughts.

Truman adjusted a word or two, but overall it worked.

"Wow. Did we just write a song together?" Chantel seemed shocked at this whereas Truman wrote all the time.

"I think we did. You think it'll work?"

"Maybe." She teased him. "With the right partner. I'm sure Flye would be happy to rap with you on this one." She laughed but stopped suddenly and turned around. "Someone's waking up." She set the lyrics next to Truman and moved to the backseat.

He split his attention between the road and the rearview mirror to make sure his son didn't need him.

"Hey, buddy." Chantel tucked the blanket around Gage. "You okay?"

His son nodded, then tapped Chantel's arm. "Miss Evans?" Gage rubbed his eye with his small fist.

"You can call me Chantel if you like."

"Daddy, is that okay? She's my elder."

Truman heard Chantel snicker.

"What a little gentleman." Chantel brushed the back of her finger over his cheek.

"If she says it's okay, then you can call her Chantel." Truman got the vehicle up to speed and set the cruise control. Only a few more hours until they got home.

"Chantel, maybe we can sing." Gage raised his hands in the air and carried an excited look on his face.

Truman could almost feel the daggers stabbing the back of his neck from Chantel's eyes. The hairs stood on his arms as he awaited her response.

"Oh, really?" Chantel glared at Truman through her reflection in the rearview mirror.

"I like 'You Are My Sunshine.'"

Truman turned and found Gage settling back nicely on Chantel; then she covered him with his blanket. She stroked his son's hair like a mother would.

"That just happens to be one of my favorite songs." Chantel continued smiling but her voice trembled. "But you have to sing it with me, okay?"

Gage started singing the child's tune. His voice, though young, already sounded good. The boy carried a tune better than most professional singers Truman had heard. Chantel, though, slowed to join his son in the song.

Truman heard her clearing her throat several times. When the second verse came up, Gage asked her to sing it. Truman gripped his hands on the steering wheel and strained not to get a glimpse of her in the mirror or turn around.

Chantel's silence squeezed his heart. She couldn't do it. She wouldn't do it. Truman wanted to know who or what it was that caused this songbird to lose her voice. He couldn't put her through this test.

"Son, maybe Chantel is—"

Then she spoke. She sang. Quiet at first. So low that Truman had almost mistaken the sound to be a hum in the engine. Then her voice rose. She even arranged the song to suit her soulful style. Her voice created notes he'd never heard of or used.

Chills rippled down his spine the more she sang, partly because Chantel sang it so beautifully but mostly because she sang. She mustered enough strength to sing again and in front of him. He knew what a huge step this had been for her.

Gage remained quiet until Chantel finished the song.

"That was really pretty, wasn't it, Daddy?"

Now Truman sat speechless. His eyes stung and his throat felt scratchy. Not since he'd seen Gage take his first steps had Truman been this moved, this proud.

"Thank you for singing with me." After a long pause, Gage followed with, "Why is everyone so quiet now?"

Truman rubbed his eyes and snickered. "We're all pretty wiped out. A lot has happened today." He finally peered into the rearview mirror. He caught the image of Chantel wiping her eyes and it ripped his heart from his chest.

"Another song?" Gage clapped.

Truman heard her sniffling before she answered. "Why not? Right now I feel like shouting from the rooftops."

"But we're in a car." Gage shook his head.

"Good point." Chantel laughed.

They sang three more songs until the car finally went silent. Gage dozed off on top of Chantel. Lucky boy.

"You didn't have to do that." Truman spoke low so as to not wake up his son. "And before you ask, no, I didn't put Gage up to ask you to sing with him. He did it on his own."

"It felt good to sing with him, to sing again. I didn't realize how much I missed just singing, not for hits or sales."

Her refreshing honesty exposed a new, lovely layer to the woman who'd captured his heart.

"You sounded great. Your mother would be proud of how you've handled your life."

"What about your family? You've always talked about having pride in your name."

Truman swallowed hard. He didn't want to talk about his strained relationship with his father. If he had any hope of being with Chantel and to start making amends with his past, he had to be honest. Knowing how honest she'd been with him so far helped him in his decision.

"My father is an alcoholic. Was an alcoholic. Hell, I don't know. Once an alcoholic, always one, right?" A shiver went through his body as he remembered his father's screaming and embarrassing behavior at his public events. "My sisters couldn't wait to become eighteen, get married, and move out of the house so that they could change their last name. They didn't want to be associated at all with being a Woodley."

"That's horrible." Chantel stroked her fingertips down the back of his head.

Such a simple touch shouldn't have ignited his libido, but it did. Truman squirmed in his seat. He didn't want to break the connection, not just yet.

"He cleaned up his act about seven years ago, right before Gage was born. My sisters have made amends with him. My mother has stood by his side the entire time."

"You're the only one holding out?" Her simple head stroke now turned into a back of the neck massage.

"I'm the only one who hasn't forgotten." Truman closed his eyes and rolled his head back. "Damn, that feels so good."

Chantel stopped moving her magical fingers. "Make amends with your father before it's too late. Take it from someone who knows."

"If I promise to call, will you keep rubbing my neck?"

She laughed. "Promise me that when we get back home, your first call is to your father and I'll do whatever you like."

"Oh, don't promise me that. You don't know the dirty thoughts running through my head right now."

To his surprise, he felt a warm set of lips on the side of his neck. He reached his hand back and cradled her head. He kissed her forehead. "Get some sleep."

Chantel patted his shoulder and settled into the backseat.

Moments like these, Truman thanked the stars above that Chantel made them drive to North Carolina and back. Truman knew she wouldn't have sung on an airplane. At least on the plane he could have gotten some sleep.

Just a few more hours and they would be home. Nothing could go wrong now that he had his son and Chantel by his side. He had an album to finish and his bandmates to see again. Hopefully they would be understanding.

Chapter 18

What a night to work. Chantel could barely keep her eyes open going the few miles to Craig's. How in the world was she supposed to listen to music and tweak it the way it needed to be tweaked?

A dark feeling clouded over her as she got closer to Craig's house. A chill ran up her arms until she had to shake them to relieve the feeling. Either it would be raining soon or something bad would be happening. Good thing she didn't believe in superstition. She might have fallen for her own whacked out intuition.

"You have to go to the bathroom, Gage?" Shauna pulled the blanket off Gage as soon as Truman parked the car in front of Craig's.

Gage's bottom lip hung open as he turned to Truman. "It's like she can read my mind."

Truman laughed. "Maybe it has something to do with you fidgeting in the backseat."

The duo followed Shauna to the front door. Truman carried her suitcase. Home sweet home.

She opened the door and welcomed the familiar aromas of the house. Lilac, violet with a splash of cilantro. Delores put the herb on almost everything.

Nikia bounded downstairs and stopped at the bottom step when she saw Shauna and her motley crew. Nikia peered over her shoulder, then gave Shauna the look that she remembered from childhood. The look meant she had a lot of explaining to do for whatever she had done.

Nikia pulled down her miniskirt and sauntered to the group. She leaned toward Chantel and whispered, "You should have kept on driving. You missed a lot these last two days."

"Like what?" Chantel rubbed her eyes.

As though her voice triggered it, Craig screamed. "Shauna Stellar. Get it in my office now."

With wide eyes, Nikia shuffled to the door. "I'm outie. See y'all later."

"Hey, thanks for letting us use your car." Truman handed Nikia the keys as she rushed by him. "Drove like a dream."

"Cool. Might as well use it tonight." She tossed the keys back to him. "I know my man is already out and about with the van." Nikia winked before she peered down at Gage, then gazed up at Truman.

"My son, Gage." Truman put his hands on the child's shoulders.

"Pleased to meet you, ma'am." Gage held out his hand.

Nikia giggled as she shook the boy's hand gently. "Oh, girl. You are just burying yourself in trouble."

"Shauna." Craig screamed again.

"Good luck." Nikia kissed Gage on top of his head. "Nice to meet you, cutie."

Gage turned and pushed his face into Truman's legs. "She thinks I'm cute."

Chantel took a deep breath. "I think you know where everything is here, right? Bathroom is upstairs to the right."

Truman nodded. "You want me to go in there with you?"

She shook her head. The last thing she needed was a verbal beat down by Craig in front of Truman.

He headed up the stairs with Gage, and Chantel waited until she couldn't hear his footsteps before she went into Craig's office.

The dimly lit office made the room seem more sinister than normal. Only his desk lamp illuminated Craig's face. A lit cigar sat in a pewter ashtray. The smoke rings swirled around Craig's face.

"Where have you been?" The growl in his voice matched the scowl on his face.

"Nikia was supposed to tell you. Truman had problems and I wanted to go with him…to make sure he made it to his destination and back." She had to include a business angle or Craig wouldn't buy the story.

"Nikia told me. And your little trip has been documented by newspapers all over." Craig slammed *The Virginian-Pilot* on his desk, turned to the celebrity gossip column. In bold print over a tiny one-paragraph article read *Princess of Love Songs Snags Cowboy.*

Chantel picked up the paper and skimmed the article that claimed a secret source spotted the duo, meaning her and Truman, at a local eatery in North Carolina. Must have been the front desk clerks who recognized her when she checked in.

The article hadn't been the worst thing she'd ever read about herself and she knew it wouldn't be the last thing. At least the media stopped calling her crazy.

"I didn't think about how it would look to anyone else." Chantel threw the paper down. "We didn't do anything wrong."

Craig creased his forehead until it looked like gnarled tree bark. "Oh, you didn't? Maybe you let something slip your mind since you've been away."

"What's that?" She shrugged.

"Laura Smalls."

Her stomach bunched in a ball. She'd completely forgotten that arrangements had been made to have Laura sing a duet with Truman on Saturday.

"I wish you would have told me you'd planned all this. I could have been prepared. People already think we're second rate. Now they'll think we're flighty. We'll confirm that name people call us, Ca-Razy Music."

"Don't say that ever again." She pointed to her manager. "I don't care what other people call us but, damn it, you had better believe in this project." She'd made a mistake but she wouldn't trash her own company. "Where is Laura now?"

"Thankfully the guys laid down the tracks to the song so she's been practicing since yesterday. She'd planned on flying out tomorrow morning around ten. You all have got to get your asses down to that studio and record that song in a day. No ifs, ands, or buts. Laura's only request was to record with Truman."

The industry didn't work that way nowadays. Many collaborations happened without the artists working in the same room. As a matter of fact, the standard involved one artist recording their part and have the demo beamed to another location, and have the second artist lay their vocals over that.

Maybe country musicians liked to do things differently. Or maybe the woman had a thing for Truman. A jolt of jealousy stung her insides.

"No two AM recording session today." He glanced at his watch. "Consider yourselves lucky to have a dinnertime slot."

The earlier time would be good. Truman seemed fresh even though he'd been driving for hours. He could get the recording done, then figure out what to do with Gage.

"Why are you still standing here?" Craig pounded his fist on his desk, breaking Shauna's concentration.

"Absorbing your pleasant nature apparently." She strolled back through the door and bounded up the stairs. Hearing the shower and Gage giggling in the main bathroom, she knew Truman and his son had to be in there. After a quick glance at her watch, she didn't have much time to shower and change but she had to make time. Maybe the shower would wake her up. It certainly couldn't hurt.

After her minute-long run under some streaming water and a quick change to jeans, a T-shirt, and Keds, Shauna darted from her room where she spotted Truman standing at the top of the stairs staring at his phone. His wet hair exaggerated his few curls. He needed to shave around his goatee but he still looked sexy in his black T-shirt and jeans. Just gazing at him proved to be a better pick-me-up than the shower. As soon as he looked up from his phone and spotted her, he shoved the phone in his pocket.

"Ready?" He gazed down at her.

Not hardly, she thought. Yet she smiled and faked it anyway.

Chapter 19

When Truman walked into the studio, he felt like he'd been away from it for far too long. It felt foreign to him. It didn't help that the guys looked at him like a traitor.

"Hey, guys." Truman waved.

They all gave slight nods or barely acknowledged him. Sully kept his back to Truman the whole time. They treated him like this for getting his son? Amazing.

"Look who I have with me." Truman stepped aside, letting Gage hop in front of him.

"Hi!" the boy screamed.

That brought a light to their faces, especially Charlie.

Charlie lifted the boy into his arms. "How are you doing, tough man?"

"Great, Uncle Charlie. Where's Molly and Hannah and Little Charlie and—"

Charlie cut him off before he ran down the whole list of his kids. "They're home with their mama." Charlie flashed Truman a harsh look. "We all can't bring our kids to the studio."

Charlie put the boy down and returned to tuning his bass guitar. Tony patted Gage on his head.

"Good to see you, buddy." Tony glanced at Truman. "We lost so much studio time. It's going to cost us a mint."

The more things changed, the more they stayed the same.

"Little dude." Ervin held up his hand for a high five. "How's it hanging?"

The child slapped his hand.

Truman's eyes nearly popped out of his head when he saw Ervin. Ervin had changed in the couple of days Truman had been gone. He ditched his usual fitted jeans for baggy jeans that couldn't stay up over his narrow behind. He had on a Pittsburgh Steelers jersey, a surprise to Truman who knew Ervin to be a diehard Falcons fan. He had a diamond stud in his left ear that had to have been worth more than they ever earned in a year as a group.

"Is that you, Uncle Ervin?" Gage wrinkled his little nose. "You look different."

"It's all me, little dude." He did a little spin to give a complete view.

"What's this new look all about?" Truman pointed to him.

"You like it?" Ervin strutted around in circle.

"No." Truman shook his head.

"Nikia said I'm on fleek now. After she took me shopping, we went back to her place and—"

Truman covered his son's ears. "Hey, clean it up around here in front my kid, okay?"

"I'm talking about her fixing me lunch." Ervin rolled his eyes.

"It's good that we finally agree on something, although this is the first time in a couple of days that you talked about her. I thought the two of you had broken up." Sully made his way to Truman. He peered down at Gage. "Hey, Gage, why don't you go over to our engineer, Clayton, and ask him about his special apple?"

Gage wrinkled his little eyebrows but ran over to the thin man.

"I'm glad you got your son back, Tru." Sully put out his hand and Truman shook it.

"But?" Truman knew his friend would say something negative. He braced for the bombshell.

"No buts, man. Maybe one. Laura Smalls."

Not the bombshell Truman thought Sully would drop.

Sully nodded behind himself. "She's fit to be tied. All she kept talking about is you. Truman this and Truman that." He leaned in close to Truman and whispered, "Whatever you did with Shauna, I hope you got it out of your system. I'm sure there's an appeal to doing a woman, um, like her."

Truman's stomach knotted as he listened to Sully. If Sully meant a talented woman who had a great sense of humor, was compassionate, caring, smart, and gorgeous, then yeah, he recognized the appeal of doing a woman like that as Sully had said.

Sully knew nothing about Chantel's true heart. She'd been great with Truman's son.

"I'm telling you." Sully nodded his head back toward the studio. "If you play your cards right, you and Laura could be the next big country couple. Like Tim McGraw and Faith Hill."

"I'm not thinking about a relationship right now." Truman lied. As soon as he got to touch Chantel intimately, he wanted her in his life for good.

Did she want that role particularly after she had admitted that relationships between couples that work in the same industry don't work out? "I just want to sing and perform."

"And sing you will," said a female voice behind him.

Truman turned around and within a few feet of him stood Laura Smalls. He'd seen her on magazine covers and her mega-selling CD covers for the last three or four years. Country's newest princess. With her blonde hair piled on top of her head in a loose-fitting but apparently stylized hairdo and sheer top so that her rhinestone-covered bra could be seen through it, she definitely played up the part of princess.

She held out her hand; each finger had a diamond ring on it. "Hi, I'm Laura Smalls, the woman you've kept waiting." She pouted.

The look alone turned Truman's stomach. He wouldn't have tolerated that expression from his child. He certainly wouldn't take it from this one.

Truman took off his baseball cap, an older one he'd long retired, but since he left his other cap in the motel he fled from he had to go for his backup. Then he shook Laura's hand. Her soft hand melted into his, especially since she didn't grip his for a proper handshake. Touching her didn't give him the spark that Chantel's touch had given him.

"I apologize, Ms. Smalls." Truman bowed his head.

Laura waved her hand. "Call me Laura. If we're going to be working together, we'll have to be on a more intimate level, don't you think?"

Truman peered over to Sully who only raised his eyebrows and walked away with a smile.

"Something like that." Truman nodded. "I had to pick up my son."

Laura looked into the control room at Gage. "Cute kid. You know I would love to start a family of my own. Even though I'm only eighteen, I see myself being a mother very young."

Eighteen? She hadn't even lived a full life yet. What in the world would she have to offer as far as common interests?

Chantel stepped into the room. From the way she stared at Truman and Laura, he could almost hear her assessing their situation and running a scenario in her head. He took a step back from Laura to change Chantel's perception.

"Oh, good. You're here." Laura turned to Chantel who smiled brightly. "I need a bottled water and my little dog, Snoopers, walked every half hour."

Truman's ears felt hot and tingled. If *he* felt embarrassed, then he knew Chantel had to be livid.

Chantel's smile dropped and she folded her arms. "I'm Shauna Stellar."

"Oh my God. I'm so sorry." Laura shook Chantel's hand. "You look so different without makeup and hair. I mean you have hair just not all done up like I'm used to seeing you."

"Some of us don't do the whole hair and makeup thing when we're working. That look is for the public." Chantel put her hands to her hips as she stared at Laura who seemed to be getting smaller and smaller by the moment.

"Right." Laura tucked a few strands of her curls behind her ears, showing off more diamond studs going up the shell of her ear.

"I'm sure you have people here who can get you what you need." Chantel hung a Mona Lisa smile on her face that would have cracked anyone. "I know we have a lot of work to do. I'm sorry for the delay."

"You should be." Laura jutted out her chin, finding her strength. "I dropped a lot of other obligations to be here." She gazed at Truman and put a smile on her face that appeared damn near obscene.

"Fine. Let's get started. If you need to go somewhere to warm up your voice—"

"No. I'm good. I find that my best take is the third or fourth one anyway." Laura looked at her manicured fingernails and smoothed her thumb over each nail.

"Oh, so you record to warm up."

Truman heard Chantel's sarcastic tone, but he liked it.

"We don't have much time to waste two and three takes, Laura." Chantel headed to the boards. "I prefer that you warm up."

"And I prefer to have been done with this yesterday but we can't all get what we want." Laura picked off some nonexistent piece of lint from her shirt directly over her breast. "Not all of the time."

"Look, I need to do my scales." Truman put his hand to his chest. "We can do warm-ups together. Save some time and we can see how we harmonize."

Laura beamed. "Oh, sounds perfect."

Chantel directed them to the conference room or the roof but, Truman said he preferred the men's bathroom. He liked the acoustics it offered. Plus he really wanted to see how grossed out Laura would get with the thought of going to a men's bathroom. Turned out that as long as she got to be with him, Laura didn't mind the less-than-ideal location. Perfect.

* * * *

"Let's try it again." Chantel slammed her hand down on the microphone button to talk to Laura and Truman. After Truman and his band banged out the music for the song he and Chantel had written on the way back from North Carolina, he attempted to sing that song with Laura.

Every time they sang 'Meet Me Halfway,' something sounded off. Chantel couldn't put her finger on it. The sound had nothing to do with Laura warming up her voice.

Chantel closed her eyes, thinking that maybe watching Truman sing about a love compromise with Laura, a half-wit with a voice, clouded her judgment.

She fought the impulse to believe she could be jealous of anyone. It hit her whenever Laura touched Truman's hand or arm as she sang. Shauna wanted to slap the woman's hand off him every time.

Not only did she close her eyes, but she turned her back on the duo. Truman's voice held each note with a strong hold. His powerful but compassionate tone gave the song what it needed. But Laura. Maybe it had something to do with her age. What would a teenager know about making compromises in a relationship? She probably filled her days with shopping and getting her hair and nails done to think about making sacrifices.

Chantel opened her eyes at the end of the song. She sat face to face with Truman's band who sat on the couches that lined the walls. Tony had fallen asleep with Gage sleeping on top of him. The rest of the group had the same confused look on their faces.

Chantel heard a crunch and turned to the side toward Clayton. He'd taken a bite of his own apple, his protected timepiece.

"It's going to be a long night." Clayton shook his head.

"Let's try this again." Chantel took her spot at the control board next to Clayton. Clayton started the track and Chantel closed her eyes.

Truman opened the song. His powerful voice melted over the lyrics like butter on toast. He felt each word and that came through. Then Laura sang.

Maybe that was the problem. She sang. She didn't feel any of the words.

"Stop." Chantel interrupted Laura's vocal acrobatics. "You don't need to overdo that part. Just sing it like you mean it."

"That's what I'm doing." Laura shook her head.

"No. You're shouting like it's a gospel tune. Reel it back in and sing it like you're whispering to your lover."

Chantel saw Truman's eyes get wide.

"That's exactly how I wrote the song as though a couple were talking to each other, like on a car ride." Truman fixed his stare on Chantel.

Chantel heard Sully groan at the statement, but she didn't turn around to acknowledge him. She kept her focus on Truman.

"Oh, I get it now." Laura adjusted her headphones.

When the track started, though, she sang it the same way.

"Stop." Chantel rubbed her eyes.

"What is it now?" Laura put her hand to her slender hip.

You're too thin. You're over-singing this song. And Truman would never fall for your bottle-dye job and fake boobs in a million years!

"You're not changing your style. Instead of singing it like the way you have, sing it like this." Chantel cleared her throat and sang one line. She cracked it at the end but it still sounded better than Laura's version.

The smile Truman had couldn't be blasted off with dynamite. Although Shauna's heart pounded until she thought she would faint, she felt good.

"Do you want it with or without the crack?" Laura asked in a smarmy tone.

"She wants it with heart and feeling." Clayton's statement came out of nowhere. So the nebbish did have a backbone.

Chantel nodded to her engineer. "Couldn't have said it better myself." Chantel made sure to cut off the mic that went into the recording studio.

Laura sang the line again, and again it sounded flat and emotionless.

"God, what's it going to take?" Chantel leaned back in her chair.

"It's going to take a miracle." Clayton looked over at her. "Or an expert. Someone who knows what the song needs."

Chantel stopped the music again. "Let's try something, Laura. Sing it like this." She sang a line, then waited for Laura to follow suit.

The young woman rolled her eyes, mumbled something to Truman, then finally obliged.

"Good." Chantel meant that.

Laura didn't hit the note exactly like Chantel wanted, but she suspected the young woman had been singing that way for years and this recording session wouldn't break her of her bad habits. Even Mariah Carey stopped doing that dog whistle note in her singing. Singers could change. People could change.

"Now sing this line like this." Chantel sang more but this time she noticed Truman joined in with her. She stopped when it sounded too good. She noticed Clayton sitting up straight.

No. God, no. She shouldn't have put herself out there.

"I think that's the best damn thing I've heard all night," Ervin said from behind her.

Chantel chewed the inside of her bottom lip. Her hands trembled over the control panel.

Breathe. Just breathe. It'll be okay.

"How about over this line?" Truman shuffled in his spot. "Shouldn't it be more like this?" He sang the line and Chantel couldn't help but join in.

Their voices melded in a beautiful harmony as though they had been singing together for years.

"Why don't you go into the booth?" Clayton nudged her with his elbow.

"Because I'm not singing. Laura Smalls is. She came all this way. And she'll sell more records than me." And because Chantel couldn't stop shaking long enough to record a decent vocal.

"Do it to show her how it's done then." Clayton continued nudging her arm. "It's apparent we aren't going to be leaving today with a good recording unless she knows how it's supposed to sound."

"I can't." Chantel kept her head down and shrugged away from him. "What if she gets offended?"

"Laura, honey, why don't you take a break?" Clayton smiled bigger than a beauty pageant host. "There are some video games in the back. Make yourself at home."

She took off her headphones and stretched her arms over her head. "Good. I could use a quick yoga session." She looked at Truman. "I'm very flexible."

Truman nodded but kept his mouth shut.

"Come on." Laura attempted to take Truman's hand.

Now flames filled Chantel's vision. It took all her willpower not to scream, "Get your hands off my man!"

"No, Truman has to stay." Clayton shook his head. "We need to work on his vocals."

Laura looked at Truman, then to Clayton and Chantel in the control room. "Oh, okay. I'll see y'all in a bit."

As soon as she sauntered out of the room, Clayton wasted no time in hustling Chantel from her seat and scooting her into the recording studio.

"One take. That's all I'm asking." Clayton put his hands together in prayer form.

Chantel stood next to Truman who beamed.

"I think he heard what we all heard." Truman moved in close to her. "We're good together."

"I shouldn't be doing this." Chantel fidgeted in her spot. "I haven't warmed up."

"You'll be great." Truman held Shauna's hand.

She felt immediately safe.

"Sing to me the way you felt when you wrote it. Sing from your heart." He nodded. "I know you will."

When the track started, Chantel didn't need to look at the words. She knew them by heart and knew exactly where to come in. When they sang the chorus together, they sounded like a couple making love. His voice mixed with hers until it didn't sound like a song. They transformed it to a musical conversation.

She kept her gaze on him the entire song until she blocked everything out around her. When they stopped singing, the booth went quiet. Neither one said or did anything, but they stared at each other. Then she heard the applause.

She looked into the control room and saw Truman's band as well as Nikia, Flye, and the Skillz Squad all clapping. Nikia wiped her eyes like she'd been crying.

"You did it, Chantel." Truman whispered before hugging her. She'd done it.

The crash at the window stopped the revelry. Chantel covered her head, but luckily the window hadn't broken. With Truman's arms around her, she turned to the soundproof glass that faced the hallway.

Laura stood there behind a large spider web-like crack on the glass that must have occurred when Laura hurled whatever object she had thrown. Chantel couldn't hear her through the glass but with the doors open, she heard her screaming.

"Bitch! Bitch! You backstabbing hoe!"

Oh, yeah. Chantel had done it all right.

Chapter 20

The scene reminded Shauna of a bad soap opera. Horrible. Laura screamed and screamed some more and kept screaming until her people shuttled her and her little dog out of the studio.

Although Chantel had stood proud through the whole ordeal with her head cocked as though ready for a fight, inside she wept.

She never wanted to be one of those artists that would backstab another. When she'd been hauled into the recording studio with Truman, she couldn't deny the connection, both physically and musically.

When Craig stormed into the recording studio, he had an expression that screamed "I told you so" on his face.

"You tried to fight me on this." Craig wagged his finger at her.

"I know." Chantel walked past him and into the control booth.

Big mistake. Flye and his crew filled the space along with the Sliders. The one time they decided to agree on anything and it had to do with her singing the duet with Truman.

"And I told you it would work." Craig looked like he wanted to leap out of his skin.

"You did." Shauna gathered her things together.

She had enough of work especially since she managed to piss off a major artist and lay down substandard vocals for a duet. Chantel could have done better. Much better.

"And now the country will know what we all know. Shauna Stellar is back." Craig clapped his hands in an over-the-top way.

Couldn't this day end any faster?

"No. We're putting Laura's version on the album." Chantel shook her head.

"Over my dead body." Truman stormed into the booth after her. "I'm coproducer and we put the best person on this song. I'm not going to buckle because her feelings got hurt."

Chantel shook her head. "But—"

"But nothing." Truman interrupted her. "I know what I want and I want you." Truman didn't amend his statement. It seemed like he didn't care what his friends thought.

Chantel tried hiding her smile but her insides felt like pure sunshine.

"You sang it beautifully, Ms. Stellar." Clayton patted her hand.

Chantel scanned the roomful of people. They all had hopeful expressions on their faces. Couldn't they understand that one fluke didn't make it a comeback?

"As much as we would like to stand around and talk about your phat R&B-and-country collabo, we have some hits to make." Flye and his crew gave each other high fives as they strutted into the recording studio.

"Our stuff's packed in the van, Tru." Sully nodded back toward the door. "Let's roll."

Truman took Gage's hand, then stopped on his way out the door. "I can't." He cursed under his breath.

"What are you talking about?" Tony shrugged.

"I called your sister when we got the studio." Truman directed his statement to Charlie. "She said she has no room for—" Truman patted Gage's head. He motioned his eyes down to his son. The group all nodded and raised their eyebrows as though they knew what he meant without actually saying it.

Chantel crouched down to Gage. "Would you like to have a sleepover at my house?"

Gage's eyes went wide. "Would I?"

"Not fair, Chantel." Truman put his hand on Gage's chest.

"Chantel?" Flye and Craig said in unison.

She kept looking into Gage's eyes. Chantel figured out Truman's weak spot. He would do almost anything for Gage.

"Craig's wife, Delores, makes the best pancakes in the world." Chantel smoothed her hand over the boy's head.

"Not better than Grandma Jackie." The boy shook his head.

"Maybe a close second. What do you say? Want to come with me and color and draw and cook and—"

Gage cut in. "And sing?"

Chantel glanced at the three men looming over her. Even Truman wanted to hear what she would say, so much so that his pulse raced.

"Sure. We can sing a little." She conceded.

"Yeah." Gage looked up at Truman. "Can we stay with Chantel, Daddy?

Please?" Gage gripped Truman's hand as he jumped around.

"Delores and I would like to have you there." Craig looped his thumbs into his suspenders and reared back on his heels like he thought up the plan.

Chantel sighed in relief that Craig accommodated her offer. She didn't have a Plan B if he had said no.

"Yeah, man. Meet her halfway." Flye nodded, proud that he thought to use Truman's own song title against him.

Truman's smile to his son looked forced. "Fine. One day."

The child cheered. "Race you to the car."

Craig peered at his watch, then smoothed his hand over his shiny head. "I have appointments to make this morning and Delores is at the restaurant. You think you can make up that bedroom for Tru and his son?"

"We'll be fine." Chantel gathered her things.

* * * *

It took them no time to get back to Craig's home. Silence filled the car the entire trip there. Truman didn't know if he should be angry at Chantel for overstepping her bounds or happy.

When they arrived at the house, Truman had already made a mental plan to bathe his son and get him to bed. Then he would steer clear of Chantel. If left alone, he wouldn't be able to keep his hands off her.

"Whoa. This place is like a palace." Gage stood in awe in the foyer.

Truman had thought the same thing the first time he'd stepped into the house. He still felt overwhelmed whenever he scanned the home. He guessed that even if Chantel had lost all her money that Craig had invested well.

"Are you hungry?" Chantel crouched down to Gage's level when she talked to him. "Doesn't look like Delores is here. But I can make you something."

"You cook?" Truman immediately felt silly for asking it.

He needed to let go of his preconceived notion of her, which included images of her being pampered and fussed over. She'd proven several times over that she didn't exactly fit the diva image.

"Yes." Chantel stood and glided toward the kitchen. "Delores taught me."

"I keep hearing my name out here." Delores emerged from the kitchen.

Chantel put her hand to her chest, obviously startled by the woman's appearance. "I didn't think you were here. I didn't see your car out front."

"My head chef has gone to the wine suppliers for me but she should be back soon."

Even at eight in the morning, Delores looked put together. Her simple hairstyle gave her an almost presidential look. In her crisp white blouse and tan slacks, she looked more like she dressed for a lunch date than going to work in her own restaurant. Truman tried not to stare at the woman but he wasn't sure if Delores had flawless skin or if she had on makeup.

"And who is this?" Delores looked at Gage with a smile.

"I'm sorry." Truman snapped out of his stare. "This is my son, Gage. Gage, this is Craig's wife and Chantel's friend, Mrs. George."

Delores extended her hand to the child who already had his hand out in a gentlemanly fashion.

"Nice to meet you, Mrs. George." Gage shook her hand. "That's like Curious George, right?"

Delores laughed. "Yes, it is. That was my youngest son's favorite character in a book. Do you like books, Gage?"

The child beamed. "Do I? I read my first book by myself last month."

"What a smart boy." Delores leaned down. "And you can call me what everyone else calls me, Mama Dee."

Gage nodded.

A car horn sounded in front of the house.

Delores rolled her eyes. "She's a great chef but acts like she's been raised in a barn." She picked up her purse. "Changing the menu and I want to try out everything." Delores smoothed her hand over Gage's brown, shaggy hair, then looked up at Truman. "You guys need your sleep and this little guy seems fit to be tied. Why don't I take him with me? He'll be fine in the restaurant."

"I don't know." As much as Truman wanted to sleep, he wanted to spend time with his son. He knew Delores had the best intentions. From the way Gage jumped around, his son didn't mind at all going with her. "He might get in your way at work."

"Truman, I've had three sons about his age running around in my restaurant. If I can handle them, I can surely handle this angel." She cupped her hand under the child's chin.

"Please, Daddy? I'll be good, I swear." Gage clasped his hands together.

The thought of staying in the big house alone with Chantel filled him with excitement. He desperately wanted to touch her, taste her, feel her again…and again and again. He didn't want to push her.

"I don't think so, buddy." He glanced at Delores. "I don't want to impose on your time and generosity." When Gage's chin quivered, Truman looked away.

He never intended to hurt his son. However, this family had given him so much with asking for so little if not nothing in return. He earned his way.

The front door flew open. Truman put his hand on Gage's shoulder and stood in front of the women to confront whatever beast had burst through the door.

In the doorway stood a small woman, smaller than Nikia, with hair shorn down to a short do. In her white chef's smock with her hands on her hips, she looked like a drill sergeant.

"Are we going or not?" The woman even stood with her fists to her hips.

"Lord, give me strength." Delores gazed up to the heavens. "If she couldn't cook worth a damn, she'd be gone."

"We're going to be late. I have everything scheduled down to the minute. Two minutes to pick you up. Fifteen minutes to get to the restaurant. Eleven minutes to do the kitchen pre-inspection."

Delores held up her hand. "I get it, Yolanda." She grabbed her briefcase. "Truman, my house stays pretty empty when Shauna, or Chantel, and my boys are not here. I miss the company. I miss children. If I've put you in an awkward position, I apologize."

Why did Truman feel like a world-class ass now? Here this woman tried doing him a favor by taking his young son off his hands so that he can get some well-needed sleep, and he fought against it.

"Wait." Truman held his hand up to Delores. He crouched down in front of Gage. He wiped his son's face. "What are you crying for?"

Gage sniffed until his whole body shook. "'Cause I want to go with her and you said I can't and—"

"You have to promise me you'll be on your best behavior. If Mrs. George tells me that you even looked at her the wrong way, you and I are going to have a talk."

"Yes, sir." Gage gave Truman a hug. Truman didn't want to let his son go. He hugged him back hard before allowing the child to wriggle free from his arms and run to Delores.

"I have a couch in my office." Delores patted Gage's small shoulders. "If he gets tired, I'll let him sleep there, okay?"

"I won't get sleepy. I know I won't." When Gage shook his head, his entire body swayed back and forth.

"They all say that." Delores took the child's hand and they walked out of the house that now felt eerily quiet.

Truman glanced at Chantel. Her skin looked so golden. He wanted to touch her, kiss her again, hold her. He had to clear the air first.

"That was a sneaky thing you did to get me to stay here." He crossed his arms over his chest and tried looking as menacing as possible.

He saw her swallow uneasily before she eventually smiled. "You want me to say sorry for looking out for you and Gage?"

Truman started to open his mouth, but stopped. She had a point. When should generosity be seen as a bad thing?

"We should get your clothes. We can wash your stuff and Gage's while we're here." Chantel walked past Truman without looking at him.

Since he didn't have an answer for her previous question, he followed her to the Mercedes and pulled out the bags of clothes. Chantel slammed the trunk closed when all the bags and the bike had been removed.

He followed her into the house and down into the laundry room. He had never seen an actual laundry *room* in someone's house before. The large space had a washer and dryer on one side, an ironing board set off next to a wall and racks to hang up clothes. They even had a machine to press clothes.

He'd grown up in a place where he had to have stackable washer and dryer because they didn't have room for a side-to-side model. He had to set up the ironing board in the dining room because that room had the most space.

"Truman?"

Chantel's voice snapped him out of his trance. "Sorry. I've never seen a room like this." He brought his attention to Chantel. "This is pretty wild."

"It's just a laundry room." She smiled as she started the washer.

Seeing her doing laundry, being so normal, pumped his heart. God, who knew his dream woman would be a top-selling R&B singer who could cook and do laundry?

Chantel arranged the clothes into the washer, pressed some other buttons on the digital display, then closed the lid. He moved closer to her.

"What's all this?" He pointed to the display. He hadn't seen any other washer models other than the old crank-and-pull knob kind. When did they get all fancy like this?

She pointed to the display. "You can tell the washer what to look for when it cleans. Grass stains, oil, blood." Her voice cracked when she spoke.

"Blood? Good God." Truman leaned closer to Chantel to get a better look at the display, but ended up pressing his chest onto her back. He pointed to the controls until he lowered his hand on top of hers. With great ease, he curled his fingers around her hand. He felt her body trembling and heard her breath quicken.

Truman's skin felt hot the longer he held her hand. When her skin touched his, his body tingled. The hairs on the back of his neck stood.

"Food." Chantel said the word like it should have stopped his actions. "You must be hungry." She pulled her hand from his grasp and made her way back into the main house without looking at him.

He followed her as though caught in her magnetic field. By the time he reached her, she had her nose poked into the shiny, gray metal refrigerator. "Let's see what's in here. I could make you pancakes or waffles. Looks like Delores has what I need to make you Eggs Benedict if you want."

He observed this enigma with her back to him. Her shirt rose to expose her lower back. That gentle stirring below his belt pulsated even more as he watched her. Then the vibration of his phone broke his mood and concentration.

Ashley. Since Truman took Gage, his ex had been calling his phone nonstop for hours. Until he could get some sleep and think with a clear head, he wouldn't be talking to her. Instead he sent her a text that simply said, "Gage is fine." He hoped that would end the calls. When the phone vibrated again indicating another call, Truman turned it off. He had a woman in front of him who was worthy of his time.

She turned around, holding a lemon in each hand as soon as he shoved his phone into his pocket. "And I could make you some tea."

He stared at her until he smiled. Chantel amazed him, from her kindness to her beauty.

"Tea is fine." He reached out to grab a lemon from her hand, but ended up keeping his hand on top of hers. His thumb caressed her skin. From the way her arm drooped, he felt her melting. Her body relaxed. She closed her eyes. "Oh, God. Now I get it."

"Get what?"

"Now I know why Nikia and Ervin steal away moments with each other all the time." She connected her stare to his. "I haven't been able to stop thinking about what we did all day, especially when we sang."

* * * *

"What did we do?" Placing his hands on her hips, Truman eased her against the countertop. He wanted to hear her say it.

"The sex." She wrapped her arms around his neck as he leaned down to kiss her. Once his lips touched hers, she let the fruit roll down his back and bounce on the floor.

Her soft lips invited him to kiss her more passionately. Even in the early morning, Chantel tasted like sweet nectar, sweeter than any honey his father could produce. As his hands rested on her waist, he felt her trembling.

She ran her fingertips down the side of his face. "I want you. I don't know if you feel the same way."

To calm her fears, he took her hand and placed it over the bulge in his jeans. "You don't think I want you?"

She didn't answer. Chantel smoothed her hand up and down his hardness until the pressure became too much.

Truman couldn't help exhaling and smiling like a schoolboy. She wanted him. Out of all the men in the world she could have, she chose him.

"Where's my bedroom?"

She held his hand and led him to the grand staircase. "This way."

Truman admired the sway of her hips as she climbed the stairs to a room off to the right at the top.

At the doorway, Truman wrapped his arm around her waist and held her so tightly that he felt her heart pounding. She stepped backward into her bedroom and continued moving that way until she fell back onto the bed, pulling him down with her.

His face hovered over hers. Her clear brown eyes melted his resolve. Every part of his being wanted this woman.

On instinct, his hand roamed her body. He moved over her stomach and felt it quiver. When he stopped kissing her to make sure she wanted to keep going, she put her hand to the back of his head and pulled him down.

Chantel pulled him on top of her and wrapped her legs around him. God, she felt good. She leaned her head back and he moved his mouth down her neck. He dragged his hot tongue to her chest until she moaned.

Not trying to scare her, he eased his hand slowly up her shirt. If she objected to the touch, he wanted to give her time to say something. She put her hand on top of his.

Damn. She wanted him to stop.

Truman pulled back and had to blink when Chantel placed his hand on top of her breast over her bra. He massaged it, which produced a moan.

The sound forced him to glance at her face. "Why are you smiling, Chantel?"

"This is the first time I've done something completely selfish." She pulled up Truman's shirt to reveal his chest.

As though compelled by a force stronger than anything imagined, she ran her hand down his slightly hairy chest. Touching him awakened his senses. She treated him and his body like a novelty. The innocence of her actions appealed to him.

She curled her fingers around his chest hairs.

He sat up to remove his T-shirt and toss it to the floor. Like before, she caressed his body. In turn, he removed her shirt and bra so that he could enjoy her flesh. He groaned as he stared at her chest. The roundness, the firmness, it all appealed to him.

He placed his mouth over her nipple, suckling it so easily and gently that she writhed under his body. Not content to only have a part of her

Crystal B. Bright

body, Truman quickly worked on her shorts.

Then Truman sat on the edge of the bed to remove his work boots. He stood and undid his pants. As soon as he pushed them down his legs, he watched Chantel fix her stare on his jutting penis.

She scooted to the edge of the bed and reached out for him. One hand rested on his hip. She wrapped her other hand around the base of his shaft before gazing up at him.

Truman gazed down at her, wanting to say or do something in this moment. She didn't have to do anything to please him, but, damn, if he didn't want her mouth all over him.

His heart raced knowing the power she had, literally, in her hands. She controlled his pleasure. Chantel covered the plump, mushroom-shaped head and eased her mouth down as far as she could. When the tip of his dick hit the back of her mouth, she stopped, but continued holding him there.

"Jesus H." Truman put his hands on Chantel's shoulders before moving one to the back of her head.

Her hot mouth surrounded his cock like a vacuum. Although he didn't want to, his body reacted to the incredible sensation. He slid himself back and forth in her mouth. Truman felt her small tongue dancing around his shaft, caressing the underside until she pulled back and flicked the tip.

She kept a hold of him as she peered up. "Is this okay?"

Truman lost all control of the English language. He simply nodded. "Good."

"Really good?" She twirled her tongue around the top.

He felt his thighs shaking like they never had before. Even without answering, Chantel slid her mouth back down the length of him. This time, she coupled her oral action with massaging his sac.

"Very. Good." He gritted his teeth.

He wouldn't be able to hold out for much longer if she kept this up. Like she had done it before, she moved her mouth up and down him. It all felt too incredible to be believed.

When she held him in her mouth and hummed, his body quivered. He fisted her hair, still in a ponytail, while he stepped out of his pants. Against his better judgment, he pulled back from her.

"Okay." Truman scanned the room.

Chantel wiped her mouth. "What is it? I thought you liked—"

"Condoms. Now."

She jumped up. "Wait here."

She ran into another room, giving Truman time to kick off his jeans and wait for her.

Chantel returned to the room carrying a variety of condoms. In a rush, she threw them on the nightstand. "On the bed." She pointed as she pulled down her jeans and panties. When he didn't move at her directive, she repeated herself more forcefully. "Get on the bed on your back."

Truman looked at her stunned, but he liked this side of her. "Tell me what you want."

She stared at him. Chantel picked up a condom, ripped open the package with her teeth, and rolled it on him, which made him take in a deep breath and stand on his tiptoes. "I want to be on top." She then broke down what she really wanted. "I want to ride you."

Before she could say anything else, Truman obliged and sat on the bed before reclining back with his head on the pillows. Chantel climbed on top of him and straddled his body. She held his shaft as she stared into his eyes. Then she plunged down, impaling herself hard.

The world stopped. Her tightness welcomed him, drew him in, and kept him a happy prisoner.

Chantel rotated her hips, which curled Truman's toes. He held her waist and squeezed his eyes closed.

"Incredible." He moved his hands down to her thighs. "Don't stop."

"I'm starting to like this position." She braced her hands on his chest.

"Why? Tell me." He needed to hear her.

She smiled. "Finally I have a say in what I want." She started riding him faster. "I'm controlling this." She played with his small, hard nipple. "I'm not waiting for someone to tell me what to do." She pressed her knees against him. "Oh, God."

"That's it. Come on, baby." Truman hugged her as she came hard.

Chantel screamed. Her body shook uncontrollably. "You are so hard." She gripped his shoulders. "Deep." Then she nodded. "More. Different."

He understood her request. He sat up, wrapped his arm around her waist, and moved to the edge of the bed. Chantel wrapped her legs around him as she continued gyrating her body.

She gripped his shoulders. "I loved singing with you today."

Truman nodded, but didn't say anything. He stood, which made Chantel gasp a little, before he settled her on top of a dresser and drove into her harder.

"Tru." She chewed her lower lip. "Tru. Please."

"Come. Do it. Let me see you." He kissed her before she broke from it, leaned her head back, and released a long, low moan.

"More. Switch."

Truman pulled out of her, and set her on her feet long enough to turn her around and bend her over slightly. When he entered her again, he couldn't take much more.

"I don't want you to ever stop." She reached behind her to hold the back of his head. "Do it however many ways you know how."

He grazed his teeth over her shoulder before kissing his way up to her ear. "Do you mind losing control?"

She shook her head. Truman continued thrusting in her until she gave into her emotions. She clawed the top of the dresser and her knees buckled.

Her climax pushed Truman to the edge. He drove into her hard and held himself there all while gazing into her eyes through the reflection in the mirror.

"I need to thank Delores for taking Gage today." He laughed a little before he pulled her face around to give her a kiss. "I don't know about you, but I could definitely get used to this."

Chantel smiled. "I know I could."

She interlaced her fingers with his on top of the dresser. When she faced forward and caught their reflection, her smile melted.

"We can't keep going like this." Chantel shook her head.

"Give me a few minutes to rest up a bit and I can go for a second round." Truman laughed and attempted to kiss her cheek.

"No." She pushed back against him. With him disengaged, she turned around to face him fully. "Us." She waved her hand in between the two of them. "It won't work."

Truman's expression sobered to her statements. "Why wouldn't it? We both like each other. We work well together in the studio. We make incredible music. And I think we proved that we can't keep our hands off each other." He started to reach for her, but Chantel moved away.

What the hell happened in the millisecond when they both had an explosive orgasm?

"Your career is about to jump off. You don't need to be weighed down by stories about you dating the crazy diva." Chantel shook her head.

"Don't call yourself crazy." Truman deposited the used condom into the en suite bathroom trash can before resuming the conversation. "And I could care less about what people think of me. I'm a grown man."

"Yes, and so are your bandmates. You have to think about them. Do you think country fans will want to see you dating—" She paused as she searched for the right words. "An R&B singer?"

He didn't know how to answer that. He would like to think better of his fans, of people in general. Truman understood how the world worked. He also knew that he didn't want to spend a moment without Chantel in his life.

When he didn't answer, Chantel ducked into the bathroom and grabbed a bath sheet. She wrapped it around her body.

When she reemerged, Truman framed her face in his hands and

smothered her in kisses.

"Please, Truman." She put her hands to his chest to push him back. "You know what I'm saying is true. The world isn't ready for us. And if we're keeping this light and fun—"

"Maybe I don't want to keep this light and fun." He held her head still so that he could make eye contact. "I only care about how you feel."

She held his hand and kissed the back of it. "You do? Fine, I feel like anything more serious than what we're doing is a colossal mistake."

Before he could stop her again, Chantel ran from the bedroom.

"Wait." Truman didn't want to run around a strange person's house with no clothes on even if they had full run of the home.

He slipped on his jeans and did the best he could to tuck his slowly deflating dick behind his zipper. When he ran from the room, he saw Craig holding Chantel's bare shoulders. When did he come home? Truman thanked his lucky stars that their quick sex session ended before Craig came upstairs.

"You'll never guess what's happened." Excitement flashed in Craig's eyes.

She shrugged.

"I sent the copy of the duet to the producers of the upcoming Breakout Music Awards." Craig must not have recognized the horror in Chantel's face from the way he smiled and nearly giggled.

Truman had seen it once before when he helped her in the men's bathroom the first time they met.

"What?" Chantel wriggled out of his grip. "Please tell me you mean the duet with Tru and Laura."

"Yeah. Like anyone wants to hear that poor excuse for chemistry." Craig snickered. "I'm talking about you and Mr. Woodley."

Truman put his hand to his head. On the one hand, he wanted to jump for joy at this opportunity. On the other, Chantel didn't want to do the performance with him.

"Baby girl, I didn't think it was possible because they plan those shows way in advance. But they want you and Truman to perform. Can you believe that, Shauna?"

"I'm going to be sick." She broke from his grip and ran to a bathroom, leaving Truman alone with Craig.

Craig sneered as he glared at Truman. "Where's your shirt and why was she in a towel?"

Too many questions. The only thing Truman wanted to know involved the woman who fought against being with him. He had to convince her that they would be okay.

Chapter 21

The week leading up to the Breakout Music Awards went by in a blur. Only two days ago, Truman still worked as a construction truck driver. Now he and his friends would be performing in front of the best of the best in the music industry. If they stayed on schedule, they will complete their first album in another week. All of this happened so fast for Truman, including what he had going on with Chantel.

As Truman and the guys waited for their cues backstage, he shifted his weight from one foot to the other.

Don't play too fast. Don't get nervous. Have fun.

Yeah, if only Truman could believe his own mantra. He really wished he had Chantel by his side or at least there to wish him luck. She knew more about this business than anyone. She could have told him what to expect. He respected her word above anyone else's.

He also knew that he wouldn't be where he was without her. He was sure that the only reason they wanted him and his band to play had to do with his affiliation to Shauna Stellar.

"Hey." Ervin tapped Truman with his drumstick.

Truman turned to Ervin as he listened out for the cue.

"Just remember, dude, I'm doing this for you." Ervin winked.

"Doing what?" Truman didn't know what Ervin meant, but he didn't have time to delve deep into his comments.

"Here's Truman Woodley and The Sliders," the host said.

The curtain slowly rose and Ervin counted off the beat by slamming his drumsticks together. No time to be nervous now.

The spotlight hit Truman in the eyes until he made his way to the end of the stage. There he had to keep his composure because he became so star-struck that he almost forgot the words to his song.

His attention naturally went to all the country stars he spotted in the audience. Dolly Parton sat in the front row looking as glamorous and voluptuous as ever. Tim McGraw sat next his beautiful wife, Faith Hill. He had to turn away when he saw that happy couple.

Truman noticed smiles on the faces of each audience member. He looked up into the balcony area where he knew the fans had to sit. They screamed at him when he winked.

When he realized how much the crowd had gotten into him and the band, he smiled. They enjoyed the song and, more importantly, his performance. Even Dolly gave them a thumbs-up sign. The confirmation felt like getting ordained by God.

Toward the end of the song, the band suddenly stopped playing. Truman turned to the guys, shocked since they hadn't rehearsed it that way. What were they doing, besides ruining their make-or-break performance?

With his microphone still live, he mouthed the words, "What are you doing?" to them.

Tony positioned his fiddle under his chin and played the opening for "Meet Me Halfway."

Charlie leaned forward past his microphone and said, "Just keep going."

They didn't practice this. From the expressions on the executive producers' faces offstage, he knew he had to make the most of this sink-or-swim moment. No new band had ever played two songs in a row on this or any awards show.

Truman had to take this opportunity. Even if they cut the cameras off, he would have the whole music industry as his audience. He took off his headset and grabbed Charlie's microphone on its stand.

He started singing and worked out in his head how he could sing this song straight through on his own. The song should be sung as a duet. Seeing Laura Smalls scowl at him from the audience, he knew she wouldn't be keen on joining him on stage.

Truman took a deep breath before singing the next verse intended as the female part. Then a voice stopped him. An angelic voice wrapped itself around the words like a warm blanket and held them for dear life. He looked to the side of the stage and a vision in red approached him.

Truman couldn't hear the band, let alone hear himself think when the crowd roared its approval when Shauna Stellar stepped out on stage. Her red dress cut down to there and a slit up to here gave her a sexy but glamorous look. With her super sexy makeup, her styled hair parted in the middle and hanging straight down around her face, she looked completely different. Truman still saw Chantel Evans underneath the façade.

He kept his stare on her until she stopped a few feet away from him. While he noticed her dress and immaculate makeup, he recognized the pure terror filling her eyes the longer she stood on stage.

From where he stood, he caught her chin quivering like she wanted to break down and bawl her eyes out. Her hand shook so much that she needed them both to hold her microphone still.

He wouldn't stop. The show must go on. Maybe once they sang together she would calm down. Her being on stage now…with him…meant everything to him. He put his hand to his chest to calm his galloping heart.

The crowd cheered even louder when Truman and Chantel sang in unison. Their voices entangled like lovers getting to know one another's bodies until it melted into a perfect union. She was the right partner for him. Not for just the song or as a producer. Period.

He exhaled in relief. Then it happened. A crack. Chantel's voice broke a note. Her eyes danced from the audience to Truman's gaze as his mouth strained to maintain its smile.

Calm. He had to keep her calm. One mistake could be overlooked. It had been a while since she performed.

Although he'd heard the missed note, he hoped no one in the audience had…until she screeched another note and another. What was happening to her? She started off so strong. Why had she broken down now?

Flames ignited his skin and it had nothing to do with embarrassment. He knew the media would crucify her for this performance. No, Truman hated that someone in Chantel's past made her doubt herself so that she became this unstable mess in front of him. He wanted to end the song and get her off stage. From the tears welling in her eyes, he knew she wanted the same thing.

At the end of the song, Truman took Chantel's hand and turned to the audience. If he hadn't grabbed her, she would have bolted. No way would he allow her to leave in an undignified manner.

The audience's reserved applause paled in comparison to the welcome they had given Chantel when she first stepped on stage. They had heard her off night. Damn.

Truman and Chantel bowed together. The Sliders made their way next to them and bowed alongside of them. Not satisfied with only a bow, Truman let his true feelings be known. As soon as he and Chantel stood, he pulled her close and kissed her on the lips.

He heard nothing as his lips connected to hers. No applause. No gasps. Not even his band mates trying to tell him to get off stage. His full attention and concentration stayed on Chantel as it should.

When the curtain dropped, Truman continued holding her hand.

"Let me go." Chantel tried getting out of his grip.

"What happened?" He wanted to be reassuring and supportive.

"I knew I wasn't ready. The whole audience heard my voice cracking." With her face in her hands, she shook her head.

"I know I did." Sully laughed as he made his way off stage.

"Shh. We are still on and we're live." A stagehand pointed to the TV monitors around them.

Pulling her backstage, Truman found a spot that seemed quiet in relation to everything going on around them. "You still should be proud of yourself. You got on stage."

"Yeah." She snickered. "Because my cousin convinced me that I was acting like an idiot." She pushed herself back from Truman. "Now the whole world knows I'm an idiot. This was too last minute. I needed to be better prepared."

He wanted to erase her bad memories but he knew at this point she wouldn't have believed him. A barrage of camera flashes hit them as well as probing questions from reporters and celebrities alike.

"Too long away from the stage, Shauna?" a reporter screamed. "Will this keep you from performing again?"

She waved her hands in front of her face to keep more pictures from being taken. "Please just leave me alone right now."

"Will this be on your upcoming album?" another reporter asked.

"I wouldn't put that no-talent skank on my album again."

The harsh voice cut through the chaos backstage. Through the crowd that parted like a bad toupee, Raheem came strutting to them with his posse in tow.

Chantel cowered behind Truman. "Why won't this day end?"

The red that colored Truman's gaze couldn't be erased, not with a simple apology or reversing time so that Chantel could have another shot at the song.

"What did you just call her?" Truman had never met Raheem, a pompous jerk who could stand to be taken down a peg or two.

"I called her a ska—"

Before Raheem could get the word out, Truman landed a hard punch to the man's jaw, sending him to the ground.

"Truman, no." Chantel put her hand on Truman's chest but his gaze stayed trained on the whimpering man on the floor.

Raheem's boys left him on the floor as they split their attention between Truman and their fallen leader.

Chantel glared at her ex, then turned to Truman. In a move that screamed *diva*, she summoned security backstage to get the reporters off them and take Raheem to be attended to by the paramedics on standby.

"If I can't sing, I'm going to sue your ass." Raheem pointed at Truman.

"If you ever talk about her like that again, I'll be sure you don't utter another word for the rest of your sorry life."

Like a swarm of bees, large security guards landed on the nosey group and buzzed them away. Then another set of security guards snagged Truman.

"Wait." Shauna held on to his hand as they ushered him away.

"Find Sully. I'll be fine."

She nodded. "Talk to Ervin. He knows how to find me."

The guards yanked him back hard enough that their hands separated from their grasp.

Truman watched her staring at him being taken away through the crowd until he could no longer see a speck of her red dress.

What a way to start his career. He'd already pissed off two people in the industry even before his first CD had been released.

He could almost hear Sully and the rest of the guys saying "I told you so" about associating with Shauna Stellar.

The guys didn't know what he did. He'd felt her hand trembling and knew her fear. The stint on stage had been a huge leap for her. Would the rest of the guys be so understanding?

* * * *

With her face scrubbed of all makeup and just a T-shirt and shorts on, Chantel felt no more relaxed than when she'd been curled up on Nikia's couch at her beach home. She never sweated this much before in her life, not even when she had gotten booed off stage when she first started touring.

But tonight? The humiliation swirled in her head every time she closed her eyes. She'd made the mistake of turning the TV on to have some background noise as she paced in her hotel room only to be besieged with news stories about how Shauna Stellar flopped on stage in front of millions.

Just breathe, girl. Don't let it get to you.

Wringing her hands couldn't calm her escalating nerves. Why had she gotten on stage? She should have told Nikia and Craig no when they pressed her two days before the show to join Truman and his band for their performance. She should have stayed at home. She shouldn't have let seeing Raheem in the hallway minutes before she walked on stage bother her. However, she'd heard him snickering and pointing at her. The small bit of self-esteem she'd built up since leaving Peaceful Acres crumbled. With one look and a laugh, the creep had her doubting herself again.

Chantel hoped Ervin and Nikia hadn't talked and, more importantly, that Ervin didn't relay the information to Truman. Right now since she could honestly say that she put a stain on Truman's career, Chantel wanted to avoid the man at all costs.

Why had she told him to talk to Ervin? Maybe because she wanted to apologize. What apology could she offer that would save his name, save his and his band's reputation, and save his trust in her?

While lost in her thoughts, a knock sounded at her door. Chantel froze.

A second knock sounded as Chantel made it to the door. She looked through the peephole and saw Truman pacing back and forth. Her hand gripped the knob to keep her from falling to her knees. Hearts beating as hard as hers couldn't have been good or healthy. She didn't want to open the door, but she owed the man an apology.

Chantel unlocked, then opened the door. When Truman looked at her, she searched his eyes for some sort of emotion. Was he angry? Did he hate her? Did he want to kill her?

"Can I come in?" he asked, but walked into her room without her permission anyway.

She closed the door and crossed her arms over her chest, partly to look in control and to keep her thudding heart from leaping from her chest.

Tru stomped his cowboy boots over the floor as he kept his gaze down. Guests in the rooms below hers had to have heard his angry steps. Chantel sucked her bottom lip into her mouth to pacify herself by chewing it.

After a deep breath, she decided to take the bull by the horns. The reason she'd had the nervous breakdown before had everything to do with keeping her feelings bottled up inside. Now to give herself peace and to offer Truman some resolution, she knew she needed to be upfront and honest.

"I know you're angry," she began.

He snorted. "You think?"

She squeezed her eyelids shut and balled her hands into tight fists. "What happened on that stage was…"

He approached her and it made her take a couple of cautious steps back. "What happened was the build-up of years of oppression from your manager and jerks like that Raheem fellow."

Blinking her eyes and shaking her head didn't change what Truman had just said. Was he actually on her side? He wasn't angry at *her*?

"What?" She blinked.

"I bet you were forced by Craig to go on stage with me tonight, right?" As though wanting to make sure she told him the truth, he stared into her eyes as she answered.

"It doesn't matter why I did it. I wasn't ready. It was obvious I wasn't ready."

He put his hand to the side of her face and caressed her cheek. "You were more than ready. A couple of cracked notes here and there don't mean squat to me." He stared at her like a vision, almost as though he thought she was more beautiful now than when she was in that expensive Prada dress and Jacob the Jeweler jewelry. "What matters is that you are okay."

Placing her hand on top of his, she replied, "I let seeing Raheem get to me. I saw him before I got on stage and I choked. I'm so sorry. You worried that I would ruin your career and I've done it."

"Shh." Truman put his finger to her lips. "You are talented. What happened tonight is not a reflection on you or your incredible voice."

"But your career? The Sliders?"

"We'll have other opportunities."

She shook her head. "Why aren't you furious with me? I just made a laughing stock out of myself and dragged your good name with me."

Leaning close to her he whispered, "I realized when I saw you on that stage that it took more heart, more guts, and more strength to do what you did for me than it took me to punch out that jerk." Placing a languid kiss on the shell of her ear, he made her feel more cherished than any person had ever done. "You are incredibly strong, Chantel Evans. And I am proud of you. You could have gone on stage and lip synched your part but you didn't."

With a turn of her head, she captured his gaze until they locked in an intense stare. She tried mustering up the strength to still apologize for coming on stage but her compressed throat kept her from uttering a word. He knew exactly what to do with her lips.

As though time stopped for them, Chantel watched him lean in for a kiss. Her eyes closed as soon as his firm, warm lips touched hers. His scent seduced her olfactory senses until her body weakened from his kiss and from touching his body. Her other hand sought his hip and when it found it, she pulled him in close until her pebbled nipples brushed against his broad chest. His hot tongue slid easily into her mouth. Had she known that having a horrible night like she had would result in this passionate event, she would have sung out of tune a long time ago.

With some reluctance, Tru pulled back from her. He went to the door and opened it again. Before closing the door, he put out the "Do Not Disturb" sign on the knob, then locked it every way imaginable. To truly tune out the world, he turned his phone off.

"There's only one thing I have to say now." He stared into her eyes. "I don't care if we're broke for the rest of our lives and have to sing for our suppers. I don't want to be without you."

Chantel smiled and wrapped her arms around his neck. She wanted more. Pulling him toward the bed, she worked to undo his shirt buttons. She didn't want to come off as too eager but she'd waited her whole life for a man like this, a moment like this.

Once at the bed, he gently eased her down. He slid his shirt off his shoulders. She noticed his skin glowed. He'd been sweating. Good to know he battled nerves like her.

He leaned into her until he had her on her back. Without hesitation, he pulled her shirt over her head and tossed it to the side. Chantel felt naked in just her bra and attempted to cross her arm over her chest to cover herself.

He pulled her arm down to her side. The cool air from the air conditioner danced over her bare flesh until goose bumps formed.

He must have noticed them because he rubbed his hand up and down her arm. After giving Chantel a quick kiss he sat up and struggled to take off his cowboy boots. He even cursed when he removed the second boot.

Then he stood to take off his jeans. Chantel saw the bulge in his pants. He kicked out of his jeans, took off his socks, and pulled back the covers.

"I want to see you completely naked before we get in."

Truman's request seemed odd, since they had already seen each other naked on two occasions. She took a deep breath and stood, staring into his eyes as she eased her shorts down. Now in a bra and thong, she really felt naked. She reached back to undo her bra. When she unhooked the last hook, she paused before dropping the red lacy bra to the floor.

Chantel gazed down and noticed how big and hard her nipples were. When she returned her gaze to Truman's face, his gaze remained fixed on her breasts. He reached out and let his fingertips smooth over her bulbous flesh. The touch caught her breath.

He trailed his hand down the side of her waist to her thong. He hooked his finger into the side and eased it down. Not to be the first one naked, she grabbed the waistband of his boxers and pulled them down simultaneously. With a pool of underwear around their feet, Chantel stared at his hard penis.

"You are beautiful. Everything about you is perfect."

This time she put her finger to his mouth. "Shh. No talking."

He removed her hand from his lips and brought it down to his erection. He wrapped her fingers around him as though letting her know she owned it. Feeling him pulsate in her hand made her skin tingle. She licked her lips, and tried to control her quick breathing. What power, both in him and the fact that he let her hold him so intimately.

Her hand slid down to the base. She braced her other hand low on his waist, her fingers caressing his round, firm backside. When she drew her hand up on his hard shaft, Truman grabbed her wrist.

"If you do that, this is going to be a quick evening." He lifted her into his arms and placed her on the bed.

She reached for the comforter to cover her body but he stopped her. He scanned her body before finally slipping into bed.

When she fell into his arms, she felt like she should have been there the whole time. Stroking her cheek with his thumb, he stared into her eyes. She wrapped her arm around his shoulder and put her other hand on his chest. Now that she felt his heart pounding, she melted even more.

Truman kissed Chantel down her body. His lips pressed against her neck. When he trailed his tongue down to her breast, she sucked in her breath and arched her back. She didn't think anything could feel as good as getting her first gold album. Every nerve in her body felt electrified. His hand cupped her other breast and massaged it like he owned her body.

He slid his tongue over to the tit he'd been massaging. She thought she would lose her mind. The sensations proved too much for her to handle. She wanted to crawl out of her skin.

"Now," she moaned.

He continued moving down her body, licking her stomach until he reached right above her Brazilian wax job.

Thank God Nikia convinced her to get that at the spa.

"God, Truman, you're driving me crazy." Her body writhed under his. "Please, now."

He didn't question her. He grabbed his pants and pulled a condom from his wallet. Like a rabid dog, he ripped the package open. After slipping the rubber over himself, he hovered over her body.

She braced her hands on his broad shoulders. Truman struggled to ease himself inside of her. Chantel gasped, bit her bottom lip, but kept her gaze on his.

She yelped and arched her head back. When he slid out and made his second thrust, she dug her fingernails into his shoulders. She wanted to scream "I love you" over and over again.

She grabbed his firm ass cheek. Her legs wrapped around his body. Instinctively, she moved her body with his. A torrent of emotions swirled inside of her. Fear, hate, excitement, disappointment and love, love, love.

With such ease and precision, he worked her body like a finely-tuned instrument. She'd watched his large hands strum his guitar, those long fingers gliding over the keys of a piano, and now he mastered satisfying her body. With each thrust, each kiss, each tantalizing stare, he brought her to the very brink of ecstasy. When she couldn't take the overwhelming pleasure, she screamed.

He groaned and collapsed on top of Chantel. "You okay?"

Between breaths, Chantel said, "Again. Again."

He laughed as he rolled off her. "I see you're fine."

"Thank you for a good night." Now she would have to wait until tomorrow to see what Craig had in store for her.

Chapter 22

Chantel was having a fabulous month. Making love to Truman felt like she had been introduced to a new life. Recording with him had become more fun than before.

At home, the loving didn't stop. After she and Truman put Gage to bed, Truman would go into Chantel's room and sleep with her. They had fallen into a comfortable routine that Chantel wanted to kick herself for doing. She promised not to get herself involved, to keep it fun. With Truman, she saw so much more. She imagined a relationship with him. Damn her imagination.

With the album done, Chantel had a bittersweet feeling come over her. She wanted Truman to have the finished product, but to her it meant everything they had would end. Being in Virginia shielded her from a lot of inquiry into her life. She knew that would change as soon as they started promoting the album.

In the morning, she bounded down the stairs with a CD jewel case in her hand. She skipped into Craig's office and sat the CD on his desk. Cigar smoke swirled around Craig's solemn face.

"You should be happy, Craig." Satisfied, she put her fists to her hips. "I've done my part. I've produced this album like you wanted me to. And I hear we've gotten offers from a few record labels. All is good." She had to keep smiling to sell that feeling.

"You would think so." Craig tapped off the ash from the end of his cigar and took a puff.

"Come on. Don't smoke. It kills my throat." She plopped down in the chair in front of his desk.

"Oh, so now you're interested in singing again? Didn't have enough at the Breakout Awards?"

Chantel caught the anger in Craig's voice and she blinked. "It was a bad night. I told you that. Is there a problem? Here I bring you a finished product and you don't even seem happy about it."

He blew the smoke away from her, and leaned back in his swivel chair. He picked up the case and stared at the cover.

"I hear Delores is doing something special for the band tonight to celebrate the completion of the album." She tried to gain eye contact with her manager but he swung his chair around to face the wall.

"Looks like you and Mr. Woodley have hit it off. And with these offers coming in, I guess you won't need to stay here in my house for much longer." The gruffness in his voice matched the harshness of his ejection.

"Are you kicking us out?" She struggled to keep her voice from quivering.

"I'm allowing you to be the adult you've been striving to be these last couple of months. But I tell you this, Shauna—"

"Chantel. That's my name."

Craig glowered at her. "You aren't seriously going to change your name, are you? The public knows you as Shauna Stellar. They don't know Chantel Evans, a poor ghetto girl with a voice."

"Maybe they should know her. I'm real. I'm not some robot made in a factory. I have a heart and feelings." Thanks to Truman, she realized all of this. He'd opened her eyes to be appreciative of her name and making it her own.

"You had better think about the consequences of your actions because it's going to come down to what's right for you and what's right for your career." Craig stamped out his cigar.

"You're right. I do need to start looking at the big picture, start evaluating all aspects of my life *and* career." One thing she had to consider was the man in front of her. At this point in her life, in her career, did she still need this type of tough love? She crossed her arms over her chest. "Where is all of this coming from?"

Before Craig had a chance to answer, Truman bounded into the office. He looked good in his T-shirt and black jeans.

"Did you hear?" He beamed from ear to ear. "*The Big Ol' Barn* wants us to sing on their show down in Tennessee. It's a huge deal for a country artist to sing on that."

Chantel smiled. She knew how important a move like this would be for Truman. From the way he grinned, she couldn't let him see she and Craig had been arguing.

"That's great. I told you good things were going to happen for you." Because she had done it a million times already, she held his hand without caring about what Craig thought.

"They already have." He kissed her forehead. "So what do you think? You're going to sing 'Meet Me Halfway'?"

Craig cleared his throat in an obvious attempt to get her attention. She didn't turn to him or give him the satisfaction of seeing her expression. Honestly, it scared her to death to sing in public again. To mask her fear, she plastered a smile on her face.

"What does the band think?" No matter how she felt about Truman, she wouldn't get in between him and his band.

"We get to do a full set so this one song is not going to take away from us." Truman squeezed Chantel's hand. "I want you there. This time there'll be no Raheem to throw you. We can practice however long you want. I know you can do this. If you don't feel comfortable singing in front of an audience—"

"No. I'll do it." She felt bullied before her last performance. She wouldn't cower again. More importantly, she didn't want to let Truman down. Plus she had to redeem herself to the world.

Truman hugged her and ran from Craig's office to call the rest of the guys.

She waited a beat before she continued her conversation with Craig. "You knew about this."

"I'm your manager. I'm supposed to know about what's going on with your career." Craig slammed some magazines and newspapers on his desk. "You are not looking good to the black media. They think you're crazy again for coming back after your sabbatical by singing with a country group. Not a smart move."

"Wait. All of this was *your* idea. You wanted me to produce Truman. You asked me to sing a duet. Now you're mad at me because the song is a hit? You can't have it both ways." She stormed to the door.

"You can't either, *Chantel*."

She spun around to catch Craig's worried expression.

Craig continued. "I was wrong to push you into all of this. Don't feel compelled to follow through on my crazy schemes. I will be more than happy to admit my mistake in a press conference."

"None of this is a mistake. Don't you dare say a word to anyone. I'm doing the show. And Tru, Gage, and I will be out of your house by the end of the month."

"Fine." Craig bolted from his chair, pushing it back against the wall and causing her to direct her attention back to him. "If what you want is to alienate the family that helped raise you and have been looking out for you for years, then go ahead. But I'm going to tell you this last thing. Your boy, Truman, is not being honest with you about this Ashley woman. Ask him about what he's got going on with her."

Chantel wouldn't give Craig the satisfaction of catching her worried expression. She ran from the office and headed to the family room where she found Truman with Gage.

Truman read from a large yellow book to his son, then allowed the child to read to him. She had no idea what Craig implied about Truman. He had spent almost all his time with her and Gage. She would have suspected something by now. Then Truman did something that he had been doing for the last couple of weeks. He checked his phone and put it away without answering it. Occasionally, he would send a text.

Damn Craig for planting the seed of doubt in her head. Truman had been open and honest with her. Then again, she had asked him to keep their relationship light and fun. Maybe he had found the next woman to occupy his time.

Truman glanced up and caught Chantel standing at the doorway into the room. He gave her a wink and a big smile.

Truman wouldn't hide anything from her. Craig, however, knew about the offer at *The Big Ol' Barn* so maybe he knew something else about Truman and Ashley that Truman wasn't sharing. What was it?

Chapter 23

"Where's Chantel?" Truman hadn't seen her since that morning.

They'd started a routine of bathing and dressing Gage...like a family. Although breaking up with Ashley shortly after the birth of Gage disappointed him because he never wanted his child to have a broken home, Truman saw the possibilities with Chantel. He saw a new life for himself and his son. Too bad she couldn't see it.

"She's upstairs getting ready." Delores reached up and stroked Truman's hair in a motherly way that he appreciated.

Truman ran up the stairs taking them two at a time. When he reached Chantel's room, he eased the door open and found the light on already.

"We're in here," Chantel called back.

Truman continued into her bathroom where she had Gage in the bathtub. Bubbles covered him from his hair to his waist as he sat in the tub.

"He woke up a little early so I thought I would start his bath, since you were giving Flye his piano lesson." Chantel kept her concentration on Gage.

Truman kissed her on the top of her head. "You're too good to me."

"I am, aren't I?" Chantel winked at him.

"Daddy, you weren't supposed to come up here yet." Gage scrunched up his little face.

"Why is that?" Truman sat on the edge of the bathtub.

Gage stood in the tub and shuffled to his father. He put his hands on Truman's shoulders, leaned in, and said, "You're cuttin' into my alone time with Chantel."

Truman laughed and it echoed off the white tiled walls. "I'm so sorry. Do you think I can have just a little time with her?"

Gage rolled his eyes and sat down in the water with a splash. Chantel laughed and wiped water from her face.

"Gage. You know better than to horseplay around in the tub. Apologize to Chantel for getting her all wet." After he made the statement, Truman noticed her outfit. In a business-like skirt, cotton, and heels, she looked too dressy to bathe his rambunctious five-year old or for the party.

"I'm sorry, Chantel. Are you mad at me?" Gage pouted.

Truman didn't teach him that little trick.

"No. I'm only upset with you if you lie to me." She glared at Truman when she said that.

Truman blinked. He didn't want to say anything in front of Gage, but if she was upset with him for any reason, he had to hammer it out.

After drying and dressing Gage, Truman and Chantel took him downstairs to the pool area. Gage took off for Delores and hung with her as she plied him with baby carrots and cheesy nacho chips.

Truman pulled Chantel back into the house. Pinning her against the kitchen counter, he placed his hands on the sides of her face and kissed her softly.

Reluctantly, he pulled back from her. "I've been wanting to do that all day."

Chantel smiled. "And why is that?"

"Because I've been wanting to kiss you and you look like you've been needing to be kissed."

She brought his hands down from her face and turned away. "I'm going to ask you something and I want you to be completely honest."

The hairs on Truman's arms stood on end. He had nothing to worry about. He'd been completely honest about everything in his life to her. Except for the situation he had with Ashley, he had nothing to hide.

"Is there something going on with you and Gage's mother?" Chantel stared at him hard.

Geez, Chantel should have been one of those TV psychics. Truman took a deep breath. He made sure to make eye contact with her. He prayed to God that she wouldn't freak out.

"Yes." Honesty would be on his side.

Chantel rolled her eyes and headed out of the kitchen. "I knew it. Craig told me, but I didn't believe him. It was all the phone calls. I should have known something was up." She made her way toward the stairs but Truman ran in front of her to block her way.

"What did Craig tell you?" He managed to stop her trek.

"That you and your child's mother had something going on." She shook her head. "Nikia told me to stay away from men with kids, but knucklehead me, I have to learn the hard way."

Chantel moved around him and made it up two steps before Truman grabbed her wrist.

"The only thing I have going on with Ashley is a lawsuit. What did you think I was talking about?"

Chantel gazed at Truman for a while, studying him before she made her next move. She must have found it because she let go of her breath and wrapped her arms around his neck.

"I was so worried that you wanted to go back and make your family with her again for Gage's sake." She kissed the side of his face. "I saw you on the phone all of the time and you seemed really secretive."

"I didn't want to get you involved." He wrapped his arms around her. "I knew you had enough on your plate." When Chantel stood up straight, he continued. "She's fighting for custody of Gage and she wants some hefty child support. She has been calling me ever since I took Gage. Guess she saw me on TV and thinks I've got some money. After that, her attorney started calling me."

"You will have some money after my trip." She ran up the stairs.

Trip? What did she mean? Truman chased Chantel up to her room. He must have been oblivious to everything in her room before because now he noticed a packed overnight bag next to her bed.

"Where are you going?"

"New York. There's something I need to take care of before we hit the road to Tennessee."

"You want me to go with you?"

"Yes, I would like for you to come with me. But you can't." She shook her head.

He felt confused, relieved, and hurt all at the same time.

"As much as I would love for you to be by my side, I need to do this alone. Nikia's going to take me to the airport. I asked her while you and Gage took a nap this afternoon." She headed back downstairs the moment the doorbell rang.

"Why didn't you tell me this before?" She hadn't even left yet, and Truman already missed her.

"I knew you would try to talk me out of going or try to convince me to take you along. I have to do this." She got to the bottom landing. "Trust me. You'll thank me later."

"You know we could do like last time and drive up there, just me and you." He wrapped his arms around her waist and nibbled the side of her neck.

He felt Chantel soften but as the doorbell rang again, she tensed up and braced her hands on his arms.

"You do not play fair, Mr. Woodley." Chantel laughed.

He let her go so she could answer the door. "Will you at least tell me what you're doing? Are you some drug lord or something?"

"Yes, I'm selling Flintstone Vitamins to kids. I start them off with a Barney for free to get them hooked. Then they have to pay for the Freds and Wilmas." Chantel opened the front door. The Sliders stood on the other side.

"Come on in, guys." She stood to the side and let Truman's band enter. They still looked awestruck when they scanned the place.

Nikia bounded into the front room wearing a short sundress and no shoes. With her hair in pigtails, it looked like Ervin also influenced her personal style.

"Was that the door?" As soon as Nikia saw Ervin she squealed and ran to him, then hopped on him and wrapped her legs around his body.

"Nikia, I have to get to the airport." Chantel tugged on the back of Nikia's dress to get her cousin's attention and also to pull it down so it didn't show her backside.

"Uh, there goes my appetite." Sully held his stomach.

"Makes me miss my wife." Charlie looked at the couple and smiled.

Nikia dropped her feet to the floor and slowly removed her arms from around Ervin's neck.

"Why don't I take you to the airport?" Truman nodded. "It's obvious that these two don't want to be apart right now. And it'll give us a chance to talk."

"Sounds like a great idea." Nikia kept her gaze on Ervin as she spoke.

Truman had a feeling that he could have said that he would shoot Chantel from a cannon to the airport and Nikia would have still said the same thing.

"What's going on here?" Flye stood in the doorway of the kitchen. "The party's not in here. It's out there. And I have a surprise for you two." He pointed to Truman and Chantel.

Truman had an uneasy feeling creeping through him at the thought of a gift from Flye. He still had to get adjusted to the fact that he wouldn't be sleeping next to this woman tonight.

"Come on out to the back." Flye gestured to the pool area. Everyone followed him out and made their way around the pool.

"Hurry up, Sherman. I have a plane to catch." Chantel smirked.

"It's Flye. Flye!" For effect, he pounded on his chest.

"Whatever." Chantel giggled.

After pumping his chest out, Flye held up his hands to grab even more attention. "As you all know, Big Tru and his boys and Shaunie are supposed to be going down to Tennessee to be featured on *This Old House*."

"*The Big Ol' Barn!*" the group said in unison.

"Close enough." Flye shrugged. "So as my treat to you all, I'm going to allow y'all to use my tour bus to get down there." Flye punched some buttons into his high-tech cell phone. "I can't have my cousin riding in something beat down. And it sleeps eight so Craig can go with y'all."

Truman's friends all remained quiet. They looked like they didn't know how to respond. Then he heard an air horn blaring.

"It's here." Flye slipped the phone into his pocket and led the group around the side of the house to the front yard. In front of the house stretched a long black tour bus with red and orange flames painted on the front and sides.

"Whoa. We get to ride in that?" Tony cautiously approached the bus. He poked his head inside. "This is nicer than my apartment."

"Go on in. Take a gander at what's gangsta." Flye pointed to it like a sideshow barker.

Truman walked to Flye. "Man, you didn't have to do this. This is too much."

Flye shook his head. "I told you that if you taught me piano that I would pay you back somehow. And since Shauna don't want me hooking you up with any of my honeys, I thought this might do the trick." Flye smiled and even in the dark night his teeth gleamed. "Now I'm not *giving* you the bus. It's just a loaner."

Charlie ran off the bus. "There's an Apple TV and Netflix and a Wii and a phone and a fridge."

"Charlie, take a breath, man." Truman held up his hands to calm his friend.

Once the group toured the magical bus, they made their way back to the party area. Truman helped Chantel load her bags into the Mercedes, let Gage know of their whereabouts, and then they took off for the airport.

As soon as Truman hit the interstate, he reached for Chantel's hand. She wrapped her fingers around his and placed her other hand on top.

"I should have told you my plans." She held his hand on her lap. "I wanted it to be a surprise."

"What?" He wanted so much to see her face, but the combination of the darkness and him driving prevented him from doing so.

"Let's just say that being with you has given me the strength to fight demons." She put his hand on her bare knee and he felt an electric jolt go up his arm. "I've been doing a lot of thinking lately."

"About us?" Truman smoothed his thumb over her knee.

"You are always on my mind. But I've been thinking about my career, my next step. Your introduction to the world has been done. Your album is completed. You're pretty much set. Now it's time for me to think about my next move." She patted his hand. "I'm glad to have been a part of your journey."

Just touching her smooth skin made his heart pump. Blood engorged his lower region until he would either have to satisfy his lusty craving or pour a bucket of ice down his pants. So he thought about things that weren't sexy. The Bulls losing Jordan, Chantel believing he could be racist at their first meeting, Raheem at the award show. He snickered now reminiscing about it.

She lifted her head. "What's so funny?"

"The first time I met you." Truman tried splitting his gaze between the road and Chantel.

She covered her face. "When I threw up."

"No, when you thought I didn't want you as a producer because you thought I was a racist." He feathered his fingertips over her knee.

"Now I know different. But tell me. Why didn't you want me to be your producer?"

He stole quick glances at her as he answered. "I didn't think you would know or understand my music. I was way off. Music is music. You said that from the beginning. You get it. If I had to do it over again, I would beg to have you coproduce my album."

"You couldn't afford me." She giggled, and it sounded like music to Truman's ears.

Why did she have to make this sudden trip? He wanted to make love to her one last night before they had to be on the road.

He pulled into the airport parking lot and turned off the car. "Are you sure you want to go?"

"I'll be fine. I'll be more than fine." She kissed him but he couldn't let her leave with only giving him a peck.

He framed her face with his hands and brushed his lips against hers. He felt her warm breath tickling his lips and he bore down on hers. When she moaned it vibrated his lips.

He kissed down the side of her face and hugged her. "I'm glad you didn't tell me earlier about this trip. I would have spent the whole day missing you."

"It's just a day. I'll be back by tomorrow night. Early. My plane should land at five."

"I'll come get you. Me and Gage."

A man walked in front of their car, peered at them in their embrace, and smiled. Even this stranger knew that Truman and Chantel looked good together. Truman helped Chantel with her bag and waited with her in the waiting area outside of the security check-in area.

"Call me when you check into your hotel. Which hotel are you staying at again?" Truman bounced his knee as he held on to her hand.

"The Hilton." She appeared calm. Her long, curly lashes framed her wide brown eyes perfectly.

"And you'll call when you're on your way home." He swallowed.

The nerves he felt had everything to do with her trip, not her. Worried that she could get hurt or be disappointed in her quest. He didn't want her feeling broken again.

"The minute I get out of my meeting, I'll call you. Promise." She kissed his cheek. "I've never had anyone miss me before. Not like this." She smiled. "It feels good."

"Yeah. Speak for yourself. I'm a wreck." He wiped the sweat from his forehead.

"Aww, honey." She kissed him and stopped when she caught a flash.

Truman jerked his head away and directed his attention to the two men in front of him. One man he didn't recognize, the one with the camera. The other man he remembered as the one who had walked by their car moments before and smiled at them.

"See, I knew she was famous." The stranger pointed at both of them. "Weren't y'all on some award show not too long ago?"

Truman stood and took Chantel's carry-on bag. "Let's get you in the passenger area where these guys can't get to you." Placing his hand at the small of her back, he guided her to the metal detector.

"I'm sorry this happened." She tried peering over his shoulder as she stood in line.

"Not your fault. I'll see you tomorrow night." He kissed her forehead, then backed up as she went through. She picked up her bag and waved at him as she ran away from the prying camera.

He stormed back to the car with the two men following him. He kept his gaze forward, not giving them a chance to get a good shot.

"So are you and Shauna Stellar dating?" The cameraman nearly tripped over his own feet trying to get a good shot of Truman.

Good. Truman hoped the man fell flat on his face for breaking up their moment. Asshole. He felt no need to answer them.

"We saw you kiss her." The second cretin continued snapping pictures.

Truman remained quiet as he made his way out to the parking lot and into the luxury car, all the while with the photographer clicking away and the other jerk screaming questions.

If he had to endure idiots like this to be with Chantel, he would do it. She had his heart. Whether she wanted to stay with him or not, he had to tell her. When he finished this ordeal with Ashley, he would put his heart on the line.

Chapter 24

Chantel opened the door and sauntered into the Universe Records office. Before the men could get to their feet, she made it to the end of the table.

"Please, sit." She liked treating them like dogs, the same way they had treated her. "My time is way too valuable for pleasantries."

"It's good to see you again, Shauna." Mr. Zinner adjusted his tie. "How's your voice?"

His question oozed of smarmy sarcastic wit that she wouldn't allow to bother her. Not anymore.

"Call me Ms. Evans. In this fake business, I've decided to go back to my real name. And since this is a business meeting, Mr. Zinner, I'm going to treat you like any stranger on the street and not someone I've known for more than ten years."

Chantel watched the large Adam's apple in Mr. Zinner's throat go up and down when he swallowed. The power surged through her like a drug. With the confidence of a matador, she cocked a smile on the side of her mouth as she reached into her borrowed Louis Vuitton bag.

"My manager shared with me some wonderful news." Chantel placed the papers on the table with the offer that Universe had sent to Craig on top.

Mr. Zinner must have noticed the letterhead because he smiled and leaned back in his chair.

"After your last visit and your appearance on the Breakout Music Awards show, Universe Records has since changed its stance on picking up Charisma Music. Mr. Kyson fought long and hard to sway my opinion."

Chantel glanced at the same executive who showed up at her concert the day of her mother's funeral and had also been at her previous meeting with Zinner. He offered her a pleasant smile, which she responded in kind. At least someone outside of her immediate camp went to bat for her.

Zinner continued. "After much debate, we decided that this country artist was worth our time. And if Charisma Music can continue producing artists like Mr. Woodrow—"

Chantel corrected him. "Woodley."

"I mean Woodley. We would love to enter into another agreement with your production company. And let me just say, Shauna, I sincerely hope you harbor no bad feelings for Universe or its affiliates because of our last meeting."

"Come on, Mr. Zinner. I'm an adult. Grudges are for children and teenagers with no other means to vent their anger or frustration or, worse yet, have no other options. Me, now I have options. And in looking at the contract you sent to my manager, I see that my only option is to choose the best deal for my company, the company I was allowed to keep after my mother passed."

Mr. Zinner's smile became so wide he looked like a cartoon character. Chantel only wished that Nikia could be with her when she dropped her bomb.

"Excel Entertainment made me a grand offer, one that not only included my studio but also a talent contract for me." Chantel placed her hand to her chest. "The offer was incredible. Way more than anything I've earned here. I would be a fool or, well, crazy to turn it down."

"Whatever they offer, we can counter." Laz's response caused Zinner to whip his head around so fast that the few hairs he had on top of his head moved out of place.

"That is very encouraging to hear. I thank you for that incredible offer as well. But after a lot of thinking and soul searching, I decided to listen to someone who believed in me and my talent, who appreciated my hard work, and who I now love with all my heart. Me." She smiled so hard her cheeks hurt. "I've been doing a little research. Lots of artists nowadays cut studios out completely and have been putting out their work themselves. I'm going to go that route. I've produced a great album with Truman Woodley." She glanced at her watch. "At this point, it's up for pre-sale on iTunes and all major online retailers. When it goes on sale, all the profits will go to me and that group."

The smile dropped from Mr. Zinner's face as well as the other members of his stooge panel. Every cell in Chantel's body screamed in delight. She'd waited a long time to do something like this, exact revenge on a company that smiled in her face and stabbed her in the back.

"You see, I was amazed to read your quote/unquote new contract with Charisma after my meeting with you, and found that you made absolutely no changes to the terms. You wanted to only pay me exactly what you would have paid my mother two years ago. Times have changed and so have I." She shoved the Universe contract back to Mr. Zinner. "I'm looking forward to finding new artists and growing my business." Fatima would have loved that aspect.

Mr. Zinner twitched up a smile. "I'm happy for you that you could make such a wise business decision. But that contract is just for your production studio. You can still sign an exclusive contract with us. Come on, Shauna. We brought you to the top. We could do it again."

"No. My voice, my talent, and my drive put me at the top. You just rode my back the whole time until I collapsed." She hung her purse on the crook of her arm. "Gentlemen, I'm afraid this is the end of our relationship. I like producing, so I think I'm going to stick with that for a while."

Mr. Zinner stood. "Shauna—"

"It's Chantel." She pointed at him. "Let me give you a little advice. Know what your artists want and accommodate."

With her head held high, she strutted from the office. Once she got into the elevator alone, she screamed and danced around. She felt so free that every part of her body tingled. She'd stood up for herself and it felt good. Now she could start a life with Truman. A real life.

* * * *

After Chantel and Truman struck gold at their *Big Ol' Barn* performance, Chantel couldn't wait to go home. Not only did she perform in front of a roomful of people, but she sang. She sang in public without fear and they liked it. From the applause, she could tell they loved it. Her voice held strong throughout.

At the end of their duet, Truman capped their performance with a sweet kiss.

Gauging from the audience's applause, Truman and Chantel had been and would be accepted as a couple. Maybe she needed to stop being so afraid that Truman would reject the idea of having a relationship with her.

Chantel, Truman, and the band got on the bus after doing a couple of quickie interviews. The sooner they hit the road the happier she would be.

With pre-moistened wipes, she removed the makeup off her face. She so desperately needed a shower. She would have to wait for the bus to get going before trying to get one of those.

Once the bus got moving, Chantel eventually fell asleep thanks to the rocking. It helped that Flye had the softest sheets and a velvet comforter on the bed that made her feel weightless.

She felt a gentle nudging on her shoulder. When she turned over, she expected to see Truman, but she saw Sully and gasped. He sat on the bed, his face hovering over hers. Not knowing what he wanted and careful not to seem too flighty, Chantel smiled and sat up.

"Are we at a rest stop or something?" The undertone of her question really was "What are you doing in this room waking me up?"

"Just a few more miles from it." Sully smiled, but it came off sinister. "I wanted us to talk. Everyone else is sleeping, and really what I wanted to talk about is you so I thought, why not go to the source?"

Chantel moved over to the one side of the bed and curled her knees to her chest.

"I don't know what's going on with my group. I've known all of these guys since before I had pubic hair." He feigned an embarrassed chuckle. "Sorry if I'm a little crude. I always talk that way in front of my boys."

She smiled but her stomach churned from his repulsive behavior.

"But ever since you came into our lives, things have changed. Ervin dresses like some rapper and he's doing *your cousin*."

Chantel had a feeling he wanted to use other words than just your cousin but she nodded in agreement.

"Then Tru, who I thought was just like me, ends up going gaga over you. He's not the same guy I knew just six months ago."

"Is that a bad thing?" She had only known Truman for a couple of months, but she didn't see a drastic change.

"Yeah, when it involves our money." Sully raised his voice, then looked around and lowered it.

"Your money should be fine. Truman should have said something to you guys." She smiled hoping that would ease Sully's demeanor.

Sully nodded and rubbed his hand over his chin. "Oh, yeah. I heard. Way to go with the business decisions. I kind of think that's the reason why Tru kissed you on stage again. Yeah, it was just a big thank you for getting us paid more. And when he said 'you're the greatest' after your duet, he meant that he appreciated you for your hard work. I posted that on our group's Twitter page so that we don't lose fans."

Chantel chewed on her lower lip but kept her stare on Sully. Maybe if he saw her fear, he would ease up. Or maybe she needed to look as ferocious to him as she did when she met with Zinner.

"Maybe you should be having this conversation with Truman. He can tell you exactly what he meant." She tipped to one side when she felt the bus pulling off the main highway. At least Sully hadn't lied about the rest stop.

"No. Maybe what I need to do is to find out what it is you have between your legs that makes men lose their minds." Sully grabbed her ankle and yanked it down.

Adrenaline coursed through her body. Chantel balled her hands into fists as Sully attempted to grab her other ankle.

"So why don't you show me what I've been missing, since I haven't been fucking bitches like Ervin and Truman." Sully jumped on top of Chantel and covered her mouth with his large hand. His body crushed hers as he attempted to undo her jeans. Thank God she'd changed into those instead of leaving her dress on.

Sully grabbed one of her wrists and held it down. When he removed his hand from her mouth, he crushed it with his lips. Chantel drew her lips into her mouth to keep from touching his and turned her head back and forth. She kicked wildly, but stopped when she felt Sully's hand on her breast.

Chantel almost shut down. She felt like she wanted to leave her body and let Sully deal with the shell. The old Chantel would have gone down without a fight, acquiesced to the situation, and dealt with the aftermath later. Not this new woman she had become.

With her free hand, she dug her thumbnail into Sully's eye.

"You bitch!" Sully let her go and covered his injured eye.

Then she rolled him off her and onto the floor. With his legs parted, Chantel kicked him squarely in between them. Even with her bare foot, she managed to do some damage.

She opened the door.

The rest of the band stood outside at the front of the bus. Truman made his way down the aisle toward her, but when he saw Sully on the floor, he ran toward them.

"She's a psycho-bitch, man." Sully coughed. "She attacked me."

"Yeah, after you put your hand up my shirt and tried to rape me." She kicked him in his back for good measure.

"You tried to what?" Truman stood protectively in front of Chantel.

"She's lying. Who are you going to believe? That whore or your best friend?" Sully struggled to stand, but when he did, he looked Truman in the eyes.

Chantel watched Truman bounce his gaze from her to Sully. Then in one motion, Truman picked Sully up by the back of his collar and dragged him to the front of the bus. He threw him off along with all his clothes and his guitar.

"What the hell are you doing, man?" Sully cowered on the ground. "You can't leave me out here in the middle of nowhere. Where's your loyalty?"

"It went out of the window when you tried to hurt the woman I care about." Truman folded his arms over his chest. "I can't believe you would touch her. As much as she has done for this band, and as much crap that you talked about her, you would have the nerve to attack her. You're scum. I don't want to see you again."

Tony, Charlie, and Ervin all stood around Sully.

Ervin crouched down next to Sully. "I wished you would have tried that on Nikia. She would have cut your balls off."

"You mean like she's done to you?" Sully retorted.

Ervin reared his fist back and planted a solid right hook on Sully's jaw, knocking him back down to the ground. Then Ervin got back on the bus. "Are you okay?" he asked Chantel.

She nodded, not really knowing who to trust at this point. If Sully talked about her, he had to have talked to someone. So who agreed with him?

The bus driver asked if he should leave Sully. Everyone on the bus said "yes" in unison. Didn't look like Sully had an ally. If he did, they didn't have his back.

"Did he hurt you?" Craig asked after the bus took off.

"I'll be fine." She wrapped her arms around her body.

When she returned to the main bedroom, Truman followed her, closing the door behind them. He got in bed first and held his arm open to usher her beside him.

She pressed her back against his chest as he draped his arm over her waist and held her close.

After taking a deep breath, Chantel said what she had suspected. "I wouldn't have blamed you if you believed your friend. You've known him longer."

"I know Sully fights dirty, although I've never known him to be disrespectful to women. All I had to do was look into your eyes to know the truth." Truman kissed the side of her face and settled in closer to her. "I won't let anyone hurt you. Ever."

The strong promise sounded great. Could he deliver?

Chapter 25

"You know you can pay people to do this." Chantel rolled on another coat of Williamsburg blue paint in Truman's kitchen of his rental home.

"What, and miss out on doing this." Truman slapped his hand on Chantel's behind. She yelped and twisted her overalls around to see a nice blue handprint on the back of it.

She rolled extra paint on her roller. "Oh, you are going to get it, mister." She chased him around the house with the roller until she had him pinned in a corner.

"Just remember. I only touched your clothes. I didn't hit your skin." With his baseball cap on backward, he looked boyish and mischievous like he had a Plan B up his sleeve.

"I'll remember that." She lunged but he moved to the side and now had her trapped in the corner. He removed her roller from her hand and tossed it on top of a pile of plastic drop coverings.

"There's paint on that roller." She pointed behind him but she, like Truman, honestly didn't care about painting right now. She couldn't keep her hands off him and wanted to bang her head against a wall for not noticing him sooner.

He unsnapped her overalls and let them fall to the floor. Pressing her against the wall, he kissed her like it he had never done it before, like he had never rocked her world. His lips pressed on hers gently, then harder with his tongue sliding in and out of her mouth.

"Tru, we can't here. You don't have any curtains. Your neighbors could walk by and see us." Of course she said this while stepping out of her pants and Keds sneakers. She pulled his T-shirt over his head and worked on his jeans.

"Maybe they'll learn something." He winked.

He positioned some moving quilts on his bare hardwood floors and brought her down on them.

He kissed her again with so much passion she lost her breath. His hand roamed her body, sliding under her T-shirt and massaging her breast, then moving over her stomach. Once he reached her panties, she grabbed his hand.

"We're in your living room underneath this big picture window in the middle of the day for all of your neighbors to see." Although the stuffy statement came from her mouth, her body reacted differently. She wanted this man.

Inside she found it exciting. She loved trying new things with him, and Truman indulged her in any and all of her fantasies. Although she never thought of herself as an exhibitionist, she certainly didn't want to awaken budding voyeurs in the neighborhood.

"I love it when you get all demure and prudish." He winked.

"I'm not a prude. We just can't have sex in front of this window."

"Fine." He moved down and positioned his head between her legs. He slid her panties down.

"What are you doing? I said no sex." She made a half-hearted attempt to grab her panties, but he had them off and tossed to the side.

"According to a former president, what I'm doing doesn't qualify as sex." He spread her legs.

He kissed her inner thighs being sure to avoid her throbbing sex that begged to be licked and relieved. He blew a cool breath on her pleasure center and Chantel trembled. When he licked the length of her, she moaned so loud she hoped none of the neighbors heard her through the open windows.

He continued licking and teasing her, driving her crazy until she came so hard she clawed the floor.

"Please tell me you took your pill." He hovered over her. "I don't think I can find the condoms in any of these boxes."

She nodded and helped him pull off his jeans. Screw the neighbors. She wanted her man.

Truman slid into her and let out a low, guttural moan. When the wave of pleasure hit her, she arched her back. She loved the feeling of being with him. He always looked into her eyes every time they made love. That made her feel special, wanted.

When they both came, he lowered his head next to hers and said in her ear, "See. You're just as adventurous as me. We belong together."

He shed a light on something she'd been pondering for weeks. Would a relationship between them work? After appearing on *The Big Ol' Barn*, critics questioned Truman's country appeal. Chantel would never forgive herself if his career didn't take off because of her.

"Do we? We've been hiding out from the media." She let go of his hand.

"Yeah, because you said they would ruin us. But they're not the problem. The problem is you want to wait for something to magically change. What do you think will change?" He pulled up his jeans while still on the floor; then he stood to fasten them. "You have to learn to fight for what you want, because no one else will fight your battles for you." He peered over his shoulder out of the window and cursed.

"What?" She bolted upright.

"Doesn't your cousin ever call ahead?" He picked up Chantel's overalls and tossed them to her.

"My panties." She pointed to the rumpled pink ball on the floor.

He picked them up, but instead of tossing them to her, he shoved them in his front pocket. "Oh, no. I keep these." He winked at her and went to the front door.

"Tru."

He put his hand on the knob as he looked at her. "You had better hurry. You know how your cousin is. I wouldn't be surprised if she just tried waltzing in—"

The knob jiggled, interrupting him.

"See?" He pointed to it.

Chantel slipped on her overalls and hooked in the suspenders. It felt strange wearing nothing below. She'd never done that before. It'd always been panties or a thong. The more she stared at Truman and noticed him ogling her, the sexier she felt.

"You think you have time to take off your bra and just go with a T-shirt and overalls?"

"Open the door." She folded her arms to illustrate her seriousness.

"Anyone in there?" Nikia pounded on the door.

He opened it and let in the coifed fury known as Nikia Evans.

"Since when do you guys lock the door?" She stepped around paint cans and rollers.

"Since a certain person, who we love dearly, can't seem to remember to call before she comes by or at least knock on the door before coming in." He stood behind Chantel, pressing her backside against his crotch.

"It's a good thing I like you." Nikia wagged her manicured nail at him.

"No, you like Ervin. He's your baby." Chantel smiled.

"Speaking of baby, that's the reason I'm here." Nikia reached into her designer purse.

"The story isn't true, Nik." Chantel shook her head. "I'm not pregnant and I haven't put on weight."

Truman grabbed a handful of her ass. "I don't know, honey. You're getting a lot of junk back here in your trunk."

Chantel playfully slapped his arm and removed his hand from her bottom.

"Here." Nikia shoved an official looking document at Truman. "This came to the house for you."

He took the document and gasped. Chantel broke from his hold and stared at him.

"What is it, baby?" she asked.

"This is for arbitration about Gage. I'm supposed to be in Tennessee to meet with Ashley in two days. When did this come?" His gaze never left the paper but with each flip of the pages, Chantel felt his anxiousness.

"About a week ago." Nikia looked around the empty house. "Y'all need some furniture."

"You got this a week ago and didn't tell me?" He ran his hand over his head.

The redder his face got the more Chantel felt his rising anger. Her heart pounded against the wall of her chest. How could Nikia be so careless? Gage meant everything to Truman. Now the child meant so much to Chantel.

"It'll be okay." Chantel patted his back. "I'll make the travel arrangements. You pack. I'm sure Delores won't mind watching Gage."

Truman paced the floor. "No. He should come with me."

"Us. I'm not letting you go alone."

"Maybe Gage should stay here." He spoke as though he hadn't heard a word she'd said. "If I know Ashley, she'll try to be sneaky."

"We won't let her. At least she's going through arbitration first. She must have changed just a little bit." Chantel needed to calm Truman down a bit. Cooler heads would prevail.

Truman snorted. "You've seen her."

Nikia sucked on her teeth and sauntered back to the door. "I'll leave you two to your drama. I've got things to do. Mainly Vin." She flittered her well-arched eyebrows and left the house in the same grand fanfare that she had when she entered.

"I didn't think she would go through with this." Truman lowered his voice to a mumble. "Things were going so well. He's doing better with me. Gage is happy, right?"

Chantel wrapped her arms around him, hoping that would calm him down. The way his heart raced, he needed more than a hug.

"Let's get cleaned up here." She started picking up paint rollers. "You're keeping your son."

By hook or by crook, she would make sure of that. She'd experienced separation from a parent. She did not want Gage taken away from the one good parent he had.

* * * *

Truman's leg bounced as he sat at the table in the stifling office. Summer in Tennessee tested Truman's resolve. His nervous sweat cooled from the forced air from the air conditioner. He hadn't eaten a thing and yet his stomach twisted in knots.

Until he felt Chantel's hand on his, that's when Truman stopped bouncing his leg. He looked at her and her sweet smile made his heart slow to its normal beat. He didn't know how she did it but she always made him feel incredible.

Tired of waiting for the right moment, he had planned on declaring his love for her and asking her to marry him. Now he wondered if she wanted so much drama in her life.

"Where are they?" He looked at his watch for the twentieth time.

"We're early. They'll be here." She patted his hand.

As though summoned by her, Ashley entered the room with a tall, thin man. Truman stood, being a good Southerner, as Ashley walked over to a chair across from him.

He couldn't stop staring at her. She had dyed her normally yellow straw hair with black roots to a chocolate brown shade, and had it cut in a bob. Only lip gloss adorned her lips. Her conservative flowered dress looked like it came from a *Little House on the Prairie* catalog. Who was this woman and where was she hiding the mess who left their son alone in a dirty trailer?

"I'm Corbin Bowery, your arbitrator." The man with strawberry blond hair parted on the side with round wire-rimmed glasses shook Truman's hand, then Chantel's.

"Hi, Tru." Without its normal shrill, Ashley's voice didn't sound at all like her.

Truman nodded, too surprised to see Ashley cleaned up like this.

"Please have a seat," Corbin instructed. After they all sat, the arbitrator began. "This is a step taken to prevent going to court. The expectation is that when we leave here, we'll come up with an agreeable arrangement for Gage."

"That's all I want." Truman nodded. "I want the best for my son."

"*Our* son," Ashley corrected. She clasped her hands together and placed them on the table. Probably to keep from scratching his eyes out.

Corbin stared at Chantel. "Are you married to Mr. Woodley?"

Chantel glanced at Truman. "Um, no."

Truman held her hand. "She's important to me, and I want her here."

Corbin turned to Ashley. "Do you mind her presence here? You have the right to say you do not want her to be present."

Ashley stared at Chantel for a long, uncomfortable moment before she answered. "No, I don't mind her being here. She might have something valuable to add to the discussion."

Truman knew the underlying meaning to her statement. Ashley probably thought she could get some of Chantel's money. He knew this hotheaded woman. She hadn't changed since he'd known her seven years ago. With a new hair color and style, he didn't believe she'd made some miraculous transformation.

"I think we should get started." Corbin arranged his papers. He started asking standard questions that involved revealing their full names, dates of birth, places of residence, and medical histories.

Truman felt confident about his answers until Ashley decided to speak.

"So you finally have a place of your own?" Ashley drummed her fingernails on the table, a habit she knew annoyed him. "Last I heard you and Gage were living with some family."

Truman stared at Ashley. "It was a friend of mine. Her manager, as a matter of fact." He pointed to Chantel. "Sorry I didn't happen to have family in Virginia to move in with like you did with your mother here in Tennessee or when you visited your grandmother in North Carolina."

"I understand." Ashley nodded and forced a smile. "Maybe if you didn't kidnap your son like a thief in the night while I was away, you wouldn't have lost your job and gotten kicked out of the place you were staying."

Truman had never told Ashley about his living arrangements. Maybe she figured it out when she called to find him and couldn't reach him.

"Please." Corbin held up his hands. "Let's keep focused."

"Yeah, let's not talk about past actions like child neglect or drug use." Truman leaned forward but Ashley stayed still.

"I went two trailers down to—"

Truman cut her off. "Borrow some sugar?"

"And I don't do drugs." She gritted her teeth, flexing the muscles in her jaw. The old Ashley started to rear her ugly head. He could see her seething.

"You had drugs in your room," Chantel said, cutting through the tension.

"Ms. Evans, did you see the drugs?" Corbin poised his pen over his paper.

Chantel furrowed her eyebrows and looked to Truman. "No. Truman told me he saw pot and crack in the bedroom."

"How did he know what types of drugs they were?" The arbitrator volleyed his attention from Truman to Chantel.

Truman directed his attention to Corbin. "I'm in the music industry, buddy. I've seen it all."

"And how did you know it was Ashley's room?"

Truman paused before he answered. "My son told me that's where they slept. I didn't know for sure. I would hope it didn't belong to her grandmother." He glared at Ashley. "Maybe her grandmama has glaucoma."

Ashley sneered at him.

"Besides, it was in plain view and Gage could have gotten to it." Truman punctuated each word by tapping the table with his middle finger.

Ashley took a deep breath and on the exhale she gave a very clear and calm statement. "I realize what an unhealthy environment I had my son in. So I was making plans to go back to Tennessee when Mr. Woodley kidnapped Gage."

"Stop saying I kidnapped my son. We agreed to share joint custody." Truman felt steam coming from under his collar. He wanted so much to undo the top few buttons of his shirt and take off his ugly tie. No way would he lower himself, not while Ashley presented herself like a victim.

Ashley snickered. "Funny how joint custody to you means taking Gage when it's convenient for you and your career. What about me?" Ashley pouted.

Truman had enough of her act. The fire that swirled around his body couldn't be extinguished by being polite and kind.

"What about you? You don't work. I sent you money every week only to find that Gage's clothes are a size too small for him and he weighed as much now as he did at three. Meanwhile, I'm busting my butt."

"Mr. Woodley." Corbin tried to stop Truman's rant.

Truman continued. "I'm the one who worked a job in the daytime and recorded all night long so that you could have money for Gage."

Chantel put her hand on top of Truman's. He glanced at her and found compassion in her eyes that made him stammer.

"And when you lost your day job, you took Gage. So how were you able to provide for him to feed and clothe him?" Ashley cocked her head.

"Please, let me ask the questions." Corbin directed his attention to Ashley.

"Truman and his group had two very high profile TV appearances." Chantel tried to be the calming voice of reason in this volatile atmosphere. "One on the Breakout Music Awards and the other at *The Big Ol' Barn*. Although they weren't paid jobs, the exposure caused the pre-sales for his upcoming album to jump tremendously, which will result in a larger residual payment. He'll be able to go wherever he wants."

He squeezed her hand and opened his mouth to speak when

Ashley cut him off.

"Yeah, you two looked nice on TV." Ashley nodded her head. "I heard some reporter call the two of you Truly Stellar. I find y'all truly disgusting. I hope you aren't kissing and more in front of Gage."

"Yeah, God forbid he sees an example of a loving relationship." Truman answered her with a sneer.

"That brings me to my next point." Corbin raised his voice. He nearly had to scream to be heard over Truman and Ashley. "What is your relationship to Mr. Woodley?"

Chantel looked at Truman, then Ashley, and finally to Corbin. "What do you mean?"

Even Truman wanted to hear what she had to say. What did she think of the two of them? Did she love him?

"Are you two a couple or is it strictly business? How romantic is your relationship?" Corbin elaborated. When he saw Chantel stare at him, he quickly said, "Everything revealed here will be kept in the strictest of confidence."

"Yes, by *you*." Chantel glared at Ashley. "But not everyone values privacy. Point blank, I think Ashley will try to sell our story to any magazine offering the highest price. I find it amazing that weeks after Truman has his son and after both of his TV appearances, Ashley hadn't bothered to contact her child or seek legal assistance. Perhaps she thought she could cash in on his sudden popularity. I've seen people like you come and go. You would be poison to that child."

"Excuse me." Ashley braced her hands on the table, showing off her fingernails bitten down to the quick. "Let's talk about you, Ms. Thing."

"Yes." Corbin held his hands up to both women. "My main concern and the basis for my previous question was out of interest for how much exposure the child will have to you."

Chantel broke her glowering stare from Ashley to Corbin. "Exposure to me? What do you mean?"

The arbitrator shuffled through some papers and pulled up one. "You have been hospitalized for several months in a mental institution."

Truman held Chantel's hand tighter. He knew the reason for her break. She wasn't crazy, only stressed. He had no right or plans to share her personal story. If she wanted to tell it, she could.

Corbin continued. "You attacked a band member on a tour bus recently. An officer stopped you during a drug sting at a North Carolina motel." Corbin took off his glasses and rubbed his eyes. "Mr. Woodley, you said that you worried about drug exposure with Ashley, but quite frankly, I think you need to worry about him being around Ms. Evans."

Truman slammed his hand against the table. "Those are all lies. The media twisted all those situations around to make her look crazy and dangerous. She's not."

"So you're saying none of these things happened?" Corbin pressed.

Ashley folded her arms and leaned back triumphantly.

"They did, but not in the ways you're thinking." Truman glanced at Chantel but she had her head down. She looked defeated and this fight really had nothing to do with her. He had to save her.

"I trust this woman completely with my son. He adores her. Why should I worry about Chantel with Gage? I would worry more if he were with Ashley. She damn near said that my son was her meal ticket." He pointed to the woman who had changed for the worst over the past few years.

"That's a damn lie," Ashley snapped.

"Maybe we should come up with a plan for Gage." Frustration filled Corbin's voice.

"Fine. I want full custody." Truman had no plans to compromise with this opportunist. Attacking Chantel showed him how low she would go. He didn't want his son to be with someone this cruel.

"You're not taking my son." Ashley shook her head so that her nicely coiffed bob came undone into something wild.

"I can care for him a lot better than you can."

"So could I if I had support."

Truman laughed. "So that's what this is all about. Money. As long as you have Gage, you think you're going to suck me dry. Understand this, missy. We were never married and we never lived together, so you're not getting any spousal support from me. And you know if I have Gage, I don't have to pay you a dime. Tell you what. I'll keep him all year and you can get him on major holidays like Easter and Martin Luther King, Jr. Day."

Ashley glared at Chantel. "Gee, wonder why you picked that day."

"Perhaps this would be a good time for a break." Corbin's pale skin now had a rosy hue to it. "We'll take about five minutes. But there are some things you should consider during the break, Mr. Woodley. If you two aren't able to come to an agreement, this matter will be turned over to the courts."

"Fine. I'm willing to fight for Gage." Truman pulled his tie down and undid the top two buttons. Time to get real.

"If that's the case, the things I brought up today will be brought up in court. The drug bust, the drug exposure in your business, and your association with Ms. Evans."

"So what does all that mean? Truth is on my side." Truman undid his cuffs under his jacket.

"Sympathy might not be. Courts tend to keep the children with their mothers. You could run the risk of getting partial visitation, supervised visitation or—" Corbin paused and swallowed.

"Or what?" Truman asked.

"You'll lose custody."

Truman split his attention between Corbin and a smug-looking Ashley. He ground his teeth so hard his head pounded in rhythm with his heartbeat. As a way to vent part of his frustration, he squeezed his hands into fists.

Before Truman could give Ashley the tongue-lashing she deserved, Chantel spoke up. "We should take that break and cool off."

Ashley stood and sashayed from the room. Corbin remained seated when Chantel bolted from the table, grabbing her purse and running for the door. Truman went after her and attempted to catch her hand but she flailed her arm away from his grasp.

He finally caught up with her when she got to the stairs. "What's wrong? Don't you worry about Ashley. She's got a bigger bark than her bite."

"It's not her I'm worried about." Chantel kept her gaze from Truman but he saw tears in her eyes before she turned away. "The arbitrator is right. The longer I'm involved with you and Gage, the worse your chances are of getting even partial custody of your son. I could never live with myself if that happened."

"It won't happen." He put his hand to her chin to turn her face to his but she jerked away.

"You don't know that. Just like you don't know that being with me will affect your album sales. If your album flops, you'll have no money. If you have no money, you won't get Gage. So I'm just bad for your career and your personal life."

"How can you say that? If it wasn't for you I wouldn't be where I am today." He stroked her cheek.

She allowed that touch and sighed, which melted his heart.

"I've checked out your pre-sales so far." She finally looked at Truman. Her wide eyes were red. "Although you have had a couple of big bumps in sales, the projected sales of your new album don't look good. It's because of me. Your country fans don't think you're country enough because of me. Pop fans don't know you yet. You were right from the beginning."

Truman's gut wrenched with her words. He wished he hadn't said that her affiliation on his record would be the death of him. Although he thought news like that would have crushed him, he didn't care. He cared about it enough for his remaining bandmates, his friends. Personally, he didn't care. If it meant Chantel would be out of his life, he would rather have the album tank.

"I have to tell you something. I lied to you."

Chantel blinked at his admission.

"After the first time we were together, you asked me if I wanted to keep things light and not worry about a commitment. I told you that was fine." He shook his head. "That was a lie. I want you in my life always, not just as a producer. I was pigheaded. I love you." He didn't say it as a desperation move. He meant it.

"I love you, too." Chantel spoke so softly he barely heard her.

To hear her say she loved him made him feel lightheaded. How could she possibly leave him now?

She wiped her nose with the back of her hand. "It's because I love you that I'm leaving. You are so incredibly talented. And you are a wonderful father. Trust me. With your celebrity, you can win any custody case. But I'm just an albatross around your neck."

"Don't say that." He attempted to hug her but she wriggled from his grip.

"You were right about me. When we first met, you said that I was selfish. I don't want to be that person anymore." She hugged her purse to her chest. "Since we're confessing, I lied, too. I said I wanted us to keep it fun because I didn't think you would want a serious relationship right now." She put her hand to her chest. "I was trying to protect myself because I thought you would be off doing your thing once the album was done."

"I'm still here."

Chantel kept talking as though Truman hadn't spoken. "I care about you and Gage enough not to stand in your way. If I am the reason you could possibly lose custody of your son, I wouldn't be able to live with myself."

"Damn it, Chantel. Fight. Please. Don't do this."

Looking over Truman's shoulder, Chantel's eyes widened as she made her way past him. With a confident step, she headed to Corbin. "As Truman's business partner, only for his current album, I came here to support him." She looked back at Truman who had followed her closely. "But there's no involvement between us. He'll be raising his son alone."

"Is that true, Mr. Woodley?" Corbin asked.

He shook his head. "No. She's trying to protect me."

"No, I'm not." She backed away from the men. "I'm looking out for a child who needs the best parent he can get. Gage should be with his father. And I shouldn't be here."

Truman went after her until he heard Ashley's shrill voice.

"Are we going to finish this or not? I would hate to tell the court judge that you ran from the arbitration meeting without coming to an agreement because you're too stubborn to work things out."

Truman needed to work things out with Chantel. The sacrifice she made wasn't her decision. They could have talked about it. Knowing her, he probably wouldn't have convinced her to change her mind. Truman knew how she felt about children being with their parents. So she sacrificed her happiness to make sure Truman was happy, and she was the crazy one? Not hardly.

Chapter 26

Craig knocked on Chantel's door and walked into the room. "All packed up?"

Chantel hoisted the box up into her arms. "This is it."

Craig tried taking the box from her, but she insisted on handling her own property. She wished she'd learned that lesson years ago. It took her ten years, an album she didn't want to be involved with initially, and a lot of self-reflection for her to get to this point in her life. She took the time to stare at the man who probably knew her as well as her cousins. He'd given her the support she needed at the time. Now she had to learn to take care of herself.

As Chantel walked down the stairs, Craig followed her. She had to choose her next words to him carefully, although she had been thinking about how to do this since they talked about her doing *The Big Ol' Barn* in Tennessee. Thinking about that show brought up bad memories of Sully and wonderful thoughts about Truman. After a week of not seeing him and avoiding his calls, her body hurt. She took a deep breath to keep from crying about him again.

"You know I never really had a problem with you staying here. It was you *and* Truman that bothered me." Craig's booming voice shook the stairs.

Chantel slammed the box on the floor as soon as she reached the main level. "If Truman isn't welcomed in your home, then neither am I."

"Wait. I didn't say that." Craig held up his hands to her.

"Which brings up another topic I wanted to discuss with you." She turned to Craig. She had to do this now while her stomach knotted up and her hands shook. "You're fired."

She had never let anyone go before in her camp. If someone didn't pull their weight, Craig became the hatchet man. Although she didn't like disappointing people, she did love the feeling of taking control of her life finally.

Her manager's face dropped for a moment before he perked it back up and laughed. "Very funny, Shauna. Stop playing. We have to get started on your new album and tour soon."

"I'm not joking. And my name is Chantel. The fact that you refuse to call me that is another reason why I'm letting you go." She held his hand because she knew her next statements would hurt him no matter how delicately she said them. "You have been like a father to me. You have supported me and helped me get through some tough times. But I need to start doing things on my own. I need to start respecting myself as an artist, which means I need to make demands when I need rest. I need to speak up if I'm not feeling up to performing. I'm not a windup doll. I'm a human being. I can't assert myself with a man who still regards me as that same fifteen-year-old girl that he signed over ten years ago. I'm a woman. Despite my past mistakes, I am a smart woman. I will continue to be a success. And I owe every bit of that success to you and Delores. But I've made my decision and I have a meeting with a potential new manager tomorrow."

Craig snickered like he didn't believe her or this moment. "Where does that leave me? I gave up clients for you."

"You will be fine. Trust me." She kissed his cheek. "As far as where this leaves us? I'm hoping we can still be friends. I'll always come to you for the fatherly advice that I need sometimes. I hope you see me as the daughter you never had."

With that statement, a fat tear rolled from Craig's eye. "Was I that horrible to you?"

Chantel had never seen this type of emotion from Craig. He had always been that hard-nosed businessman who barked orders and made other people cry. She wept this time as she hugged the man. "Never. This is just something I need to do on my own. Although I don't need your support, I would love to have it."

Craig pulled back from her, tears still streaming from his eyes, and he framed her face in his large hands. "Always." He kissed the tip of her nose.

"Good." She broke from the embrace.

As Chantel started to bend over to pick up her box, Craig intercepted her. "I would do this for my daughter, not a client." He smiled.

Chantel breathed in relief knowing that she had Craig's support. If only her personal life could be this smooth.

* * * *

Truman endured the worst couple of weeks of his life without Chantel. Dealing with Ashley's custody battle wore him out. Since they could not come to an agreement during their arbitration meeting, they ended up in court.

He waited outside of the courtroom with his attorney by his side. His thoughts danced between his son and Chantel, two of the most important people in his life.

Although Chantel had refused to see or talk to him since arbitration, it didn't mean his heart didn't still ache for her. Calls to her went unanswered. She went unseen when he made trips to Craig's house until finally Delores told him that Chantel had moved and she could not give her new address to him. Truman felt lost without her.

Heavy footfalls on the hardwood floors snagged his attention. He turned to see Ashley with her attorney coming toward him.

"Excuse me." Truman stood and stormed toward Ashley. "Can I talk to you for a second?" He grabbed her arm and pulled her toward a quieter area in the hallway.

"Hey, get off me. Don't make me press assault charges on you." Ashley wriggled her arm from his grasp and folded her arms over her chest. "So what do you want to talk about?"

Truman thought about his words carefully. He wanted to say the right things so as not to anger her any further. The more he thought, the more he realized that he needed to speak from the heart. Chantel would have told him to do that.

"I love Chantel." He stared at Ashley in her eyes.

She rolled her eyes and attempted to move past him. "I can't believe you pulled me aside for that little announcement."

"Wait. I love her and I love Gage. I love them more than I love my music, more than anything in the world. I don't know what you think you're getting out of this. If you want money, I'll give you every dime I have and every dime I'll make if you just let me have my son."

"He's my son, too. You seem to forget that until it's convenient for you."

Truman didn't want to argue with her. He had to hear her out. "You're right."

Ashley stumbled back like she hadn't expected Truman to respond that way.

While he had her attention, Truman continued. "I don't think I considered your feelings in all of this. At one time, we were together romantically. We talked about building a life together once you found out you were pregnant. Be honest with me. If you weren't pregnant, would you have still wanted to be with me?"

"Come on, Tru." She turned away from him.

"Tell the truth."

She stared at him for a moment before saying, "No." She shrugged. "So we didn't love each other. That doesn't take away from the fact that we made a child together."

"Yes, we did. And we need to be the best for our boy. He deserves that." Truman held on to Ashley's shoulders and stared into her eyes.

Her bloodshot eyes had blown out dilated pupils. His first instinct screamed for him to admonish her for her appearance. Truman had changed. He had to for his son and for Chantel's sakes.

"You have a problem."

Ashley opened her mouth to refute his assessment.

He barreled on. "If you push this, I will insist that you be drug tested regularly. I don't want to do that."

Tears streamed down Ashley's face. "Why? Wouldn't that just make you happy to see me suffer?"

He shook his head. "Gage has a mother. She needs to be just as healthy as our son."

"If you make them test me, then I'll—I'll—I'll push for—"

Truman held up his hand. "I'm not trying to be mean or cruel. I'm protecting our son." He leaned in close to her. "Let me help you. I can put you into a private facility. No one will have to know. And we can work out an equitable custody agreement."

Ashley considered his proposal for a moment and shook her head. "No, you're trying to trick me. You just want to go back to Shauna Stellar, and you want to put me away in jail or something."

"You're right. I do want to be with Chantel. But I have no interest in hurting you. I want you to get the help you need." He hugged her. "Please let me help you for our son's sake."

When Ashley cried, it broke his heart. He held her tighter. "You're going to be okay. We'll be okay."

"Mr. Woodley."

Truman turned around and saw his attorney behind him.

"Are you ready?"

Truman broke from the embrace long enough to look into Ashley's eyes. "Are you ready to go?"

Ashley wiped her face and nodded. "I know what we need to do."

The fact that she said "we" calmed Truman. She saw them as a united front. He had hoped his words affected her to do the right thing.

He wrapped his arm around Ashley. "We're ready."

Once he got through this crisis, he had another hurdle to overcome. He had to get Chantel back. How to do that, he would have to figure it out.

Chapter 27

When Chantel looked at the mass of people in the MTV green room, her gaze met with Flye's, who made his way through the crowd to get to his cousin.

"You nervous, shorty?" He gripped her shoulders.

"Why do people keep asking me that? Do I look nervous?" The irritation couldn't be kept from her voice.

Chantel hadn't gotten sick because of nerves in a while. She stopped letting so many things bother her.

"Just a question, cuz. Didn't mean to get your chest all puffed out." Flye straightened the huge rings on his fingers. "You talk to your boy?"

"If you mean Truman, he's not my boy, and no, I haven't talked to him in a while."

"Shame. Brother was talented. I can play 'Heart And Soul' on the piano now, which is better than nothing."

"So he still gives you lessons?" Chantel asked, curious as to why Truman would still offer to teach Flye to play.

"He's a man of his word. He can roll with my posse any time he wants. And since he doesn't have a shorty in his life right now, I can hook him up with all kinds of fly honeys."

"Why don't you let him concentrate on promoting his album rather than pimping out your trashy leftovers?" Chantel couldn't stop the jealousy and bitterness that filled her voice.

"Dice owes me a C-note." Flye laughed. "I bet him that you were still hung up on Tru and would be pissed off if I offered to hook him up."

"I wasn't pissed off. I'm just looking out for Truman's career." Chantel tried making that sound convincing but even she didn't buy her story.

The stagehand called for Chantel to go out into the main studio. He handed her a microphone after he tested it for sound, then pointed her down a hallway. At the end of the hallway, the screams from the young fans got louder and louder until the sound filled the space.

A part of Chantel missed fan opportunities like this. When she recorded again, she would do more of these fan shows. She wouldn't have Truman but she would have her music. What a great bedfellow.

"...formally Shauna Stellar," the host began, "she now goes by Chantel Evans. Give it up for the Princess of Love Ballads."

Chantel let out a long haggard breath, smiled, and strutted her stuff into the studio. She gave high fives to the fans that lined the corridor.

"We love you, Shauna!" the fans screamed.

It would take them a while to get used to her new name, but at least they loved and missed her.

When she made it to the center stage, Chantel stood next to the host, a young man with long dreads that hung down in a ponytail in back and incredibly straight, white teeth.

The host did some playful banter, but with the crowd screaming she could barely hear him speak let alone what he had to say.

"So I hear you've gotten into the producing arena. Tell me about that." The host feigned interest by looking in her direction, but Chantel knew he kept his attention on the teleprompter behind her.

Chantel plastered a smile on her overly made up face. "It's a country album actually."

"Yeah, I heard that. Truman Woodley, right? I've heard nothing but good things about him. Except for the fact that they did a Destiny's Child move and kicked out a member right at the beginning."

Chantel kept smiling and hoped the young host didn't have the actual reason why Sully had been cut from the group. Mentioning it on live TV wouldn't do for her career, Truman's career, or her sanity.

"We have some reviews."

Oh, no. Keep smiling. If they're bad, just laugh it off as stuffy reporters with no talent.

"'The next big thing in music, not just country music.' That's from *Rolling Stone. People* magazine said that listeners have been waiting for a group like this for years. You must be very proud of them. Those are some hot reviews."

Inside Chantel jumped and screamed. Critics liked him and that usually meant awards. Now if she could only get the fans to fall in love with him...like she had.

"Why don't we go to break by showing one of Chantel's most famous videos to her song 'Love Me, Love Me, Love Me'?"

The audience went bananas as soon as the video started. Once off camera, the host told Chantel what a big fan he was of hers, then barreled through about getting Flye and Nikia on quick because the fans had been dying to see them.

"And I'm sorry about the situation with Raheem," the easygoing host said.

She couldn't believe people still talked about their breakup like it still mattered. She started to say something, but the host kept talking.

"What he called you backstage at the Breakout Music Awards was horrible." He shook his head. "I hope you take comfort in the fact that Raheem's sales have dropped hard and fast. People are having CD burning parties. If you didn't know it before, I hope you know now that you're back."

She hadn't known it. But it relieved her to hear that she was still loved and cared for by the fans, and that her threatening words to Raheem actually came true. He felt the sting of harming her. Good. Let him go away for a while and get his life back in order.

Back from break, the host asked Chantel a couple more questions, then quickly introduced Flye, Nikia, and the Skillz Squad.

In their normal loud, rowdy selves, the mass of them jumped, screamed, and took over the set as they ran around the room. Nikia sauntered her way to the center of the studio with Chantel and the host.

After a while, Flye settled down and talked to the host.

"What's up?" Flye gave the host a pound.

"New album dropped. How you feeling?" the host asked.

"Good. It's a tight joint that I think the fans'll like. As a matter of fact, y'all have the album. Play a little of each song." As usual, Flye held his arms out wide.

The fans screamed even louder.

Chantel smiled but with all the screaming her head started to hurt. She wanted to get into her limo and go back to the hotel where she could get some sleep before going back home.

Each of Flye's songs contained loud, offensive, and rude lyrics, but with a tight beat. When they got to his last song, Chantel recognized the melody. The guitar riffs, unusual in rap unless the song came from the Beastie Boys, sounded familiar. Until Flye rapped, Chantel recognized the country version of "Reeling."

Chantel looked at Flye who only winked at her.

"That's an unusual joint. What made you do that one?" the host asked.

"Yeah. What made you do that one?" Chantel followed.

"The song is written by a cat y'all were just talking about, Truman

Woodley. Brother is deep. And I heard him recording this and I told him I could do a phat remix. He played the guitar and wrote the words. But for you diehard country fans, y'all can hear this on Truman's album. It's coming out the same day as mine. Check 'em both out."

Chantel wanted to cry. How generous of Flye to not only put Truman's song on his album, guaranteeing that Truman will get paid out the ass when Flye's album goes diamond, but he gave Truman his props for being an artist and a good one at that.

"We have a special guest from Tennessee on the phone," the host said.

Chantel had been a part of these things before. Fans call in so that they could gush all over Flye and his crew.

Flye gobbled the scenery no matter where he went. This special guest had to be for him.

"Hi," a tiny voice said. The voice sounded young, way too young to be on a video show like this, maybe a teenage girl.

"Hey," the host said into his mic. "You want to talk to Flye?"

"No."

"Nikia?"

The caller giggled. "No."

Chantel furrowed her eyebrows together. Usually fans didn't play hard to get.

"Who are you a fan of?" the host asked.

"Chantel."

The voice sounded kind of familiar.

"Oh. Flye, you and your boys step aside and let the lady through." The host took Chantel's hand and pulled her forward. "Ask your fan a question."

Chantel felt silly playing this game. But if it got her back to her hotel, she would do it. "How long have you been a fan?"

"Not long."

Chantel raised her eyebrows. She hadn't released anything new except for the duet with Truman. Maybe this fan liked her old stuff.

"What's your favorite song?" she asked.

"'You Are My Sunshine.' Will you sing it with me again, Chantel?"

Chantel nearly dropped the microphone when it hit her that she had been speaking to Gage, and that he had to have been there with Truman.

Truman came out from the back. He looked good. Too good in his white T-shirt, great fitting jeans, boots, and an Atlanta Braves baseball cap. Gage ran next to his father. As soon as he saw Chantel, he sprinted and jumped into her arms.

"Ladies and gentlemen, Truman Woodley. The man we've been talking about," the host said and pointed to Truman.

Chantel held Gage so tight she thought she might hurt him. The little boy hugged her back.

"I missed you, Chantel," he said.

"I missed you too, buddy." Chantel placed the child down.

"Daddy misses you too, but he didn't want to tell you." Gage laughed as he held her hand.

Truman's face remained stoic as he approached Chantel.

She swallowed, not knowing what thoughts went through Truman's mind. Would he be upset that she left him or understanding? Did he still love her?

Truman stopped in front of Chantel who had her hand on Gage's shoulder.

God, please don't embarrass me in front of millions of viewers.

"Is this your first trip to the Big Apple?" the host asked.

Truman didn't answer. Keeping a steady stare on Chantel, he handed the host his microphone, framed Chantel's face with his hands, and kissed her so passionately that Chantel thought the screams from the fans would shatter the windows.

Chantel, not worried one bit about what anyone thought, kissed him back. She closed her eyes and tried hard not to cry in the middle of it.

"Hey, hey, hey. Break it up. This is a family show," Flye said jokingly.

Truman pulled back and smiled. "I know why you left. I love you even more for why you did it. And I want to punch Raheem's heart out for what he put you through."

"You and me both, brotha," Flye chimed in.

Truman continued. "But I can't live without you. I have to have you in my life."

"We were supposed to go to commercial but keep those cameras rolling," the host said.

Truman said, "I don't care if I don't sell one album."

Chantel smoothed her hand over his son's hair. "But Gage—"

Truman shook his head. "Ashley and I made an agreement. I'll have primary custody."

"Aren't you scared of threats?" Chantel asked.

"Anybody threaten my boy and they're going to have to go through me." Flye pounded his chest.

"And me." Nikia stepped forward.

"And me." Gage jumped up and down.

The host pressed his earpiece in, nodded, and smiled. "Looks like preliminary numbers are in on projected record sales. Flye, looks like your album is going number one with a million copies to be sold in its first week." He turned to Truman. "Truman, your album will probably be second or third on the charts with a respectable two hundred fifty thousand copies sold. That's tight for an effort you put out yourself without a major studio backing it."

"In a week?" Truman asked.

The host nodded. "And this is the pop charts."

"I'm sorry, honey," Chantel said. "I know you wanted to make it big in country."

"No, you don't get it. I wanted people to hear my music. And more importantly, I wanted you back in my life." Truman surprised not only Chantel but also the studio audience when he got down on one knee.

"Oh my God. We have a moment in TV history in the making here!" the host screamed.

"I love you, Chantel. I know I'm just a son of a honey farmer and you're the Princess of Love Ballads, but I swear I can make you happy. I'm asking you in front of the whole world and I don't care who sees it or what they think. Will you marry me?"

Too overcome to talk, Chantel simply nodded.

"I'll take that as a yes." Truman stood and lifted Chantel into his arms. "I thought for sure you would have gotten sick."

"I'll save all that nausea for when I get pregnant." She kissed Truman. "I love you. I love you. I love you."

Chantel couldn't stop saying it. Luckily with Truman, he would let her say it as much as she wanted.

Epilogue

Two years later

Truman rushed through the backstage area to get to the dressing room. He didn't even have time to take his guitar off when a stagehand informed him that Chantel had locked herself in her bathroom.

He burst through the door and saw Ashley and her husband sitting on the couch, playing with Gage.

"She in there?" Truman pointed to the bathroom door.

Ashley had a strange smile she tried hiding as she nodded, an unusual reaction considering the circumstance. Her husband, Dale, didn't even look up when Truman entered the room. Their families had been getting along great lately. He couldn't imagine Ashley going back to her old ways.

Truman would have to address that later. He stood outside the door. Before he knocked, he heard a sound he hadn't heard in over two years, the sound of Chantel vomiting in the toilet. He heard her heaving and the loud splash moments later.

"Honey? Open the door." Truman knocked and waited.

After a beat, he heard a flush before the door opened. Chantel stood on the other side. Rings lined the underside of her eyes. She poured a capful of mouthwash between her lips and puffed her cheeks out as she swished the minty liquid around.

As soon as she spat it out, Truman crowded her space in the bathroom and closed the door behind himself. "I know you haven't performed on stage since *The Big Ol' Barn*." He held her hands. "You'll do great."

Chantel smiled and nodded. "I know. You're with me." She took a deep breath. "And I love singing our songs."

After their song "Meet Me Halfway" hit bigger than Chantel's "Love

Me, Love Me, Love Me" song, she always wanted to write with him, which suited him just fine. Chantel fueled him creatively until he couldn't wait to sit down with her to bang out a tune.

To see her look so tired and pale, she didn't look ready to go back to the main stage. "I know I'm the first one to say that you should fight for what you want, but, baby, for this time, you don't have to." He nodded toward the stage area. "The Sliders and I can sing our songs and still put on a good show."

Chantel smiled. "I'm not afraid to perform. I want to sing." She nodded. "Tonight, I really want to sing."

Truman felt his eyebrows knit together. "Okay, so if you're not worried about performing, what's the problem?" He looked over his shoulder to make sure he had closed the door. Then he lowered his voice. "Is it about the baby?"

Chantel stilled.

He held up his hand. "Look. I know you and I have talked about wanting to try and start a family soon. We don't have to right now. We've been married for less than a year. Just because Ervin and Nikia have a baby, doesn't mean we have to rush." He moved in closer to her. "You don't feel the pressure to get pregnant right now, do you? Is it me?"

A knock sounded on the door. "Are you two, ready? It's show time." The same stagehand spoke through the door.

"Let's go perform." She stood on her tiptoes to kiss him.

In her gold glittery dress, she looked like the top prize of a contest. When she opened the door, Gage jumped from the couch and hugged her.

"You are so pretty." He pressed his face into her stomach.

"Thank you, sweetie." She crouched down. "You be good to your mama and Mr. Dale." She looked at the large, flat-screen TV on the wall. "You can watch us perform."

He nodded and kissed her cheek. "Love you."

Chantel hugged him. "Love you, Gagey Bear."

He leaned over and whispered something in her ear. Two years later, and Truman's son still had a crush on Chantel. He couldn't help but smile at the scene.

Whatever Gage told her, she nodded and gave him a wink. Then she slipped her shoes on, took Truman's hand, and walked with him to the stage.

"Are you sure you can do this?" He didn't want her feeling pressured to perform.

The last time that happened, she fainted off the stage. He would have to watch her just in case.

"I feel fine." She leaned her head against his shoulder. "Ready to get out there and greet the world."

He kissed her forehead as they stood off to the side. When the Sliders played the introduction music, an announcer spoke over the PA system.

"Welcome, Truman and Chantel Woodley, and the Sliders!"

Truman walked out on stage with Chantel by his side. Every day he had to pinch himself for finding and marrying this jewel of a woman. She completed him like no other. Tonight, she looked absolutely stunning.

He played the beginning of one of their up-tempo songs. He started singing. When the song got to Chantel's part, she didn't sing. She stared at him with a strange smile on her face.

Truman mouthed the words, "Are you okay?"

Chantel brought her hand up in the air and signaled for the band to stop playing. An uneasy ripple danced over Truman's stomach.

He put his hand over his microphone from his headset first. "What's wrong? You want to go?"

She shook her head, then turned to the audience. "Ladies and gentlemen, a couple of years ago, I was a broken woman."

Truman started breathing hard. If Chantel had issues, he didn't want it to be in front of the world. He took her hand, but she stayed in her position, refusing to leave the stage area. So he listened to her.

"You all may have remembered seeing me take a header off the stage." She mimicked the motion with her hand and laughed.

Truman found nothing funny. He kept a careful stare on her to make sure to stop another potential breakdown.

"I didn't think I could come back from something like that." Her eyes started to look red like she wanted to cry. "I thought the world had written me off."

He held her hand tighter to show her he would be there for her always.

Chantel took a deep breath. "Back then, I had asked if anyone knew what love was." She smiled hard. "Now I know. I met and married the man of my dreams."

The crowd cheered.

Truman nodded and rewarded his gorgeous wife with a kiss.

Chantel wiped her thumb over his lips, her usual routine to get rid of her lipstick staining him. "He's a great singer, a great leader, a wonderful husband, and a great father to a beautiful son." She looked around and stopped when she spotted one of the cameramen filming this concert event. "Hi, Gage." She blew him a kiss. "Love you." Then she looked at Truman. "And I love you so much."

"I love you, Chantel." He stepped closer to her but stopped when she moved his hand.

She placed it on her stomach. "Good, because I'm pregnant."

A wall of screams filled the arena as he stared at the love of his life. Even seeing Chantel with tears streaming down her face, he couldn't believe what she had said.

"Are you serious?" He took off his guitar finally and placed it on the stage.

Chantel nodded. "I found out today. Ashley saw me getting sick and figured it out. Gage knows and is so excited. The doctor thinks I'm about three months." She rubbed his hand over her belly. "You're going to be a dad again."

Truman screamed and it came from the depths of his soul. He wrapped his arms around her waist and swung her around. She held on to his shoulders, probably for support.

When he realized what he had done, he set her down on her feet, then dropped to his knees in front of her on stage. "We're having a baby." He caressed her stomach before he kissed it. "I love you so much."

She wiped the tears from her face. "Can we please sing and give these people a great show?" She pointed to the audience.

Truman stood. "Are you up to it?"

Chantel winked. "Just watch me." She turned to the band. "Hit it, boys." She held Truman's hand. "Try to keep up."

"Yes, ma'am."

Don't miss Crystal B. Bright's next book in the Love & Harmony series!

Love Like Crazy

Available in April 2018!

Chapter 1

"I want that asshole fired!" The petite starlet jutted her finger in Laz Kyson's direction as he sat at the opposite side of the table from her in the Universe Records office.

He wanted to react, but he knew timing was everything.

"He—he," she paused for effect, "told me that if I didn't do certain things to him, he would make it difficult for me here." Then the sobbing came…without any tears.

Laz shifted in his seat. The heat under his collar started to get a bit unbearable. He started drumming his fingers on the table until he saw Mr. Zinner's stare go directly to his hand.

The man had been salty to him since Laz went to bat for Chantel Evans, or Shauna Stellar, as Zinner continually referred to her when he would lament about the money lost from not signing her and Truman Woodley to the label. Zinner had his chance with her, and he blew it.

Zinner raised his hand like he wanted to pat the young woman's hand, but he stopped as though thinking better of his actions, especially considering what she was accusing Laz of committing. He, instead, spoke in soothing tones. "There, there, Kat."

To punctuate her hurt feelings, she responded to Zinner's sympathy with a protruding bottom lip. Her raven hair along with her sky-blue eyes and pale, clear skin made her a sexy beauty. Coupled with her rotten insides, Laz only saw a monster at the end of the table who had now made it her mission for the summer to get him fired. Not happening.

"Although I don't want you to relive this traumatic moment again, for the record, I'll need to know what happened. Will you please describe for me and the attorneys present the details of this alleged sexual harassment?" Mr. Zinner leaned back, probably to allow his gut freedom to breathe away from the table.

As much as Laz wanted to tune the woman out, he made it a point to listen to each and every word that would come out of her mouth. His livelihood depended on it.

"I was doing my pop-up show at that little venue in Norfolk, Virginia." She wiped underneath her nose with the back of her thumb. "Then he shows up." She pointed at Laz again.

At least Kat didn't say Laz's name. Keep his name out of her mouth and he would be happy.

Kat continued. "I thought it was weird that an A&R rep was there at my show."

"Yes, that is unusual." Zinner cut a harsh look at Laz.

Laz glared back at the man, hoping he picked up his unspoken complaint about doing more for the studio. When Zinner returned his attention to Kat, Laz released a long breath. His boss didn't get it.

"He starts showering me with compliments at first, telling me what a great singer I am and all."

Laz tried hard to suppress his laughter but it puffed out. He covered the sound with a cough, and then took a sip of water. He didn't need her stirred up any more.

No way did he think her vocal chops matched that of the great singers out there like Aretha, Christina, Adele, and Chantel. This pop star needed to stay in her lane as far as what she offered to the music industry, and she needed to start being honest. He didn't know how long he could hold out not saying anything while she massacred his reputation.

Kat sniffed. "Then he pulled me into a room."

"Mr. Kyson put his hands on you?" Zinner sat up taller.

So did Laz. He heard his heartbeat pounding in his head and it shook his body. It took every bit of his strength for him to not scream that this woman had lied about everything so far.

Kat nodded. "When we got in there, he said that if I didn't—" She hesitated and leaned over to her attorney. "Do I have to say it?" She whispered it to her but said it loud enough for Laz to hear.

The older woman next to her nodded and patted her hand.

"Fine." Kat took a deep breath and tucked a wavy curl behind her ear. "He said if I didn't put my mouth down there that he would make my life miserable." She pointed down to her crotch to really drive the point home.

A gasp echoed throughout the room. Kat's attorney stared at Laz with her mouth agape. Zinner couldn't even look at Laz now. The studio attorney adjusted his tie, and Laz wanted to scream.

Laz could count to a million in his head and still wouldn't be able to calm himself down. He pressed his hands against the cold table while he bounced his knee. He had an ace up his sleeve. He just needed to wait for his moment.

"That's the reason I haven't been in the studio to record. And because of all this, I'm not sure if I'm up to going in there for a while." She wrapped her arms around herself and shook her head. "I'm too shaken up." With her head down, she peered up at Laz. "That man is a monster. If he's not fired, I'm walking. I have ten million Instagram followers. They'll boycott this studio if I tell them to."

Zinner shook his head, letting the sweat that poured from it fly. "Let's not be hasty, dear. I'm sure this is all a misunderstanding." Finally, Zinner directed his attention to Laz. "Mr. Kyson, is there anything you want to say on your behalf?"

The air in the expansive boardroom went still, yet felt heavy and made it difficult for Laz to breathe. That wouldn't prevent him from responding. He had his name to clear. Before he did that, though, he would have a bit of fun.

"Yes. I have always preferred tea over coffee." Laz took a deep breath, relieved to finally say something.

"Excuse me?" Zinner braced his meaty hands on the table.

"And I would rather have a cat than a dog. Cats are quiet." Laz, realizing what he had said and the name of the woman across from him, amended his statement. "An older cat though. No kitties." He glared at the pop star.

"He's making this out to be a joke." Kat's pale face turned crimson. "I'm prepared to go to *TMZ* and *People*."

Laz reached into his front jacket pocket and pulled out his phone. "I'll be glad to help you with your story."

"I think you've said enough." Zinner held up his hand, then directed his attention to Kat. "You can take as much time as you need to record your fourth album. We can push the tour out as well."

Kat leaned over to her manager sitting on the other side of her this time. She whispered something in his ear.

The manager nodded. "For her inconvenience and mental trauma, Kat would also like a five million dollar kicker to her contract."

Hush money. No way would Zinner agree to that. He had kicked out Chantel Evans, a far superior singer and entertainer, when she asked to be fairly compensated.

"Done." Zinner slammed his hand on the table.

Unbelievable.

"Hold on." Laz held up his hand. He clipped an attachment to his phone so that he could project a video on the wall. "I think you all need to see this."

He pressed play and made sure to turn the volume up as high as it would go. Even though Laz had only been in the music industry for a couple of years, he knew enough to cover himself.

The stories about Kat's predatory behavior ran rampant throughout the industry. She played virginal, but she had a voracious sexual appetite. In Laz's younger, immature days, he probably would have taken her up on an offer or two. Now, he had his mind solely on business.

The night in question, Laz had set up his phone to record in Kat's dressing room where he had been told to wait for her after her show. He had his phone on a high shelf so it would tape the full scene below. It showed him in a full suit, pacing back and forth in her room with her hair and makeup people.

When the door opened, Kat walked in wearing her trademark sparkly leotard, sky-high booties, and her hair piled high on her head.

"Get out." She waved her hands in the air to get everyone to leave the room. The people started to go, including Laz, but she put her hand on his chest to stop him. "Not you." She laughed.

"We don't need to see this." Kat started to stand.

"Sit down." Her attorney held her client's arm and pulled her down to sit. "I need to verify if this is authentic."

"He had this video doctored. I already told you exactly what happened."

Kat's screeching voice pierced Laz's eardrum. He continued playing the video, especially since Zinner couldn't stop staring at the image.

"Thank you for seeing me. It's great that you want to talk about the progress of your next album. We have a pretty aggressive schedule planned, so it would be great to get the ball rolling on the music. I was fine talking to you afterward on the tour bus with your manager." Laz took a few steps back from her.

"I'm not really down for a threesome, not tonight." Kat pushed Laz down on a couch in the room, and then straddled him.

"Um, that's not me. I think that's one of those drag queen impersonators." Kat pointed to the image on the wall.

"I'm not sure what you think you're doing, but this is not happening," Laz replied as he stood while trying hard not to touch her.

Kat had her arms wrapped around him. She kissed his neck, chin, and cheek. "I haven't had you yet. I think this will be fun."

"Oh, God." Kat hung her head down in the conference room.

The video continued. Laz pried her arms from around him. "Let's chalk this incident up to your performance high. I won't say a word about this to anyone."

Kat cocked her head and crossed her arms over her chest. "What? You think I should be embarrassed or something, like I did something wrong? I'm a young woman. I have needs. It gets lonely out on the road."

"Stop the video." Kat waved her hand in the air.

Laz didn't. He wanted his name fully cleared.

In the video, Laz said, "All I want to do is talk about your music. You owe Universe—"

"Universe can kiss my ass." Kat punctuated her point by slapping her small ass cheek.

Zinner cleared his throat. Laz enjoyed this moment. Vindication felt good.

In the video, Kat's phone rang. "You wait right there. I'm not done with you."

"We are done here." Laz headed toward the shelf area.

Kat answered the phone. "Hello?" She paused. She clicked a button on the phone first. "It's my bitch attorney. This will be quick. Don't you dare go anywhere or I'll make your life a living hell." She ducked into a room next to her dressing room.

The end shot showed Laz grabbing his phone. "Insurance just in case." He winked in the camera and stopped recording.

Kat let her feelings be known about the video and her statement by throwing up on the floor. The stench of her vomit stung Laz's nostrils until he had to turn his head away for a moment and breathe through his mouth.

Laz, confident that he got his point across, ended the video. "You want to go to a gossip site and a magazine with your claims?" He pointed his phone to Kat. "Go ahead. One word, and I'll release this video." His gaze dropped down to Kat's hand. "Young girls wearing purity rings to emulate you would be disappointed to see what a sexual predator you are."

This time when Kat cried, real tears rolled down her cheeks. She stood from the table. "Next week. I'll be in the studio next week." She waved her hand wildly in front of her. "No kicker needed."

"Wait." Her manager tried holding Kat's clean hand.

"No. No more games. I tried holding out to get more money. I tried a lot of things." She glared at Laz. "I'll do what I agreed to in my contract. I'm sorry." She turned to her attorney. "I don't think you're a bitch."

Her lawyer must not have believed her. She collected her belongings and walked out before Kat.

Kat started to leave. When she got behind Laz, she grumbled, "Asshole."

"Hope you're feeling better, Kat." Laz slipped his phone back into his pocket.

When Kat's team vacated the conference room, Laz finally smiled, a first since hearing of Kat's accusations a couple of days go. He turned to the staff attorney, expecting him to share in Laz's delight. He looked more pissed than Kat.

The attorney shook his head. "Should have kept your mouth closed." He picked up his tablet and left Laz there with Zinner.

When the attorney closed the door behind himself, Laz faced his boss. Surely this man would have his back.

Wanting to get Zinner's opinion on the situation sooner rather than later, Laz spoke first. "I didn't do what she accused me of doing. I never touched her."

Zinner snickered. "You idiot." He shook his head. "Do you really think you're the first person in the music biz accused of sexual misconduct with the talent? Hell, you're not even the first person Kat has been with on this *staff*. This is not unusual, and you're not special."

At that moment, Laz didn't even feel heard.

"I knew what she was trying to do." Zinner swung himself back and forth in his chair.

Laz nodded. "Yeah, take down my career."

Zinner held up his hand. "Bigger picture, kid. She wanted more money. It's always about money. Nothing more. Nothing less."

"And you were willing to pay her more money for a delayed album and tour?"

Zinner slammed his hand on the table. "Five million is nothing compared to the revenue we could have generated from her. She is a pop music money machine. The pre-sales for the album she has yet to go to the studio for has already sold a quarter-of-a-million copies. Her tour would have paid us even more, on top of lucrative endorsements for the sweet-as-pie, goody-goody act she puts on so well. We could have gotten her to sign an additional contract with us...until today." He snickered. "Thanks to you, more than likely she'll fulfill her obligations to this contract and then move on to another company or, worse yet, pull a Shauna and put out music on her own."

Laz shook his head. "Paying her for a lie meant that my reputation would have been tarnished, and I would have been out of a job. She wanted me fired."

Zinner didn't blink, didn't react.

Laz was not special.

"I could have talked her out of seeing you let go. I would have made sure to keep you away from her, which, by the way, why did you even approach her anyway? You're A&R. I just need for you to acquire talent. We have people on staff to talk about contract obligations. Those people are attorneys, not you." When Zinner pointed at Laz, it looked like he wanted his finger to be a gun and he wanted to blow Laz's head off his shoulders.

"I told you I wanted to do more here. I've been here a couple of years. I've earned the right to go into management." Laz sat up taller. "I can be used more."

"You could have." Zinner stood. "Not anymore. Pack your shit and go." He pointed to the door.

Laz stood with him. He hoped his towering height over the already tall man would give him a little bit of an intimidation factor. "What the hell? You saw with your own eyes that Kat lied. I never dragged her into a room and asked her for oral sex. She jumped on me. Why am I getting let go if she was the one in the wrong?"

The automatic blinds in the room started to lower on their own, casting an ominous shadow in the room.

"You're poison to us now. The threat that you may release that video will keep Kat from saying anything publicly, but privately, with other up-and-coming talent, our business will be mud. They'll associate Universe with perverts and creeps, whether it's true or not." Zinner strolled toward the door.

"Then I'll sue her. I've worked too hard to be—"

Zinner put his hand on Laz's shoulder. "It's over, unless…"

Laz peered down at Zinner's hand before redirecting his attention back to him. "Unless what?"

"I can have you doing another position. You remember Mable?"

Laz blinked. "The older lady in HR?"

Zinner nodded. "She's retiring. Or she died recently. I can't remember. Anyway, she used to oversee the interns. You could do that. You could wrangle the intern pool here, which will keep you away from the talent."

Laz took a few steps back, which broke the hold Zinner had on him. "With my education, experience, and years of service here, you want to bump me down to a babysitter?"

Zinner exhaled like he needed to, not out of exasperation. "You'll still work for the company."

Laz shook his head. He didn't do this to have his name associated with a company. He had something to say, something to prove.

"I'll be gone in five minutes." He stormed to the door.

"You won't make it out there," Zinner called after Laz.

From this point on, he would have to keep moving.

* * * *

Avery Shields leaned on the mop handle she'd just used on the women's bathroom floor as she peered down to read her statistics book. She needed more hours in the day to get it all done.

"Avery, you done in the bathroom?"

She heard her father's voice, but she had a few more pages to review first. She glanced at her watch and cursed. In a few more hours, she would have her first of many exams. Life wouldn't be life if it didn't include tests.

The door to the women's bathroom creaked open.

"Did you hear me, gal?" Her father came up behind her and tapped her shoulder.

"Yeah." Avery didn't have to look at Leo Shields to know that he disapproved of how she responded. "I mean, yes, sir." She broke away from her book to give him her full attention. "The toilets are cleaned. The mirrors are all shiny. I just mopped. I'm good in here."

As though not believing her, Leo scanned the room. He dropped his gaze to the floor first before proceeding to inspect the rest of the place.

In the meantime, in the quiet, Avery continued reading until she heard that disappointed groan she had heard from her parents before. Each time, it gave her an uncomfortable tickle up her spine to the back of her head.

She heard the sounds of plastic crinkling before she saw her father coming around the corner with a full bag of garbage in his hand.

"All of the garbage receptacles. You have to empty them all." He shook his head as he walked by her. "I swear sometimes you don't think."

"I was going to get it." She winced at the lie with good reason.

Leo didn't make it out of the door. He returned to her and cocked his head. "So you thought it would make more sense to mop the floor before emptying out the trashcans?"

"When you put it that way, I guess it doesn't hold any logic." She shrugged.

"My name is on this cleaning business."

When Leo started on his rant, it could wear on a person's nerves.

"I know, Dad." She understood the sacrifices her parents had made for the family.

Leo drove taxis, cleaned office buildings, and even had his own pressure-washing business at one time. Avery's mother usually worked alongside him until she started taking classes to become a nurse.

Avery really had no reason to complain. She had a job, too many jobs, actually. Her father didn't have to hire her, but he did. That didn't mean she didn't see more for herself like her mother. Her dream, though, didn't involve another high-level profession like nursing.

Leo's gaze dropped down to her opened book. "The sooner we get this place cleaned, the faster you can get home to finish studying."

"Yes, sir." She slammed the book closed and slipped it into a side pocket that Avery had made to hang from the rolling cleaning cart that carried all her supplies.

Her father carried the same warm honey skin tone color, but on him on long days like today, he looked ashen and tired. His gray coveralls stretched tight over his rounded belly. The scowl he carried spoke volumes. He, nor Avery's mother, could easily hide their expressions.

Avery bent down to roll the cuffs on her oversized coveralls to keep from tripping on them while she walked.

"You get that end and I'll get this end, and I think that'll be it." Leo nodded to the area behind Avery.

"Yes, sir." She watched him walk away before she pushed her cart to the end of the top floor where she knew magic had to happen.

Avery scanned her identification badge over a reader to open the door first. As soon as she stepped inside, her shoulders relaxed. The place already smelled like flowers and fragrant candle wax. She loved stepping inside Charisma Music's studio.

She got the place on a good night. The studio sat empty, which lately had been a rare occurrence. On the nights when artists filled the studio space, Avery tried keeping away from the area. She didn't do it out of embarrassment because of her job. She worked hard. She just didn't like seeing others going for a dream that she at one time had.

Avery left her cart in the center of the room so that she could start her work. No use lamenting about what could have been. She dusted the surfaces. When she got to the control boards, she dragged her fingers over the knobs and buttons.

"Maybe." She snickered. "Probably not."

After dusting, she adjusted her headscarf over her hair, styled with two-stranded twists all over. Then she tackled the thick glass panes that surrounded the recording booths. She let her hand rest on the glass that was rumored country singer Laura Smalls once smashed with a chair. Strange what people will do for love, or even lust.

To make sure she didn't leave any handprints, she examined the glass thoroughly. She didn't need her father catching her slacking off on her duties again.

When she got by the piano that sat off to the side, Avery hung around it longer than she should have. Like the control board, she danced her fingers over the keys, allowing one to dip down on one key so that the sound reverberated throughout the compact space. When the sound came, so did the involuntary hum that rattled her chest.

Avery peered up to make sure her father didn't pop up all the sudden. When she didn't see or hear him, she took a seat at the piano bench. She took a breath before tickling her fingers over the keys. She tried doing it ever so lightly, but then she got into playing a Stevie Wonder song and found herself getting into it more and more.

She smiled, her body not feeling like her own as she played the melody. Before she knew it, Avery had started singing.

She closed her eyes and imagined her life recording music in a studio like this and with people like Chantel and Truman Woodley. If Chantel could make it out of her humble beginnings to be a major power player in the business, Avery held out hope that maybe one day after finishing her business degree and getting a job her parents would be proud of, she could really pursue her dream. If she did that, would they still be proud of her?

When the thought hit her, she stopped playing. She hovered her hands over the piano keys. What was Avery doing besides torturing herself? This life could never be hers.

Avery stood from the piano and returned it to the condition she had found it. She vacuumed the carpet and made sure to empty out all the trash bins around the recording studio area. With that done, Avery started to push her cart out to get up with her father. Getting done by two AM seemed like a gift. She would still have some time to go home, study a bit more, go to work at the diner, and get to class on time.

Thinking about her schedule had her sighing. She shouldn't complain. At twenty-two, she had time and energy without sleep to work hard.

Right when Avery opened the main door to go back out into the hallway, her father met her face to face, which startled her. She had hoped with the soundproof walls that he hadn't heard her playing only moments ago.

"All done in here." She smiled to ease his concern and keep the conversation going in a different direction. "I would say you don't have to check behind me, but I know you." Avery laughed.

"I should've had you do the business offices and I should have taken care of this area."

Busted.

The relaxed feeling Avery had felt earlier behind the piano disappeared. She felt her shoulders tense up around her ears. She balled her hands into fists. When she realized the position of her hands, she shoved them in her pockets.

"I didn't—" She had almost said she didn't touch anything, but she couldn't lie to her father…again. "I didn't break anything. Everything in there is fine."

Leo nodded toward the bank of elevators. "I'll check your work. Go put your cart away and wait for me downstairs."

"Dad, do you want me to—"

He pointed. "Go."

With a single word, her father reduced her to a trembling child again, or worse, that same scared sixteen-year-old with a real fear that she might be a parent soon. Some mistakes would never be forgotten—no matter what she did to rectify them.

On the elevator ride down, Avery thought about the situation. Sure she had made mistakes as a teenager. Who hadn't? Since her break up with Kenan, she had done everything she could to get in her parents' good graces, with one exception. She moved out and got her own apartment despite her parents wanting her to stay while she pursued her degree.

Avery realized years ago that as a woman, she needed to start acting that way. She no longer needed to feel shame for her past mistakes. She worked hard. She earned her own money and paid her own bills. She hadn't had a serious relationship in six years. She needed to be cut some slack.

She secured her cart in the storage closet on the lower level. Avery removed her coveralls and hung them on the crook of her arm to take home and wash. She tried making the garment smell like something other than bleach and ammonia.

Avery had her arguments ready in her head by the time she heard the elevator doors ding and she saw her father coming out of the darkened location. The sounds of the wheels going over the tile floors echoed off the walls until he got to Avery at the closet.

She took a deep breath before she prepared to tell her father to respect and understand her. Despite past mistakes, she could be trusted. Even though she had her eye on a more professional career, that didn't stop her passion for music.

"Dad, I—"

"You want to sing? You can do it in church. You're still going, aren't you?" He shoved the cart in the closet and closed and locked the door. "You move out and we don't see you on Sundays anymore." He placed his fists on his hips. "This life, the one you desire that involves music, will only break your heart. It's not a business that can guarantee you'll get to eat every day or have a roof over your head." He held her shoulders, which made her gasp. "Promise me that you won't think about pursuing a life in music."

He shook his head. "I'm not saying you can't sing. We both know that God blessed you with a voice. This music life is something you don't need."

Avery had so much to say. She hated feeling suppressed and hiding her true feelings because of fear and past regrets.

"Promise me," Leo said again.

She swallowed. Every argument she had running around in her head disappeared. "I promise."

So did her dreams.

Meet the Author

Crystal B. Bright graduated with a BA from Old Dominion University with a major in Creative Writing, a minor in Communications, and an emphasis on Public Relations. She earned her MA from Seton Hill University in Writing Popular Fiction. She is a member of Romance Writers of America. For more information about Crystal and her writing, please visit her website at www.CrystalBrightWriter.com. You can also find her at https://www.facebook.com/crystal.bright.397, or follow her on Twitter @CrystalBBright.

CPSIA information can be obtained
at www.ICGtesting.com
Printed in the USA
LVOW12s1124120218
566114LV00005B/149/P